SAN ANDROS FAULT

A JAKE STORM NOVEL

WILLIAM JOHNSTONE

TAYLOR

DEDICATION

My great appreciation to the following folks without whose support these books would not be possible.

K.H. Koehler, "Editor Extraordinaire"
Helen McGonigle, Attorney
Adria Henderson, Editor
Gail H. Johnson, Research Assistant
Foster Gamble, Editor
Paul Nelson, Technical Assistant

CONTENTS

FOREWORD

It has now been seventy-five years since the end of World War II, and through this novel, William Johnstone Taylor affords the reader a look deep inside one of the 42,500 Nazi ghettos and the personal side of concentration camps during Adolf Hitler's reign from 1933-1945. These camps, just as they are described in *San Andros Fault*, were used for the most barbaric and horrific actions ever taken against humankind. Some were war supply factories where prisoners were forced on a daily basis to manufacture the very weapons that the Germans would use against them. By the end of the war, these camps had imprisoned somewhere between fifteen and twenty million innocent people.

Ghettoes were an integral part of Hitler's Final Solution—a plan begun in 1941 to remove and murder all European Jews.

Now, in *San Andros Fault*, we have Joel, a Jewish man who endured this dreadful event and lived to face his absolute worst fear, the commandant of his internment camp, who is known as "The Ghost."

Jake once again takes you beyond the norm and into a world with unbelievable circumstances—a place where only Jake Storm and his trusted comrades could possibly go! The twists and turns will keep you on the very edge of your reading chair as you try to put this novel down. But, time after time you will be thinking, *There is no way Jake is going to make it out of this depraved mess he is in this time...*

And, does he?

As demonstrated in his first novel, *Stolen Angels*, Jake and his one-of-a-kind elite team venture into uncharted territory. In the case of *San Andros Fault*, the territory in question is an island where criminals of war live their lives in leisure—at least until "the Storm" hits their beaches like a Category 5 hurricane and all hell breaks loose!

Don't miss this incredible novel journey that will fill your mind with wonderment, your heart with joy, and your soul with the understanding that, truly, "what goes around, comes around" in life. Everyone should read this book. It will change your view of the world and its politics!

Gail H. Johnson, Investigative and Security Consultant
Former Walt Disney World Executive
Orlando, Florida

PROLOGUE

Something was burning at the back of my brain. I could feel that old sensation of doom washing over me. I hope it wasn't some poor soul reaching out for my help, as has happened so many times in the past. I did have a habit of getting people dead! For some strange reason, I pictured Nancy's beautiful and nearly perfect face, and, at the same time, one of my burners vibrated in my pocket.

A feeling of dread washed over me. I was nearly relieved that it was Top saying he could see a boat on the horizon heading straight in our direction. The men were heavily armed and looked very, very hostile. I thanked Top and asked him to haul anchor and head north in case we came in second in this skirmish and needed to be picked out of the warm Gulf Stream— assuming we survived at all.

He said, "I am already underway and I'll be there as fast as I can!"

I put the phone away in the dry storage bin and asked Sorensen to pass my long gun up to me. He was busy checking his own rifle and passed me my weapon. I checked the chamber and the action on mine. It was ready.

I was ready. Insofar as I would always be ready.

As the hostile's boat rapidly approached, I dropped the sails and kept the engine running at full throttle. When they were just within range, I turned hard at them and Sorensen made a sound of surprise. He didn't expect a suicide run. Then, not waiting for an invitation, he aimed his rifle in their direction, though the wind—and our speed—was surely going to play havoc with his aim.

The men in the boat also had guns, and I could clearly see them aiming them in our direction as our two boats headed for a collision.

Bang-bang…!

Two weeks earlier…

Lord, this gets tougher all the time.

I have learned not to look directly at the Wall. If I have to, I blur my eyes so I won't focus on any one name. It helps that the Wall is shiny and picks up reflections, blurring the names, but those ghosts draw me in anyway. How could one man recognize so many names that belong to so many faces, so many reaching hands, and so many pleas for help?

Nearly everyone I got close to, everyone that meant something to me…gone. Their spirits reach from beyond and through this wall as if it's their window to get out—to come back to this world. I wish I had the compass, the way, the power to lead them! It sucks the very soul out of me every time I look at the names.

Now, my ghosts use the survivors from the Nam who patrol the Wall to force my attention on them. Their embraces, their words of love, and the camaraderie they display and pass onto me.

What a war! What a nightmare! And, what a daymare it is for me. For me to feel guilty for surviving those three years and the more than a thousand chances to have had my name engraved here. Well, my ghost friends, I gave it my best shot. The bullets could have just as easily hit me. I was right next to you, Johnny. I was standing up, directing fire, when you were hit, Smitty. I know I should have been the target. I don't know why it was you.

Why don't you guys look peaceful? What is it that will finally make you rest? What is it that I can do to make it right? Who can I blame? Why do you call me here and then just reach out? Talk to me! Tell me who to go after. I will just keep moving along this line and hope your messages will eventually break through this thick skull of mine.

I wish I could change my choice of meeting spot with the Major. The Wall is bothering me far more these days than it did years ago. I guess my age is finally wearing on me. All those people I pass along the way, and, on occasion, embrace, look so troubled. My whole life, I have found myself in the wrong place at the right time. Maturity has not changed that.

My name is Jacob Storm. My friends call me Jake. My family calls me Scarce. My enemies don't call me at all. They just drop in from time to time.

As the Vietnam Memorial fades from my right peripheral, I take in the steps of the Lincoln Memorial looming in front of me. One more time, I run the memory tape in my head of the strange story I'd been told the night before on the Ellis Island Ferry by the son of the man currently the subject of my investigation.

His name is Paul Keis. There is no doubt in my mind that the story he related to me is true. It is too bizarre not to be. I even remember the quiet buzz about the incident last month when I was visiting with my friend Calvin Green in Nassau. Calvin is a Bahamas government agent and one of my close friends whom I have known for many years. We have shared more than a few adventures together. It just goes to prove that if a news article or a story catches my attention, somehow, I will become involved in it before too long. Calvin will be invaluable to me in this matter.

When Doug Parton, first signaled me that we needed to talk, I was reluctant, as usual. Our last mission was hairy, and it has taken me nearly six months to heal, both physically and mentally. Doug is an attorney who deals with "less than conventional cases." He has been referred to as the "Don Quixote" of the legal field, and he, in turn, refers to me as his "Help Button."

Over the years, we have been through a great deal together. He mostly handles cases involving civil rights violations, some murder defenses, and many battles against officials of large government agencies that use their position and power to grab money from the average citizen—usually causing great hardship. In some cases, the cause and effect are death and destruction.

I call Doug "The Major" as a code name. I took the name from an old Robert Redford movie we once saw together. It reminded me of what he and I do for a living. The movie was about a group of civilians working for a government agency who were trying to right the wrongs in the world. Only, in our case, we can only "hope" we work for the good guys.

Doug was a Captain in the Army Reserve in college but resigned his commission when they tried to teach him to use a garrote during his Ranger training. He couldn't quite get the hang of it. He thought it was too barbaric.

I felt anxious to get going on this case. The funding was available but would be tight, as usual. But, if I used the *Slim Molly*, I could cut my expenses to a minimum. The *Slim Molly* is my thirty-eight-foot Catalina sloop sailboat with a swing keel, modified with a larger-than-usual engine. The swing keel allows me to float over very shallow water. The *Big Hat*, my fifty-eight-foot Hatteras, was far too expensive, and it would draw too much attention in the area I was heading to. I needed to draw up a plan in my mind and follow it through.

Who was I kidding? I knew as sure as dirt that any plan I devised now I would alter at least ten times over before I even got there. Ol' Murphy's Law would bite me on the ass as everything changed for the worst—every time it possibly could.

Just then, I spotted the Major, a big man in his own right. I had met him many years before when we both worked for the same law firm in Boston. That wasn't long after he had graduated from law school and before he became the foremost civil rights attorney in the world. He makes a difference in this world, and it's my job to keep him from getting dead and upsetting the balance of the universe.

As he cleared the ridgeline above the wall, I recognized his long gate and surefootedness. I was standing in a shadow with the bright lights of the Lincoln Memorial to my rear as he approached.

After his affectionate hug, he started briefing me on the case. I had already met with the son the night before and had the basic story from him, but the Major filled in the blanks, reemphasizing the importance of a quick and successful conclusion to this matter. He always said that, but I realized he was dead serious this time as the clock was running out on a poor lonely man sitting in a Bahamian prison.

It seemed there were secret goings-on on Andros Island, and the Bahamas government did not want anyone to know about them. It involved the U.S. in a way that would shock the world. The Major was reluctant to speak of it but, finally, after being reminded that I was his best source and comrade in the universe, he filled me in on a long-held U.S.-government secret that there were former Nazi officers living on Andros and that they had been there for many years. I already knew some of the San Andros story but felt it good manners to act as if he was filling me in on incredible new stuff! However, the next bit of information was a shock, even to me. The Major informed me that there were Middle Easterners living there as well and that they had been there since just after the 9/11 World Trade Center disaster!

As quickly as the Major arrived, he disappeared by doing a military about-face and quickly marching into the shadows of the surrounding trees. Before he left, he shouted above the din of the traffic skirting the Capitol Mall, "Don't get dead!"

A common parting wish from him.

En route to my island home, I went over the electronic files that the Major had sent me earlier. He had requested I catch the next flight up to New York City and meet with the family of an imprisoned man in the Bahamas. The moment I read the Major's email briefing, written in our common code, I was hooked.

The following narrative is the story of Joel Keis, as I know it today from the numerous interviews and documents retrieved from our research. This, to the best of my knowledge, is what Keis had lived through during his tortured and long life.

* * *

Joel Keis, now known as Joel Kelsey—not his legal name but his American adopted one— was a Polish immigrant who came over from Europe after the Second World War. His family and everyone he knew had lived in Kazimierz Doliny, a little Polish town on the eastern banks of the Vistula River in the Lublin Province. Most were Jewish. Under an order from Nazi administrator Adolf Eichmann, all were rounded up in January of 1942 and brought to camps at Treblinka, Belzec, or Sobibor.

These camps were specifically constructed for the extermination of Poland's Jews. All were held in conditions worse than animals. Most were barely clothed, even during the fierce and violent winters. Joel and his family were imprisoned at the Belzec camp. The Germans placed the men

13

in one barbed-wired section and the women and children across the way behind another fenced-in area. Joel could see his wife and three children every day, but he was absolutely forbidden to talk to them or to do anything but make quick eye contact each morning as he headed for the small repair shop where he was forced to work.

Joel and his family were among the millions of Jews and other ethnic people who had been interned in one of the over 42,000 concentration and extermination camps throughout Eastern Europe during the late 1930s through to the middle of the '40s.

Joel would wake up every morning on his hard, wooden bed and, oh so slowly, open his eyes only to realize that his nightmare was a reality. He would glance around at the other half-starved men, careful not to make too much eye contact with them. Most of them resented the fact that he had a job serving the Nazis. What they failed to realize was that Joel's job might be his only chance to save his family. Joel hoped and prayed that he might be able to reach into the hearts of at least some of his captors by cooperating with them.

Joel's job in the small shop was separating gold, platinum, and silver. Some of the precious metals came from the teeth of fallen Jews in his and other nearby camps. He also tested and melted down gold jewelry and separated gems from glass. Joel had been a successful jeweler and gemologist before the Nazis began their campaign of terror in his town.

Nearly every day, Joel would learn that another friend or relative had vanished from the sheds they lived and survived in. Joel worked extremely hard at his task to try to keep in good graces with the camp commandant, a cruel man named Colonel Stefan Braun. It was rumored among the prisoners that Braun's mother was a Jew from Berlin. However, after many months of constant long hours of work, his worst fears were realized. His wife was moved to another shed and, soon thereafter, his children, as well.

He tried frantically to persuade the commandant to bring them back, but he was sent back to his work area with threats of punishment and death if he asked any more questions about his family.

Commandant Braun was a big man. He stood about six-four and was very broad at the shoulders. His tailored uniforms with pads, special cuts, and pleats made him appear even bigger than he actually was, and the highly polished, sterling silver insignias and buttons made him look superior. With almost white-blonde hair, he was often referred to as "The Ghost" by even his own troops. He was younger than Joel by some years and was far younger than many other officers of his rank.

His fierce looks and evil demeanor seemed doubled by the menacing tattoo on the inside of his right forearm depicting a striking snake wrapped around a double-edged dagger—a decoration he proudly wore exposed, keeping the sleeves of his tunic folded up at all times, including on the most severely cold days of the Polish winters. Braun took perverse pleasure in tormenting his prisoners. Every prisoner was made to stare at this ugly display of painted terror as he toured the shacks and work areas of the camps, making sure his supremacy was understood—but mostly feared.

One day, as Joel was scanning the faces of the people being forced into the open-backed trucks near the perimeter of the camp, he spied his wife looking back at him. She was, as were many of the others, completely nude and being struck by one of the guards as she tried to call to him. Joel broke from the work line and ran to her across the field as she was thrown into the bed of the truck.

As he approached the truck and saw how tortured her face looked, he knew she was probably being transported to one of the many death pits he had heard about from the other prisoners. As he ran to her, a guard struck him on the back of his head with his rifle butt and knocked him to the ground. All hope left Joel that day. He never saw any member of his family again. And, every night, Joel dreamed of Braun's snake tattoo. He knew it was probably the last thing his wife and children had seen before they were placed alive in the death trenches of the camp and then burned.

Joel thought he would never forget that day in 5702, a date based on the Hebrew calendar, as it marked what he thought was the end of happiness for him. The years drifted by like a nightmare as Joel barely survived starving to death. His skills were the only reason they allowed him to live, but he prayed for a quick death every night.

One day Joel woke up to the sound of shouting by the guards and people screaming for mercy. Joel quickly ran to his little shop only to see it had been ransacked of all the gold and precious stones he had divided the day before. He looked through the window to see the guards forcing hordes of prisoners into the death trucks and driving toward the death trenches at high speeds, a sight he had never seen before. There were far too many prisoners running from the wooden sheds to fit in the trucks, even though there were many trucks staged for loading.

All of a sudden, the guards fired their rifles into the crowds of prisoners just as fast as they could. The guards kept reloading their rifles and firing at point-blank range at anything that moved. Joel ran from his shop and picked up a long-handled shovel and began swinging and pounding and slicing the guards from behind until the prisoners, the ones still able to walk, rushed the guards, whom they outnumbered twenty to one. The prisoners tore the guard's limb from limb with their bare hands. The entire camp became a bloody battlefield as the prisoners picked up the guards' weapons and began shooting every uniform they could see.

After what seemed like hours of horrific battle, Joel and the rest of the prisoners—some two or three thousand of them—found themselves standing in the blood-soaked field at the center of the camp with no guard left standing. The only sounds were the crying and whimpering of those dying and the sounds of some of the prisoners who had turned the weapons on themselves.

In the distance, Joel could hear artillery booming and the sounds of explosions as the rounds struck their mark. The prisoners figured it was the Germans coming to finish them off.

Joel re-loaded the rifle he was carrying and ran over to the headquarters building to look for the commandant and his staff. When he entered the building, he saw the commandant's office was empty of all memorabilia and files. There wasn't a trace of the monster left anywhere. Joel looked at the rifle he was holding and thought of his family and friends lying in the cold, dark earth beyond the barbed-wire fence that still loomed from horizon to horizon. One small pull of the trigger with the barrel to his head and he would join his family, but he quickly put that thought out of his head and focused on the missed opportunity to put the monster down. Joel felt robbed once again as he looked out the window at his last chance for revenge.

Within a couple of hours, some small fighter planes flew over—not German but American Bell P-63 King Cobras and British Hawker Typhoon fighters. The pilots were taking photographs of the people on the ground from the canopies. It seemed as though there were hundreds of planes flying toward the east in the direction of the Germans' retreating lines of military trucks and small Volkswagen cars.

Later that day, an American Army group came to the camp. It took a while for the Americans to convince the armed prisoners that they were there to help. Eventually, they let them into the camp to treat the sick and wounded.

Although many of Joel's campmates died in the coming days from wounds received during the take-over battle or just disease in general, the American forces fed, clothed, and nursed many of them back to health. Joel needed very little care, as he was one of the few who'd been given a steady diet due to his value as a tradesman.

Joel found himself the center of attention, as he was one of the longest-lived survivors in the camp. It was also soon discovered that he had a vast knowledge of the Germans' business dealings, as well as their leadership. Joel was quickly transferred to the area command center and eventually to the Allied Operational and Occupation Headquarters in London, England.

Before he had left the camp, he searched endlessly through piles of dead Germans for The Ghost and his staff but was unable to find even one member of the camp command.

Joel stayed in England for a number of months after the war as an advisor to the Allied Forces. He was then given the opportunity to return to Poland or relocate to the United States of America, where he had a distant cousin in Brooklyn. Joel had been briefed by some late arrivals from Poland that the Russians were now taking over Poland and were not much kinder to the Jews and the Poles than the Germans had been. It did not take Joel long to choose the United States as his new home.

Joel moved in with his cousin and his family in New York. As the economy once again began to grow and prosper, he soon found employment in the vast diamond and jewelry district of Manhattan on West 47th Street.

Joel met a young Jewish girl named Adrian, whose husband had been killed in the war in Europe some years before. Their relationship flourished, seemed to take on a life of its own, and soon they were married with three children—Paul, Josh, and last, but certainly not least, sweet little Katy.

Joel worked very hard at his trade and his hard work paid off. In the late fifties, he started his own business. Fifty years later, his children finally convinced him to work fewer hours and spend more time at home with their mother.

Joel and Adrian had many friends in Brooklyn. Many had lived through the death camps of Europe and migrated to the U.S. for a new start in life, but hardly spoke of the horrible camps. As the children of the Holocaust survivors grew up and began asking questions about the numbers tattooed on the adult's arms, the survivors began to share some of the stories. Many of the children hid in corners and covered their eyes and ears on hearing the horror stories. Joel and the others' stories of "The Ghost" and his sadistic tattoo especially enthralled them.

Joel, Adrian, Paul, Josh, and Katy all had good lives. His sons both became attorneys and his daughter Katy was the wild one. She was more of a tomboy than her two brothers. She became a firefighter for the City of New York. They were a happy family.

Then came 9/11. At about 9:00 AM that morning, Adrian called Joel to tell him to turn on the local TV channel. That evening, two firefighters from Katy's unit knocked on the door to tell them Katy had been inside the North Tower when it collapsed. Joel could hardly breathe.

As Joel fell to his knees, the question: "Why me again?" ran through every vein of his being.

The following days, nights, and weeks after losing Katy were agonizing. It was all a grim reminder of his days in the prison camps when he knew his entire family was gone and that he would never see or hold them again.

Joel's faith and his wife, Adrian, kept him going, but the hatred he felt inside toward the monsters, whether they were Arabs or members of a great conspiracy who had perpetrated these events, was overwhelming.

Ted Lowell and his wife, Debbie, were close friends of Joel and Adrian. Ted was a concentration camp survivor like Joel. Joel trusted Ted completely and they often consulted one another in matters of personal feelings and family.

Since Ted was retired, he and Debbie had decided to do some traveling. They went to their local Thomas Cook Travel Agent regarding a trip they were planning to the Caribbean. The travel agent told them that she and her husband had stayed on Andros Island within the past year and enjoyed its remoteness and lush, sandy beaches. She explained that Andros is the largest island in the Bahamas—104 miles long and forty miles wide, with the third-largest barrier reef in the world. She highly recommended it. Ted and Debbie took an off-season trip to the coastal village of Nichols Town near the northeast coast of Andros Island in the southern Bahamas.

Ted and Debbie traveled to Nassau on Bahamas Air and then on to Andros by commuter plane landing in the small San Andros Airport a few, short miles west of Nichols Town. Ted was able to rent an old Volkswagen Beetle from a local resident who happened to be a German. He happily took the car rather than rent a moped, as he would surely injure himself.

On the day before they left to come home, Ted put a small, but quite visible, dent in the right rear fender of their rental Volkswagen. Ted inquired of the motel manager where he could find the German fellow who had rented him the car so he could pay for the damages before he traveled back to the US. After receiving the directions, he left Debbie at the motel and drove toward the town of San Andros.

He was surprised to find that the village of San Andros was a fairly modern housing area equal to many housing developments in the rural USA. He noticed that many homes had garages, carports, and front porches. Ted even saw a modern general store. The only difference was that most of the directional signage, street signs, and window ads were written in German and Arabic.

Ted stopped at the store and inquired of the men relaxing on the porch where he could find the VW's owner. He was instructed in very broken English to drive to the Community Center down the road and inquire there. Much help they were not!

Ted drove a bit farther and came to a sentry shack with a closed gate. The sentry only glanced at the old VW and motioned him through as he opened the gate. Ted turned the next corner and saw what appeared to be a Mosque. There were men and women in Arabic garb walking toward the Mosque. Many of the homes were modern and looked like elaborate U. S. homes. Some of the men waved at the car as Ted drove by but didn't seem to pay much attention to who was driving. Ted figured that was why the guard at the gate did not stop him.

He drove to the end of the road but still did not see any building that resembled a Community Center. Ted turned around and drove back toward the sentry gate. As he passed the Mosque, he saw a man who looked remarkably like Osama Bin Laden standing with two other men. At least the man looked like the pictures Ted had seen of Bin Laden, just not as tall.

Ted had his camera on the seat next to him as he had been taking shots of the local landscape. He picked up his camera and shot a number of quick photos, keeping the camera low. As he started to drive off, one of the men with the Bin Laden look-alike who appeared to be the size of a Detroit Lions linebacker looked directly at Ted and started to run toward the vehicle. Ted drove off quickly, heading directly to the gate.

Ted stopped in front of the gate and asked the sentry, who appeared to be an American soldier, where the Community Center was. The sentry became wide-eyed and asked him to exit the area immediately!

Ted drove to a large building with a group of men standing outside talking. Once again, he inquired about the whereabouts of the car owner. He was directed to a small house just down the way. As he left the men in front of the building, he saw a large man walking toward them from the other direction. The man, elderly but still huge and muscular, glared menacingly at Ted as he approached. As Ted drove off, he noticed something that turned his blood to ice water. The man had a tattoo of a snake wrapped around a dual-edged dagger on the inside of his right forearm.

Ted stared too long. The man began walking toward him. Ted placed the car in gear, hit the gas pedal, and drove toward the small house the men had directed him to. When he stopped a short distance away he took out his camera, snuck back between the houses, and snapped five or six pictures of the group in front of the store, including the large, elderly man with the tattoo.

Ted returned to the car with the camera and quickly changed the film, placing the exposed roll neatly under the seat where it was hidden but easily accessible. As he climbed out of the car, two large young men grabbed him and forcibly relieved him of his camera.

The men spoke to him in German, popped open the back of the camera, and pulled the film from it. They then threw the camera into the car, breaking it into three pieces. They strong-armed Ted and pushed him back into the car. Despite the men's German, which he spoke very little of, he understood they wanted him to leave the area immediately. In the rearview mirror, Ted could see the large man with the tattoo speaking with one of the Arabic men he had seen earlier. The Arab was pointing toward Ted and the car.

Ted drove quickly out of the settlement and back to the motel.

Ted and Debbie flew home the next day. Ted continually spoke of his encounter with the muscular old German with the tattoo and the Middle Eastern men near the Mosque. Ted had thankfully retrieved the film from under the seat of the old VW and had it safely stored in his carry-on bag. This film was not leaving his side!

After arriving back in New York, Ted had all their vacation film rolls processed. A couple of weeks later, Ted and Debbie contacted their friends and invited them to view their wonderful vacation photos of San Andros and to celebrate Joel and Adrian's wedding anniversary. The Saturday night get-together was well underway when Ted took out the envelopes containing the vacation photos. All were amazed to see the land crabs that crawled all over Andros Island like large insects. They were just as amazed at the beauty of the island edged in sugar sand and surrounded by turquoise-colored water with coral reefs visible just below the surface.

As Ted randomly flipped through the photos, he came upon the ones he'd shot in the village community of San Andros. When he flipped to the picture of the large German man, Joel gasped, grabbed the photo from Ted with both hands, and fell to the floor next to the coffee table, his whole body shaking. He would not respond to Adrian's pleas to tell her what was wrong. Everyone was convinced he was having a stroke.

Ted suddenly realized the photo was of the monster that Joel had described in the camp during the war—"The Ghost" who was such a brutal part of Joel's nightmares. Ted got Joel off the floor by telling him, "Now justice can be served and God will lead the way."

All that night and through the next day, Joel locked himself away in his office and pored over every reference book he could find regarding the Bahamas. He called the Bahamas' Consulate Office in New York City to inquire about the village of San Andros on Andros Island. He called Ted many times throughout the day to question him further about the tattooed old man and to see if there was anything else Ted could recall of his encounter

Ted had consulted a lawyer friend, named Chris, about the Arabs and had found that the Bin Laden look-alike could possibly be Osama's older brother, Salem Bin Laden who had been living in Orlando at the time of the attack on the World Trade Center. Mysteriously, he and a group of Middle Easterners had been allowed to fly out of the Orlando International Airport after the attacks, when all the other flights were grounded and all U.S. airspace had been closed. Chris had a source within the government that helped him often with information for his clients.

The plane must have flown all those Middle Easterners directly to the Bahamas under our government's sanction since all flights had been grounded at that time. Chris said he would contact one of his friends to see if he could find out anything. He told Ted to be patient as information of this nature took time to uncover.

Joel's research on San Andros wasn't very useful. The town magically appeared without any fanfare around the end of the 1940s. There were no resident listings, just a post office reference in nearby Nicholls Town. There was, however, a mention of a Canadian consulate contact in San Andros at Morgan's Bluff, in the Nicholls Town tourist reference.

The next morning, Joel went to the Canadian Consulate's Office in Manhattan and inquired about their knowledge of the village of San

Andros. No one at the consulate knew anything about San Andros or had any contacts there.

Joel knew that he was going to have to go to Andros to see for himself. Adrian came home from work to find Joel packing. She asked him if she could go with him, but Joel explained that this was something he just had to do alone. He did not know what was going to happen and did not want to place Adrian in harm's way.

The next morning, Joel left JFK for Miami and then secured a private charter to San Andros airport. The flight was shorter then Joel had anticipated. Suddenly, he was on the tarmac at the San Andros airport. A feeling rushed over him like something he had not felt since the day the American troops entered the concentration camp and he realized the Nazis in charge of the camp had slipped by the troops and wiggled their way to safe passage.

Once Joel got his motel room there at the airport, he arranged for a moped and secured a full-face helmet. The full helmet was going to work well to hide his face and protect his identity, but with the searing San Andros heat, it was going to be like wearing Hell on his head!

Back in Brooklyn, Ted received a call from his lawyer friend Chris. He asked Ted if he would mind sharing his vacation photos with another lawyer he knew in Washington, D.C. Ted agreed and asked to be kept in the loop about any information.

In San Andros, Joel drove toward Nicholstown. As he rode along the bumpy asphalt road, he passed only one other vehicle coming the other way. It was dark and quiet like a cemetery feels at night. He slowly came to a stop on the side of the road. He could make out a slight reflection, not much light but just enough to know something was up ahead. Joel pulled off the road, parked the Moped deep in the trees, and continued on foot.

Soon, he could hear voices speaking German. It made his stomach turn. Joel crept through the brush and recognized the voice of the "The Ghost," something Joel thought was never going to happen until he chased him to hell after he passed away!

A group of about ten or so men stood next to a building, arguing in German, which Joel spoke fluently, about expenses for some kind of travel they were planning to take in the near future. They were talking about flights out of Miami and New York.

Joel cautiously moved as close as he could to the voices and found a car parked near the first building. He was relieved that no interior light or sound gave him away as he slipped inside the rear seat. As he peered up through the window, he saw, standing no more than ten feet away, Commandant Braun and two other men coming from the building. As he stared at the Monster, Braun turned and stared right at the car as if he sensed Joel's presence and his loudly beating heart. Soon, the commandant and his mates walked away into the night.

Joel was sure he had been detected, and he knew he had to leave immediately or he'd be caught.

As Joel slid out of the car and to the ground, he felt a hard, steel rod lying on the floorboard. He carried the tire iron with him to the brush, and just as he arrived at the edge of the woods, he heard the breaking of twigs. He turned just in time to see the commandant swinging a long shiny blade of sorts at him. It happened so fast that it was like a bolt of lightning and it nicked his left shoulder and struck the tree next to him, nearly cutting the sapling clear through. Joel tried to duck and run, but the blade nicked him a second time as he turned.

The aging man's condition caught Joel off guard. He had to be in his late seventies, but was still agile enough to keep swinging the sword repeatedly! But, as Joel stumbled backward, he noticed the Monster's legs seemed to weaken with every step and his eyes appeared to be clouded with cataracts. Still, he could clearly see the fury in the commandant's face.

Joel kept stepping backward faster and faster in the brush but lost his footing and fell backward. The commandant took one more huge step and lifted the shining blade over his head to finish Joel off...when he tripped and fell forward. Instinctively, Joel threw his hands up to block the huge man from falling directly on him, holding the tire iron up to protect himself. As the commandant fell, the tire iron jammed into the commandant's left eye and continued to pierce his head, nearly coming out the back of his skull. The sound of the bone shattering in his skull was like nothing Joel had ever heard before.

Joel was terrified! He had always dreamed of killing this Monster, this beast, who had robbed him of his life and family in Poland. Now, he had killed "The Ghost" and, at present, he was pinned under the large man's lifeless body.

It was getting harder to breathe. He strained to push the dead body off him and nearly slid out from under the weight when flashlights seemed to be coming from all directions, shining on him and the prone body on the ground. One of the older men with a flashlight began to shout to the others standing near the community building. Soon, all came running. Joel mustered up as much strength as he could, crawled to his feet, and ran as fast as possible toward the Moped hidden in the trees. Joel realized he was feeling extremely weak and his thoughts were getting foggy as he moved through the ambient lights of the nearby buildings. He could see his clothes were turning red from his blood loss!

Joel was only able to take five more steps when he ran out of energy and collapsed face-first to the ground. He could see the back reflector of the moped in the bushes just a few steps away but someone struck him on his back with something hard. Just before he lost consciousness, he heard someone screaming that Braun was dead.

Joel woke up lying on a steel bed with the smell of antiseptic in the air. He was handcuffed to the bed with an IV running into his arm. He attempted to sit up but was far too weak to move.

A small black man came over and examined his arm and shoulder. It was then that Joel noticed he was in great pain. Joel asked the man where he was and why he was handcuffed to the bed. The man introduced himself as Dr. James Whittington and explained to Joel that he was in a village clinic near Nicholstown on Andros Island.

The altercation with the commandant came crashing back to Joel. The doctor explained that Joel had been unconscious for two days and that as soon as the doctor felt he was strong enough to make the journey, Joel would be transferred into the custody of a constable coming in from Nassau

Although the doctor did not know the exact nature of the charges against Joel, he explained that they were serious enough that only the doctor and his nursing assistant were allowed to treat him or speak to him directly. That included the local Constables from Andros Island.

The doctor told Joel that the night before, an expensive-looking twin-engine aircraft had flown in from Miami and a number of very important looking men met in one of the hangars next to the airfield. He said the men were Americans, wanted to take custody of Joel. The Doctor told him that he had to threaten them with a call to his family, who were very important people in Nassau, to prevent these men from moving Joel out of the clinic.

The doctor had put 140 stitches in his arms and shoulder and told Joel that he had very serious, life-threatening injuries. He advised Joel to move carefully or the stitches wouldn't hold. Although Joel heard most of what the doctor was saying, with all the medication and pain, he fell back asleep, never imagining what the future held for him.

Back home, Adrian was frantic. She had been calling the motel every hour only to be told that Joel had not made it back to his room in the three days since he had checked in. The desk clerk said that Joel rented a moped, but that was all Adrian could gather.

After speaking with the desk clerk, the hotel manager, Paul Messing, realized that something was wrong. He contacted Adrian and told her that he would call a friend of his in San Andros to inquire further and would update her when he had any information.

Messing reported Joel missing but the local constable told him that they had no knowledge of Joel's whereabouts—or any other information regarding him. Meanwhile, Adrian called an old friend, Mary Koskoff, whom she had known many years ago from Harvard College and asked for advice. Professor Koskoff was the Dean of The Harvard School of Law and had always been a great advocate of Human Rights, especially regarding governmental abuse of power.

After Adrian explained what Joel was doing in the Bahamas and about his mysterious disappearance, Mary immediately agreed to assist Adrian. Mary called a friend of hers at the State Department and learned that there was, in fact, an incident in the Bahamas. He told Mary that although he did not have any additional information, the Secretary of State herself was personally involved and he would try to learn more.

Later that same day, an orderly led Joel out a back door and into the bed of a small truck. Joel saw two black men wearing brand-new suits standing about ten feet away, speaking American English—no accents. He quickly walked to them, but one of the black guards who were with the suits struck him violently from behind. As Joel fell to the ground, he saw the two men look the other way. He was beginning to feel a very old but familiar fear. The location had changed, the men had changed, but these men pulling him to his feet were just as callous, vicious, and dangerous as the ones in Poland.

Two large black men forced Joel into the rear of the truck and told him to lie down and not to look up. They drove off, and when they stopped a few moments later, Joel could see through a crack in the aged, green canvas covering the back of the truck that the two men in the suits were now speaking with one of the old men from the little German settlement, as well as an Arab man wearing a turban. They did not look at all happy as they watched the truck drive away.

Joel could tell that they were driving toward the airport because the turquoise blue ocean was to his right. Soon, they slowed and Joel could see his motel where his few belongings must still be located. That was the least of his worries as they passed into the airport. As they came to an abrupt stop, a propeller plane engine coughed to life. The next few hours would match any horror Joel had ever experienced in his life.

Adrian received a call back from Mary Koskoff about ten o'clock that same night telling her that her source had been informed that an unnamed American was being detained in the Bahamas for the murder of a Canadian citizen living in the Bahamas. The U.S. State Department was not releasing any information at this time and was leaving the matter to the Bahamian officials to handle as they saw fit.

It wasn't until two days later that Joel was informed that he was being officially charged with the premeditated murder of Stephan Braun. He was not allowed to make a phone call or speak with a lawyer. Still in handcuffs, he was flown to a small airstrip and then transported to a large, gray cement building balanced on a coral reef on the shore of a large island. Once the handcuffs were removed and he could see around him, Joel realized he was alone in a small cell. He could see out of a small, barred window toward the open ocean. The view was peaceful, but the rest of the accommodations and level of service was not.

Adrian took the morning train into the city to confront the Bahamas consul in person. She had been put off long enough by telephone. Paul Keis, Joel's eldest son (he had rejected the name change to Kelsey), flew to New York from his home in London to be with his mother and to try to find his father and bring him home. The Bahamians at the consulate were just as confused as Adrian was and claimed they could not help.

Paul Keis was a barrister in England with many influential friends in the legal community. One of these friends was Doug Partin. Paul called Doug from the airport as soon as he landed and explained what he knew so far. Doug had visited Paul's father and mother many times over the years and was concerned by the news. He immediately offered to help.

Joel, meanwhile, was sitting in his cell, going over the events of the past three days. He kept thinking back to the two Americans at the clinic and the way they turned and looked away when the guards assaulted him. He was sure they were U.S. officials and were there because of him. The more he thought about it, the more confused he became.

He asked the prison officials if he could see someone from the American Embassy, but he was told repeatedly that they had been notified and that they did not want to get involved. He was also told that he could see an attorney as soon as one was located to take on his case. Joel asked them many times to call his family. He even explained that his son, Paul, was a lawyer in Great Britain and could represent him here in the Bahamas. They did not allow him any calls—and told him he would lose any future privileges if he persisted in asking. Silence seemed to be the best policy, at least for the immediate future.

Paul met Doug Parton near the front door of the Bahamas Consulate Office in New York City. As they waited for Adrian to arrive from Penn Station, Paul filled Doug in on everything he knew at this point. Paul had called the Bahamas Prosecutor's Office before he left Heathrow for Kennedy, but he was told they had no knowledge of a Joel Keis and did not have him in their custody. They said they would look into it and call him back before his plane left. Paul never received the call. He called them again as soon as his plane touched down on the tarmac. After being rerouted through numerous people at the Prosecutor's Office, he was told that they had no knowledge of his father.

Doug took out his cell phone and called a familiar number from memory. Jake Storm! While Doug spoke, Paul heard his old friend speaking in some form of code as they arranged to meet near "the curbstone." Doug turned to Paul and said that he would know much more by the end of the day. Doug seemed pretty sure of himself...and confident in the man he had called.

* * *

I called Dave, my right- and left-hand man, at his little house near my island in the Banana River near Cape Canaveral, Florida, and asked him to prep the *Molly* for a two-week cruise. I also asked him to load my weapons into the secret compartments in the gunnels. Dave knew exactly what I would need for this kind of trip.

Dave and I had planned to fly up to Ashburn, Georgia, in my Cessna 182 for a couple of days relaxing and eating at the best barbecue restaurant in the south, Keith-A-Que's, and I know Dave was disappointed in the change of plans, but he would never show it. Keith's place is a safe meeting place for my sources and me in that section of the south. Not only is Ashburn a safe and relaxing hideaway, but it is also surrounded by military bases and some of the great intelligence minds in the entire world. After I got underway, Dave could fly up and smooth things over with the folks there and also see if they had any knowledge of the goings-on at Andros Island.

For me, my first stop would be Andros to see what I could find out about this German village and why there were Arab folks next door. The second part of the case would involve backing up Doug as he wound his way through the legal process in Nassau. Watching Doug is always interesting. He appears to grow more and more knowledgeably clever every year. Doug gets himself into lots of bad spots and very seldom cares what it costs. He has little regard for his own safety as he wallows in the legal mud. This time it was far more intriguing than the normal everyday venture.

I could sense that someone in a high place was nervous about this matter and was already gathering information about my whereabouts. I had received a text message from a good friend with Homeland Security that my name had become more prominent on the watch list with some obscure government agency.

As soon as I arrived at my parking spot on South Tropical Drive opposite my island, Dave picked me up in his boat and excitedly told me about a black helicopter that had buzzed the island with four passes and then flew toward the Tech lab at Patrick Air Force Base.

I immediately called my friend Gage Copeland from the Intel office at the Tech Lab on Patrick Air Force Base, and he told me that a couple of spooks were down from D.C. and had asked a lot of questions about me. Gage is one of my very best and most trusted friends, as well as my "information guru." If information is out there to see, hear, know—or even if it is not—Gage can and will find it.

I figured the spooks were trying to decide if I was ashore. That did not bode well for our safety. Somehow, we had stepped into a hornet's nest by my preliminary inquiries, and we hadn't even started our formal investigation yet.

It was about 23:00 and a good time to slip anchor and head out. With any luck, I could be gone and fifty miles out to sea before first light. That meant that I would have to shoot Sebastian Inlet in the dark. With an offshore wind, that was going to be rough!

stepped the mast of the *Slim Molly* forward about six feet and fastened it to the pulpit. That way, I wouldn't have to have any bridges opened. I gave Dave some further instructions on the nature of my mission and hauled in my anchor so I could begin my journey. I don't like to call Gage so late in the evening, but on this day, I thought it better to be safe than sorry. I rang Gage up and he told me to be extra careful. His exact words were, "Be extremely cautious like never before, Jake!" Coming from him, that meant a lot to me.

As a rule, I would have flown into the Bahamas and snooped around. It would have been faster and less complicated. But, seeing that I had already aroused so much attention, I felt that I should use the stealth method even though it would take three more days to see what was shaking. Having to be extremely cautious takes more time and keeps you on your toes every step of the journey.

My trip through the inlet was smooth. I hoped that the entire trip was as good. I reset my mast and was delighted to find I had a great northern wind to push me against the Gulf Stream current. I also cranked on my engine and had it going three-quarters throttle. I was now making about eleven knots. When I crossed the stream and headed south along the shallower water on the Bahamas side, I would average about seven to ten knots. That would bring me to the north coast of Andros in about sixty-one hours. I needed to stay in international waters to avoid the interest of the Bahamas Navy—or even our own Coast Guard. Now, if I could avoid the drug pirates, I'd be in the clear to see what we could do to save old Joel!

I stayed awake the rest of the night and avoided the numerous cargo freighters running the Straits of Florida. I also had to avoid all the trash thrown overboard by the ships. A fifty-five-gallon drum can ruin your entire day when it slams your hull! My boat is equipped with a forward-sensing sonar that gives me a little warning when there is an object with any density in my path. Unfortunately, you have to be awake and nearby to quickly swerve to avoid the collision. The boat is also equipped with a very sensitive Decca radar system that has saved the day on more than one occasion. I have learned to rest in the cockpit with the autopilot on and half my senses working. This way, I am at least partially rested.

About 1400 hours, (2:00 PM for the landlubbers) I spotted a well-worn game fisherman open boat turning in behind me about a mile off my stern. There were two men in the boat looking in my direction. The boat followed at that same distance for about an hour as if it was doing a fast trawl. I made a slanted turn to the southeast and, after a while, the boat did the same.

It certainly did not look like an official government boat or a sport fisher. That left only one other possibility—a drug pirate. They're a fairly uncommon breed in these waters, but not unheard of. There is a strict law in the Bahamas regarding weapons. No guns of any kind without a permit. So, these fellows had little to fear if they decided they wanted your vessel to use as a drug boat. Unfortunately for them, I have a permit to carry weapons in the Bahamas and far more armament than my permit allows. If only they knew what I had on board, they would be hightailing it in the opposite direction, full steam ahead!

I decided that I needed a persuasive remedy for this boat's curiosity before it radioed to any possible comrades it may have over the horizon.

Years ago, I was given the gift of a World War II British Enfield rifle. It's basically a 30.06-caliber round that is not only accurate but does powerful damage when it strikes an object. I allowed the boat to get about a hundred yards off my stern. I turned slightly to the east so I could run parallel to the swells for a few moments to calm the movement of my boat for accuracy and popped my first round perfectly into the stem of the boat's bow about one or two inches below the waterline.

The round apparently penetrated the bow stem and found a can of fuel on the deck or in a compartment. To my surprise—and the two men who were now holding long rifles in their hands—an explosion blew the entire boat and its occupants into a red, yellow, and black ball of smoke and flames. No reason to search for any survivors in that mess.

I have learned through the many trials in my life not to look back. I do feel some guilt for some of my actions, but not in a case like this. I knew who they were and what they were up to the minute I saw them slip in behind me. I have worked a number of high-seas cases of missing boaters, and although I've solved some of them, it's never a happy ending for the families of the victims.

I decided to run closer to shore just in case the Bahaman Navy came to investigate the black smoke slowly sinking into the sea behind me.

On the third day of my run, I cut toward the north shore of Andros. I had about eighty miles to go, by my latest calculations. I am pretty familiar with these waters. With my custom swing keel partially up, I can run over some fairly shallow water.

I radioed Dave a few times on the trip. He told me that the chopper had made a few more passes the next day and then disappeared. No one had been to the island or his house on South Tropical Trail to inquire about my whereabouts. Dave thought we might have bluffed them for a while. I was concerned that the occupants of the copter would have seen, at first light a couple of days ago that my boat was gone from its mooring and start searching the offshore waters for me. I hadn't seen any sign of them on my journey and they had come back to the island a few more times according to Dave, which told me they hadn't figured out where I was yet.

Unfortunately, I had not heard back again from Gage. Until I heard from him on specifics, I'd wait. I knew there were challenges lying in wait for me here in the Bahamas. I also knew I had to control both the time and the place.

The northern coast of Andros Island is actually a great plain of meandering coral reefs. My GPS system has a built-in avoidance mode that has taken the place of most yachtsmen's navigational skills. That includes me. At one time, I could feel my way around these waters with keen accuracy and a steady hand on the helm. That skill is now ancient with these days of modern technology. I can plug in my destination and my GPS devices will park me at the dock! I specifically said "devices" because I always have three working at the same time. A lazy navigator I may be. A dumb one I am not!

When I arrived at the little village of Nicholls Town on the northeast coast of Andros, I topped off my fuel tanks with diesel and then waited until the sun went down over the Straits before I motored into a snug little cove on the north shore. I wasn't far from what I believed to be the German village of San Andros. I did not clear customs with the local Customs Office, as I had never checked out of the Bahamas the last time I was here about two months ago.

I dropped anchor so the boat would swing on the tide and avoid the shallow reefs. The boat would be difficult to see from the coastal road and anonymous to any of the boats that passed out beyond the reefs.

I had been dragging my Zodiac black rubber dingy the past hundred miles. So, it was available as soon as I dropped anchor. Before I got too comfortable, I checked my GPS to see if I was close enough to the village to take care of my first order of business.

I paddled the Zodiac inflatable all the way to the beach so no one near the road could hear me. Not that there should be anyone around these parts at this time of day, but, again, "extremely cautious" was the rule of the day. I pulled my inflatable up into the bushes, covered it with some brush and palm fronds, and found a path to a small dirt parking area just off the road.

I figured that put me about a quarter-mile from the village to the west. That also put me about a half of a mile from the little commercial airport beyond to the west. I had heard a number of twin-engine planes landing as I came in close to the island, but none had taken off since my arrival. I cut across an old logging road toward the airport and, as I walked along the side of the road, I could hear a car coming from the direction of the airport. I cut back into the woods on the south side and ducked down as it passed. It was a small, dark-colored sedan. Four men were riding in it. As it traveled down the road, the shocks on the car squeaked and made it sound like an old Model A Ford. It went about two hundred yards farther down the road when I saw the reflection of its brake lights on the surrounding trees and saw that it turned right. I figured that must be the road to the village.

As I approached the narrowly paved road leading into what I thought would be the village, I saw lights in the sky and heard some voices in the distance shouting in what sounded like German. I have a difficult enough time speaking good ol' English, much less any foreign language, so, as they say, "It's all Greek to me."

I decided to go through the brush and pine forest to get a better look at the area where the voices were coming from. My survival instincts are far better than my language skills, thank goodness, and my senses stopped me short about fifty paces in.

I could feel a definite energy in front of me that could have caused my demise had I not stopped and focused on what was in my path. Squatting down about twenty-five yards ahead of me was a camouflaged sentry looking toward the east as I approached from the north. I could make out the outline and reflection of his rifle. He was wearing a U.S. Military-type war helmet. I realized that if he was here, there might be far more sentries scattered about in a defensive circle around the village. I did not know if I was out-numbered, but I did know I was not outsmarted.

Why would these foreign-speaking people on this island, out here in the middle of nowhere, rate the protection of uniformed soldiers with U.S.-made gear? This was getting more interesting by the minute! If you don't ask yourself the questions and put them on a wish list, you will never get the answers you are looking for until it's too late.

I had come on this first recon without any survival gear and decided to retreat to the boat so I could wrap my mind around this whole affair and come up with a plan of action.

As I headed back to the boat, I heard the low rumbling of a large turboprop plane at the nearby airfield. I recognized its sound as a KC 130 transport plane and that, for sure, meant military. This was not looking good for a single-man surveillance operation, and I knew that at first light, my boat would easily be spotted off the beach. I had some rethinking to do, and if Gage had any new intel, I needed to know everything he knew and more!

Back on the *Slim Molly*, I made a radio call to Doug's cell phone and left a message on his voicemail. Because it was fairly clear that one agency or another was monitoring most of his communications, I left a cryptic message in a language we had developed over the past thirty years of working together. I told him the water was warm but the sun was hot. It was 11:10 PM EST. He would immediately understand that there was something out of the ordinary going on here.

I powered up my engine and put a little strain on my anchor chain to keep the noise low. The Perkins diesel pulled me off the beach nicely and I decided to find a less conspicuous mooring.

I was fortunate to have found a few more sailing rigs to the east just above Nicholls Town and, set off about a hundred yards north of the most northerly sailboat, and dropped anchor again. Now, I was just another sailboat enjoying the waters just off the island.

Not being aware of the current state of communication monitoring, I decided to wait until morning to go ashore and use a landline to fill Doug in on this adventure.

During the remainder of the night, I heard a number of aircraft come and go from the airport and two helicopters buzz to the north. It sure was a beehive of activity for such a quiet little community.

At first light, I climbed out onto the deck and saw about fifteen boats of various sizes anchored out from Nicholls Town and a few more moored at the docks in the marinas. The most interesting boat was a Bahamas Navy, shallow-draft frigate anchored out about a mile from shore and about a half-mile from my current position. Using my binoculars, I could see two black sailors scanning the surrounding boats with large, post-mounted high-powered binoculars.

I had changed the name of my boat by hanging stern-mounted and side-mounted varnished signs that read the *Big Mamoo*. I even had International Registry papers to back up the new name. Although these papers were for a thirty-four-foot Morgan sloop, no one would know unless they were anal enough to break out a tape measure and stretch it from stem to stern. It would also stand up to an International data check because there was such a boat with the same name that belonged to an old friend. The real *Big Mamoo* sank off the coast of Mexico twenty-five years ago, but I have maintained its registry ever since. My friend never reported it gone, as he did not care to have it located and refloated. Something about an unfortunate fellow's demise during a questionable sailing expedition. Not for me to question.

As I watched the Frigate, I noticed a launch leaving its port side and heading in the direction of the mooring area where I was anchored. I decided that now was as good a time as any to inflate the big Zodiac I also carried, and head ashore. I had just hooked up my 6 HP British Seagull outboard when I heard the rumble of the launch about a hundred yards away. I pulled the starter rope and she fired up on the first pull. Dave's maintenance program for my gear never fails. I was off toward the town landing and out of the area of scrutiny. I never looked back.

As I slowly buzzed the little marina, I spotted two soldiers walking past the marina toward town. These guys were Caucasian and looked to be what you would consider good, young, average Americans. This was getting stranger by the minute. I pulled my rubber boat up on the sandy beach and went ashore. I guess it was as good a time as any to meet the other side.

As I passed the inside area of the marina, I saw a U.S. Coast Guard Class E Cruiser. The E is a small boat that the "Coasties" use to patrol the outer islands for drug smugglers. I noticed the young soldiers were looking at the Coast Guard boat, so I angled myself across the dock so as not to be noticed and then stepped on and off the launch as if I was coming off the Coast Guard boat and belonged there. Along with my camouflaged trousers, white t-shirt, short haircut, and close-cropped beard, I could have been a senior Coasty enjoying a little liberty, as were the soldiers just heading to shore for some island time. I saw that they had watched me climb off the launch and so walked toward them.

I caught up with them about a hundred yards from the marina and greeted them from behind. We exchanged small talk while walking toward the local area pub and café, and I asked them if I could buy them a drink. After buying four rounds of beer, along with a couple of whiskey shooters, these young men were more than willing to blab a blue streak about their mission and really anything else I wanted to know about them. We were sitting in the corner of the small outdoor café where I could easily monitor the road from the airport, as well as the village, and even see the *Slim Molly/Big Mamoo* in case the Bahamas Navy became too interested, or just nosy.

The taller of the two militants was named Thompson. He told me he was from New Hampshire. He had been in the Special Forces when he'd been discharged and then recruited by a company called Mentor Corporation, located in North Carolina. He had been with his section of Mentor for all of three months when they were called upon to fly to San Andros from Fort Bragg, North Carolina, to secure the safety of some American interest here in the Bahamas.

The other militant, Brewster, was less talkative but was annoyed to be away from his new girlfriend back in North Carolina. Brewster pulled out his wallet, took out a picture of his new girl, and said, "Now, she is a looker, isn't she?" Well, I had to agree, but I have seen prettier girls waiting for last call back home on a Friday night and yet, according to Brewster, she was "all that and a bag of chips!" Brewster was from Arizona and had been with Mentor for only about a month. They were happy to be on a five-hour pass. He was the first to state that the only thing they had seen that would be of American interest was an entire community of Stateside-type homes with a bunch of old foreigners living in them. "In grand style, nonetheless," he commented.

I urged them to talk more and another round for the table didn't hurt. They obliged by saying there were U.S. State Department suits meeting with the old-timers and a number of spook types carrying enough firepower to start a war with them. They also stated that there was a group of folks from the Canadian Government staying at the motel out by the airport. Sure seemed like an international congregation was going on here for some reason.

Thompson related that their job assignment was to provide security for the suits while they were here meeting with the local folks. The only thing they'd been told was that these were very important people and they were not to listen to any of the conversations at the risk of being fired on the spot. They asked if I was patrolling the coast. I had nearly forgotten they had believed I was off the Coast Guard boat in the marina. It was not far from the truth to say that I was, so I just nodded and took the last sip from my glass.

I told them that I had heard that the old folks at the village were former German soldiers. These young men were not that briefed on the goings-on and were not familiar with the language, so they just agreed, I guess, to pacify me. They were also just as puzzled about the Arabs living to the south of the German village. They had been instructed not to interact with any of the residents, and they'd both had their cameras and cell phones confiscated before they left North Carolina a few days before. They had also been forbidden to discuss any of the strange things going on at San Andros with one another.

I asked how Mentor had recruited them, and they said the Army provided them with a pamphlet when they were getting ready for their discharge. They both thought they were working for a top-secret government organization! The pay was very good and the assignments allowed them to travel on the company expense account, so neither of them had anything bad to say about Mentor.

I told them I was fascinated to see U.S. troops on this island. I told them that I had also spent ten years in the Marine Corps, did three tours in Vietnam, and had worked with the Army on numerous operations. I couldn't discuss any details with them, but I wanted them to know I was "one of the guys." At this point, they seemed to become even friendlier and wanted to buy me a drink. Finally!

The most interesting thing they said was that they had heard that three people were killed in the village, and one of the dead was a very important guy.

I asked, "Important in what way?"

But, neither of them knew the answer. The other two dead were just locals, not important. They said a fourth guy who worked at the airport was missing and it was rumored he was involved in one way or another with the deaths. They said that the Bahamas Police had someone in custody at the prison in Nassau.

"What for?" I asked.

They both looked at one another and tipped their glasses of beer at the same time so as not to have to answer my question.

A few minutes later, a black Hummer with custom top lights for night searches and a heavy-duty front winch pulled up out front and the two soldiers ran out, now half in the bag, and jumped in—I presumed for the ride back to San Andros. I had learned some valuable information, but now I was puzzled by the other deaths and the missing person. I needed to call the Major on a landline and report in while I was still able!

First, I called Dave on his cell phone. It had an out-of-state number and he changed it every couple of weeks with a burner phone. Dave told me that a civilian boat had cruised around the island twice over the past few hours and he had heard a Coast Guard call on the marine radio asking for help locating the *Slim Molly* in and around the east coast of Florida. It did not appear that anyone had landed on the island to look for me, but Dave is not an expert on these things and may not have seen the telltale signs.

Next, I called the Major on his safe phone and filled him in on the details I had so far. He told me that the Bahamas had finally admitted they were holding Joel and had charged him with three counts of first-degree murder. He was waiting for the State Department to receive and then to forward the charging documents. He would fill me in on our next call. He wanted as much information as I could get about this village and needed it as soon as possible. Because I needed reliable and accurate information, my next call was to none other than Gage.

First, I asked Gage to check into Mentor Corporation and get as much information as he could on where it had been established, who owned it, who was currently in charge, and what dirt he could find on them. I needed him to get back to me just as soon as he could. Gage said he knew about Mentor Corporation, actually knew a few guys within the organization from the good ol' days, and so would dig deep, move fast, and contact me with intel I could not only update the Major with but also use to my advantage.

After hanging up with Gage, I decided to go over to the little store/post office combo and see if any of the locals hanging around outside had any helpful information. Locals like to talk, but most of what they tell you is not worth the paper to blow your nose.

A handful of Bahamians were sitting on old, plastic, sun-stained chairs in the sandy lot in front of the store. All became quiet when I approached. I greeted them, showed them respect by making small talk until one of them jumped in and asked if I was here specifically because of the recent killings. Without affirming or denying anything, I asked what they knew of the subject. Most of them knew the two locals who'd been killed, and one knew the old German fellow. I prodded them to talk more and it appeared they were ready and willing.

They said all of the men were shot in the head. They had heard that the two locals were shot through the back of the head execution-style and that it was an absolutely horrible sight. They did not know how the old man had died but they had assumed in the same manner.

The strange thing was that Charlie Ambrose, who worked at the airport, had told a local deliveryman that he had seen one of the deceased, Paul Nelson, alive and quite well long after they had the old American in custody at the local Medical infirmary. Charlie must have known too much because he never came home that night from the airport. His wife, Leota, and eldest son had gone to the police, but they were told that they had no information regarding Charlie, and the police certainly disputed the information regarding the American. Both Leota and her son were told by the police that if Charlie had mentioned anything to them that they were not to be spreading rumors of any kind around the island and to just go home and wait for Charlie to return.

I had a bad feeling that good ol' Charlie wasn't coming home anytime soon!

I thanked the men for their friendliness and told them I would leave a few bucks with the bartender at the little café in case they got thirsty. I finished with the café keeper, who thanked me for my patronage and asked me to please come back anytime I had a pocket full of money. Upon leaving the café, I strolled over to my inflatable and pushed it off the beach.

As I cruised to my boat, the inflatable bouncing on each wave and throwing splashes of cool water on my sun-tanned face, I noticed that a few more boats had dropped anchor during the morning. I was glad I had picked this location, as it turned out to be a favorite spot for many boaters and now I was just one among the crowd. I decided all was safe there and

The Big Mamoo looked handsome among the other crafts, so I headed northwest around the top of the island.

I found a few tight passes in the coral that I could slide through with the inflatable when I did my next midnight recon, so I made mental notes and stored the info until I needed it. It was too far to walk from the north shore to the airport, so I headed back to town. This time, though, I was going against the tide and it took almost twice as long to get back. I finally made it and rode my Zodiac backup on the beach again. I thought it was time to get rid of my sea legs for a bit and ride around the area to see what I could see.

I rented a small scooter from the local bike shop for fifty dollars for half-day. It wasn't worth fifty dollars on a good day! I pushed the beaten-up old, white helmet with some Harley-Davidson stickers over my head and took Queen Ann's Highway, the road to the airport that passes by the San Andros village road. I was thinking whoever put these HD stickers on this helmet was either a jokester or thought maybe he was part Hell's Angel.

I rode along at a slow pace, looking like all the other tourists in these parts. Except for my special helmet, of course! I noted that the old road I had crossed over last night was a secondary road going a little farther north on the island called the Main Lumber Road.

As I passed the end of the village road, I saw there was a military-style blockade across the road manned by four militants. There was also a small, rubber-wheeled tank vehicle just beyond. The tank was equipped with a set of fifty-caliber machine guns on top. I could tell by how all the tires were flattened that there was a lot of ammo and extra gear inside the tank. Was this some serious affair going on here or what? None of the militants paid me any attention and I kept up my pace toward the airport.

As I turned to the south, I saw the end of the airstrip. Parked with tie-downs were two KC 130 aircraft just off the tarmac. I continued on to the motel restaurant and walked inside the lobby. Whenever I enter such an area, my first instinct is to glance around and take note of anything that seems out of place, make a mental note of it, and then carry on.

I approached the check-in counter, greeted the clerk, and used a pseudonym that I had an ID to back up. I carry numerous identifications, but my favorite is my authentic press credentials. I have an online news site called *The Florida Islands Gazette*, or *FIG News*. The site is legal and a Delaware Corporation pays taxes on it to make it so. My pen name is Jackson Place. So, after I introduced myself as Jack Place, I began to ask about the strange goings-on over the past few days and why so many American soldiers were hanging around the island. Of course, I was prepared to play the press card, if I had to, but it wasn't necessary. This clerk was not only talkative but also the cousin of the missing airport worker Charlie Ambrose. On islands like this, many of the locals are related to one another.

The clerk's name was Paul Ambrose and he was not buying any of the official's line that his cousin had just gone away for a few days. He knew Charlie better than that and knew he was either dead or being held against his will. I had to slow Paul down so I could keep up with the information he was relating. He told me that an older American guy had checked in a few days ago and rented a moped from the vendor next door. He said that the old man stayed in his room for hours and pointed to the far end of the line of rooms. He said that just after dark, the old man drove the moped toward Nicholls Town and he never saw him again. The next morning, his cousin Charlie said the old American was at the clinic in Nicholls Town under heavily guarded conditions. He appeared to be very badly hurt and bleeding, as his clothes were soaked with blood. Later that same day, one of the maids said that two of their friends who worked at San Andros were killed the night before, along with one of the old Germans who had lived there for many years. She said a crazy American killed them all at about 10:30 PM!

Charlie said the American was brought to the clinic at about nine o'clock. By chance, Charlie looked at his watch and so thought the maid must have had it wrong. Charlie called the constable's office from the motel lobby telephone and told them that he had seen the American brought to the clinic at 9:00 PM. Charlie was told by whoever was on the other end of the line to come to the constable's office right away and give a written statement. Charlie left in a hurry on his motorcycle and did not even wave as he always did when leaving his cousin. That was the last time anyone heard from him!

I decided that Paul was just about tapped out and headed back to my boat to get my satellite phone for better and more secure communications.

I'd always been random in my travels and decided to take the northern Main Lumber Road back. On my ride back, while the wind cooled my face and chest, I made plans to anchor my boat a little farther west than I did last night, which was farther away from the village and safer for my recon. I figured I could also stash my own moped, which I keep in the boat's hold, in the brush there. One of Gage's mottos is "Plan your work and work your plan," but, hell, my plans change so often and so fast, my own motto is more like," Plan to live and live another day to plan." It works better for me!

I took the rented moped back to the vendor, paid him in cash, and thanked him for that special HD helmet. He laughed and said that not many people he rented to looked like they could wear it and actually defend themselves if anyone kidded them about it. I had a chuckle on my way back to where the Zodiac waited, then another across the still waters and back to my boat.

The *Big Mamoo* seemed secure and none of my markers had been moved, so it appeared no one had been on board while I was away. I thought to myself, "Self...be extremely cautious the way Gage always recommends and tomorrow will be another day to plan."

As I moved my boat to the west and waited for nightfall, the sunset was just starting to draw its wonderful multicolor just above the horizon and over the green-blue waters. The mix of reds, oranges, yellows, and violets that embraced the ocean's colors was incredible. Actually, it was breathtaking, so I took out my Sony F828 and took what must have been twenty-five shots, each one a little different than the last. As the sun melted into the sea in front of me, I realized that even in a place like this, where things were happening that didn't make sense, there was still beauty to be appreciated.

I managed to drift over the shallow reefs and found a deeper area to drop anchor about the size of a football field. If there was any bad weather, at least now I didn't have to worry about being stretched to the end of my anchor line over a reef head.

I settled in to get a little R&R and to wait until two or three in the morning before my next movement. I had already loaded my moped into the Zodiac and decided to use that to travel to the woods near the village. I'd had Dave put a special muffler on the moped, as well as add a few other tweaks. Dave knows his business, and his business is to help keep me alive!

Just after midnight, I heard a helicopter fly west from the Morgan's Bluff area. It was patrolling the coast with its blinding searchlight. Looking for what or who, I was not sure. Just before it got to my area, it turned to the south, thank goodness, and flew west back toward the airport. I was anchored just far enough from the village to be of little interest to anyone. I started up my Onan generator to keep my batteries and satellite phone charged. I turned it on, let it warm up, and checked for messages left on my safe phone line. What I found was a message from the Major. He had been trying to reach me since the early afternoon. I told him I would call him as soon as I had some new information, but the Major calls whenever he feels like it.

I got the Major on my first try only to find he was clearly agitated about current events. He quickly laid into me. He had been visited by a team of suits—not ordinary suits, but ones that really meant what they said. They claimed to be representing the interests of a person or persons that did not want the Bahamas matter to cause an international incident. They had been quite clear that they would stop at nothing to bring this to a quiet end! This warning included dealing with "the Major's agent"—that would be me—who was currently snooping around the Bahamas. Well, I told the Major this wasn't the first time we were warned about one of our escapades, now was it?

I returned a few more important calls before shutting my eyes for a couple of hours. Upon waking—if sleeping with one eye open could be called sleeping—I grabbed a couple of bottled waters, an energy bar, and prepared to go ashore for a look around the village. I decided to put the Zodiac ashore about a quarter-mile east of the village just in case I had to run and swim. I should enter Triathlon events because I sure get the training for it.

I ran the inflatable ashore where I could still see the boat to the west in the twilight. I carried the moped to the Lumber Road. I had no doubt it would start on the first kick and it ran as smooth as silk. The little four-stroke engine was very quiet. Dave's muffler helped and I knew it would allow me to power in close before I had to shut her down and walk the rest of the way. I pulled out onto the road and turned east. The road had many potholes but this little breakdown bike was equipped with good springs to keep my butt from getting seat bruises. I hate to think of Dave when I am thinking about my own ass, but good springs don't just grow on trees, you know?

I left the bike about a hundred yards north of the village road and hit the heavily wooded area to the south. I used my super quiet feet this time. Of course, when you get to be my age the old ears lie to you. If you can learn to walk Native American-style (toe-to-heel) instead of normal steps (heel-to-toe), it is extremely quiet. You feel everything under your feet and can adjust your footing. I only hoped that the sentries on duty tonight were as bad and as half asleep as the ones I'd encountered last night. Heck, I hoped they were all snoring.

I spotted the first sentry about thirty yards off the road to my left. He was listening and moving to his iPod. I would have smacked any of my men over the head in Nam with my rifle stock if I'd caught him pulling that trick! I guess it was a good thing that iPods had not been invented yet—at least for my troops.

I took my time, made it by him, and then encountered the sound of voices and the scents of human activity. Food, soap, aftershave, and cigarette smoke are the most common. One of the most important lessons to learn in preparation for combat is to smell like your enemy or you'll walk into an ambush every time. It seemed a little early for so many people to be awake and moving about at this early hour. Then I remembered that the Arabs would be up praying before dawn and anyone within earshot would have been woken up by the call to prayer. It isn't something you would put on your iPod or play at a party, that's for sure.

I edged up to the big bush next to the largest building and kept myself low so as not to be detected. I could see two men wearing suit coats talking and could just barely hear snippets of their conversation. They said something about not worrying about a trial. It wasn't going to happen if they had it their way. I guessed that was not a good thing. I found it interesting that the first actual words I was able to overhear were about my guy Joel. A third man, much older, with a very strong German accent, soon joined the two. He was agitated over the prospect of having to move from San Andros or the islands in general, if this all became public. One of the Americans told him that the old man being confined would not make it to trial and his family would be dealt with if they knew anything at all about this matter. This was pertinent information that I needed to get to the Major right away.

I turned away slowly so as not to disturb the bush when I saw another large man walking up to the suits. This man was clearly a Middle Easterner. I took out my small night-vision camera that takes pictures in pitch-black conditions as if it is midday and took about ten rapid photos on quiet mode. As I studied the guy's face and recollected other photos I had seen of this man, I realized he was one of the most wanted men on planet Earth. It was Mohammad Zistubi!

I told myself that this couldn't be. I have seen a lot of crap in my life, but this was a total shocker. In the middle of nowhere, on an island in the

Bahamas, is this guy who is wanted for being one of the 9/11 masterminds. The Administrations had been telling us for years now that he was traveling with Osama Bin Laden in and around Afghanistan. If he was here, who else was here with him? And, what in the world were U.S. citizens doing here, protecting them? So many questions and, with this now embedded in my thoughts, so little time.

As I turned to head back to the road, a sentry walked right up to me casually and hesitated for about two seconds until his brain computed who I was or wasn't. That hesitation cost him a real bad Excedrin Extra Strength-type headache and a bruised temple from my right fist. He went down like a bag of lead, but, thank God, without a sound except for a slight click from his rifle as I caught it with the top of my foot. No one seemed to pay it any attention. Because of his lack of professionalism—or his lack of paying attention while on patrol—I now had an M16 rifle, eight magazines loaded with rounds, and a portable radio tuned into the security's frequency! I dragged the poor bastard into the tall grasses along the side of the houses and figured that hit to the head would keep him out of the picture for at least a few hours. So far—me: one, them: zero!

I managed to get back to the road. I could not help but notice that the rounds in the magazines were hollow points. This was totally against the rules of war. (Can you believe that there is actually a rulebook for war?)

As I was riding my moped toward the beach where I had stashed the Zodiac, the walkie-talkie came alive with shouts of alarm. I guess they'd found Sleeping Beauty a little faster than I had hoped they would. As I intently listened to every word of the alarm orders on the air, I realized they had no idea of what had actually happened. They were shouting something about searching for one of the old men from the village and warning that he was heavily armed and dangerous. This was so bizarre! Either they were dumber than I thought or someone had thrown them a curveball! Either way, I was now sure that they had no idea that I had been there.

I left the bike neatly concealed in the bushes and paddled oh so slowly out to the boat. As soon as I had boarded her, I heard several vehicles' engines racing down the Main Lumber road and some fading shouts. No one sounded happy. The radio was completely quiet now so they had finally realized that one of their radios was missing. Smart as they were, or think they were, anyway, I started scanning all the frequencies and found them soon enough. They were conducting a thorough search as they headed toward the airport and another group was moving toward Morgan's Bluff. I was debating if I should haul anchor or sit quietly for the night. I didn't want to leave my little bike behind—boy would that piss off Dave after all his hard work—so I decided to stay and make contact with the Major. I hauled my anchor line in a few feet and secured it so I could pull out faster if I had to leave in a hurry. Fast getaways are one of my specialties.

When I contacted the Major and told him about Joel not making it to trial, he blew his stack with typical Doug Parton legal-speak. His next order was nothing short of exactly what I was expecting: "Get Joel covered or break him out. Just make it happen!"

I told the Major about the crazy mix-up of soldiers looking for an old man instead of me. He replied that a number of U.S. agents were working this matter and they may be going after someone who knew that I was involved.

I seem to run into old friends and acquaintances all the time in this business. Most of my old friends are police or government agents. That someone in the area should recognize me wasn't impossible. I'd thought I was being clever. (Of course, it was possible that I was the old guy they were describing and I looked a lot older than I thought!)

Now, I had to figure out how to get into the big, cement prison over on New Providence Island and make this right. I was sure that the Major had told the family that it was all going to work out perfectly. One of these days, I was going to mess up really bad and the Major would have a great deal of egg on his face!

I decided to set up the GPS GoTo, the little gizmo that navigates for me, for the sail to New Providence Island, and I had to leave before sunrise. It was a clear and star-filled sky and, with the help of my forward-looking sonar and my depth recorder, I was able to slip out of the little harbor without as much as a scrape to the keel. Technology is so wonderful, and good old-fashion luck is even better.

Once I cleared Morgan's Bluff to the south, I let the autopilot and GPS take over for the trip to New Providence and Nassau. I pulled the mainsail in tight and let out the jib to catch the stiff breeze from the northwest. These were perfect conditions for the run to the east. The sun was climbing the horizon and shone like a flaming, orange ball, making it difficult to see dead ahead.

As I watched the radar screen, I spotted two blips due east closing in. From the size of the return, I could tell they were not just wooden fishing boats but large, dense boats of metal with some height from the surface. I knew I was encountering a couple of Bahamas Navy cruisers. Not a good sign.

A quick check of my cockpit and a glance down into the cabin told me that I had properly concealed my weapons and any other thing of interest to the Coast Guard or police, so I kept on sailing.

I tried to split the difference between the two boats, hoping they were not interested in me, but the hail from the loudspeaker on one of the ships was not a good sign. Even worse, I was told to drop my sails and prepare for a boarding party. I've always enjoyed a little party, but this wasn't going to be one of them.

I dropped the mainsail and let out the jib. As the sun cleared my vision, I saw a big naval cruiser blocking it and four Bahamian sailors pointing M16 rifles in my general direction. Now that wasn't good!

I let the sloop drift close enough for the sailors to gaff my boat alongside theirs. I was ordered to stand back and place my hands in view. Two sailors boarded the boat and searched it thoroughly, not asking any questions. They seemed satisfied that I wasn't carrying any contraband and ordered me to board the cruiser.

After being led to the bridge, they ordered me to stand fast on the forward deck. After about ten minutes, I was escorted into a small room behind the bridge. Sitting at a small table was a large man wearing Military style, multi-pocketed camo trousers, and a green polo shirt. As soon as I was inside the door, Polo Shirt ordered the crewmen out and kicked the door shut from his chair. He looked up at me with a broad smile and jumped up to hug me like a massive bear.

My fear drained out of me as I hugged back a man who had served alongside me in Vietnam and, since then, a few times in Central Africa. Ron Sorensen! CIA, NSA, Former Marine Corps Intelligence, and any number of lettered, named organizations you can think up. This guy was the real McCoy. Everything anyone ever imagined in books, movies, or fantasy stories—this guy had done many times over. Anytime an agent was missing, captured, or stranded in a hostile environment, Sorensen went in and snatched him out. And, here he was, squeezing the breath out of me as if I had just made the winning touchdown for my high school football team. This was a reunion of friends and a bit of a rescue for old' Number One!

Sorensen explained to me that he had received word late yesterday from our mutual friend Calvin White, of the Bahamas Intelligence, that I was in trouble and may need some help. Sorensen lives in the Miami area and he flew his small Cessna to Nassau right away and, with Calvin's influence, boarded the cruiser and steamed all night toward San Andros. When the sun came up and my boat appeared on the western horizon, Sorensen recognized the *Slim Molly,* now the *Big Mamoo,* right away. It made no difference what I'd changed the name to.

He knew to look in the North Andros area after hearing that a militant working for Mentor Corporation had been assaulted there a couple of hours earlier. Only one person would have been deep inside a secret U.S. operation, knocking out soldiers and slipping away. He knew just where I would be when he learned of my involvement in this matter.

This is probably a good time to mention that Sorensen is known as "The Tree" to his close friends. The reason being obvious. The Tree explained that there was a top-secret group of safe houses on San Andros and that these people had been protected for a good long time. He himself had only learned about them in the past few days when the American showed up and killed the German and the panic button had been pushed. He received a call from Calvin as soon as he heard what was going on in San Andros and knew I would need help.

I decided to trust Sorensen with my additional sighting of the Middle Easterners and my positive ID of Zacharias Musaki and had photos to prove it, in the same compound. I also told him about the Mosque and bodyguard types with the Arabs.

The Bahamians on board the Navy cruiser were in the dark about my involvement and only knew what Sorensen had told them. They thought I was another agent and had been in some kind of trouble with a possible hostile passenger, thus the search of my boat. Tree thinks of everything.

Sorensen requested that the cruiser tow my boat back to Nassau Harbor so he and I could meet and come up with a plan. Why ride the rolling waves in a sailboat when you can have a real cabin and fresh-cooked food? Of course, Sorensen wasn't aware that I preferred my little sailboat to any other form of residence.

He announced that he was taking a few days off to work with me on this matter. Didn't ask, just announced. Over the years as friends and working partners, we've sort of worked out a system of watching over each other. If he went off the radar, I would go and find him. It was the same with him. He has assisted me in almost every major case I have ever worked.

We arrived at the naval berth near Nassau and pulled my boat alongside. I boarded the *Big Mamoo* once again, as I preferred to anchor her off the beach and use the inflatable to go ashore.

Sorensen and I made plans to meet a little later near Cable Beach to work out a plan to help Joel. As I powered out of the shipyard, I noticed one of the cruiser's officers speaking with a white tourist-looking fellow near the dock. It would not have been that unusual except that they were in a restricted zone and I and my boat appeared to be the center of their attention.

I decided then to move my boat around to the east side of the island instead of off Cable Beach. There were coves on the northeast side where I could nestle in between a few of the fishing boats for some cover.

After running about ten miles north, I noticed a small speedboat with two men on board running behind me and gaining quickly. One of them was standing in the bow and appeared to be holding a camera with a long lens. There wasn't much wildlife out here to photograph, so I was pretty sure I was their subject of interest.

I decided to tact toward the east so I was broadside to the boat's bow. The small boat slowed but kept its course north. The cameraman began taking photos of me and the *Big Mamoo*, which I really wasn't too fond of, and he moved the camera slightly to take in every inch of viewable surface. I turned to the north again and they broke off and headed back toward Nassau. Hopefully, they were satisfied that I was leaving the islands.

The eastern sky was darkening with the close of the day. I was busy preparing to turn to the east to find suitable anchorage when I again felt those old, familiar impulses on my skin that I was about to find the near future a bit uncomfortable. Never a good sign!

I heard it before I saw it. A small, high-wing plane on the horizon was flying north at low altitude along the same path I was on an hour before. There was no doubt in my mind that they were searching for me. I did have the advantage of enough wind to cover my easterly wake line. In ten more minutes, I would have all the cover of darkness.

I watched them in my peripheral vision and willed them to keep their northerly course for just a few more moments. I also pulled down my mainsail and shortened my jib to change my boat's profile as much as possible. I could see a number of trawler fishing boats to the south and east of me and I might just fool them enough at this distance.

I watched through my binoculars as the plane turned slightly east and then banked to the south. I could now see it was circling a sailboat anchored near a small island. The plane flew in low over the sloop and automatic rifle fire erupted out first one side and then the other. The boat rocked back and forth from the impacts and the mast collapsed like a huge, fallen tree into the water. The rifle fire tore the boat to shreds and it leaned to port a bit and then started down to the bottom. The water must have been very shallow because the boat settled, bow up, and stopped sinking. The plane circled one more time for a confirmation view of their efforts and then flew off to the west. There was no doubt in my mind that the boat had been sadly mistaken for mine.

I changed course, came about, and headed for the sunken boat, keeping an ear out for a returning plane or any other new friends I might have made. There seemed to be little hope for anyone surviving what I had just witnessed. I came alongside the stricken boat but saw no sign of life—or, for that matter, signs of death. I searched through the holes in the cabin roof with my waterproof flashlight and saw no bodies or signs of blood.

I dropped my anchor, stripped down to my shorts, dove into the warm water next to the wreck, and looked closely through the portlights to see if anyone was lying in the air pocket near the overhead. There was nothing at all to indicate life or death. I then noticed that the hatch into the cabin was latched and padlocked. This boat had been at anchor and the owners were either out in their dingy or ashore on the island. I was happy that no one was hurt and could now refocus my attention on the matters at hand.

I swam back to my boat and inflated the small Zodiac. It was a short paddle to the beach, but instead of grounding the inflatable, I paddled around the shore, looking for any signs of life. About fifty yards around the north side of the small island I saw some fresh footprints and what appeared to be a pile of towels and bathing suits. The footprints led into the brush. I paddled a little closer to where the small breakers rolled up toward the sandy beach. I called to the bathers I could now plainly see ducking down in the bushes and told them that I saw what happened to their sloop and that I was not connected with the shooters on the plane. I introduced myself as pleasantly as I could and gently warned them that whoever was in that plane may have a shore party on the way to inspect their dirty work.

Once all of us were safe aboard the *Big Mamoo* and I had calmed them down from their adrenaline rush, we had time to get to know one another.

My new friends were John and Suzy Nelson from Melbourne, Florida. I explained to them without giving too much detail that their boat had probably been mistaken for mine, as I was involved in an investigation on the island that may have almost cost them their lives.

John explained that they had been sunbathing late in the afternoon and had fallen asleep due to the coolness of the afternoon breeze. The sounds of the low-flying airplane and then the thunderous gunfire woke them. When they ran to the side of the island where their boat was moored, they saw it was completely destroyed.

John told me that he was a freelance reporter for the *Today* newspaper in Brevard County, Florida. He was a crime writer and was currently working on a book about tourists being victimized in the Caribbean area. He'd certainly not expected to get this kind of research experience. But he did say it would make for good print. I told John he better be careful about what he put in print about this episode. I also told him not to get too carried away about speaking about it openly, except to the authorities. John agreed.

Suzy was a clerk for the Senior Circuit Judge of Brevard and Seminole Counties in the Melbourne area. I could tell they were both still in a state of shock. They were talking fast and telling stories about themselves that they would probably later find embarrassing.

We talked a little longer had some cold water and then I sailed with them to the north side of the island so they could get a taxi back to Nassau and report the incident to the local authorities. It would not have been in my best interest or theirs to sail back into the harbor and announce that my boat and I were still safely afloat. Others not knowing this gave me an edge.

I gave John three hundred dollars cash, as everything they had was on their sunken boat. After they reported the incident to the local authorities, they could rent a small boat at the marina to attempt to salvage the few things from their boat that may have escaped the bullets. Jake said his wallet and Suzy's purse were in a waterproof satchel in the hold of the boat. That was all that really mattered to them at this point, as they were grateful to have their lives and each other. The Nelsons said they would try to keep my name out of it for a few hours until I could find a hidey-hole in some hidden cove. We promised to get together when I got back to the Melbourne area.

After dropping them at a long dock near a small shopping area, I motored south toward some little coves that I was familiar with from previous cruises. Although the thoughts running through my mind were disturbing, I still had many pleasant memories of past outings in these islands. Never let one thing cloud the mind or darken thoughts of good memories of the past. I always try to tell myself that when confronted with situations of this nature.

I found a cove where I had spent some time a few years ago. The old weatherworn sailboat wreck with half of one side buried in the sand was still on the beach, and no one had built any structures here yet. I had plenty of food and water aboard and no need to shop for a few more days. I had left my moped in the bushes on San Andros, so I had only the inflatables to use for transport around the island. I knew that walking would be the best choice, anyway. I spent the rest of the night in my comfy bunk and slept fairly well, given the circumstances.

T he next morning, I inflated the big Zodiac and cruised south a few miles and then west until I was in view of the big, gray prison on the south side of New Providence Island. The monolithic-looking structure was still as bleak and unnatural looking as I remembered it. I couldn't believe anyone could survive in that place for very long. I had been in there some years ago with Calvin to interview a drug smuggler who was a witness to a case I was working at the time. There was no air-conditioning whatsoever—not even for the guards or in the few office areas. There were very few windows or outside ventilation ports to circulate the air within the walls. It sits on an old reef bed that is three or four hundred yards from shore. It towers over the water as if it's floating.

It's a great conch collecting area, but of little value to anyone. You can walk up to the back of the prison and barely get your feet wet at high tide.

I floated with the current for about a mile south and held my cheap Zebco fishing pole in my hands in case the guards from the prison watchtowers were watching me. I had my ball cap pulled down low on my eyes to disguise my looks as much as possible. It also helped me to see past the glare off the water.

I had my compact, digital, high-definition movie camera pointed toward the prison next to my fishing rod so I could play it later and study every facet of the walls and drain systems on my flat-screen HDTV back on the boat. I could clearly see two large, rusted discharge pipes snaking into the water across the coral field. They appeared to be about five to six feet in diameter. Because it was a prison, I was sure there were metal screens welded on the ends and a few random bars welded in along the length to deter escapees from venturing too far down one of the pipes. At least, that is what the prisoners would have been told upon entering this hellhole.

I also noted two small trucks with large, oversized wheels and tires parked at the edge of the water on both sides of the prison. From what I could make out, there were two people in each truck. There were also a few other bonefish boats along the reef near me, so I did not think I was of any concern to anyone looking in my direction.

I cruised back and forth about a mile past the prison in both directions for about an hour and then headed back to the *Big Mamoo*. I had seen enough to know that there did not seem to be an easy way onto the prison grounds. I'd have to make contact with Calvin tomorrow to see if I could get in through the front door. I didn't like to put my friends in jeopardy, but it would be worth asking. The worst he could say was no.

As I arrived at the cove where my boat was moored, I noticed a small boat heading toward me from the north. I kept my northerly heading and cruised past the inlet so I would not attract attention to my boat sitting in the noonday sun deep inside the cove. The small boat had one occupant, as far as I could tell. It changed its course and headed right toward me. I had not brought any weapons with me except for a small pocketknife. But, with this particular Zodiac, I did have the ability to skim over the shallow reef near the shore, whereas his boat would strike the bottom ten feet in. I cruised safely on.

I was about to take evasive action and turn left across his bow when I recognized Sorensen. He was sporting a bigger-than-usual grin and he offered a hearty wave of his arm. He was certainly a welcome surprise in light of the last few dire days!

I drifted up to his gunwales and shook his hand gratefully. His face was good to see for a second time in the last two days.

Sorensen explained that he'd become worried when I did not show up at our Cable Beach meeting yesterday afternoon. When he received word that a sailing vessel had been sunk off the north coast, he sought out the owners at the Nassau police compound and questioned them as soon as they left the site for a hotel. He said it was not easy to get them to acknowledge my existence. He commented that I must have done a good job making them understand I would be in harm's way if they acknowledged my interaction with them, but, finally, did so after Sorensen related a few stories that only a close friend of mine could tell. I couldn't wait to hear what those stories were!

Sorensen told me that the shooting of the sailboat had attracted attention from a couple of returning fishermen and that they had alerted the Bahamas authorities. Upon arriving at the scene, they found no bodies or signs of injury on the exposed parts of the sunken boat, so they thought the boat had been abandoned and shot up as an insurance scam. The shooting part is not common, but people desperate and in financial straits do sink their boats for insurance purposes more than you think. It was not until the Nelsons showed up at the Nassau Police Depot that anyone realized the extent of the circumstances.

Sorensen knew as soon as he heard about the incident that I was somehow involved. In fact, he first thought it was my boat and that I had been the missing victim. As soon as he heard about the Nelsons, he hung around the depot until he saw them leave and then confronted them. After hearing their story, he knew I would be skulking around in one of the northern or eastern coves. That was how he'd found me so quickly.

Sorensen had looked into finding the small aircraft used in the rifling and sinking of the Nelsons' boat. It was last seen flying west toward Andros Island. Two fishermen read the numbers on the plane.

The tail numbers were United States issued, beginning with an "N," but were incomplete and didn't match any numbers issued by the FAA.

From what he could find out, the tower at the airport did not have any planes on their radar in that area and no radio calls announcing any arrivals or departures. Many drug smugglers used these small, single-engine planes to evade detection by the shore surveillance and fly into U.S. territories. It was easy if you had the government helping you—as I now believed was the case. Sorensen was diligently working on finding the aircraft and its occupants through his sources, but all I was concerned about was coming up with a plan to help Joel.

I called Calvin on his safe phone and left a message giving him a specific time to meet near the Straw Market next to the port. Sorensen and I took his little skiff around the island to a dock about a half-mile east of downtown Nassau. We walked the rest of the way down tree-lined roads that were obviously not used much for travel from the loose dirt that bore no tire tracks or footprints. When we got to the Straw Market, we each bought a set of hats and sunglasses and some horrible, flowered button-up tourist shirts—mine had parrots all over it—to blend in with the folks off the cruise ships.

I was interested in the Bahamas Naval officer I had seen speaking with the civilian after we docked on the naval cruiser. I was curious about why he would be speaking to a white civilian as soon as we docked

We went to the bayside of the Straw Market where we could clearly see the Navy cruiser. There were a number of sailors and officers standing next to the docked ship, but I did not see the officer in that group. As we walked with the tourist crowds along the seawall, looking here and there as if sightseeing, I finally spotted him walking out of the Nassau Government Building. He walked east toward downtown and then slipped into a small bar next to a bank.

Sorensen waited outside while I went in to see if the officer was meeting with anyone in particular. The bar was almost completely empty except for a young girl wiping the tables in the rear, a tray of empty beer bottles and a few used ashtrays in her other hand. She looked directly at me and then turned her head toward a door in the rear. I nodded a thanks to her and walked to the door.

Before I even opened the door, I could hear talking and some island music playing at low volume. When I opened the door, I found it led to the establishment's restrooms and kitchen in the rear. The door to the kitchen had a small window in it and gave me a perfect view of the officer and two white men in short-sleeved shirts. I walked back out to the bar as if I had used the restrooms—just in case anyone else saw me—and gave the waitress a twenty-dollar bill and left the bar.

I looked around and quickly found Sorensen speaking with a moped vendor across the way. He did not say a word to me. He just handed me a blue helmet. I was happy it did not have any damn stickers on it. Together, we rode through the crowd around the Straw Market and then around the next bend to the Cable Beach road.

As we approached the old Cable Beach Hotel, we passed an official-looking car going the other way. It was moving fast and nearly forced us off the road. Behind it was a similar car, only much bigger. This car was sporting an American diplomatic flag on its front bumper. The windows were blackened out but it did not take much imagination to realize it was a very important U.S. official and they were in a hurry to get to Nassau.

Calvin was waiting for us right on time on the beach area where they once filmed the James Bond movie *Thunderball* in the Sixties. This has always been a secure spot as it was off the main road and had a number of dark, shaded areas under the numerous trees planted in an oasis-like setting for use by the cast working on the movie set. The rest of the beach and coastal areas are littered with low-rise condos and resorts. The people who own this lot must be die-hard sentimentalists.

Calvin motioned to us from the porch area of the old house. We embraced, as was Calvin's custom. We had been like brothers since we met in the late 70s. He had lived with me in the States for a while as an exchange student. During that time, I got him interested in the intelligence business that later helped him make good choices while climbing the career ladder. When your ladder is leaning against the right wall, you can climb faster and go farther. Now, he is near the top of Bahamas intelligence and, someday, may well be Prime Minister.

Calvin knew the details of the shooting and boat sinking from the day before and was busy tracking the parties responsible. He knew without a doubt that it had to involve some of his own people because it could not have happened without a sanction from his small government. He suspected that it might even reach into the Prime Minister's office. That was very troubling to Calvin.

He found out that the small plane involved had flown all the way back to the Tamiami Airport in west Dade County, Florida. Calvin had been able to track it with the help of his people who worked for the FAA at the Miami Airport. The plane had been allowed to fly under the radar and land without challenge by the Coast Guard and the Customs Bureau. That meant there was a lot of muscle behind this operation.

I have worked many odd cases and have seen a lot of corruption in my days. This was the motherload of all corruption cases. This San Andros matter had to reach to the highest levels of both the U.S. and the Bahamas governments. It appeared that many different agencies might be cooperating in this matter.

With all that had been going on, I was just beginning to feel the depths of this case. At least three governments were involved: The U.S., Canada, and the Bahamas. Not just a few individuals, but entire agencies. This might include an international policy greater than Operation Paperclip and Operation Overcast!

I thought about contacting Gage for an update, but first I made a safe call to my friend at Homeland Security. His code name is Mountain. His real name is Brody. He is near the top of most law enforcement activities all over the globe. I received his voice mail and left a brief message that I was out of pocket but needed answers to some puzzling questions. He called me back not three minutes later. He already knew about most everything I'd told him.

He said that most of the underground Washington buzz was in an uproar over this matter and that it went far deeper than Sorensen and I could possibly imagine. Brody stated that what I had stumbled upon was decades old and reached back through many administrations to the early Fifties. He told me that there was an actual, permanent secret committee that was set up to handle this matter and that it became much more of a chore for the committee after the 9/11 disaster. He told me he would keep his ear to the track and would update me as he heard additional information helpful to us.

Sorensen was busy making his own phone calls and briefed me on his information when I finished telling him what Brody said. Sorenson and I looked at each other with almost the same expression and said, "Time to touch base with Gage, isn't it?"

But, before calling Gage, Sorenson wanted to finish briefing me on his most recent information. First of all, he said that he had been ordered back to his station in Miami. This was not a request but an order! He was told to stand down with regard to any further relationship with me on this matter. We had a great laugh at that. Sorensen would rather die than let me down for even a moment. He was also told that when he arrived back in Miami, he would be meeting with some people who wanted to debrief him on everything he knew about my actions and whereabouts.

The last thing I heard him say before he hung up was, "Truck you very much, sir!"

Both Calvin and I knew "The Tree" could say almost anything he wanted to his superiors, as he was the greatest asset they had in the intelligence community. Sorenson commanded respect from all corners of the world and was not about to be canned or disciplined for his often-crude remarks. Most believed that without him our country would fall completely apart.

With that business out of the way, the three of us sat down and sorted out what we really knew at this point. We also bantered back and forth with our reasons for getting involved with this in the first place. The bottom line was, "Because it was the right thing to do!"

My next phone call was to Dave so he could be on the lookout for snoopers, and then to Gage for a much-needed update.

Gage told me that Mentor Corporation catered to a variety of executive clients with high-profile security needs in locations all over the world, and that they, by all accounts, were extremely discretionary and exuded an air of "quiet professionalism" that was above reproach. We had been aware of the folks who made up Mentor, as that organization had had numerous names over the years but basically did the same type of missions. Some good and some not so hot, in my opinion. That was until a newcomer appeared on the scene a little less than a year ago who became Chief Operations Officer almost before anyone knew what was going on. Along with such a high-level, executive change had come many other changes.

Gage said that some of the best-trained individuals that we'd both known from the old days were terminated from their employment almost overnight. They had also had all of their equipment, weapons, and gear confiscated as if they were criminals.

The new guy's name was Bruno Weiss. Background checks on him revealed that he did not exist before 2002, and Gage only knew that he was from Wurzburg, Germany. There was no information in America, or anywhere else in the world, relating to this guy. And, Gage knew where to look when it came to finding out information on people who did not want to be found. But, try as only Gage might, there was nothing.

Gage went on to say that one of his insiders who still maintained a position with Mentor told him that it had dropped important clients all over the place since Weiss came on board. Their focus over the past year was the Bahamas, the surrounding islands, a few remote places in the Middle East, and parts of Africa. Gage said that unless I personally knew a Mentor person from the past, I wasn't to trust them for a second. I was also to be extremely cautious when I was within their sights. That is just one of the reasons I love this guy so much. Gage isn't just a friend; he is blood!

After speaking to Gage, Sorensen and I turned to Calvin, who had been gathering his own intelligence while we were hunkered down in the sand dune. He had just found out that the old American had been moved from solitary to general population. This was a bad sign for Joel's health. If someone had set a hit on Joel, there was no way to prevent it. We had to move fast!

The first thing Calvin did was call his office on his government phone to see if he had been associated with us yet. After getting normal messages from his office, he called his wife and told her he would be a little late getting home for dinner. She acted normal and had no messages for him, nor did she mention any unusual incidents at home. It seemed all was good from Calvin's point of view.

Next, we all climbed into Calvin's official car, as cramped as it was for Sorensen. He may be one big lug, but his size has gotten us out of many a fix, so I'll give him the extra room in a crowded vehicle anytime. We proceeded to drive to the old prison. We decided to play it as straight as we could by using Calvin's official position within the government.

We were allowed right through the gate to the inside parking lot. Calvin led the way to the warden's office and found a Captain with whom he was familiar and, introduced us as American agents. He told him we were taking Joel Kelsey into our official custody. Calvin did not think that Joel's real name—Keis—would be used, and he was spot on.

The Captain never flinched, answered, "Yes, sir," and called a guard outside his door to bring the prisoner Kelsey to his office immediately. Everything was going well so far!

After making some small talk with the captain and getting an offer of coffee, the guard came back—but with no Kelsey. He informed us that Kelsey was in the infirmary and could not walk after falling down some stairs about an hour before. That was a real problem.

Calvin thought about it for a moment, made eye contact with me, and then ordered the captain to have Joel carried to his vehicle. He told the captain he was not concerned about the prisoner's health and did not care what condition the prisoner was in. He just wanted him gone from his hair.

We stood firm as if we had intentions to get him ourselves, should the Captain not follow Calvin's request. I knew what Calvin was thinking. *If we did not get him out of here right now, Joel is a dead man.* Joel had not fallen down the stairs; he was pushed. We were lucky he was still alive!

The captain hesitated only a moment, thought better of it, and ordered the guard to take whatever measures necessary to have Kelsey carried out to the parking lot. He then called another guard in and asked him to prepare and bring in the release papers.

Calvin said that would not be necessary, as the prisoner had never been officially checked in. The captain looked confused but did not argue with Calvin. It suddenly dawned on me that Calvin might have been throwing away his entire career.

The Captain walked us to Calvin's small car. Just as we arrived in the parking lot, I saw two guards were carrying Joel from another exit. He was in bad shape. He had been beaten and looked practically dead already. His two guards looked puzzled as they surveyed the small car, but Calvin had them prop Joel up in the middle of the rear seat and put a seatbelt around him to hold him in place while Sorensen and I squeezed into the space on either side of him. Calvin started the car and we returned to the gate leading out.

The gate guard let us out of the compound with no hesitation. We were on our way!

As we passed the first small village just west of the prison facility, Calvin's official cell phone rang. He looked at it, let it ring three times, and then canceled the call. He looked in his rearview mirror without speaking. His eyes said it all. He turned down a small road and up to an old wooden house painted sky blue with darker blue fascia trim and white shutters at the windows. As we came to a stop, Calvin told us we were changing vehicles and almost did not wait until the car stopped before he climbed out.

As he ran into the house, we had our first opportunity to look Joel over to see if he was going to make it. He sure looked bad, and he was making strange noises as he breathed. There was no doubt that if we did not get him medical attention soon, this would have all been for naught. As I spoke his name and focused my energy on him, he responded by making eye contact with me. I told him who I was and that I was working for a friend of his son, Paul. I then told him he had to fight and hang on for Adrian and his two sons. They needed him back with them more than ever. He perked up and seemed to pull more energy from me.

Calvin came around from the back of the house and motioned for us to get Joel and follow him. We carefully pulled Joel out of the car and carried him to the rear of the house where Calvin was talking to a man driving a jitney bus. We hauled Joel into the jitney and covered him with a large blue blanket the driver had thrown to me. Calvin gave Sorensen and me large straw hats and told us to hide our white arms the best we could as we drove the opposite way toward the north side of the island. Before we left, Calvin pulled some wires out from under the dash of his government car and threw the keys to a young boy who could not have been more than twelve years old standing by the house. The boy ran to the car and, as we drove off, I saw the boy driving the car through a field of grass and into some thick woods. Calvin told us that his car had a locating device installed and he'd just disabled it.

It was not long before we heard what we thought were the sounds of large vehicles racing toward the prison from the direction of Nassau. There was also the sound of sirens in the distance. We crouched low on the seats of the open-sided bus and tried to hide our faces from any of the passing cars. A few people walking by the side of the road tried to flag the jitney down for a ride, but the driver shouted that he was off-duty.

The driver pulled into a funeral parlor with the name "White and Bixby" on an old sign near the road. He pulled under a canvas awning at the rear of the building and stopped.

Calvin pointed for us to carry Joel to the door at the back of the building under the awning and ran to open the door for us. As Calvin approached the door, it opened from the inside and an older, dark Bahamian came out and hugged Calvin while motioning to us to get inside quickly. The older man pointed to a stainless-steel table and told us to lay Joel down on it. Calvin quickly introduced the man as his uncle but did not offer his name. I then realized that Calvin had not introduced us to the jitney bus driver, either. I had a feeling that these people were all his relatives or part of a highly trusted network of sources.

The older man, who was either White or Bixby, began examining Joel much like a doctor. He took his blood pressure and checked his pulse. He looked down his throat and into his eyes. He then began pressing on Joel's abdomen and extending his arms and legs, feeling each bone and joint thoroughly. He then called to a young woman who had been hovering nearby at a table and gave her instructions and a list of medical supplies he needed. She silently left the building, and, as I walked to the front door, I watched as she climbed on a bike and peddled away. There were many people walking in both directions down the street in front of the funeral parlor, but none of them gave me even a passing look. In fact, they appeared to be making an effort to look away. I knew that Calvin was very popular and highly respected here, but I was amazed that he had managed to unite all these folks to protect us—and in such a short time span. The young girl came pedaling back a few moments later with a satchel of medical supplies.

I went back inside and watched the old gentleman work on Joel. I wished I had brought along my satellite phone so I could find out when Doug was arriving. I needed to get Joel out of here and to the States for better care.

The old gentleman was placing an IV line into Joel's arm and a bag of clear liquid was on a post next to the steel table. Joel whimpered a bit as the needle went into his wrist. Then he opened his left eye a slit. I went to his side so he could see me, and he tried to speak. I told him to save his energy for our next journey. He continued to make small sounds that I could not understand. He finally blurted out the word "Monster" and then fell into unconsciousness.

After about half an hour of the IV drip, Calvin said it was time to leave. He had just found out that there were some police and white guys in suits going door to door in the next village west of here.

I thanked the old guy, whatever his name was, and lifted Joel off of the table and carried him to the rear door. I pushed the door open with my foot and was surprised that all I saw was an empty driveway, a wide field of dry grass, and little else. A moment later, a small pickup turned off the road on the other side of the field and drove straight across the grass toward the funeral parlor. It was towing a large open wood fishing boat. The back of the truck and the boat were stacked five feet high with fishing nets. An old Bahamian wearing a straw hat like the ones the jitney driver and Calvin had us wear on the trip from the prison was driving the truck.

The truck pulled up behind the building and stopped right in front of us. The driver pushed a board up that was sticking out from under the nets in the back of the truck. Calvin came out of the building and told us to place Joel underneath the nets and for one of us to get in with him.

As I lifted Joel into the truck bed, I heard the thumps of the rotary wings of a large helicopter heading our way. I dove in and the nets fell on us lightly shutting out all light. I heard the truck start, the driver grinding the gears a little, and we lunged forward, bumping along the rough driveway and finally onto the road. From the direction of the truck, I knew we were again heading due east. I hoped that Calvin and Sorensen were making the trip with us in the truck. I could hear the boat bouncing back and forth behind the truck as we turned the corners. Joel was not taking the rough ride well. He made moaning sounds as we hit more bumps.

As we bumped along, I could hear horns blowing and then some shouts of people that I could not understand. I held Joel close, and, as we slowed and came to a stop, I whispered to him to be strong and not to cry out. I told Joel that this was a matter of life and death.

The truck began to slow and I heard voices shouting orders and horns honking. As we came to a stop, I realized we were at a roadblock and some of the voices were American. I held Joel tighter as the voices got louder and came alongside the truck.

I could feel the nets being poked over and over, and then something hit my leg one time hard and then moved on. My prober must have felt me, but it seemed he had chosen to ignore it and kept probing. There was some more talking and then a Bahamian told the truck driver to move along. We jerked into a slow speed on the smooth road.

Joel let out a faint moan and a great rush of breath. "Are we safe?"

I said, "Yes, for now."

We drove for about ten more minutes and then turned left onto what must have been a dirt road or path as the bumpiness was almost intolerable. We stopped two minutes later and the door to the truck opened and closed quietly. About thirty seconds later, someone pulled the fishnets back and I saw Calvin and Sorensen standing there with grins on their faces. There was no one else around.

The driver had vanished into thin air. Sorensen pointed behind me, and, as I turned around, I saw my boat bobbing in the cove beyond the beach. What a beautiful sight the *"Big Mamoo"* was!

Calvin helped me lift Joel off the back of the truck and laid him down on the grass. I put the back of my hand on Joel's head and found he was now burning up with fever.

Our next course of action was to get Joel to the boat anchored in the water some three hundred feet away. Not an easy task without a dingy or a raft.

I looked around for something to float Joel to the boat. There was nothing—not even a garbage bag to use as a floatation device to offset his weight. The boat on the trailer was unusable, as it was mostly being used as a trailer. Too many holes in the bottom.

Sorensen set out south and Calvin took off north to look for a solution. I stayed with Joel and tried to comfort him as best I could with reassuring talk of being home with his family very soon. I could still hear the big helicopter in the distance getting louder all the time as it moved in our direction.

I placed Joel next to the water's edge behind a bush and looked for Sorensen and Calvin. Neither was visible. I wished they had not gotten out of my line of sight. I scanned the beach and then across the water where a number of fishing boats were drifting out beyond the reefs. One of the boats was heading toward the cove at a high rate of speed. I figured that Calvin had summoned yet another of his mystery contacts and we were about to get a ride out to the boat.

I then saw two men riding the bow like George Washington crossing the Delaware River. They were both armed with long guns. One guy drew a bead on us. There was no place to drag Joel for better cover. Only scrub bushes and some low-level coral reef. I dragged Joel to a part of the reef and lay down on top of him to protect him the best I could as the men on the boat started firing. I could tell they were on semi-auto and shooting at random. I had no weapon at all—not even a stick to defend myself.

Just as they passed my boat in the cove, I saw a slight movement in my boat's cockpit. All hell broke loose! It was Sorensen with the M16 I had stashed under my gunwales. He tore all three of the men on the speedboat to shreds in a matter of seconds.

The speedboat rammed the beach at high speed just in front of me with the engine churning up the sand and throwing water wildly up into the air. Calvin heard the ruckus and came running down the beach but passed us and went directly to the boat and shut down the motor. He then grabbed the men, tossed them out of the boat and to the beach, and yelled at me to carry Joel to the boat.

Calvin was pushing with all of his might to shove the boat off the sand so we could use it for transport to my boat, but it would not move. He motioned for me to help him. I left Joel for a moment, jumped in the craft, and tilted the engine out of the water so we could get the boat afloat again. There was so much blood in the bottom of the boat that it looked like tomato soup.

I lifted Joel and placed him on the bow to keep him from drowning in the pool of blood. I helped Calvin move the boat into deep enough water to restart the engine, put it in reverse, and then idled out over the reef heads. I could see Sorensen stepping the mast and, as we came alongside, heard the motor running under the deck.

Calvin and I lifted Joel over the port gunwales so Sorensen could lay him on the deck of the cockpit. He wasn't looking any better and I was worried we were losing him rapidly. There was no way we could get the kind of help Joel desperately needed back on New Providence. There was also no way we were not going to be searched for in this boat and on this side of the island.

We needed to get creative, so I made a decision and told Sorensen to take the mast back down. While he was doing that, Calvin and I carried Joel to the V-berth in the bow of the boat.

I grabbed a bowline attached to my boat and swam to the speedboat that we had put adrift. I climbed aboard, put the bowline to its transom, and told Sorensen to man the tiller on my boat. I cranked the speedboat up, checked the gauges, and, after Calvin hauled in the anchor, started towing my boat as if it was broken down. I scooped as much seawater into the boat as I could to dilute the blood and body fragments so I could, in turn, start bailing them out of the boat while I towed the *Big Mamoo* east.

I signaled Sorensen to fire up the satellite phone so I could find Doug. When he signaled me that it was ready, I killed the throttle and drifted back to the cockpit of the boat. Calvin was using my binoculars to scan the horizon, shore, and waters for anyone interested in our whereabouts.

"All clear for now, guys," Calvin stated. "But, remember we aren't here on holiday."

I got Doug's voicemail and left him a cryptic message that we were all having a great time in the sun and could use some aspirin for a major hangover. Hopefully, he was in the Bahamas and would check his messages soon. I hoped he got the gist of my message.

I pulled away from the boat again, took up the slack on the line, and continued to pull the boat east toward the outer islands. At this point, we were about five miles off the east coast of Grand Bahamas Island. Looking back over the top of my boat, I could see two large helicopters in the distance. They were slowly circling the area where the men in possession of this speedboat first discovered us. We hadn't taken the time to conceal their remains—what was left of the poor bastards—so it was only a matter of time before someone discovered them.

The men that had just met their maker were definitely Americans since they were all as white as snow and, as they yelled at one another, as they raced toward us, I heard their accents sounded like they were from the Bronx. The helicopters were new model Sikorsky choppers. The Bahamas government may have a couple of military choppers, but not new ones like this—and certainly not unmarked, as these were.

Off to the north, I could see a large grey boat, possibly a Bahamas Naval cruiser. I sure hoped not as we had had enough excitement and fun for one day. I truly didn't believe Sorensen could talk us out of this one. I just continued to tow the boat on a dead east heading on the small compass fastened to the dash on this shot-up, borrowed speedboat I was piloting.

I played out more line and let the boat drift back and forth with the slight breeze that was coming from the northeast. I figured that if someone were watching us with a long lens, I would appear to be towing a broken-down old sailboat in the direction of Eleuthera Island. My boat was internationally registered, so it had no numbers or letters on its side. I never looked at the side of the speedboat I was pulling it with to see where it was registered. I was pretty sure it had a Bahamian registration, but it was too late now to check. I watched the big grey ship and thought it was turning to starboard back toward New Providence Island and away from us. It did and now I had to turn my thoughts back to Joel and his emergency medical needs.

We were about five or six hours from Eleuthera at the rate we were currently traveling. If we set the sail on my boat and turned back to the west toward Florida, we were at least twenty-four or more hours from any medical help. I towed my boat about two more miles to make sure the cruiser hadn't changed its mind and dropped back alongside the boat. Luckily, the waters had been calm so far, and when I checked the fuel gauge on the speedboat, I saw we had plenty of fuel.

Joel's condition had not changed much for better or for worse, but Calvin was able to get him to drink some water and had managed to pour a little sugar into his mouth for some much-needed energy. I got the guys together and discussed the route we needed to take to get him aid as soon as possible. Calvin had a few relatives in the Eleuthera Islands and suggested we keep running east for those islands. We agreed and recommenced the tow.

After about three hours and two fuel tanks, the speedboat motor started sputtering from lack of fuel. Well, I guess I can be wrong once in a while. I didn't correctly figure just how much fuel it takes to tow another craft when weighted down with three passengers.

I cut the throttle, shut the engine down, and let the sailboat drift alongside. I took the three rifles and all the extra magazines and passed them to Sorensen. I untied the speedboat and set it adrift. It would be found free-floating with the currents, and the assumption would be that the owners were hijacked or that they had met with some other unfortunate fate. It would not be long before the dead guy's leaders figured out that it was their boat and that we were their unfortunate fate. They would know that we were headed to the Eleuthera's. I hope Calvin's relatives there are as dependable as the ones we had already met. The right family members in a time of need are truly a godsend!

I stepped the mast and set out my jib sail. The wind was out of the west southwest, so we had great sailing. We were making about nine knots and the hull was riding high. About two hours into the sail, the sun was over the western horizon. The sun was actually so orange and beautiful that I almost thought even with everything that was going on that I should snap a few photos, but hesitated.

We could now see some lights on the top of the eastern water. We needed to run a little south, according to the GPS to Hatchet Bay. That was where Calvin had folks waiting for us with medical supplies, a few much-needed energy bars, and an EMT to play doctor with Joel. I had heard Joel mumbling some words from the cabin and thought that he was about ready to regain consciousness. At least, I hoped that was what it was and not just fever making him babble. It was a wonder a man of his age was able to survive the physical punishment he had been through over the past few days.

It was extremely dark as we approached the first markers to Hatchet Bay. I did not want to use my spotlight and draw attention to us coming in. We all knew we were right in the crosshairs of a Bahamas Island dragnet and may have police and U.S. Federal Agents all over us in a matter of minutes. As I studied the outside markers, I spotted a smaller boat with its running lights on coming in from the northwest toward the channel. I dropped my sails and drifted for a while until the smaller boat passed by my bow about a half-mile in front of me. As it passed, I cranked my motor and followed it at a safe distance so as not to be seen. The leading craft did a great job of staying between the markers and coral heads, taking no shortcuts through the shallower water. I was glad about that.

In fifteen minutes, we were passing into the bay and safe waters. Calvin started looking at our exact position and motioned to me to steer toward the north as he spoke with someone on his cell phone. While he spoke, I saw a bright light flash two times in our direction from the shoreline just as Calvin pointed me in that direction.

We pulled into a long, wooden dock that had some boards missing but appeared to be stable and safe enough for docking. I let the transom drift about until the bow was pointed back toward the bay. A couple of very large Bahamian men came down the dock and greeted Calvin with the customary hug. Calvin said something to both of them and they jumped into the boat, went below deck, lifted Joel out, and down the dock they went.

I properly secured the boat to the dock and jumped out, watching my step due to the missing boards. I saw Sorensen setting up the satellite phone on a nearby table on the shore. I could hear the familiar chirp of its low battery signal, a sound I always dreaded, especially when out in the middle of nowhere. I jumped back in the boat and retrieved a fresh battery pack from the cabin. I took the phone from Sorensen, hooked up the new battery pack, and reset the phone so it was able to receive as well as send.

It was signaling that I had a number of messages from clients, but the most important one was from Doug Parton. He was in Nassau and officials had just informed him that Joel had escaped custody. They believed he might have murdered three American citizens. He gave me a safe phone number and said he needed to speak to me as soon as possible. I called the Bahamas exchange and Doug answered immediately on the first ring.

I filled him in on what had happened over the past two days, and then I explained that we'd had no choice but to put the three Americans down as they were trying to blow us away. Doug said that he had passed the Princess Margaret Hospital earlier that morning and said there was an army of agents trying to act casual at every exit of the building. He said he knew Joel needed medical treatment and the Princess Margaret Hospital and a few clinics were all that was available on the island. Doug asked me not to tell him where we were right now just in case our phones were being monitored.

I knew beyond a shadow of a doubt that my phone was safe as it went from direct satellite to a station in Germany and then back out by satellite to my destination call. I communicated to Doug in a code that only he would understand that I was taking Joel to Sanctuary as soon as I could. He knew exactly where that was. He stated that he was meeting with a U.S. legal officer at the U.S. Embassy the next morning at 0900 and expected to get the runaround. He cautioned me about contacting Joel's family, as he knew they were being monitored and watched.

He stated that he was not convinced that this ordeal was a government-sanctioned operation. He said he would explain more when we got together.

After I signed off, I realized I was standing all alone on the dock and had no idea where everyone had gone. I walked up the dock, almost falling through where a board was missing, and saw a number of small multi-colored houses in a row along the narrow dirt road. As I stepped off the dock, I turned right toward the east and walked along for a while. The houses were small but arranged neatly and well cared for by the occupants, showing their respect for their dwellings.

As I reached the last row house, I could see headlights in the distance heading in my direction. I saw that the vehicle, a jeep, had a powerful spotlight shining from a bar mounted on the roof. It was scanning the water and around and between the houses—anywhere someone might hide. Without a second thought, I quickly stepped into the bushes and lay down as flat as I could. When I think about it kiddingly, I call this my "pancake position." I knew enough about human senses not to look right at them, as they might feel my energy, but I did watch them from my peripheral vision.

The first thing I noticed was that they were not Bahamians but white military types. The second thing I noticed was that their rifles had been pointing out the sides of the vehicle as if they meant to use them before asking any questions. These men had the hard look of hired killers, something I had seen many times before. Men who were just itching to kill someone.

For some reason, I am never wrong about these types of people. I vowed to myself that no matter the outcome of our mission to save Joel, I was going to get to the bottom of this Bahamian mystery—even if it killed me. As soon as they passed, I leaped up from my hiding spot, quickly and quietly ran to the rear of the open jeep, grabbed the man standing aft, and pulled him to the ground. He hit with a thud, and I grabbed his rifle and fired three quick rounds into the back and head of the jeep driver. My next two rounds hit the third rider in both legs, as he was standing up. He went down just as hard as the first guy. I leaped up, grabbed him out of the jeep, and slammed him backward to the ground. I smacked him hard in the side of his head and left him lying there. With my other hand, I grabbed the other moaning man on the ground and dragged him into the brush and down to the water's edge.

I could hear the people coming out of their houses now, and then a woman screamed like a hurt cat, as she saw the gore of the driver's head on the windshield of the stopped jeep.

I floated the groggy militant through the water toward a group of boats floating just off the beach, lifted him up and over the side of the second boat, and splashed him with a handful of cool seawater. I climbed aboard to have a favorable position over him. He came alert quickly and made an effort to sit up. I smashed him hard directly on his nose and told him I was going to ask him some important questions and every time he hesitated or argued, I would break something of his that he might find extremely painful.

He did not flinch so I could tell he—and probably his friends—were hardcore killers. I was not about to give him a break. With a look from me that I have been told is "bloodcurdling," he realized that I was deadly serious. He then nodded. He covered his face with both hands and started to talk before I even asked him my first question.

The man's name was Richard Rolf. He worked for Mentor Corporation, headquartered in Dallas, Texas, and he had been employed for four years. The company did diplomatic security in foreign countries and he had worked previously in Iraq escorting green-zone personnel around the country. So far, what he was saying seemed to match what Gage had told me earlier about Mentor.

Rolf said he had been on his way to Afghanistan three days ago when he was diverted to the Bahamas in the middle of the night for what was known as "Zero Dark Thirty." He had been dropped at San Andros Island by a U.S. Military KC 130 and was flown here to Eleuthera about three hours ago in a different KC-130 along with four jeeps and their weapons. His specific orders were to hunt down and kill me and an older man who would be traveling with me. He said he was shown a photo of the older man lying on a floor somewhere and the photo he was shown of me, which he had in his inside waterproofed pocket, was a very old one that showed me with brown hair at a very young age.

I believed that a *People* magazine photographer had taken the picture many years ago. His having that photo was strange because I had been photographed numerous times since then for passports and various licenses, including concealed weapons permits and a private investigator's license.

Was someone still out there looking after me as I ran this gauntlet?

Another thing Rolf told me was that he and his squad were ordered to shoot me on sight. His extremely agitated supervisor told him that I could bring down a lot of very important people in high places. Rolf was told that his and many other's jobs would cease to exist if I was able to get to the media and tell the lies they thought I would tell.

He said that once he arrived, he began to have doubts about the job because he was told by a soldier over on San Andros that there were some Arabs living there who may have been part of the 9/11 terrorist group. He admitted that because of his orders, he would have killed me anyway. At least he was brutally honest about it. He said there were two other squads on the north and south ends of the Eleuthera's working their way toward the middle so I would have had no possible avenue of escape whatsoever, or so they thought. He also said that there were numerous other search squads on the other islands around the Bahamas looking for us. That gave us about two hours, maybe a little less, to get off the island, out of the surrounding waters, and back to the States.

I was not sure what to do with Rolf. I should have just put his lights out then and there, but I was getting soft in my old age. I told him I was going to tie him up on the bottom of the boat. I told him that I didn't want him to get stupid when I left and start screaming and he told me that since I didn't just cut his throat and leave him to bleed out that he would be quiet. I did not gag him as I could see he meant it—and because his nose was badly broken and full of blood.

I secured him to the bottom of the boat where the fishermen coming back to the docks the next morning would find him.

I slowly climbed into the water so I wouldn't make any splashing sounds and swam to the beach. I walked from the water and then away from the voices of the people still excited about the carnage down the street. I was now listening closely for the sound of a vehicle coming from the north as Rolf had explained would happen.

I needed to find Calvin and Sorensen as soon as possible so I could brief them on the past few minutes of madness that I had caused. I stayed close to the side of the road, hugging the tree line and bushes, as I made my way back to my boat. When I arrived, I saw a young boy sitting on the dock near the transom of my boat. He signaled me to stay on the shore as he jumped up and ran toward me.

I moved back into the shadows and scanned the area around the little harbor. I didn't see or sense anything threatening in the immediate area. The boy came up to me, looked me directly in the eyes, and asked me to follow him. I tagged along beside him until we got to the road. He looked both ways and then crossed as we took a path through the bushes to the next road over. We cut behind a house and entered a bamboo and grass structure where I saw Joel on a cot. Standing over him was a tall, shapely, and beautiful Bahamian woman.

Calvin came in seconds behind me. He told me that his people were handling the mess I'd made down the road earlier and asked where the third member of my party was stashed. I guessed I wasn't as discreet as I thought, as they already knew there was a third person in the jeep. I told him he was alive and presently floating in a boat about a hundred yards south of my boat. He stepped outside the hut, whispered to someone, and then came back in.

With a surprised look, he asked me why I let two of the men live. He said it was totally unlike me to shut down my killing machine once I got started. I just shrugged and asked how Joel was doing.

The very tall and remarkable looking lady with Joel was Calvin's cousin, a doctor who ran the small clinic in nearby Alice Town. She was an Emergency Room Doctor who had done her internship at Jackson Memorial Hospital in Miami. She went into private practice in Miami for a while and then made enough money to settle back home in Alice Town. She earned a good living working for the government. All Bahamians enjoyed nationalized health care the same as they did in England, where everything is paid for by the government. She knew her business, as the first thing I noticed was that Joel's eyes were partly open and he was trying to focus on me as I approached.

I looked around and realized that Sorensen was not among the folks standing around. Calvin told me that as soon as we'd arrived, Sorensen disappeared into the dark like the blowing out of a candle. Poof! Calvin had no idea where he was but suspected he was making someone's life miserable.

I told Calvin about the patrols coming from the north and south of the island and that we needed to get Joel and Sorensen and be on our way. I thanked the Doctor for her help and taking the chances she was taking. She just smiled.

Considering our options, I decided we had no better mode of escape than my boat. The airport was certainly under surveillance, as were the charters or any other larger boats. The small fishing boats I'd seen earlier that were owned by Calvin's family were too small to use to cross the Gulf Stream. I told Calvin to hang tight. I quietly slipped out of the small yard and headed north, staying to the right side of the road and in the shadows while the new day was opening to the east.

I spotted the young boy who led me from the boat and asked him if he had any idea where my tall friend was. Smiling, and without saying a word, he nodded to the road running north. I had to look twice to believe my eyes. There was Sorensen, walking down the middle of the road with two men in camouflage gear, hands tied behind their backs. Both were bleeding from their noses and looking extremely unhappy.

Sorensen marched them right up to me, forcefully shoved them to the ground on the edge of the road, and introduced them with his often-used nicknames, Tweedledee and Tweedledum. These were two of Rolf's buddies coming from the north island. They looked about the same size as Rolf and were both dressed in night-camouflaged attire of the kind they used for night raids. They both had bloody faces just as Rolf did. Not a pretty sight!

According to Sorensen, he had found them walking around the local marina about a mile or two north. They had been roughing up some of the nice folks who live in the area to find out what they knew about a couple of white guys who had newly arrived on the island. Sorensen said one was possibly injured and needed medical care. Apparently, Sorensen had questioned them in about the same way I'd questioned Rolf. We refer to this method as "Rough & Rougher"—a way to get answers quickly to necessary questions.

They told him the same things I'd learned about from Rolf. They left out the part about the two patrols to the south.

Sorensen asked Calvin if any of his friends wanted these guys to use for chum while fishing for sharks. The two tough guys looked extremely worried, and, based on what they had already been through with Sorensen, I knew they figured he wasn't kidding!

I looked at the trees around us to get a feeling for the wind direction and its current speed, as we needed to set sail and soon. There was another patrol on its way toward us and, we were told, the local constable would be along any moment. So far, neither Rolf nor these guys had a radio for communications. They all had cell phones, but there was very little coverage out here. Millions of dollars had been dumped into paying these mercenaries, and they didn't even have cheap walkie-talkies that might have saved them from their current fate.

Calvin told us that his people would hold Rolf and his buddies until we were far to the west. He guaranteed us that the constable would also hold them for questioning for a while longer because they were carrying firearms in the Bahamas. It was illegal to have even a small rifle on these islands. Meanwhile, I couldn't help but notice the automatic rifle Sorensen was carrying and that all his pockets were filled with ammo magazines. Someone was going home a lot lighter!

We told Joel we had to move him again and carefully carried him over to the *Big Mamoo*, once again placing him in the V-berth. I was surprised to see him looking at me with much clearer eyes than I had seen before. He was trying to speak but I told him to save his energy, rest, and that we would speak later, once we were away from the island and on our way back to Miami.

I thought it best to leave the phony name across the stern of the boat and set out for deeper waters. I laid the mast down again to give the impression that we were leaving the bay in a powered boat. The less obvious we were the better. We cruised west directly from Eleuthera toward New Providence Island and, as soon as we were over the horizon and there were no other boats in view, I stepped the mast and headed northwest to clear the Nassau area. We had a good wind and we were making progress.

About noontime, I turned the helm over to Sorensen and we talked briefly about Calvin, who had stayed back at Alice Town. He had to get back to Nassau to see if he could salvage his career. Calvin wasn't one to worry, but he had really overstepped his authority this time. He was going back to do damage control.

I stepped down into the cabin and checked on Joel. He was sleeping soundly and his fever was down. As I tucked the sheet around him more snuggly, he woke up and asked me my name. I told him to call me Jake. Joel told me that he thought he was having nightmares but was beginning to realize that they weren't nightmares at all but actual memories.

He told me about seeing the "Monster" from his Concentration Camp during the war. He said he had never really thought about the nickname "The Ghost," that the commandant was known by until it was like seeing a ghost right in front of him that night.

After killing The Ghost, he remembered being caught, dragged, and then beaten repeatedly by some men. Suddenly, he stiffened and said that he just remembered something very important. As he was lying there after being beaten, he looked up and saw the face of a man who looked just like Osama Bin Laden. A face that was burned into his memory forever from so many newsflashes since 9/11. He said that the men with him were also Arabs and that they were heavily armed with military-type rifles. It was like looking at a newsreel from Afghanistan.

American men interrogated him but they didn't question him at all about killing the German. He, of course, did not bring it up to them. As brutal as the German's death was, he thought it was very unusual that they should overlook something this important.

He said that all the American interrogators were interested in what he saw and remembered of the Arab area of the community. He said he kept telling them that he saw nothing except some old men near the Community Center and that one old man attacked him. They continued to beat him in the face and stomach as they asked him about the Arabs. He said it seemed as though the men did not believe him.

When the Bahamas Police had him in custody, they refused to answer his questions and did not ask him any questions in turn. All the beatings he got before he arrived at the prison were by Americans. His beatings continued in prison and always from Americans pretending to be inmates. There was no doubt in his mind that they were trying to kill him and make it look like other prisoners did it. Some of the real prisoners whispered to him that they had been offered money to beat him, but they refused.

Every few hours, new prisoners came into his cellblock and assaulted him. Afterward, he was strong-armed and taken to a stairway near his cell and beaten until he must have passed out. He said that he often pretended to pass out to stop the kicks and punches, but it usually didn't help.

When he was first brought to the police station on San Andros, he remembered one man whom the other Americans addressed as "Yes, sir" and "No, sir." Everyone addressed him if he was a high-ranking official. All the Americans referred to each other as Mister—no first or last names.

I was beginning to believe that these bad guys were a part of the government that I had read about that was referred to as OGAs—Other Government Agency or Unknown Government Agency. Even the most knowledgeable government employees did not know about all the secret provisions in the Patriot Act enacted after 9/11, but whoever these folks were, they had been around for far longer than 2001, as they apparently had been hiding Nazis for over fifty years on this remote Caribbean island.

Joel asked if there was any way he could speak to his wife. I told him that I had both a cell phone and a satellite phone. I recommended that he call one of her friends, as I was sure Joel's home phone was being monitored. He gave me the number of his wife's sister Mary on Long Island. I made the connection and passed the phone to Joel.

After many shouted words of glee and then some crying, Joel told his sister-in-law the reason he was calling her. After explaining that Adrian's phone may be tapped and their house under surveillance, he asked Mary to go to his home and without mentioning anything about Joel, tell Adrian to go to their temple and stand just inside the door. He asked Mary to give Adrian her cell phone at the last minute before she left and to keep it turned off until she reached the temple. If their house was being bugged and they heard her tell Adrian that she had spoken to Joel or received any word from him, they would know. These were professionals. Her actions and demeanor would tell them she was excited and not acting normal, and they would connect the dots.

Joel asked me what time it was now and I told him it was eleven o'clock Eastern Standard Time. He thought for a moment as he calculated the timing and told Mary to make sure Adrian was there at or before 2:00 PM. Mary said she would handle it, be very discreet, and after a few more words of thanks and encouragement, Joel passed the phone back to me. I was amazed at the quick wit and fast thinking of this old man. He'd survived numerous years in a German concentration camp, so perhaps I shouldn't have been surprised.

About 2:00 PM, I set up the satphone again for Joel and dialed the number he gave me. As soon as the phone rang on the other end, an anxious lady answered. I introduced myself as Jake and explained that she was to show as little emotion as she could as someone might be watching her. She said she understood and I passed Joel the phone. I had already advised Joel to speak to her in general terms, keep it short, and save his story for when they were reunited.

Joel and his wife spoke for about ten minutes. He explained that he could not tell her where he was or where he was going. He said they would be together soon and that he just wanted her to know he was safe and with a new, trusted friend. Joel said he loved her dearly, a tear ran down his cheek, and he handed the phone back to me. After listening for just a few seconds to make sure there were no additional clicks on the secure line, I hung up.

After Joel was finished with the phone, Sorensen asked if he could use it to call a friend of his in Palm Beach. He took the phone from me and disappeared onto the deck. Joel and I continued to talk about his ordeal.

A few moments later, Sorensen came back into the cabin and announced that we could be expecting a seaplane to land near us within the next hour and a half. He had called a friend and he volunteered to come right away.

We were now a little northeast of Nassau. We were under full sail and making great time westward. This was the most dangerous area for us. We were now a very big target, even with the low radar visibility because of the fiberglass hull. The mast was aluminum and very tall. It was taller than most boats this size because the previous owner had modified it for his purpose of cocaine smuggling. To help, I had lowered the radar reflective ball to the deck, but my own radar and radio antennas were large and lined up across the mast spreader. This made us very visible to those seeking us—and they really wanted to know where we were. I had been searching the horizon for another boat all day that we could shadow to reduce our radar image, but so far no luck!

At about 1500, we received a radio call on our marine ship-to-shore radio. It was Sorensen's friend in his plane. He was closing in fast but needed our exact coordinates. We gave it to him in a code that Sorensen had worked out with him earlier.

Moments later, we could hear his plane in the distance. This was not just a small seaplane, but a large, vintage, 1930s- or 1940s-style dual-engine seaplane like Jimmy Buffet flies. I'm still not sure who was behind the yoke on that beauty. It could have been Buffet himself, for all I know. One thing was for sure—whoever it was, he knew how to fly that plane.

It came in fast, struck the water with hardly a wake, and coasted up to us with the greatest of ease. I dropped the mainsail and then the jib. As we came to a turning stop, the plane was right next to us. I thought, *Poetry in motion.*

A crewman positioned in the side hatch threw us a line and I pulled us transom-first right up to the hatch. I turned around and Sorensen already had Joel in his arms. He just stepped up into the hatch, waved, and said he would meet me in Miami the next morning. He cast off the line and the plane blasted off into the sky. I swear from landing to take-off, the exchange didn't take three minutes. I hoisted the mainsail and continued on my way.

I continued my easterly heading toward Miami. The weather was perfect, the wind was perfect, and it seemed I was the only boat on the ocean. As I settled in with a hot cup of English breakfast tea, I felt the worst was behind me. Boy, was I wrong!

I made a sat phone call to Dave up at Merritt Island. He did not answer his cell phone, so I left him a brief message. I next called Calvin's cell to advise him that Joel was safely out of the Bahamas. His phone went right to voicemail, so I left him a message that I was alone, westbound, and would call him from Miami the next day.

I was beginning to have a bad feeling about how quiet things were. The silence was almost deafening. Not seeing any sign of patrol boats or low-flying planes when I knew we were subjects of interest was just not making any sense. Then it dawned on me. I was heading right into a trap as soon as I crossed into the Gulf Stream and was out of Bahamian waters. Before I hit U.S. waters, I was going to go down to visit old Davy Jones's footlocker!

Working on mere instinct, I altered my course on the compass heading and headed due south. I planned on cutting between New Providence

Island and Andros. All I needed now was luck and lots of it!

I was hoping I could sail south, then west of Andros Island, sneak up the west coast and then cut across to the point of Key West Florida. A few moments later, my suspicions became a reality when Sorensen called me on the sat phone and informed me that he could see a number of small, military-looking boats on a picket line at the edge of the Gulf Stream. He said there was a Bahamas Naval cruiser right in the middle of the line with its radar blasting away on full power. He said they had been challenged by radio as they flew west, but his pilot had a special clearance with the Bahamas government and flew past with no problem!

I informed him that I had just figured that all out before he called and was taking evasive action now. He asked me to inform him as soon as I was clear and on my way to Miami. I signed off and let my sails out for more speed.

About an hour later, I spotted a large ketch sailing west from the Nassau area, so I altered my course once again to slide in behind her to use her radar reflection as a shadow and mask my movement when I cut south. I also noted that the lettering across the transom of the ketch was *Semper Fi*, the Marine Corps motto!

It was about that time that I saw what appeared to be a small plane on the horizon, flying low to the water toward the west from the direction of the Nassau Pindling Airport. It flew parallel to my course, turned north, and disappeared over the horizon. About a half hour later, it was back on the same course. There was no doubt that I was the subject of its interest.

I picked up the sat phone and put in a call to my voicemail. There was a message from Doug saying that he heard that one of the Bahamas' officials was in custody for aiding an escapee from the Bahamas Prison. I placed a call to Mrs. White, Calvin's mom, who answered on the first ring. She said she had been anticipating my call. Bahamian authorities and some white men had detained Calvin after he landed at the Nassau Airport. She said that one of the men was Bahamian and was dressed in civilian attire. One of his friends told her this, and to patiently wait for a call from me.

This was not good, although I can't imagine that he wasn't expecting it from the onset. He never hid his identity, so he had to expect they would catch up to him. I needed to go back and get him out of this mess. There was no doubt Calvin would do it for me.

The first order of business was to continue on to San Andros and drop anchor outside of Nicholls Town as I had done the other day. I contacted Sorensen on his cell.

He was in Palm Beach, where he had just arrived with Joel. They were going to take him to a safe house in Broward County where he could get more medical attention. When he returned from Nassau, Joel planned to give an official statement to Doug for his use in his defense. I asked Sorensen if he could ask his pilot friend to fly back and pick me up for a ride to Nassau. I explained that Calvin needed my help and the seaplane was my best option. Sorensen put me on hold, made a call to his friend, and came right back, gave me a phone number, saying his friend would wait for my call and then pick me up at a safe location of my choosing.

As I continued sailing in the wake of the big ketch, I noticed the helmsman turning to look at me about every two or three minutes. I was paying so much attention to him and his boat that I failed to check aft to see a large speedboat driving right up my ass. That was what Mr. Ketch was looking at, not me.

I was keeping my course and heading directly toward the ketch when the first shot from a high-powered rifle nearly parted my hair and punched a large, nasty hole into the transom of the ketch in front of me. I could see the shooter lining up another shot from what looked like a lever-action 30-30 or larger from the bow of the speedboat. At that same moment, as I was diving for the deck, I saw the shooter's head disappear in a bloody explosion!

The speedboat veered to the south and then turned away, picking up speed. As I lay on the deck, I heard another shot that sounded like a cannon blast. I looked over the gunnels to the south and saw the speedboat turning in tighter and tighter circles until it came to an abrupt stop. I pulled my mainsail over to the far right and turned to starboard as tightly as I could. I was too far away from my cache of weapons to grab a long gun to take up the battle, so I kept peering over the gunnels, looking at the now completely stopped speedboat. It was about a hundred yards aft of me, and it was getting farther away as I sailed north.

I looked west and saw the large ketch turning to run along my same course. I also finally gave the boat a good look and saw a man and a young woman standing in the cockpit. The man, about my age, perhaps a little younger, was holding what appeared to be a rifle that looked like a small cannon.

I continued to stay low in my cockpit until I saw the man in the ketch give me a military-type salute and place the rifle at port arms. I slowly stood up, reached over, released my jib, and then dropped my mainsail. The ketch came alongside and dropped his massive sails, which caused the great boat to nose dive into the water for a moment and then settle off my port side as neatly as I had ever seen it done.

The man smiled at me and recited a slightly different rendition of a great line. "I love the smell of gun smoke in the afternoon."

He introduced himself as retired U.S. Marine Corps Master Sergeant Frank Kaiser and said his friends called him "Top."

I looked at the long rifle he held and yelled out, *"Semper fi!"*—a greeting from one Marine to another. I hoped that I could be his friend. He certainly would be my friend forever. Talk about being saved in the middle of nowhere!

I tied my lines to the ketch, then reached up to shake the hand of my special savior. He excused himself for a moment, pointed his rifle back toward the idling speedboat, and fired three quick shots. I saw the holes blown into the boat's side just below the waterline. The boat quickly began to list to its starboard. It went down so fast that I found it hard to believe!

Top turned to me and gave me permission to board his boat. I made sure the lines were right and climbed aboard. The first thing I said to him was that we needed to move out of the area as fast as possible. I explained to him that they were not pirates but security agents from some quasi-U.S.

government agency.

Top never even batted an eye. He told me that he saw me pull into his shadow and was watching the speedboat following me for the last couple of hours with his radar. The boat was staying over the horizon to my rear and he could tell that they were up to no good. He explained that he had worked with some black ops' folks over the years in the Marine Corps and knew if they were going to blow me away with him as a witness, they planned to do him in, too. This far out in open waters, no one would ever know.

He had also seen the plane on the horizon that appeared to be paralleling me. It had disappeared just before the speedboat appeared on his long-range radar. He knew it was skullduggery as soon as he watched me try to hide in his radar shadow. He was not sure who was going to be the receiver of his fifty-caliber rifle until they shot first. That was his deciding factor.

I helped him place a couple of boat fenders between our boats and then went onto the transom and assessed the damage done to his boat from the rifle shot. It had gone through the hull and into his aft master stateroom. He found the round embedded in his mattress. He nonchalantly plugged the hole in the hull with some plastic putty and said it would hold until he could get back to the States. He pushed a red button on his helm and the two massive sails rode up in their channels. The boat leaped forward as if he had pushed a throttle. With my boat snuggly tied alongside, we were full steam ahead without the steam!

He introduced his daughter Patty to me and explained that they had lost her mother to breast cancer last year. Father and daughter were taking a Caribbean cruise to celebrate Patty's recent graduation from The University of Central Florida. They lived in the Central Florida area near Orlando.

"Top" had retired from the Marine Corps five years ago. I had been out of the Corps for more than thirty-five years, so that meant I was out before he went in. Marines never really get out unless they get a dishonorable discharge or die. The dead part may be questionable. Once a Marine, always a Marine!

I decided to come clean with Top and explained all I had been up to for the past few days. I left out a bit of the incriminating things so that neither Top nor his daughter would be party to knowing and concealing criminal acts.

I spoke of Joel and my friends but kept their names confidential. Top had heard about the prison break and Patty had overheard some talk from a couple of Bahamian girls she met that a high-ranking official may have been directly involved.

I told them that one of my friends needed my help and that I needed to get to the north shore of Andros to secure my boat and meet a friend. I also told Top where my scooter was hidden in the bushes off the old logging road. He told me that he would be glad to pick it up and hold it for me.

Top said that he had read about me in some books and newspaper stories written about my cases over the years. Being former Marines, we were always drawn to stories about our comrades. I've had my share of publicity over the years and, as you can imagine, it is not always invited. Getting your name and picture in the news can have a negative effect on your caseload. Not many folks are eager to let the general public know that they have hired a private investigator.

As the sun set, we continued to sail west. After a few hours, the night turned as dark as the bottom of a well and we finally arrived off the north coast of Andros. It was about three o'clock the next morning when I set off from Top's boat and dropped the *Slim Molly's* anchor about a quarter of a mile off Nicholls Town. I had removed the *Big Mamoo* plaque the day before to mask my identity as best I could.

Top suggested I leave my boat there and catch the seaplane from his boat. We sailed north for about an hour. I had already called Sorensen's friend and told him the approximate coordinates to pick me up. The seas were nice and flat and I could just see a faint glow of sunrise to the east. Sunrise, when you are on the water, is such an awesome sight. The glow reflecting off the water looks more like an oil painting than real life.

I put my ear to the wind and could hear it before we saw the plane come low over the horizon from the northwest. It was so low that it seemed as if it were skimming the surface of the water.

The large seaplane landed across our bow like a huge, graceful bird and taxied alongside us. Top had lowered his sails and was drifting with the current to the west. The pilot eased the side of the float skids close to the aft swim deck. I leaped across before the wing struck the aft mast.

Top gave me a Marine salute, and, as he hit the button to raise his sails, he yelled, "I'll be back off the coast of Nassau the day after tomorrow." I must have looked puzzled because he then said he had to send Patty back to Orlando but then wanted in on the action. I smiled and saluted him back.

I felt far better today than I had yesterday. The pilot, whom I still had not met, ran up the engines, turned into the wind, and blasted into the sky. I was on my way back to New Providence Island.

Sticking to his silence, the pilot flew just over the surface of the ocean. I had never flown this close to the water at high speeds before. He announced the island was coming up in ten minutes and told me he would drop me at the Westside Beach. He landed, spun the wing over the beach, barely stopped, and I was out and running for cover by the road. I turned, watched him skim over the waves, and then he was gone as fast as he had arrived! I wondered who was paying for all the aviation fuel.

I walked for about an hour toward the airport and finally caught a jitney to Nassau to begin my hunt for Doug. I did not want to activate my cell phone—at least, not just yet—and the sat phone was in my duffle, waiting for a recharge. I came across a small drugstore and decided to buy a burner phone, switched it on and dialed the Major.

He answered after the first ring. Not knowing if his cell was being monitored, I asked him if he was enjoying the balmy weather in Nassau. He said he was. I asked if he was able to get a nice hotel on such short notice. He said he was staying at the Atlantis on Paradise Island. I told him his cell transmission was all fuzzy and that we had a bad connection. I would call him on his landline. He gave me the hotel number and his room number. I said I would call him in "about thirty-three minutes"—our code that I would meet him shortly. If a meeting were not possible at that time, he would have told me thirty-three was too exact a number. Not a foolproof code, but a code nonetheless!

I caught a very rundown taxi across the bridge to Paradise Island. I actually wondered if it was going to make the trip. Before reaching our meeting spot, I climbed out to walk the rest of the way. I roamed in and out of a few stores and used a back or side door each time one was available. I did not see or sense a tail along the way, so I proceeded to the Atlantis Hotel.

I told the atlantis guard that I was going in to inquire about the rates, as I was unhappy with my current hotel. A U.S. twenty bought me admission. I wandered around the side near the water park and slipped in the side of the massive main lobby area. I saw Doug standing casually at the front of the gift shop. I passed to his rear and made a razz sound, then continued to the men's room off the lobby.

A few moments later, Doug entered and looked under the stalls. I told him I had already checked and it was clear. I leaned against the inside of the entry door to keep others out and proceeded to tell him, in detail, the events of the past few days. I finished by telling him Calvin was missing and presumed to be in the custody of the American Mercenaries.

Doug had been meeting with some Bahamas government folks, trying to work out a deal for getting an official release for Joel. Even though he was now out of the country, there were still murder charges against him. So far, they were only considering execution as an option. He needed me to start putting together a defense investigation so he had some bargaining tools.

He was beginning to believe that the majority of the Bahamas' government had been kept in the dark about what really went on in San Andros. Calvin knew about the Middle Easterners living there, but most residents of the islands were under the impression that they were employees of the U.S. Government or Canadians.

My first order of business was to find and release Calvin from his captors.

Doug agreed. He said he would see if any of the legal folks he was dealing with had any helpful information. Calvin was liked and respected by all who knew him.

I left Paradise Island the way I had come—in a taxi and then on foot! I stopped at the Straw Market and again bought a straw hat and a lightweight pullover shirt. The colors did not do me justice, but a fashion show this wasn't. After rounding a corner and stepping into an alleyway off the beaten path, I pulled the shirt over my head and put the hat on. I split the straw a bit on the front brim so I could walk with my head tilted down and still see forward. As long as I kept my hands inside my pockets, I could pass as a local from a distance.

I walked to Calvin's mother's home and went around the back. Mrs. White was sitting in the kitchen area with a female friend I recognized from an earlier visit. We embraced and she offered me a cold Coke. I gratefully accepted it. I could not remember the last time I'd had any sugar down my throat. Everyone was always trying to pour booze into me for some reason. She also offered me a peanut butter sandwich, which tasted incredibly good. I explained as much as I could about what Calvin and I had been up to.

Mrs. White told me that her niece, who worked at the Airport, saw Calvin get off a small plane about mid-morning the day before yesterday. Her niece saw two white men approach him, took him by his arms, and escort him to a small car. She told Mrs. White that they were very muscular and had close-cropped hair like soldiers.

After assuring Mrs. White that I would bring Calvin home soon, I thanked her for the Coke and sandwich, left the house, and walked toward downtown Nassau. A woman who had been standing on the corner across from Mrs. White's caught up to me and told me she was a very good friend of Calvin's and had some information regarding his whereabouts. I watched closely as she reached into her purse for something, but only removed a small wallet and showed me her credentials. Her name was Pearl Simpson and she worked for Calvin.

I walked Pearl to a shaded area in a small park and we sat down on a bench under a big tree. My disguise clearly wasn't working too well and we were attracting a lot of attention from everyone passing by. Pearl told me I looked like an advertisement for some cruise line. My goal was to hide my identity—not necessarily blend in like a native.

Pearl learned that Calvin had been taken by helicopter to San Andros just an hour before. She said that, since yesterday, one of her fellow agents had been tailing the group that was holding him. The politicians controlling her agency were afraid to interfere with the Americans, as the American presence was stronger than ever right now in and around the Bahamas.

I thought about contacting Gage but instead used my new burner to call Sorensen, who was now in Miami. I told him Calvin's whereabouts and that my boat was anchored off Nicholls Town. My plan was to pick up a few items and be on my way to San Andros.

Pearl said that she had a friend who had a small seaplane and was sure he would fly me there, especially as he was another one of Calvin's cousins. I wasn't keeping count, but his guy must have been related to everyone in the Bahamas! Sorensen said he should be there before me and hung up. I accepted Pearl's offer of her friend's plane ride and we set out in her little green Honda for the west side of the island.

I called Doug, briefed him on the latest events, and then told him where I was heading. He had made contact with an attorney friend of his in New York City and they were working on an agreement with the U.S. State Department and the Bahamas regarding Joel's fugitive status. I was not sure what that meant, exactly, but let it go for the time being. I did not want to get into any more details due to the lack of secure communication.

Pearl parked her Honda next to a small cove on the beach and we walked over a rise. There, floating next to a small dock, was what looked like a plane—at least, I thought it was a plane. It resembled a dinosaur skeleton in a museum. It had to be a hundred years old. Its frame had very little outer covering, with only two seats bolted—or maybe wired somehow—to a platform used as a floorboard. The engine was huge compared to the rest of the plane and there was what appeared to be a fuel tank hanging from the frame behind the seats. The plane had huge tall pontoons under its long, wide wings. The plane stood about fifteen feet above the water like a flying crane.

A man, I hoped was not the pilot walked toward the dock wearing the thickest glasses I had ever seen on a human. Pearl called out to him and he looked in the wrong direction until Pearl told him we were on the dock.

He was the pilot and Pearl introduced him as Lefty Smith. It was then that I noticed he was missing his right hand. He extended his stump, and as I shook it, he looked me up and down through those coke-bottle glasses and told me I couldn't wear my new outfit on his plane, as I looked ridiculous. Was he kidding? This day was not looking any better!

It turned out that old Lefty was a former pilot for Air Bahamas who had lost his hand in a contest with a large shark while fishing off Key West some years ago. His so-called airplane was purposely stripped down to carry cargo to the smaller islands and villages around the Bahamas and the upper Caribbean Islands. He could carry twice as much cargo with the fuselage off—as well as oddly shaped items such as large-screen televisions and even pool tables. He said he once transported an entire double-wide modular home in several pieces to a small island off the Exuma's.

We watched as Pearl drove off to see what else, if anything, she could do to help us bring Calvin home. I was left alone with good old Lefty and his fantastic flying wreck.

I helped him load fuel into the exposed tank. Then, after he made some adjustments and tied my two small bags on a side rack, he said, "Climb aboard—she's safe."

I sat in the right seat and buckled in tight—oh, so very tight. He released the lines from the dock and, with his foot, pushed the plane away from the dock.

I then realized that he was not actually on the plane, but then felt better when the plane suddenly spun around so it was pointing toward the open water. Lefty, using his one hand, pulled the plane back to the dock, jumped aboard, and climbed into the left seat.

I noticed that all the controls were on the left side of the yoke, which had a fork-like extension sticking out the right side so he could turn it with his right arm stub. It definitely looked homemade, but it all looked in good working order.

As we drifted away from the dock, he turned the key and the engine turned over and started on the first revolution. That engine was the biggest and loudest I had ever seen or heard in a small, single-engine aircraft not used for stunt flying. That's when it dawned on me that this plane's first life was as a stunt plane and that it was probably homemade

We took off west into the breeze. The plane was solid and cut the water as if it was on wheels. We lifted off and without making a single turn headed right toward San Andros. Lefty never made a radio call and stayed about three hundred feet above the waves. It was a great plane and seemed to glide along at about one-quarter of the throttle my Cessna needed to stay aloft.

About thirty minutes out, we passed two sailboats, and then I saw the *Semper Fi*, Top's ketch, sailing east below us. Above the roar of the engine, I shouted to Lefty that I needed to signal Top to tell him I was on my way back to San Andros.

Lefty yelled back that he could land next to him and I could transfer to the boat. Why didn't I think of that?

We turned about and made a pass by Top. He looked closely at the antique airplane and its passengers and then waved as soon as he saw me. I noticed he had his deadly rifle right next to his helm in readiness for action.

Lefty dropped his altitude like a rock falling from a cliff and skimmed the top of the small swells as the plane drifted to a halt. Top swung his ketch around and dropped his sails right alongside the plane like the pro he was. I shook hands with Lefty's stump, slipped him a hundred-dollar bill, and climbed out onto the pontoon.

The small swells were lapping at the pontoons and my shoes got wet. But, being back on Earth, even wet, was a relief. The fantastic flying machine was definitely an experience I'll always remember.

Top swung his helm a bit and the transom drifted close enough for me to jump aboard. Lefty cranked up the engine as soon as I was on board. The seaplane roared away and took to the sky. With a gentle swinging wave of the wings, he was gone into the eastern sky.

Top had sent Patty home to Orlando by private plane from San Andros as he did not want her directly involved in any of the things we were about to get into.

He told me he had seen the road to the community and could see what

87

appeared to be a military blockade gate across the main road. As far as he could tell through his binoculars, there were at least four heavily armed white men at the gate near a military-type vehicle parked inside.

We turned and headed back toward San Andros. I told Top what I knew about Calvin being transported to San Andros and that my intention was to get him out and to a good safe house until this matter was concluded. Calvin was priority number one!

We sailed for about three hours until I saw some fishing boats that told me we were about a half hour out from Nicholls Town. Top's cell phone was still out of range so I cranked up the sat phone. I thought I'd better check in with Gage before too long but called Sorensen on his personal cell first.

No surprise he answered on the first ring. Sorensen said he was sitting on my boat, drinking an ice-cold beer. He said he had some news and would tell me when we arrived. He had flown back in on a small seaplane and had to swim across to the *Slim Molly* because the plane's wings were too low for the pilot to get alongside it.

He said he showered on the deck and that I needed to put some more freshwater in my holding tanks before too long. I figured if I was looking to shower or get cleaned up, I was out of luck, but that was the least of my concerns right now.

As we approached the mooring area off Nicholstown, we saw a Black Hawk helicopter approach from the west and settle into the trees just about where San Andros would be. The airport was farther to the west than where the helicopter had landed.

Sorensen was standing in the cockpit of my boat, holding a line ready for us to come about. As we came alongside, he cinched it up tight, jumped aboard the ketch, and gave me my usual bear hug.

I introduced him to Top. It was a hardy handshake between the two of them and two "Semper Fi's. "

Sorensen noticed the large rifle lying in its holder next to Top's helm-stand. "So, Top, are you going elephant hunting?" he asked.

I said, "Don't even ask."

We let my boat drift away to its mooring position, moved farther out from the other boats, and dropped anchor.

The salon on Top's boat was a ballroom compared to my boat, and the galley was first-class. Top stood in the galley, putting some good-looking food together as Sorensen and I sat at the long, solid teak table. Sorensen sat with his ever-present beer and me with bottled water.

Sorensen told me that our little escapade in the Bahamas was the talk of the town among the intelligence circles. He added that odds were against us living any more than two or three more days, tops. He said that there were some very powerful people being lobbied to turn their backs while this group of private soldiers made us go away forever. I told him that at this point, that was not news to me. Our first task was to free Calvin. Survival was number two!

I was exhausted and could not remember the last time I'd slept for any considerable period of time. I needed some rest or I would start making every mistake possible. I asked Top if I could borrow a rack for a few hours for some R&R and suggested they do the same. I knew after we all had some rest; we would have clearer minds and could plan our next moves with more certainty.

About six hours later, I woke up to the sound of a powerboat coming very close to the hull of the ketch. I heard Top, using his best Top Sergeant voice, ordering someone to stand clear of his craft and move on. Top was serious and his bark suggested he meant business.

I peered out the portlight and saw four white, heavily armed military types in a large, open-assault boat. I could not hear what they were asking, but it was clear that Top wasn't having any of it. They looked Top up and down, reluctantly pushed off, and drifted toward another boat.

Top came below and told us the patrol wanted to search his boat. They claimed there were known terrorists in the area and they wanted to search his boat for his own safety. He asked them what authority they were working under and what military unit they were with. They didn't answer either question.

Top said they were armed with the most advanced weaponry he had ever seen. They were also wearing electronic bio-collar devices that signaled real-time combat physical analysis back to their units. Top related that U.S. troops were not outfitted with these devices yet.

I wondered what kind of government influence had the power to outfit American civilian, paramilitary types with this kind of advanced technology and weapons. I could tell that Top was troubled by the same thought I'd had.

I asked him if he had ever seen anything like it before. He said, "The civilian paramilitary guard at the Green Zone in Baghdad always had better weapons than my Marines did." He then suggested that they had bought their own fancy modern equipment. He said our government was buying those mercenary's stuff and that it was better than the things they were giving their own Marines.

The three of us were rested enough to start throwing around some ideas about how we were going to get Calvin out. After some discussion, we decided that all our ideas required that we do some recon of the San Andros area.

At this point, we were unable to even get out on the deck with that patrol still snooping around in the nearby waters. I watched the patrol pull alongside the *Slim Molly* and look in her portlights. I had a big, heavy-duty padlock on my hatch that Sorensen had refastened before he came aboard the ketch. They would know that no one was aboard because of the outside padlock. If they were doing their job properly, they would call the International Registry on the boat name, but that would have come up legitimate on their books. If they checked the hull for a serial number, they would find it missing and glassed over.

One of the para-soldiers looked around the cockpit area, lost interest, climbed back into the assault boat, and then they moved on to the next boat. It seemed that most of the boaters felt they had to submit to the search since we watched the searchers climbed aboard all the boats we could see.

If they had performed a proper search of my boat by looking under my gunnels, they would have spotted the hinges that swing the hatches over the fasteners used to hold my rifles, cartridge magazines, and holsters for my two pistols. A search of the interior cabin would have revealed the two military rifles and cartridge magazines I had ripped off over the past week as I encountered their comrades around these adventurous islands.

My other weapons would be a bit more difficult to find as they were hidden in specialty-molded compartments in the galley. I remembered that I had a few more items hidden in the hull. A night-vision scope and a couple of flash-bang hand grenades. There could be a couple of old M-26 fragmentation grenades hanging around there somewhere, too. Gage had once tried to talk me into putting a fifty-caliber long rifle like Top's in the forward hull that I could remotely fire from the helm.

My response? "If I needed that kind of firepower, I would have bought a refurbished PT boat, dude."

About an hour later, the patrol boat moved away and vanished over the horizon to the south. The three of us checked our gear before climbing into

Top's Zodiac rubber boat. Along with our other supplies, we had two HD digital cameras and a night-vision scope compliments of Sorensen's brief visit back in Miami. We also had some medical supplies in case we needed them. Better to be safe than sorry when it comes to first aid.

We motored to the beach northwest of Nicholstown near Morgan's Bluff, pulled up onto the beach, and checked our supplies one more time.

We had about an hour before dark so we hung around on the beach perfecting our plan.

As soon as it was dark enough, we planned to slip the Zodiac back in the water and hug the shoreline until we came up to the cove where I'd stashed my scooter. Top didn't have time to look for it yesterday and left it there for another day.

Top would stay with the Zodiac and keep it idling so we were ready to take off, should we come running out of the trees. Sorensen and I would take the scooter down the road to the entrance to the San Andros community and stash it in the bushes as I had before. I remembered the spot and it was a perfect hiding place.

Our first order of business was to locate Calvin. We could plan the rest from there.

About an hour after sunset, with the sky filled with bright orange colors that made it look like it was on fire, we pushed the Zodiac off the beach and headed west. We had discovered while sitting on the beach that there was a converted cabin cruiser patrolling the northern end of San Andros. What appeared to be a machine gun was mounted on the forward deck but covered with a fitted tarp. This cruiser would make it a bit more difficult to conceal our activities.

Top raised the outboard motor on the boat so it was barely pushing water and we skimmed along the inside of the barrier reef next to the beach. The patrol boat established a pattern of about two hours to make its run back and forth, so that gave us about an hour and fifty minutes of safe time to get in and out ahead of them.

We idled along the beach and came to the little cove I had discovered last week. Top ran the boat up on the beach and we sat there in total silence for a few moments to see if we could detect anyone stationed in the brush. There were no unnatural sounds. The critters were squeaking, chirping, and hooting as normal. Those sounds told me we had an all-clear.

Sorensen and I climbed out of the boat, walked ashore with our gear bags over our shoulders, and slipped into the darkness of the brush. I walked ahead of Sorensen, as I was a bit smaller and made less noise with the branches and ground cover.

I found my scooter in the spot where I had left it. I checked it over for any booby traps, found none, and carried it into the clearing. I saw Sorensen's face and knew he was trying to figure out how it was going to carry both of us. I knew my little bike's capacity for hardship and knew it would carry us a long way, though not in great comfort.

I sat forward as far as I could on the seat and kicked the starter. It came to life on the first kick. I let it warm up a bit and told Sorensen to sit behind me on the flat carry rack and put his feet on each side of the rear axle. I kept the tires overinflated on purpose so I could carry heavy loads. Four hundred pounds was a bit much, but the rear tire stayed inflated, stayed off the rims and the shocks, and the heavy-duty springs kept the tires off the inside of the fenders. I rolled the throttle forward and we were off.

I got the scooter up to about twenty-five MPH and cut over onto the main road from the Old Lumber Road. We only had about a mile to cover and we were there in five minutes. I pulled to the right side of the road, stopped, and Sorensen got off, making a remark that he hoped no one saw him on the scooter. It would have been humorous except that we were about to slip into some crap and may not come out of alive.

We stashed the scooter in the brush, covered it with branches, and headed west of the San Andros road. Everything was quiet. We could see the dim lights of the makeshift gate about fifty yards up the road. Through the brush, I could make out some movement from time to time. I hoped for some rain to mask any sounds we might make, but the sky was clear and the air a little too cool for any rain. We were also limited by time as the coast patrol was going to spot Top and his rubber boat at first light.

Just then, we heard a truck coming from the direction of the airport. It sounded loud but I could tell it was slowing down as if it was preparing to turn onto the San Andros road. I looked at Sorensen and winked.

As soon as it came alongside our position, we crossed the road and started moving through the light brush west of the southbound entrance road, using the truck's sounds to cover our progress.

We continued to skirt the road about twenty yards west, heading in a southerly direction as we watched for tripwires and infrared detectors. With all the fancy expensive equipment they had at their disposal, I would have expected mini robots crawling through the woods, but there was nothing that amazing. Making things even better was an animal path or old trail that we were able to follow right to the village.

We continued south for another hundred yards and turned slightly west to avoid the clearing around the village. From this position, we could see the German village and the driveway to the Arab area the same as Joel had described to us earlier. There were a couple of people standing near the Community Center, and there appeared to be some paramilitary types at the entrance to the Arab area. We also noted that there were two men wearing Middle Eastern turbans standing with the guards. Both of them were holding rifles. The rifles were AK-47s!

Now we had American paramilitary and Arab guards working together with German Nazis and possibly Arab or Middle Eastern militants on an island in the Bahamas about a hundred miles from the United States! This was becoming stranger by the hour.

Sorensen and I sat there for a while and studied the buildings to see if any of them appeared to be a jail—or, at least, a holding area. Nothing jumped out at us so we continued south until we could see into the Arab area more clearly. There was a house with two cars and a black Hummer parked in front of it. Two American guards were standing near the front door with weapons at the ready. We could not see the rear of the house, but if the front was covered, then so was the rear.

As we studied the building, we could see three windows on the north side and two on the west. The house faced west and had a small porch with three steps up to the front door. The two guards we could see were facing each other and appeared to be casually talking. We could only hear about every third or fourth word from our current position. They seemed to be discussing a sports game on TV that they were missing and they hoped their fellow troops were taping the game for them. One was complaining that someone was monitoring him as he made a call home to North Carolina.

After observing the house for about half an hour, two men came out the front door and one of the men told the guards to be alert and to pass on special orders to their reliefs when they came on duty. The taller of the two guards asked the man when they were to be relieved. The man responded that he had no say so in the matter and that he should ask his Section Chief. He also told them that no one was allowed to see the detainee without his permission.

The two men walked off toward the interior of the village. I heard the taller guard ask the man if he knew the man's name who had just spoken to them and he said, "No."

The tall guard kiddingly said, "Then how do we get his 'expressed orders' if we don't know his name or how to reach him?"

The other guard said he didn't know anyone here and had only been with the company for one month.

I looked at Sorensen and winked. He just smiled at me. We'd just found our best chance to get in there to see if Calvin was the detainee.

Sorensen and I quickly made a plan to become one of the unknown leaders of this little army of spooks. We circled back around to the entrance area of the Arab camp. We put our clothes back together as neatly as we could and walked out of the brush.

As we hoped, no one paid any attention to us whatsoever as we walked down the road toward the little house with the two guards. As we walked, we made conversation about everyone getting out of this damn place and going back to the States, possibly tomorrow. We made ourselves loud enough for the two guards to hear us as we walked directly toward them.

As we'd hoped, they stopped talking and looked and listened to us.

Sorensen led the way right up to the door and said, "How is it going, men?"

The taller guard said that all was quiet and that the other men had left only a little while ago. Sorensen asked them if they needed a break to make a head call or to have a smoke, and they both replied that they did and appreciated a break.

I told them to take ten minutes but not to roam too far away as we would only be here for a short time. Grateful, they thanked us and walked to the south where we thought the guards and spooks were being housed.

Sorensen walked up the steps to the door, took some keys from his pocket, and acted as if he was opening the lock on the door. As he put the key up to the doorknob, he locked his massive hand around the doorknob and twisted it over, breaking the knob and the locking mechanism inside. He pushed the door right open and we walked in.

The front room was empty except for a chair against the south wall under a table. There were some soup cans and a bowl next to them. There was a hot-plate burner on the floor next to the table and a gallon water jug next to it. There were two doors on the back wall right across from the front door. There was no alarm system and no lights to turn on. There was a ceiling fan in the middle of the ceiling, but no light.

I closed the door as Sorensen crossed to the right-hand door. He opened it quietly, as we still did not know if there were any guards in the rear of the house. As our eyes adjusted to the dim light, we saw a narrow bed against the right wall. The window above the bed had a piece of plywood nailed over it from the inside. There was a wooden card table in the middle of the room with two chairs on opposite sides. There were three or more chairs along the left wall. Something moved on the bed and Sorensen stepped over and then waved for me to come over. There was a young black man—not Calvin—handcuffed to the bed. He just lay there, terrified, looking up at us.

It wasn't Calvin, but I guessed it was Paul, the airport worker who'd gone missing last week at San Andros Airport. Sorensen did something to the handcuffs and I heard a sharp crack.

I asked the young man if his name was Paul and he nodded yes. I explained to him that we were going to get him out and to safety. He started to whimper and fall apart, but I told him to save it for later, that he would need his strength and energy now.

Sorensen stayed with him and I went out and opened the other door. Calvin wasn't there, either, but there was a large desk covered with papers and two laptop computers. Sorensen came in, turned both of the laptops over, and, with his Swiss Army knife, took the hard drives from both and stuffed them in his pockets. I grabbed a couple of piles of letterhead memos from the paper piles and placed them inside my shirt. I had no time to read anything right now but I would take the time later.

We half carried and half pushed Paul to the front door and leaned him against the outside wall. I looked out through the window and saw the two guards just walking back up to the house. I looked at Sorensen and he had the same *aw crap* look on his face. At least the guards had come back without an army behind them.

We placed the handcuffs back on Paul loosely. I walked out ahead of Paul and Sorensen and asked the guards if they'd had a good break. They looked at Paul and acted as if they did not recognize him. The taller of the two guards thanked us for the break and smiled. I told them we would be back in about an hour, not to leave their post, and that when they went off duty, they should inform their reliefs. We then walked Paul toward the gate and Sorensen motioned for me to turn left between two buildings and walked briskly west into the brush. No one had said a word to us or paid us any attention other than a brief glance as we had walked parallel down the street.

We walked a little farther and west into the brush and Sorensen took the cuffs off of Paul. We squatted down to talk and further informed Paul he was with friends. I told Paul that we were taking him to our boat, where he would have to hang out for a while until things quieted down. I told him he could tell us his whole story then. I also told him we would get word to his family as soon as possible that he was alive and safe.

The sun was rising on the horizon and we were losing the cover of darkness, which meant we were not safe in the bush any longer. We didn't know what time the leaders of this group came to work each morning, but judging by the time they'd left for the night, they would probably be in late this morning.

We quietly moved farther toward the road leading to the airport. Based on our previous plan, Top had to have left the beach by now, as we were about an hour overdue. We would have to hide out until after dark to get back over the beach to either my boat or Top's. This was going to be a long day.

Paul was getting stronger by the moment. He was moving on his own without our help, thank goodness. This made things a bit easier. Sorensen took point and started angling northward. Occasionally, we could hear a car or truck pass on the airport road, so when we were in sight of the road, we stopped when we heard them and waited until they passed.

Because I knew the lay of the land a little better than Sorensen, I felt we were better off crossing the road and waiting in the brush between the airport road and the old logging road. That way, we could change our position to avoid being seen—or, worse, being found.

We did not hear or see any signs of tracking dogs while we were at the camp, but that did not mean they weren't there. Having two roads to cross back and forth over would not only mess up their search pattern, but it would also make it a bit harder for any dogs to track us. We split up a couple of times to confuse any tracking dogs and we crossed the road and went into the brush on the other side. Paul stayed with me at all times.

We finally stopped in a small clearing near the south side of the Lumber Road, close to the path that led to where Top could pick us up after dark. Darkness was by far our best friend at this point. My scooter was still in the brush next to the San Andros road, and I knew I had to leave it there for the greater good! It was only a scooter.

I managed to get a quick call to Top and he confirmed that he was still on his boat. He told me that he had left just before sunup but had placed some fresh water and energy bars in the bushes where he had been waiting with the Zodiac. He said the water patrol did four passes in the night but never put a spotlight on while patrolling.

I told him I was fairly sure they were using night-vision goggles to scan the shoreline and beach area. He'd figured as much and had kept to the brush when they passed each time.

I told him, "We have Paul, the guy missing from the airport, but there was no sign of Calvin."

At that moment, Paul turned to Sorensen and told him he knew exactly where they were holding Calvin.

I signed off the call to Top and moved closer to Sorensen and Paul to listen to what Paul had to say. Paul stated that two days ago, a black man was brought into the house where he was being held. The man had a black hood over his head and his hands were bound behind him. He appeared to be okay physically, but he did have some blood on his white shirt.

Paul said he could see through the open door to the front of the house. The men escorting this man took him back out and turned left toward the interior of the Arab compound. There was a small hole in the board covering his window, but it was big enough for him to see through it and to watch the man being brought to the house across the street. From his stature, Paul thought it might be Calvin.

As we waited in the brush, a helicopter, flying very low, flew over the area a few times throughout the day. Two Hummers, black and dark green, passed on both roads going west. They soon returned, but there did not seem to be an organized search.

Top called us from his boat to say that he had seen the two Hummers pass through Nicholls Town a couple of times but there did not appear to be any search of the town. Paul said he lived near the Marina in Nicholls Town, so if his house was being searched, Top would have seen it from his boat.

We stayed in place most of the day, watching, waiting, and listening for any sign of a search. It seemed impossible that they would not have pushed the panic button by now! We could only assume that no one in authority knew about it and the guards had gone off duty and not mentioned our visit. It may be possible that they did not know their prisoner was missing yet! From their actions, it appeared that Mentor Corporation wasn't hiring the sharpest tools in the shed anymore.

As the sun was settling into the ocean, a small, twin-engine, turboprop plane circled overhead and then landed at the airport to our south. Top was on his way to pick us up in the Zodiac inflatable and called us to say, "That was one very impressive airplane that just went by, and there were no markings on it at all, boys. I've seen the same type of plane used by the no-name folks who took detainees from Bagdad off for a chat before Gitmo!"

Sorensen and I talked about it and decided to get a better look at who was coming or going on the aircraft, so we brought Paul to where Top was waiting for us on the beach, loaded him on the inflatable, and told Top to take him back to his boat and wait for us to call. Top gave a salute and off he went with Paul.

Sorensen and I cut back through the brush and trees to the airport road. We walked inside the bushes until we were about a hundred yards from the road to San Andros. We waited until we could hear vehicles moving toward us from the direction of the airport. We moved as close as we could to the road to see if we could make out who was riding in the vehicles.

There were a number of small cars and one old truck with a wooden bed and side rails that passed our position, but the occupants just looked like locals on their way to Nicholls Town to the east. We heard a large helicopter in the distance but could not tell what direction it was traveling in. As we patiently waited, the helicopter became louder and louder until it was right over us. It then flew into the San Andros compound before we could scramble and get a view of it. The helicopter came from the west so it must have flown in directly from the Keys or Miami, as it never stopped at the San Andros airport. The copter's engine wound down as we moved through the brush. Its noise masked our movements as we approached the clearing at the Arab compound. For this, we both were grateful.

At first, all we saw were the helicopter rotary wings slowly turning down. Facing the copter were three men wearing tan desert fatigues with their backs to us. The door slowly opened and three security-looking types rushed down and stood at attention at the foot of the stairs. A figure stepped out of the shadows and onto the steps. With the exception of his height, it could have been Osama Bin Laden himself but I knew it had to be his brother, who once lived in the Orlando area up until 9/11.

This man walked toward the men waiting in the field. Two more men emerged from the copter. One man in an expensive business suit without a tie and one in chinos and a polo shirt. The man in the suit was not familiar to me, but the sporty guy in the chinos I knew well. He was the Special Assistant to the Secretary of State.

This man was seldom seen out in the public sector, but he always hovered in the minds of the people in my business. When a person or persons disappear and, if they were a significant political figure or a foreign agent of some kind, I always looked at him for some dirty part of the problem. His name was Jason Patrick, but he was known as just Patrick. He was now about fifty-five years old and had been a Special Assistant for the last four administrations

It did not matter the political party. He was a dirty little secret used time and again to carry out the jobs no one wanted to be associated with. You might refer to him as an "interrogation expert."

Apparently, our current problem was far graver then we had imagined because I knew he was there for Calvin.

Torture was this guy's tool and, according to his followers, he never failed. Of course, I knew better than that, as I and some of my associates had disrupted his efforts and foiled his plans a number of times.

This time, however, I was worried. A very good friend of ours was the object of his talents, and even if Calvin had a short meeting with this guy, it could cause a lifetime of stress and nightmares. I spent a very unpleasant hour with him a few years back, and even though I tend to get over most of my occupational trauma-related memories, just looking into the eyes of this maniac gave me the shivers. Unfortunately, he knew me and, as you can guess, I was not his favorite person!

Patrick and one of his companions walked over to the military types and began talking. No customary greetings and no one shook hands, but they seemed familiar with one another. Sorensen and I recognized one of the military guys as one of the men we saw leaving the house where Paul was being held last night.

Sorensen moved like a sniper back into the brush and motioned for me to follow. I knew what he was going to say before he said it. We needed to act and do it fast before Patrick got to the house where they were keeping Calvin. If we could create a diversion, it may buy us the time we needed.

We needed to be creative since we had not taken any additional weapons with us past our pistols. I looked around and saw a pile of trash with some paint cans thrown on top. One of the containers in the pile was a can of paint thinner that I hoped still had some liquid in it.

Sorensen produced some matches from his belt pack and we slipped closer to the trash pile. The area around the Arab compound was tall, dry grass and fallen pine needles. The wind was a soft breeze out of the east blowing the grass slightly westward. If we were to light a fire, it would spread into the pines and keep going until it reached the ocean. I was sure the Andros Island Forest Service wasn't capable of fighting any real fire.

We looked around and noticed that the house they had held Paul in was no longer being guarded. I picked up the paint thinner container and checked it for contents. Fortunately, it was half full of paint thinner. We crossed the road and came up behind that house. It was amazing that no one paid any attention to us. You would think a compound this new, with so many strangers, would have internal security set up, but from what we could tell, not yet. Sorensen and I appeared just like another pair of unfamiliar strangers—two of the many new faces. We also looked like military types so we fit right in.

We walked all around the house and looked through the rear windows to make sure it was completely vacant. I told Sorensen to walk out front and stand guard while I took the container of paint thinner and poured what was left of it on the rear door jam and into the open rear window.

When the time was right, Sorensen nodded. I lit the paint thinner and it quickly spread from the door inward. As soon as I knew it was going to stay lit, I crossed the backyards of the adjacent houses to the south and came out right in front of the house where we believed Calvin was being held.

Sorensen walked slowly up the street, picking up his pace until he was right beside me. Two serious-looking sentries were guarding Calvin's prison. No one was watching the rear of the house or the woods to the west. As we moved closer to the house, Patrick and two of his militant escorts walked from around the corner of the house next door. Surprised, our eyes locked in a moment of recognition.

He looked as if he was going to faint and, as he turned to inform his escort of his "daymare," there were loud screams of "Fire, fire, fire!" and, immediately, more shouts as people reacted to the huge flames shooting into the air from the burning house.

Patrick looked at me one more time as if he didn't believe his eyes and, in that moment, he was swept up in the near panic of the people running by him. With all the commotion, I popped Patrick a hardy left, caught him as he started to fall, and propped him up against one of the structures to keep him from being trampled.

Sorensen grabbed my right arm and pulled me toward the small house where we believed Calvin was being held, but the two rather large, muscular sentries blocked our way with their rifles at port arms. I started to tell them we were ordered to take the prisoner to another location when Sorensen clobbered one of the sentries with a left cross. The man went down like he had been shot. I waited about two heartbeats, slammed the other man to the ground, punched him twice, and grabbed his rifle. He lay there, not moving a muscle, but with his eyes wide open. I told him to get up and open the door to the house. He did so right away and stepped back for me to see inside.

There were two men standing next to a desk. On the desk was a laptop with what appeared to be a video feed showing an empty table with numerous chairs on both sides and one chair at the end of the table. I quickly took my eyes off the computer screen and moved over to the two men at the desk. They were not armed that I could see, and neither of them appeared to be a physical threat.

In my military drill sergeant tone, I ordered them to move to the wall directly behind them and then looked into the room on the right. Calvin was sitting in a chair in the middle of the room. He was zip-tied to the chair and wearing a gag. He was bleeding from his nose. There was blood on his shirt and trouser legs, and his eyes and mouth were swollen.

He managed a smile with his eyes, a distinct trait that I recognized right away. I removed the gag and he said exactly what I expected him to say.

"What took you so long, Jake?"

I quickly cut the zip ties from his arms and legs and slowly stood him up so the blood would not run to his legs and make him dizzy. He wobbled just a bit, then stretched and said he was ready to go.

Sorensen had already tied the two men back to back and secured them to the desk leg. It would not be necessary to gag them with all the noise going on outside with the fire.

We opened the back door, looked for anyone in the immediate area, and slipped out and into the brush to the west of the village. It seemed like a cakewalk until I happened to look back and saw about ten well-armed militants gathered around Patrick. He was pointing toward the house we had just left. I pushed Calvin's head down and the three of us ducked down under the brush level. We only had two pistols and one rifle that Sorensen had lifted from one of the guards we had disabled. No extra ammunition and no place to go except through the woods.

As we watched, Patrick frantically yelled and pointed at the woods where we were hiding. Another house went up in flames like a matchbox and dozens of Arab-dressed men, women, and children ran from the newly burning house. The fire was quickly spreading across the dry grass and moving toward the west—right toward us. Many of the panic-stricken people were running ahead of it and right in our general direction.

We waited until some of the people had passed us and then joined them running toward the north. We were able to angle back to the San Andros road and through the German village to the road to the airport.

By now, there were about twenty-five or thirty people all around us turning around to look back at the black smoke coming from the houses going up in flames. Sorensen, Calvin, and I knew this was our best opportunity to avoid anyone noticing us, so we kept going through the sentry gate to the main road. No one was paying any attention to us, so we turned west and walked quickly to where I'd hidden my scooter.

There was no way it would carry all three of us, so Sorensen told us he would run beside us until we reached the area where Top was picking us up in the Zodiac. As we headed west on the old logging road, I heard the helicopter crank up and lift off from the village behind us. I nodded to Sorensen to jump in the side brush as I steered the scooter to the side of the road and laid it over.

Calvin had been extremely quiet since we rescued him. I suspected that he was suffering from shock and that, even being a seasoned tough guy like Calvin, had to break down sometime. I asked Calvin if he was okay and helped him into a sitting position.

I fired up the sat phone and called Top to see where he was. He answered on the first ring and said he was in the Semper fi off the coast about where we were, but three miles out from us. Briefly, I explained the situation to him and he said he could see the copter flying slowly in our direction. I told him to stand by with the Zodiac until we called him. He said he had Paul with him and that Paul could climb into the inflatable, put on a hat, and drift toward us acting like he was fishing. It sounded like a plan so I told him we would make for the shore and hide out until we could safely jump into the Zodiac with Paul.

We could now hear the helicopter working its way back and forth in its search pattern for us, getting closer and closer with every pass. We were pretty sure ground troops were spread out under the copter, searching the brush. We'd only heard two vehicles so far on the road from San Andros. That did not make a lot of sense under the circumstances. Sorensen crawled on his belly out onto the beach and looked in all directions. He didn't see any searchers or boat patrols looking for us. Patrick was keeping the knowledge of us limited to very few people. Good for us. Bad for him!

As we lay there, waiting for Paul to arrive in the Zodiac and signal us, we heard some movement about fifty yards east of where we were lying. The noise turned into footfalls and quiet whispering. Calvin was now sleeping under some thick bushes and Sorensen was about ten yards to the north of me, squatting down with the rifle at the ready. I motioned for him to be ready, but I pointed at the rifle and then to my ears, telling him what he already knew. If we fired a shot, it would bring an army of troops down on us in minutes.

The first two troops came down the path where we were hiding. Sorensen acted first and knocking the legs out from under one and slammed him to the ground. A moment later, I grabbed the other one and hit him with a round-off punch to the side of his head. He went down like a rock. Sorensen hit his guy twice and the guy was out cold. Quickly, we grabbed them up and dragged them into the thick brush.

Seconds later, two more passed by about twenty-five yards south of us, so they weren't of immediate concern. All of a sudden, one troop walked out of the brush and confronted us before we even heard him. We could tell he was as surprised as we were. Sorensen grabbed him off his feet and before he could put him out, the man whispered, "I am a friend and we need to talk, please."

I grabbed Sorensen's arm as it flew by me and toward the trooper's face just in time to soften the blow.

I took his rifle and sidearm from him and dragged him into the brush where his partners were. Sorensen held him close with his hands around his throat just in case we needed to shut him up quickly. He appeared calm and ready to talk.

He told us he was an employee of Mentor Corporation and that his name was Wilson from California. He said the troops at the compound were all former military men and women. They were headquartered out of Arkansas and had contracts just like in the service. He said he'd been sent down here last week on a high-level security detail for some foreign dignitaries.

He quickly realized that this village was not a legitimate area of American friends. He was told not to speak with anyone at the village unless spoken to first, and then only if he first consulted a supervisor. The Arabs were resentful of him and his fellow troops and acted just like the Taliban did in Afghanistan when he was there. He could see that some of the younger men were militants and were definitely against any Westerners.

Wilson told us they'd been dispatched like in a war zone and were given orders to hunt us down and shoot us on sight. They were told we were terrorists and had planted a firebomb to disrupt the exercises there in San Andros.

He saw the civilian arrive earlier and could tell he was a spook. He also knew they were holding a black man in that house and that he was a Bahamian official. Wilson spoke with his supervisor about going home and putting all this behind him, but his supervisor told him he was under contract and could not leave until his assignment was over.

Wilson was not about to shoot anyone on orders from a bunch of civilian wanna-be soldiers. He said there were more guys working with him who felt the same way he did, but they were all suffering the same dilemma since some of the senior leaders seemed to be crazy.

He said that when the civilian team arrived a few hours earlier and he saw the guy who appeared to be their leader, he knew this was an "off the books operation." He had to get off this island as soon as possible. Contract or no contract, life is more important than money!

Sorensen and I stepped aside to discuss Wilson out of his earshot and agreed to take him along until we figured out what to do with him. I told Wilson he could stay with us, but without his weapons. Without hesitation, he agreed and sat down next to sleeping Calvin. I should have done it as soon as we had secured Wilson, but I now noticed that he had a cell phone clipped to his ammo belt. I reached over and pulled it off him.

When I opened it, I discovered it was on and transmitting. I asked him where he'd gotten it and he said they'd issued it to him when he left for the Bahamas. I quickly shut it down and pulled the battery pack from the back. I was sure it was a traceable phone and would signal Wilson's exact location.

Wilson said he had no idea what it did but that they were all instructed to keep them charged and in the "on" position at all times. He received text messages with announcements every couple of hours, as did all of the guys.

I asked him if they were required to respond when they received any communications and he said no. I checked and the phone did have a locator GPS installed, so they knew where Wilson was before I took the battery out of his phone. There was no time to waste. We needed to move to a different location right away.

We decided to move back east in the light brush along the beach. They were searching to the west in the direction where they'd last seen us. Calvin still seemed out of it but was walking on his own and was curious about Wilson.

When I asked Wilson if he wanted to join us in getting Calvin to safety or go back to his outfit, he said, "I would rather stay with you guys, if that's okay?"

I had him move away from us for a minute and asked Calvin and Sorensen what they thought. They both agreed to trust him a bit, keep him on a short leash, and let him stay. I gave Wilson back his rifle without any rounds in the magazine and told him to walk behind us as if we were his prisoners. That way, if we came upon another patrol, it would give us the element of surprise to overtake them.

We moved slowly and diligently along the beach. We tried to walk on the hard surfaces of the old coral formations so as not to leave footprints or many scents for any dogs to follow. Calvin was getting better as we moved along and, knowing the terrain better than we did, took the lead, keeping us in the brush that skirted the beach. We came upon two different groups of tourists who were swimming at the small sandy beaches between the coral heads, but they did not even look up as we passed by.

Getting his wits about him, Calvin called one of his people from Sorensen's cell phone and briefly told them what had happened to him. He asked them to hold off making anything public or filing a formal complaint until we were able to figure out what was really going on here on San Andros. He said to someone on the cell, "I want a gag order put on this until I personally give the okay to release any information, got it?"

I advised Calvin to get in touch with one of his relatives and go underground for a while, as he needed to heal physically and mentally.

I now had Joel in a safe house outside of Miami, Calvin in poor health tagging along with Sorensen, Wilson behind us looking for sanctuary, and

Top waiting for our call with Paul out on a boat waiting to pick us up. Doug was next on my list to contact for a briefing.

We made our way about a half-mile east and were now extremely close to Morgan's Bluff. There were a few houses near us but only some were occupied, as far as we could tell. I called Top and told him our exact location. Top signaled Paul, who was to the south of his position in the Zodiac, waiting for us. Considering everything, we decided that we should wait a while longer before we chanced a pickup by Paul—at least until the helicopter landed or disappeared.

Wilson had some energy bars packed with him and he shared them with the rest of us. He also had two bottles of drinking water that he also gladly shared. We had passed on digging up the energy bars that Top had left, so Wilson's offering was very welcomed.

We were nested in, waiting for a break in the search, when we heard an unexpected change in the helicopter direction. It sounded like it was heading right toward our hideout. We dove under the brush to conceal our position from the air and pulled the small branches over our exposed light skin. The copter kept coming like a bat out of hell, and it was over us in an instant.

Sorensen began to shift his rifle up to fire at the pilot when Wilson stepped out of the brush, looked directly at the guys in the copter, and waved to the machine gunner manning a .50 caliber in the door of the bird. Wilson then turned his back and walked away, turning from time to time to look up at the copter. The copter hovered for just a few seconds, then finally turned and flew back toward the west. The machine gunner saluted to Wilson as they flew off.

The three of us turned with a look of *What in the hell just happened?* We looked at Wilson, who smiled back and said, "I gave them the okay sign and they bought it."

It did not explain why the helicopter had been alerted to us in the first place. We looked all around us and then it dawned on us that the copter arrived moments after I called Top from Sorensen's cell phone. I quickly turned the cell off and took the battery pack out. Someone with some technical savvy on the ground was monitoring the cell signals and had gotten a reading from our phone. Either NSA at Fort Meade, Maryland, was pitching in on this operation or the folks over in San Andros had tapped into the four cell towers here on the north side of Andros. They could then read the signal directions from the towers and could zero in on our approximate location, but they did not have the capability to listen in on our conversations or they would never have turned away at Wilson's signal. Wilson had just made new friends and proven himself valuable to our cause.

We decided that this event was a good enough reason to move our position again as they would soon figure out that Wilson was missing, but we had to hug the beach so Paul could pick us up as soon as he saw us. I could see that we were now as close to the *Big Mamoo* as we were to Top's boat.

Just off in the distance was a beach house that looked abandoned. We slowly crept up to it from the southwest and watched it for a while. The house, held up by weathered, round wooden pilings, had a small enclosed area under the main structure. Sorensen got on his belly and crawled up to it, checked out the sandy area under the platform, and then he signaled us to come over.

By the time we got there, he already had the door open to the little house. It was filled with numerous beach chairs and lots of kids' beach toys. We all came up with the same idea: *Let's set it all out on the beach to make it look like we're a family spending time at our beach house.* This would keep the suspicion down if they came snooping around or flew over for a closer look-see.

Calvin even rolled the charcoal grill out and lit some charcoal in it for effect.

Jokingly, I said, "What's for dinner Cal?"

Sorensen laughed, went upstairs, and picked the lock on the door to see if there was any food we could borrow. There were some canned pork & beans that we opened and ate right from the cans. I didn't remember canned beans ever tasting so good. There was also some bottled water left in the small refrigerator that had been left on a cool setting. We were happy campers, but we slowly came back to reality when we heard voices out in the side yard. I placed my hand on my weapon.

It was a sunburned man and a well-tanned woman. They were walking around the house slowly and purposefully. The man had a golf club in his right hand and the woman was standing behind him, egging him on. I looked down and on the floor was a scrap of paper. It was a piece of an envelope. On the front, I saw the names "Peter and Marjorie Mason" and, as I had to think fast, I thought it was our best shot at not upsetting these folks.

I stepped off the back porch just as they rounded the corner and said, "Hello! What a beautiful day." I offered my best smile, introduced myself and the others using our real first names, and then told them that we were friends of Pete and Marg.

The man switched hands with the club, shook mine with a guarded smile, and said they were the next-door neighbors and had seen us in the yard moving about. I told them we knew the Masons from Atlanta, as that was the address on the envelope, and said that we were staying a couple of nights at Pete and Marjorie's invitation.

They introduced themselves as Barb and Jim Hanson. They said they had not talked to the Masons in a couple of weeks and so had not known that we would be arriving or that anyone would be staying at their beach house.

I told them it was a last-minute offer from the Masons as we were meeting our friend Calvin here to look at some property to purchase.

The Hansons seemed to buy into our story, but I knew that they would be calling the Masons as soon as they got back home. I figured that gave us about an hour before they called the local constable.

The Hansons told us to have a delightful stay and left to walk home. We immediately put all the patio and beach items we had taken out back under the overhang. Sorensen checked around inside the house for any evidence of his break-in, and we proceeded back to the west. We needed Paul to pick us up and get us back to my boat as soon as possible.

I turned on my sat phone for a brief call to Top and told him we would watch for Paul in the Zodiac and that when we saw Paul, one of us would signal him with a small LED flashlight three times.

It was just about dark now, so we had a better chance to get off the shore safely. We could hear vehicles moving down the road and heading east from the San Andros road. There was little doubt that they were responding to a phone call from the Hansons.

Top said he would send Paul and to watch for him to come from the west and, within ten minutes, I saw the small stern light flick on and off on the Zodiac. Sorensen slipped onto the beach and flashed his small blue LED three times toward the shadow of the Zodiac moving slowly on the outside of the reef heads. Paul spotted it and turned toward us, bumping over the reef toward the beach. I took one last look up and down the beach and the four of us ran into the surf.

I grabbed the bow of the rubber boat and pointed it back toward the surf. We all climbed aboard as Paul put the outboard in gear and skimmed back across the reef to deeper water. I told him to continue north away from the beach and then called Top on Paul's small walkie-talkie. I asked Top to head west and to turn due north after about three miles out. We would meet up with him over the horizon.

We floated to the north as slowly and noiselessly as we could be. I watched the beach as it shrank from view and saw what looked like a few people with flashlights walking east toward where we had boarded the Zodiac. We also kept an eye out for patrol boats in all directions, but, so far, nothing appeared to be moving on the water except us—a good sign, for now.

After about an hour, we spotted the tall mast on Top's big sloop coming from the west. Paul pulled the throttle back and turned to intercept Top. We all climbed off the Zodiac into Top's boat and flopped down on the deck like freshly caught fish. I introduced Wilson to Top and told him he was with us for the time being. I had other plans for Wilson's testimony.

Top set his autopilot for due north and we all sat down in the cockpit to discuss our next move. I called the Major and left a message on his cell phone. Then I called Gage, got no answer, and left a message. I called the folks at the safe house to inquire of Joel and they said he was better and had spoken to his wife and son a few times.

The guardian of the safe house, a prominent law enforcement officer in South Florida, told me he had been given the word that Joel may have to return to the Bahamas to testify before an inquiry hearing.

I told him that under no circumstances was Joel to be moved without Sorensen or me there. I added that even our own lawyers were sometimes fooled by the system, and we did not want Joel to run into an ambush!

He agreed and said he would keep me informed.

Paul told me he had spoken with his wife. She cried but was glad to hear his voice and that he would call her once a day at her sister's house in Nicholls Town. She told him that two Americans dressed as soldiers had been to their house, inquiring if she had heard from him. She told them no and made a big deal about him being missing and that she felt she had been lied to. That seemed to satisfy them and they left without searching their home.

Top, always one step ahead, had two prepaid burner phones he had picked up in Nicholls Town, so I used one of them to call the Major again. He answered this time and told me to hold while he walked somewhere private where he could speak freely.

The Major had been in court hearings in Nassau for the past two days and said it appeared that Joel had a number of witnesses against him. They all had the same story, which sounded fishy and rehearsed to him. They saw Joel come up behind the German and strike him with a "death blow" as soon as he turned around. How many people use terms like "death blow" unless coached? This also did not explain the sword wounds on Joel. They said he must have already had the wounds prior to confronting the German. All the witnesses against Joel were, surprisingly, American—no Germans or Bahamians.

The Major said that he had requested an interview with each of the witnesses but was told they were out of the country and could not be reached for questioning. He did secure their names. He gave them to me and asked me to check them out as soon as feasible.

I asked him about needing Joel there to testify before a hearing in Nassau. He said that the Bahamian prosecutor was insisting on it. I told him that I thought that could be signing Joel's death certificate.

He stated, "I know that and I will fight it at every angle to protect Joel!"

I told him that I was totally opposed to having Joel there and would fight to stop any such move. The Major knew my resolve when I was in that state of mind and did not press it any further. I said that I would look into the witnesses, who they were, where they were from, and their backgrounds, and then I'd get back to him. Since we were pressed for time, I thought I might need to enlist Gage to help us on this one.

Meanwhile, somehow, we had to get back to San Andros and gather some hardcore evidence for Joel's defense.

As we got under sail and headed north by northeast, I looked across the cockpit and saw that Top had loaned Wilson some civilian clothes—shorts that looked a little tight and a sky-blue polo shirt. I let Wilson dress, then asked him to tell us as much as he could remember about San Andros. We needed as much detail in every facet of their operations as he could possibly recall. I could tell he was ready to help.

Wilson started by saying that he had flown in with a group of men who had gathered at a camp in northwest Arkansas. He and the others were told that they were going to perform a security detail on an island off the coast of Miami. Before they left, all of their personal cell phones were confiscated. They were issued new phones without caller ID and were not told their own numbers. The new phones rang a few times before they left and everyone's phone rang at the exact same time. They all had recorded messages instructing them not to use them to make personal calls, check email, or send messages. After the call ended, the phones went into a "stand-by" mode.

They were flown in on a KC-130 military-type aircraft that had no markings. In fact, it didn't even have the normal warning signs instructing personnel where not to step or to stand clear of the propellers. The aircraft appeared freshly painted in a gunmetal gray color as if it had been dipped in a vat of paint to completely wipe out all of its markings.

They were instructed to not talk to each other about the mission as they each may have been given different instructions or assignments.

Wilson was confused from the beginning because it appeared that the supervisor giving them the instructions didn't really know anything. The supervisor kept making calls from a radio mounted on the rear wall of the aircraft. He would then come back to tell them something else or change something he had already told them.

Wilson believed without a doubt that the supervisor was talking to someone in authority because, although you couldn't hear what he was saying, he nearly stood at attention when he spoke on the radio.

At one point, the supervisor must have been told to stand down, because they circled around what he believed to be south Florida for about an hour before they leveled out and landed at a small airport on what he later found out was San Andros. Since no one could see outside the plane, some of the guys thought they actually might be going back where they came from, but no such luck!

They had been able to keep their rifles and personal sidearms, but they were not given any ammunition until they got off the plane and onto two trucks at the airport. On the ride from the airport to San Andros, they were told that there were terrorists in the area and they would be guarding some Middle Eastern families that this group was threatening. They were warned not to speak with these people at all!

When they arrived in San Andros, he saw what looked to him to be a rather upscale U.S.-type community of Arabs. He noticed that two or more of them looked to be relatives of Osama Bin Laden from pictures he had seen. He said that the women wore traditional Arab clothes and covered their heads. The children wore expensive American clothes. For the most part, the men wore Arab clothing, and most were wearing Rolex watches that probably cost thousands of dollars. Some of the Arab men were soldiers in uniform and carried AK-47 rifles and sidearms under their shirts all the time. He believed they might have been working as security for the man who resembled Bin Laden.

The most significant thing he told us was that there was some kind of a training camp hidden in the big pine forest south of the Arab village. Wilson said that yesterday, early in the morning, he had been assigned to a security post on that end of the compound where a narrow road led south from the village. He had to relieve himself so he walked down that road a short distance and saw it opened onto an obstacle course. There were three or four small buildings like the "John Wayne Course" he had trained on while in the Army. The same kind of buildings used to train for urban warfare. He also described in detail that there were some military ammo boxes on the side of a small shack and they looked like smoke-grenade containers.

At that point, Paul spoke up and said, "From time to time I heard gunfire coming from the area east of the airport." He added that late one night, he also heard a loud explosion when he was working on a damaged section of the runway. He told the local constable, and the man told Paul to mind his own business.

op turned the boat to the east-southeast as we made our way back toward Nicholls Town to position ourselves for our next move. Calvin was calmly sleeping in the master stateroom but was running a low-grade fever. Earlier, Wilson had fed him some chicken noodle soup. We decided to let him rest as long as possible.

As we rounded the bend around Morgan's Bluff, I could see the tall masts of some sailboats surrounding my moored boat. A few fishing boats were also moored alongside each other closer to shore. A storm was moving in from the west and the wind was starting to pick up. At that same time, a large speedboat came around the Bluff from the Nicholls Town area and seemed to be heading straight for us. We could see two men on the bow—and they were carrying rifles.

As the speedboat approached us, Paul and Wilson went below and out of sight. The patrol boat came within twenty-five yards of our starboard side. One of the men near the helm was looking us over with his field glasses. He apparently spotted the Marine Corps flag flying from the spreader on the mast and yelled out, *"Semper fi!"*

With that, the patrol boat turned back to the west and then kept going.

Top remarked, "That was a little too close this time, Jake!"

We slowly sailed into the mooring area. Sorensen and I took the Zodiac to the *Big Mamoo* to inspect it. We circled around and approached from the marina side since we weren't sure if it had been linked to me and might be under surveillance. No one seemed to be paying any attention, so we pulled alongside and prepared to board her. All my tells were in place and the deck was damp and unmarked. I had not cleaned the boat in so long that it would have shown footprints and scuffs on the deck if anyone had boarded. With the clarity and calmness of the water, we could see clearly all the way down to the keel, and there were no booby traps on the hull, so we went aboard.

I fired up my sat phone and checked in with Dave back on Merritt Island. He answered after a couple of rings and said he was glad to hear from me. He said two men posing as government agents came to the island. He kept them in their small boat at the end of the dock and refused to answer their questions. They couldn't show him any identification so he sent them on their way.

I told Dave I would be home in a few days and asked him to stay on the island as much as he could until my return. Dave said that all was well and that my "critters" were well fed and happy. Things appeared in good shape at the island under Dave's watch, so I signed off and called the Major.

Doug was still in his meeting with the legal folks in Nassau and said he would call me back in about two hours. I told him that was not possible as we were leaving our phones off so no one could trace us. I would call him back this evening.

With most of the administrative business out of the way, I turned off the sat phone and removed its battery again. I thought about calling Gage for an update but decided to contact him later on in the day. Sorensen was whistling as he cleaned our weapons and reloaded our ammo clips so they were ready if we needed them again. I could see through the other moored boats that Top was on his boat, also doing some cleaning. Wilson and Paul must have been in the cabin, staying out of sight.

When I turned to look toward the marina, I saw a young woman standing on the dock and looking around at all the boats. I had a feeling it might be Paul's wife. Sorensen and I put our equipment together and went over the side into the Zodiac. We decided to motor over and speak to the lady.

As we pulled up to the dock, the very pretty Bahamian lady of about thirty spoke to us first. She knew who we were since she asked if her husband was safe and if he was on the big sailboat anchored out beyond the other boats. I introduced myself as Jake, introduced Sorensen, and told her that Paul was there and that he was just fine. I told her he was very brave and had been helpful in trying to clear our friend of the wrongly charged murder.

I explained to her that once we cleared Joel, Paul would be free from these guys who had been holding him, too. I gave her three hundred dollars and told her it was Paul's money and she should use it for any essentials she needed until she and Paul were back together again. I would have given her far more, but I was low on cash. I gave her the number of one of my pre-paid burners and told her Paul would be waiting for her call at six o'clock this evening. I asked her not to call from her phone so to keep the possibility of eavesdropping low.

She knew how important it was to remain alert and not tell anyone about our conversation. I asked her to fill Paul in on any rumors or news that concerned us or the folks at San Andros when she called Paul later. She said that the only change was the frequent patrols by Americans in the area.

Sorensen and I powered back to Top's boat. I still did not want to arouse any more attention than I had to with our comings and goings.

Top was on the bow, working on the anchor winch, looking and staying busy as sailors do so everything appeared normal should someone be watching us from shore. He told us there was fresh coffee and sandwiches in the galley. Right now, that sounded wonderful.

When we walked down into the galley area, we saw Paul was writing in a notebook at the dining table. We told him we had met with and talked to his wife at the dock in the marina. I told him she was gathering intelligence for us—in a safe manner, of course—and that we had arranged for them to speak at six o'clock tonight. He said Top had given him the notebook and recommended that he write down everything he could remember about his detention, as well as any memories he had of San Andros and the related people coming through the airport since he had worked there.

He always believed the folks passing through the airport going to San Andros were up to no good. When the Arabs arrived after 9/11, he knew there was no good to come from it for their little community. Because of all the American officials who visited over the years, everyone felt it was a legitimate American-Bahamian settlement. The settlement might have been questionable, but it did bring in a lot of jobs and money for the local economy.

I checked in on Calvin and found that his fever was finally lower. He smiled at me when I asked if I could have his watch if he died. Humor always made me feel better.

Wilson asked me if he could call his brother to explain why he hadn't called in a couple of days. He said that even though it was against the rules, he had snuck in a cell phone call at least once or twice a day so they would not worry about him. I gave him the cell phone and told him to make it very brief and to be careful about what he said.

Wilson sat at the galley table and greeted his brother as soon as it connected. From his side of the conversation and his body language, we could tell there was a problem at home. He was only on the line a few minutes and stopped his conversation told us both his brothers had been questioned by the local police and had been told that Wilson was missing from his place of employment and was suspected of some undisclosed crime. While the police questioned them, a civilian who was present refused to be identified. According to Wilson's brother, the civilian was definitely "running the show."

The police threatened his older brother with arrest if they found he was hiding any information regarding Wilson. His brother was relieved that Wilson was safe but was extremely concerned about why he was in trouble and was puzzled when Wilson could not tell him why.

I asked Wilson to let me speak with his brother and he handed me the phone. I told his brother that I could not identify myself at this time as a precautionary measure for both of us, but we were working with an attorney and his brother was helping us with a matter of international importance. I also told him that his brother had discovered some information that would soon be revealed to the world, and that it may be one of the most important news events since the September 11 terrorist attacks.

I requested that he tell only those members of his family that he trusted, and under no circumstances was he to gossip or to put any information online or in an email. I explained, in my serious voice, that the people we were up against were capable of eavesdropping on any communication device we had. Wilson's brother seemed receptive and said that he now knew how important it was to be careful of what he said. He was still confused as to the reason why and could not understand how his brother could be in danger when he worked for a company that did so much work for the government. I assured him that we would tell him everything as soon as we could. I thanked him for his understanding and told him I would do all I could to keep his brother safe. We signed off after promising to call every couple of days.

It was coming up on six o'clock now and I could see that Paul was getting anxious to speak to his wife. I gave him his pen and notebook and reminded him to write down anything she reported.

Top had put the satellite dish up on the bow so we could watch some CNN and catch up on news with the rest of the world. The reception was really good. We watched but there really wasn't much to catch up on, and there was no mention of our Bahamas ordeal on international or local news.

It was now 6:00 PM, so I signaled to Paul to stand by the phone. The time came and went. He waited patiently, but there was no call. It was now 6:10 and I could see the worry on Paul's face as he handed the phone back to me. No call! Why?

Sorensen looked at me, then spoke to Paul to reassure him that we would act immediately to locate her and to stay calm. I picked up the field glasses, scanned the beach and small-town center, but saw nothing out of the ordinary. There was a white man standing near a small building behind a little store. He was smoking a cigarette. He looked normal except for his skin color. The lights were out in the little store and that was all wrong! I asked Paul to look at him with the glasses. He said he did not recognize him. I then asked Wilson to look at him. He stated right away that the guy was one of the civilian security men from the camp and was one of the guards who had come with some hotshot civilians the day before yesterday. We now had a pretty good idea of what had happened to Paul's wife.

We all sat down in the salon of the boat and hashed out some ideas. Paul was hard to contain and wanted to charge in there and give himself up to get them to release his wife. I told him to calm down and to think rationally. They had no authority to hold her in the first place, so she was in the same situation he had been in. She now knew too much, as did he, and they were not about to let her go. This was getting stranger by the moment. How could they keep an entire village quiet about this situation?

Sorensen, Wilson, and I put on black wet suits provided by Top and climbed into the Zodiac. Paul came aboard and took the helm. The plan was that Paul would drop us south of the harbor and stand by to pick us up when we signaled him. This time, Sorensen and I were well armed and ready to do anything it took to get Paul's wife to safety. We had been far too gentle with this situation up until now. All it had earned us was far too many people being hurt.

It was just about dark as we slid up to the little sandy beach just south of Nicholls Town. The black wet suits helped make us disappear as night started to fall. There were large storm clouds moving in over the western sky, and the heaviness of the air was a good indicator that we were going to get some rain, and soon. Every now and then, there was a distant clap of thunder, and we welcomed the noise as it hid the sound of our movements. We shoved Paul off the beach, instructing him to stay about 150 yards off shore and wait for us to signal him with three quick flashes of our LED flashlight. I had previously told him that once we had her safely in our custody, we would take his wife to her sister's house, not far from the little village center.

Sorensen took the west side of the village behind the small houses and camps while I walked right down the middle of the paved road. I had Wilson's hat and military-looking jungle shirt on. They were dry as I had them in a plastic bag on the Zodiac. I also had Wilson's M16 rifle slung over my shoulder. I could see Sorensen pass behind the buildings as I walked north toward the small building and the sentry. He was a little ahead of me but marking my progress step for step.

When I got to the short alley where the sentry was standing, I said, "Hello," and walked toward him.

At that moment, Sorensen grabbed him from behind, threw him down, and clobbered him with the butt of his rifle. I caught him before he bounced to the ground the second time and dragged him behind the house next door. Sorensen tied his arms behind his back and then looped the rope around his legs in a modified hog-tie so he would not be able to move far when he regained consciousness. I placed a couple of strips of duct tape across his mouth and punched three holes through it with my pen so he could breathe through his mouth.

We snuck up next to the house and tried to see through a side window. There were curtains in the way but we could see there was a light on and hear voices. I could make out a female voice sobbing quietly while at least two men were talking.

I went to the rear of the building and tried the rear door. It was locked but I could see through a small window to the right of the door into the kitchen area and part of the room in the front. Jason Patrick had his back to me. I would recognize him in a crowd of a thousand! I could see Paul's wife sitting in a wooden chair with her legs and arms taped to the chair and her head bent back by a rope fastened around her neck.

I knew by the voices I'd heard earlier that there was at least one other man in the front room, but I could not see him from where I was. I motioned to Sorensen to go to the front door and knock lightly as if he were the guard we disabled. I prepared my weapon, listened for the knock, and as soon as I saw the second man answer the door, I kicked the rear door open and put a round into both of his legs and two more into Patrick's. They both went down like lead balloons. Another, bigger, man, whom I had not seen with Patrick, quickly turned toward Paul's wife and raised his pistol in her direction.

I blew the top of his head off with one quick round and then pointed at Patrick again in case he was foolish enough to try to take her out or shoot at me. He laid there and whimpered like a child, begging for a doctor. I whispered to Patrick to be very quiet or I would take out both his arms next.

Sorensen had been keeping watch but now slammed through the locked front door and quickly observed that the situation was well in hand. I cut the bindings from Mrs. Paul's hands and legs and gently lifted her to her feet. She stared with shock and disbelief at the body of the dead man on the floor. There was blood everywhere, as well as on a few pieces of the dead guy's head. I was sure that she had never seen anything like this before in her life!

There was a piece of metal that they must have been using as a torture device laying on a small table next to her chair and, before I could react, she grabbed that metal bar up and slammed it down on Patrick's head with such force that it split the top of his head in two like a ripe watermelon. She calmly placed the bar back on the table, turned around, and began to walk toward the front door.

I looked at Sorensen, who looked back at me, smirked, and shrugged his shoulders with a shake of his head. I knew he was thinking the same as I— that ol' Patrick made a grave mistake by messing with this lady!

We quickly grabbed her, stopping her from leaving through the front of the house, and moved her out the rear door to the wood line. She was weak and shaking now, so we helped her walk with us to where we'd asked Paul to meet us.

For the life of me, I still could not understand why there were no townsfolk milling about, especially after the loud reports of our weapons. Sorensen and I agreed that we would have to get Mrs. Paul to safety, then deal with the remains of Patrick and his sidekick.

Mrs. Paul looked at us and said not to worry. "Their remains will never be found and the young guard will wake up tomorrow on South Beach in Miami and have no idea how he got there." She added, "My people are very efficient and will handle it all and no one will ever speak of it again. Really.

Don't worry."

Sorensen looked at me and said, "We need this gal on more of our missions, Jake."

As we approached the small beach area, I signaled Paul out on the water with three quick flashes of our flashlight. I noticed that Sorensen was carrying a small brown briefcase. Patrick had been carrying the same case when I saw him back at San Andros.

I said, "I sure am glad you grabbed that, buddy. Now, please make sure it stays dry."

The three of us jumped into the Zodiac and Paul and his wife embraced like there was no tomorrow. I grabbed the helm so they could stay together and backed the boat into the oncoming surf until I could turn it about to head out to open water.

We headed east first, then north back to the offshore mooring area where Top and Wilson were anchored. We helped Paul lift his wife into Top's big sailboat. I jumped aboard and told Sorensen to bring the briefcase down below. Top had his generator running and the air conditioning felt like a cool New Hampshire evening. Sorensen placed the case on the galley table and I looked it over for any switches that might cause us some grief in the life department. I saw none but still cautiously unfastened the two clasps.

Thank goodness no explosion and no poisonous gas. However, it did have numerous documents and hand-written notes with various names and notations that jumped out at me like an explosive vision. There was a small laptop nestled among the papers, and when Sorensen opened its cover, it woke from sleep mode. Still being on allowed us access to its contents. I grabbed the power cord from the briefcase, plugged it into the outlet next to the table, and then plugged it into the laptop so it wouldn't lose its charge. It needed a password and if it shut down, we would have to wait for one of our talented hackers to discover what we needed to know. I knew this was going to be a wealth of information. It was a shame about what had happened to Paul's wife, but this information might just provide us some insight into the goings-on in San Andros.

Top suggested that we move away from the area for a while. I suggested that we head for Nassau to meet up with the Major. We first had to figure out what to do with Paul and his wife. They couldn't go back to San Andros, as every house and building would be searched as soon as they discovered Patrick's disappearance.

Paul said his brother, whom very few people knew about, lived near Cable Beach on Grand Bahamas Island. He was sure he would be safe there for a while.

While we were still in range of a cell tower on San Andros, I called the Major and briefed him on the past day's events. Patrick was no favorite of the Major's, but he knew his disappearance was going to shake up the intelligence community in a very big—and bad—way. I was not too sure that Paul's wife's prediction that his remains would never be found was realistic.

As I sat there in front of Patrick's computer, I couldn't help but punch my name into the search slot in its Windows-based program. I hit enter and even I was shocked at all the references to my name! There were thirty-two separate articles listed in its memory and fifteen pictures. Sorensen looked over my shoulder and asked me to click on the most recent entry dated the day before. As tempting as that was, I decided it was far more important to download the entire hard-drive onto CDs before Murphy's Law bit us on the tail and we lost everything to old Davy Jones. Top had about four packs of blank CDs and DVDs in a bin next to his navigation and plot table aft of the salon.

I asked Top if I could use a few and he said, "Certainly. Be my guest."

As the Sony laptop was backing up its hard drive in the galley area, Sorensen found some saltine crackers and started heating up some soup for everyone. Paul and his wife were resting together on the pullout bed in the salon. Top was with Wilson at the helm of the boat, under sail and with engine assist as we made our way east toward New Providence Island.

There were far too many references to my name on Patrick's computer, which meant there might be even more on other computers out there! It also told me I was far too cavalier about my own security. Little did I know I was underestimating the information by a long shot!

Top and I took two-hour shifts at the helm of the big ketch as we closed in on the west coast of New Providence. We decided to circumvent the island to the south and then come up the east coast to the small harbor near where Calvin smuggled me out a few days earlier. This specific course would take far more time but give us more cover as few used this route due to the dangerous, shallow reefs and added distance.

We rounded the east coast of New Providence Island around daybreak and found a little cove deep enough to clear the *Semper Fi's* keel. It also had enough room to swing the anchor without the fear of dragging the bottom.

When I went below, I found Calvin up and walking around in the galley, looking for something to eat. This was a good sign. Sorensen filled him in on the events back on Andros that he had slept through. Calvin said that Patrick and his goons' deaths all seemed to fall within the realm of self-defense but was sure they would try to make it out as murder. I told him about Paul's wife saying it would all go away as a great mystery and never be revealed.

Calvin agreed that the people there were quite capable of covering up just about anything since they'd kept the secret of San Andros for so long.

However, I said that when San Andros was exposed it would have the potential to raise political havoc within many governments around the world. Calvin said this may make it necessary to tell the truth when the time came for a major investigation. I agreed. But, for now, we needed to stop the conspiracy against Joel and expose the people responsible. Some needed to pay for their actions, but Joel was not one of them!

When we finished entering the cove, Top dropped the anchor and I called the Major on one of my burners. He was still at his hotel in Nassau. He asked me to standby while he walked out of the lobby to the outside patio. When he was alone, he asked for a detailed briefing.

I briefed him on Paul's wife and said we would be putting them ashore shortly.

He told me there was a lot of noise in the press about three missing Americans over on San Andros Island, and that they were searching for a fourth American thought to be working with some U.S. terrorist cell. I told him there were some things he didn't want or need to know right now except that, at present, we were close to his location.

I went down below and told Wilson that we could try to arrange to get him back home to the States. Although he had some mixed feelings about what had been going on while he was with us, he asked to stay with us to help right some of the wrongs his outfit had inflicted. I asked Sorensen and Top what they thought about Wilson staying with us, and they both agreed that it would be a good idea to have his help for a few more days.

Calvin needed to speak with a couple of his people and asked if the Major would contact one of them to stand by for Calvin's call. The Major agreed.

The Major and I made a tentative face-to-face meeting time of 1300 that afternoon near Nassau. I asked him to be extra careful with his communications and to watch his tail. I told him to start walking east from the Nassau side of the Paradise Island Bridge at about 12:45. As he walked, I would choose the meeting spot. I told him to listen for my whistle and then signed off.

C alvin made three calls to his most-trusted co-workers. He explained what had happened to him from the time of his abduction to his rescue by Sorensen and me. He asked them to keep it quiet right now to give us an element of surprise when we exposed what these folks were up to in their country. They all agreed to stand down for now but said they would be working overtime to gather all the information they could to prosecute any Bahamas government officials involved. Calvin gave them some ideas about where to start digging for information.

I grabbed the rope floating in the water and pulled the Zodiac to the side of the boat. Sorensen and I helped Paul's wife over the side and into the Zodiac. Paul immediately climbed in behind her, looked at us, and said, "This girl is not leaving my sight for some time, so make room for me, boys."

I turned and told Wilson and Calvin to stay below deck as much as they could in case a nosy shore patrol came along. Top had a small "honey-do list" that his daughter left behind and a few repairs to deal with but would be monitoring the phones at all times. He said we should call if we needed anything.

Calvin told me he remembered another shallow cove about two miles north that would bring us close to the main road to Nassau. The shorter the distance, the better, as far as I was concerned. I told them that I would be looking for the boat a little farther north when I came back.

We fired up the powerful outboard motor and turned east out of the cove and then due north to try to find a good landing spot to go ashore.

I explained to Paul that he had to be extremely cautious since many people knew he would have knowledge about our whereabouts. Paul said he would be very careful and understood the seriousness of this whole ordeal. He still looked so frail from his captivity and abuse that I didn't think he could have taken any rougher questioning.

We came upon a small cove and sandy beach with heavy, thick foliage where we could hide the boat. After watching the shore for a while from a distance, we pulled in and ran the Zodiac up on the beach. We all jumped out and pulled the craft as far as we could into the thick brush. Sorensen pulled up some bushes by their roots as if he was picking carrots from a garden and replanted them behind the boat to give it some camouflage from the waterside. I brushed the sand with a palm leaf where the boat had left skid marks. It was mid-tide, so the rising tide would cover the rest of our tracks in the sand.

Looking west, I could see a few small houses near the road. No people were around that we could see, so we made our way to the brush at the side of the road.

It wasn't but a few minutes later that a jitney bus came along. We decided that Paul's wife should go alone on this one as, after he went missing, Paul's picture had been in some of the local newspapers. We waited another fifteen minutes and the next jitney took Paul on his way. I gave Paul one of my burners so we could reach him if necessary. I also had him give me a few of his relatives' contact numbers, should we need them for any reason. Another one of those "better to be safe than sorry" moments!

Sorensen and I began walking to the north on the same road to Nassau. We let a few jitneys pass us by before we boarded one for the outskirts of the city. After arriving about a mile east of Nassau, we got off at a small café and went in. The great thing about the Bahamas is that even if you're from a different part of the world with different colored skin and a different language, you were always made to feel welcomed and at home by the locals.

As we sat down, no one gawked at us or said anything more than a casual hello. We both ordered coffee and some sweet rolls and took our time thumbing through the local paper. It didn't take much thumbing because, sure enough, there on the front page was an article about some missing Americans over on Andros. It said they were last seen sightseeing around Morgan's Bluff. I thought to myself that Patrick might still be sightseeing around Morgan's Bluff, just not from the direction he would have preferred. And, who knew at what depth!

At 12:30 sharp, I called the Major and told him to keep walking east on the outer road. I told him that when I felt it was safe to do so, I would approach him and we could meet. I watched the road in front of the café to make sure that no one had taken an interest in us. After a while, it was clear to me that no one had.

About ten minutes later, we paid our check, left a very good tip, and walked out onto the street. We walked east away from Nassau and away from where the Major was coming from until we found a small clearing under some trees. We could see quite a bit of the road in both directions and, in about three minutes, I saw the Major walking toward us.

We watched the road behind him and saw no one was following him. We let him pass us and walk about fifty more feet, then I whistled my special sound. He stopped and bent down as if he were tying the laces on his sneaker. Sorensen jogged up to him on the other side of the bushes and told him to walk casually into the brush. The Major sidestepped into the brush and they both walked back to the clearing where we had been waiting.

I embraced the Major as if we had been apart for years. It had been a grueling few days and, at this point, I was mentally drained. For his part, the Major was humorous, as usual. "You two are the most wanted fugitives in a circumference of five miles," he laughed.

After a good chuckle, we got down to business. I gave him one of the disks I copied from Patrick's computer and explained that I had not had any time to look at them yet. The Major advised that if anyone was in possession of an article, such as a computer, that belonged to a missing and possibly dead person, it should be gotten rid of as soon as possible, as it could be considered incriminating evidence of that person's demise! Hypothetically speaking, that is!

"Of course," I said.

The Major related that the Bahamians were insisting Joel be returned to their custody before they would begin negotiations on his case. He reiterated that they were relying on statements from what they called "eyewitnesses" to the killing of the German. The Major requested a witness list from the Bahamian prosecutors, but, because of Joel's escape from custody, the prosecutors denied him access to documents. I couldn't run any backgrounds on the names he had given me previously without some background info on them—even if they really did exist!

Doug had been in touch with Joel at his hiding spot outside of Miami and assured him and his family that Joel would never see the inside of a Bahamas' jail again. If this case were to go to trial, it would not be with Joel in custody.

While the Major and I were talking, Sorensen was on the phone with one of his sources in the Bahamas. When he finished, he turned to us and said there were two former American Intelligence Agents working with the Bahamian prosecutor on this case. He knew both of them to be less than honest fellows. According to Sorensen, one of the men, Carl Pettit, was a former Naval Intelligence Officer from Seattle who had been involved in a double murder and drummed out of the service. The other, Ben Matthews, formerly of Homeland Security, was fired on an assault charge involving the alleged torture of a U.S. citizen. The incident made the evening news all around the world and then was hushed up when Matthews resigned and vanished—until now.

I had never met either of these two men, but I was well aware of their dirty deeds. I was involved in the Seattle investigation and had uncovered some of the foul play involved. I could only imagine what these two sociopaths were doing in this matter.

The Major left after about an hour of discussions. We followed him from the brush, watching his back until he was safely back on the outskirts of Nassau.

Sorensen suggested we take a recon on Pettit and Matthews, the two Americans assisting the Bahamian prosecutor. I agreed. The more we knew the better off we would be. We decided to take the back roads and alleys until we reached the center of town near the government buildings. We again bought a couple of touristy shirts and ball caps so we would blend in. If we kept buying tourist junk, I would have a whole new wardrobe by the time I left the Bahamas.

As far as we could tell by the happenings around us, there was no concentrated effort to arrest us. At least, not yet!

I was pretty familiar with the government buildings as I had spent a few days some years ago tagging along with Calvin while he went about his duties with the Intelligence Department he worked for. I also knew a woman who was in the same business here. In all this mass confusion, I had nearly forgotten about her. Her name was Sara Greene and she was in charge of tourist-related intelligence. It was her job to make sure everyone who visited the Bahamas had a good time and left wanting to return. It sounds like a funny job, but it is extremely important to a country that entirely relies on tourism for its existence. Sara was a good friend and I felt we could depend on her for help in this matter. I needed to contact Calvin and find out if they were still close friends and how we could reach her.

As Sorensen and I were approaching the rear of the Government Building, we saw three men standing in the shade of a large royal poinciana tree covered with its vivid orange flowers. Near them were two small Toyota SUVs parked under the tree with the windows rolled down. The men looked like military, and all of them were wearing light jackets. In this heat, it was a perfect sign that they were carrying weapons under their coats. We ducked into a small shop and acted like tourists so we could watch them out the front window.

It wasn't long before Pettit and Matthews came out through a side door of one of the buildings and walked up to the SUVs. They both climbed into the rear of the same SUV with one of the bodyguards as their driver. The other two guards followed in the other SUV.

Sorensen and I watched them drive off and could only guess where they were headed. There were no taxis in the area so we followed on foot and cut through a couple of alleys until we could no longer see them as they drove out of our sight. It looked like they were heading for the airport road. As soon as we could, we jumped on a jitney and stayed on it until it reached Cable Beach. There we caught a taxi in front of one of the hotels and directed the driver to take us to the airport. We acted as if we were late meeting someone, so we asked the driver to step on it.

His reply: "No problem, man."

When we arrived at the outskirts of the airport, I asked the driver to drive up and down some of the access roads to the airport. I told him we were looking for some friends who flew in earlier but did not know where they had parked their plane. The driver said an American company on this side of the airport serviced American planes. He had seen numerous Americans around there earlier in the day.

I asked him first to bring us to the facility but then directed him to let us off a couple of blocks away. The entire airport was within walking distance and, if we did not find these guys there, we could walk around and just keep looking.

When the driver let us off, he pointed to a specific structure and told us some strange things were going on at that hangar. He had driven a number of folks to that area over the years, but in the past couple of weeks, they had instructed him to stop outside the gate instead of driving up to the building entrance. He also told us that recently the Bahamian guard had been replaced with at least two American, military-looking men in civilian clothes.

He added, "Usually people either ask me about my island or for directions to good eating places, but not lately. Now, I'm often told to turn up my radio when the passengers are talking in my taxi."

I tipped him double for his help. Grateful, he gave us a big, toothy smile as he drove away.

There were four planes at the hangar that the driver had pointed out to us. Sorensen and I were looking at the area from behind a fence three buildings to the north. We noticed that there were at least four guards outside the hangar. They were facing toward the fence and the approach road we were on. It would have been impossible to get any closer without someone seeing us from this angle.

We cut around a couple of other buildings and then found an abandoned building that must have been an airline's office in the past that had gone out of business. This building was just east of the American hangar, and it would give us a good view if we could get inside. The lock was not in very good shape so we forced the door open and entered. The room we were in must have been a computer room as the windows facing the hangar were painted over from the inside to keep out the afternoon sunlight. There were numerous cables still lying all over the floor.

I took out my pocket knife and cut a small hole through the flimsy sheet metal wall. I saw the two SUVs parked right next to the hangar. There was no sign of Pettit or Matthews, but I could see their security escorts through a large window.

One of the planes, a Cessna, had its side door open with the stairs extended. We couldn't see into the interior, but the auxiliary power unit was hooked up to the plane from the side of the hangar. We could hear one of the turbo engines whining as if it was producing power for the air conditioning unit on the plane. That indicated there was a meeting going on inside the plane. I wrote down the tail number and continued to watch for any movement on the plane.

While we were intently watching the plane, we heard the front door of the building open in the room behind us. Sorensen quickly moved to the side of the door and I stepped behind one of the steel support pillars. Someone entered the building and then walked toward the room we were in.

I heard a loud grunt and then saw a Remington 887 Nitro Mag Tactical shotgun fly by me and hit the floor. I turned just in time to see a paramilitary-dressed man hit the floor like a sack of bricks. Sorensen leaned over and relieved him of his sidearm and knife. I grabbed the two-way radio Velcroed to his left shoulder while Sorensen turned him over and tied his hands together with an old phone cord.

Within seconds, he came to and clearly became aware of his unfortunate predicament.

Sorensen stepped on his back. That definitely wasn't comfortable. "Be quiet and hold still or I will place you back in dreamland again. Get it?"

He was still and did not make a sound.

The radio chirped in my hand, and then I heard *click, click.* There were two more clicks. On impulse, I clicked the talk button on the mike twice. That told us there were at least two more guards roaming around the perimeter of the hangar. The question was where.

I bent down behind the prone guard and asked him how many other guards there were.

He quietly said, "Two. And one guard at the desk in the hangar." He also stated that he was only doing his job and would not cause any trouble, the same as Wilson. He was not at all motivated to oppose us!

He stayed lying on the floor, looking away from us, and told us that he had just been out of the Army for a month when he applied for this job with this outfit. He went through three weeks of training, and then his superiors sent him here last week without even allowing him to go home first. He was not allowed to call home and tell his wife where he was or what he was doing. He and his fellow troops were watched as if they were criminals, not employees. He said his name was James Wood from Riverdale, Georgia.

I looked at Sorensen and whispered that morale in this outfit was apparently really low, as we had not even questioned him when he offered all of this info!

We told Wood we were investigating the arrest and detention of a number of people over on San Andros Island. He said he had flown through there a couple of days ago. He was then flown here to stand security for the company suits who parked their planes here and had meetings. He also told us that there were two men in the hangar now meeting with some suit from Washington. The suit looked familiar but he didn't have a name.

They were all told not to look at any of the people there or to ask any questions. Wood said that, in his opinion, the two guys visiting were really bad guys. One of them stared at him with a sick grin on his face that gave him the creeps!

Wood told us as much as I believe he knew about what was going on there at the airport facility. He said he and his fellow troops were briefed that a group of terrorists had kidnapped and killed some of the members of his outfit over the past few days. There were also some Bahamian citizens missing from San Andros that they all believed to be dead. Wood said that his superiors offered no explanation as to why they were in the Bahamas or who the folks were that they were protecting. He thought it was strange that some of the residents at the small town over on San Andros were Arab looking and that some carried military-type weapons.

I looked at Sorensen for a moment until he read my thoughts. He nodded and I untied Wood. We told him we were leaving and he should go back to his job. He said he would not tell his superiors that he had seen or spoken to us. I told him it was his call, but he would be buying himself a lot of trouble if they knew he had talked to us even if he told them he said nothing. He agreed.

Wood said the strange men he had seen there today would probably enjoy trying to break him down and that he was planning to go home at the first opportunity following his first payday. He said, "They pay everyone by money order at the end of each week. I'm going to make up some excuse to go home for a few days and just not come back."

I warned him not to be surprised if they did not let him go home right away or investigated his reason for doing so before they released him. I explained that he might be better off staying and not doing anything illegal. I also told Wood that there was a court hearing coming up and that I would tell the lawyers involved that he was very cooperative and to give him any help he needed.

He thanked me and said he would testify truthfully to what little he knew if called upon. I wrote down his full name, date of birth, address, and Social Security number so we could reach him, if necessary.

I watched Sorensen give Wood back his shotgun, knife, and sidearm. He stood close to Wood and a little sideways, in case he decided to change his mind.

Wood put the pistol in its holster and snapped it in, dropped his knife in his leg pocket, and hung his shotgun away from us. It was a friendly and non-threatening gesture.

As Wood walked away, Sorensen stopped him, fished out the rounds he had in his pocket, and passing them to Wood. "You may need these in the future."

Wood smiled, put the rounds in his pocket, and said, "Thanks, guys, for trusting me."

Sorensen and I watched as Wood left around the side of the building. We quickly left as well. I half expected to be challenged, but we made it out to the main airport road with no problem.

I asked Sorensen what his take was on the meetings at the airport. We both agreed that the reason for it was that the bigger, civilian-type planes needed for long-distance travel were unable to land at the smaller San Andros airport due to the length of the runway there. The officials coming in must also have been concerned about keeping their distance from the crap going on at San Andros.

We were about to jump on a jitney to head back to the boat when a large Eclipse 550 twin-engine jet bearing an American flag on its tail passed overhead and landed. The Eclipse is the quietest jet in general aviation-perfect jet for these types of operations. I looked at Sorensen and he nodded that he understood exactly what I was thinking.

We hurried back to the hangar area to see if the Eclipse was carrying a passenger for a meeting with the folks already there and noticed three security guards near the building we had used before. We did not see Wood with them. We skirted the surrounding hangars and saw the Eclipse jet taxiing toward the American hangar. An old beat-up plane that looked like it hadn't been flown in some time was parked next to the fence that surrounded the field. We climbed over the fence by stepping up on the wing from a fifty-five-gallon drum next to the fence. We crossed over the wing and into the plane through a small escape hatch in the fuselage. There were still a few seats in the passenger compartment and the portholes were hazy but still clear enough to see through. I sat in a window seat that faced the hangar and had a clear view of the approaching jet as it taxied to a spot on the apron.

The side hatch opened and we counted four security men coming down the stairs. The door from the front office area of the hangar opened and two men walked out and over to the stairs of the plane. It looked like they were going to board. Instead, a man stepped out of the hatch of the plane and walked down the stairs to greet the two men. I immediately recognized him as John Holt.

Holt was an Under Secretary of State and was known to handle many controversial matters over the years for numerous administrations. Both Republican and Democratic parties used him for "dark work." I knew him from a matter about five years before that I was involved with regarding a peace activist who'd gone missing.

A group in D.C. had hired me to find her. They believed she was in danger and the authorities had taken little action, though they traced her to a remote location in West Virginia. I bumped around town for a few hours, then got lucky when I found out the only gas station in town had a video camera pointed at the fuel pumps.

The station attendant allowed us to view the video. Reviewing the footage, I saw the girl's car pull up to the pumps. As she pumped gas, Holt and another man stepped out of a van and grabbed her from behind, though they had parked their van so close behind her car that it blocked the attendant's view in the office.

That night, nearly a year after she disappeared, I contacted the FBI in that jurisdiction and they met me at the gas station the next morning. But, the station was closed and the owner was nowhere to be found. There was no sign of the gas station owner or the disk I had him make of the footage. The FBI asked me a few more questions and then took the copy of the disk I had in my possession. Neither my clients nor I heard anything back from the FBI or the local authorities.

About a year ago, I'd heard on the news that the bones of the girl and the station owner were found when a nearby lake was dredged to clear a blocked streamflow. I contacted the FBI and local state authorities and repeated my story of the video but never heard back from them either.

Sorensen and I took a number of photos of Holt and his entourage with our smartphones. I sent a mass picture text to my other phones and a number of my friends to prove Holt's presence here. I made sure Gage got a copy. I could not wait to hear what he had to say about this episode unfolding right before our eyes.

If Holt was involved, it meant this Bahamas matter was getting someone's full attention. It also meant that someone was worried about what was going on in San Andros. I was beginning to see why Joel—from their point of view, anyway—would be better off dead than going to trial. I placed a message on the Major's voicemail and warned him about this latest information. I also sent him the photos of Holt in the Bahamas so he could see for himself. He himself needed to be more careful, as these kinds of people were unpredictable.

The Major was also making a lot of noise and the news media would soon start to report on this case, airing allegations on the record in open court. I was hoping he would not become the target of Holt's attention!

It was steamy hot in that old aircraft, probably ninety degrees and getting hotter by the minute. Sorensen and I climbed out of our free steam bath and went back over the fence. We needed to get back to the *Semper Fi* and brief Top. We also needed to make sure that he still wanted in now that there was some official government involvement. Technically, Top was still on the government payroll since he was a retired Marine receiving a pension.

We took a jitney to Cable Beach and walked for a while until we were sure we were not being followed, then took another jitney into Nassau. We picked up a few supplies at a local grocery store that we needed back on the boat. I also ran into a nearby clothing store and bought some new white socks, skivvies, and four new shirts. You can't beat the prices here, and since I needed this stuff anyway, I thought, why not? I had been wearing the same clothes for about four days now and did not want to burden Top for any further hospitality. His boat had a great washer and dryer on board, but the clothes I was wearing needed to be buried at sea, not only because of how dirty they were but also because they were the ugliest clothes I had ever purchased at a straw market.

As we passed the Government Building, I saw one of the black SUVs that we had followed to the airport earlier. It was parked in the same place. This time our new friend Jim Wood was standing sentry duty.

I asked Sorensen to walk over to him and engage him in conversation to see if Holt was in the Government Building. I could not do the talking, as Holt would recognize me right off if he came out the door. I watched Sorensen speaking to Wood and return with what I hoped was good news.

Wood did not know Holt's name but confirmed that the man who'd flown in from the States a while ago was definitely inside the building. He did not know who he was meeting with but did know that that person was already inside before the new guy arrived. I asked Sorensen to walk through the building to see if he could find out where the meeting was being held— and with whom Holt was meeting. Holt would not recognize Sorensen, and the Bahamians inside would just think he was one of the American officials.

Standing in the welcomed shade of a large tree and holding the bags of goods I had purchased; I watched the Government Building to see if I recognized anyone as they passed by the windows. Another black SUV pulled up behind the one near Wood, slammed on its brakes, and four security types piled out and rushed into the building. This was a bad sign, so I stashed my bags in some bushes and quickly walked up to a side door and slipped into the first floor of the building.

I saw the four men running up the stairs across the rear lobby. One of them had his pistol in his hand, which he was holding down next to his leg. I ran up the side stairs from a side door. When I reached the next floor, I could see the four of them walking away from me, one of them on a cell phone or radio speaking quietly.

Just then, Sorensen grabbed me, covered my mouth, and pulled me into a side office. He released me and said that the Major appeared to be in the custody of two Bahamian police officers in the office at the end of the hall. He said that Holt was also in the room and appeared to be directing the entire show!

All Sorensen could hear as he walked by was the Major saying he was in the Bahamas representing a U.S. citizen and that he had the right to do so under International Law. I had a bad feeling that whatever Bahamian official was at the center of this matter was trying to get the Major out of the country by claiming he was there working illegally.

Nothing mattered except getting the Major out of Holt's hands before Holt had a chance to get him back to the airport—or some other remote spot for interrogation. Holt was a horrible man and, if I had anything to do with it, the Major was not going to have to endure any of his dastardly deeds.

While I tried to decide what our next move was going to be, I noticed the fire alarm fixture on the wall. I pointed at it and Sorensen nodded to me and held up one finger while he walked briskly down the hall toward the raised voices. When he reached the door where the Major and the other folks were, he dropped his hand with his finger extended, I pulled the alarm switch down, and all hell broke loose. The clatter of the bells and sirens was almost deafening. People started to file out of the doorways of the offices on the floor. Real panic set in as traffic backed up at the staircases leading down to the exits.

I forced my way through the people toward Sorensen just as he pushed his way into the door where the Major was and disappeared from my view. When I arrived at the door, still fighting people going the other direction, I saw Sorensen and the Major were pushing through the crowd toward me. I could see two of Holt's sentries coming toward the door. They were trying desperately to get to Sorensen and the Major but were meeting great resistance from the hordes of people blocking their way.

When Sorensen and the Major reached me, I motioned for them to step into an open doorway. The Major had a small grin on his face, as usual, and gave me a quick pat on the back. "What took you two so long, anyway?"

I smiled and moved to the window to see what our best avenue of escape would be. I could see a small overhang sticking out from the building just below the window. We were on the second floor and it would be a short jump to the ground from that roof. The three of us dropped down to the overhang. I lowered the Major to Sorensen so he would not hurt his ankles or knees and we dropped to the ground just as three fire trucks with sirens blaring arrived.

We slipped into the waiting crowd, made our way to a side road, and cut through a couple of alleys until we were safe. We talked about what our next moves should be. The Major had to get out of the Bahamas and back to the States as soon as possible. We knew his briefcase was still in the office in the government house and his clothes and personal belongings were in his hotel room not far from where we were. We talked about the pluses and minuses but decided to risk it and headed for his hotel room to retrieve his belongings.

The Major's hotel was on Paradise Island, about a mile from where we were. We took a roundabout route to get there and went through the back door to the rear staircase of the hotel. We didn't see anyone who appeared to be looking for us, so we went up the stairs of the hotel to his third-floor room. When we got to the door, the Major stopped us and pointed to a small piece of paper lying on the carpet by the door. It was the marker he'd left earlier. He whispered that his room had already been cleaned before he left and that there was a "Do Not Disturb" sign on the knob that he had not placed.

The door to the room adjacent to his was partially open, so Sorensen went over to it and pushed it open. There was no one inside. The room had not been cleaned since the guest left. There was an adjoining door into the Major's room. The rooms also shared an exterior balcony. I slid the balcony door open from the room we were in, hugged the wall, and crept over to the door leading into the room where the Major was staying. There were two men, both in blue jeans and polo shirts, sitting in two chairs facing the entrance door with their backs to the window. The balcony door was partially open and the drapes fluttering in the breeze from the bay. The bottoms of the drapes were rubbing against the doorframe, causing a rustling noise that would cover any noise we made as we opened the door.

I slipped back into the adjoining room and described the layout and the position of the men inside. The men were fairly relaxed looking, probably from boredom, and would be easily surprised. One of the men was only about three feet from the door that adjoined the rooms and the other man was close to the bed, about ten feet from the balcony door.

I asked the Major to go back out to the hall and wait thirty seconds, fumble with his key in the lock without actually opening the door, and then step back away from the door until we came to get him. I said I would take the balcony door and told Sorensen to listen for the Major's noises before coming through the adjoining door.

I positioned myself next to the door and slowly slid the balcony door open until I could clearly see the two men. I heard the entry doorknob wiggle and the key jingling. In the same moment, as the men stood to face the door, Sorensen kicked the side door open with such fury that all I heard was *boom!* It sounded like a bomb going off.

Sorensen was through the door in a flash and was all over the nearest guy like white on rice. I leaped through the balcony door, tackled the second guy to the floor, and hit him with a rapid volley of punches until he lay still on the floor beneath me. I must have broken his nose as it had made a disgusting crackling sound under my fist and blood was pouring out of it. I grabbed a pillow and threw it over his face, then jumped up, opened the hall door, let the Major in, and quickly closed it before we drew any attention to ourselves.

Sorensen's guy was conscious but very still and definitely confused about what had just happened. He was in a state of shock that I took advantage of right away. I asked him what his orders were. When he hesitated, I smacked him his nose and eyes with my open hand and asked him again.

"What exactly are your orders for today?"

The look of panic was obvious on his face and I could see the fight draining out of him. This was no inexperienced sentry. I could tell this was a seasoned agent with some real-time combat experience under his belt.

Despite imaginative movie writers, even these guys know when to give up the ghost.

He said they were to wait for Mr. Parton to get back to his room and contact Mr. Holt or his assistant when they had him contained.

I looked around the room and saw a small satchel on the bed. I opened it and dumped the contents on the bed. I found zip-ties, duct tape, and a large folded-up piece of black plastic. The plastic is commonly used to protect the floor and surrounding area from blood splatters during interrogation and torture sessions.

I looked over at the Major sitting on the edge of the bed. He was staring at the articles as in a trance. I stepped over to him and shook his shoulder.

He looked up at me and said, "I find this all so unbelievable, Jake."

I told him to believe it and to get over it because we needed to handle this and get him out of here.

The thug on the floor whom I had knocked out came to, pushed the pillow off his face, and sat up in wide-eyed puzzlement. He then reached into his pocket while cursing about killing us. What a stupid move!

Sorensen kicked him in the face so hard I wouldn't take any bets that he was still alive. I reached down, pulled his hand out of his trouser pocket, and found his fingers wrapped around a small North American Arms Mini Revolver.

Sorensen stood the other guy up and shook him down, but found no other weapons. The Major stood up, walked calmly over to the thug, looked him up and down, and then punched him so hard on the side of his face that the man did a complete backflip and landed out cold on the floor.

I said, "Guys, now I am not sure that we don't have two dead thugs on our hands."

The Major and Sorensen looked at me, looked at each other and then Sorensen said, "So what?"

In all the years I have known the Major, I had never seen him use violence in any manner. In all matters, he has always been the peacemaker. In fact, he always admonishes me for going "too far" when I deal out the paybacks. Both Sorensen and I were shocked but also awed at his strength and power.

We silently decided not to even mention the blow. We picked the Major's clothes up from the floor where the thugs had thrown them earlier during their search. The Major went to the small closet, lifted the corner of the carpet, pulled out a large manila envelope, turned, and winked at us. He had the important documents and discs that I was sure the almost-dead bad guys had been looking for. He said he had nothing in his briefcase, back at the Government building, of any importance and they could keep it.

Sorensen and I dragged the two thugs into the adjoining room and laid them together under the covers of the unmade bed. (Always fun to throw a little humor into the mix when possible!)

Sorensen and I carried the Major's two suitcases, ushered him down the back hall to the exit staircase, and together we left the hotel. As we exited the door and rounded the corner, two black SUVs pulled up to the side of the building in the guest parking lot.

We had just made it to a side alley without drawing attention to ourselves. We rushed to a large tourist store that we had scoped out earlier and cut through it to the door on the other side. We continued east until we came upon a stopped taxi. We climbed in and rode it back to Nassau. From there, we set out toward the beach where Top had anchored his boat.

As we approached the beach, I saw Top's boat, the *Semper Fi*, peacefully sitting at anchor in the little inlet. I pulled the Major aside and told him we needed to talk before we went aboard the boat. The Major was quiet and had not mentioned the hotel room incident once. He was in a depressed funk that I never recalled seeing him in despite the many years we had been friends. I assured him that what we did, including his striking of the thug, was not barbaric or out of line under the circumstances.

I said, "Major, I have done far more for far less in my time, and there were few regrets."

Doug turned to me and said, "Jake I never realized until today, when I saw the instruments of torture lying on the hotel room floor, that all your warnings were such a reality. He added that he had always done what he felt was right and had always strived to help all people with his actions and feelings. It felt so surreal to him that anyone would want to hurt him for looking after humanity.

With that said, he smiled and asked me, "So, did you enjoy my first act of actual violence today?"

I said I was delighted to see that he had it in him, and I told him could have put even Goliath down with that punch. We both laughed and headed down the beach.

We needed to explain to Top and the others on board what had occurred today, and I needed the Major's opinion as to the facts.

Sorensen had already contacted Top and had pulled the Zodiac out of the brush and down to the waterline. As soon as we were sure there was no surveillance, we pushed the boat into the water. I had the Major jump into the inflatable before he had to walk in the surf with his expensive, tailor-made suit and fancy dress shoes. As we pushed off from the beach, I could already see Top in the cockpit of his boat. He looked both ways, waved, and gave us an all-clear thumbs up.

We pulled up on the seaward side of the boat to mask our presence as we boarded. The larger Zodiac was tied forward of the *Semper Fi's* starboard side. It appeared that Top had gone ashore while Sorensen and I had been gone. I knew we needed supplies, so I figured Top had made a run into Nassau. I didn't mention having to leave the stuff I bought near the Government Building!

As we climbed over the side into the boat, Top and Wilson greeted us with big smiles and took the Major's suitcases from him. I introduced the Major to Top and Wilson and suggested that we all go below for a debriefing. Sorensen said he would stay above deck to stand watch.

Feeling grimy from the day's activities, the Major asked if he could take a shower and change into some clean clothes. Top took him aft into his stateroom and returned moments later.

Calvin came aft from the front berthing area and greeted us in the galley. He had been sleeping, as he was still not completely recovered from his ordeal.

I sat them all down and told them about our past few hours, from the airport discoveries to the incident at the Government Building and the showdown at the hotel. I left out the part where the Major punched the thug as I figured he could tell that part if he chose to. Why steal his thunder?

Calvin said that the hangar we were talking about was a sort of U.S. neutral zone where most of the visitors had diplomatic immunity. He said the ambassador and his staff parked their planes there and that over the years, even Air Force One used the hangar as its parking place after dropping off the presidents.

He said they once had it under surveillance for a drug sweep, but the American State Department shut them down after complaining to the Prime Minister. From that point on, they were ordered to stay away from all activities going on there and to curb any investigation or intelligence gathering that started or ended there. Calvin said that all of his records and those of his other departments for this area—including the police—were confiscated and turned over to the Americans.

Calvin added, "It is tough trying to keep law and order when my government gives so many passes to various countries diplomatic corps and their intelligence agencies."

He knew that a lot of drugs came through the Bahamas, aided by certain law enforcement agencies from the U.S., but he was told to turn his back on these dealings, as they were none of his business. He knew for a fact that he could have arrested some of the most wanted drug lords in the world right here in Nassau but his own superiors prevented him from doing so.

The Major came out of the aft stateroom in clean clothes and looking more normal than he had just a few minutes ago. He said the first order of business was going through the computer we had lifted. He asked for a few minutes alone so he could scan the info on it, and then we would sit down for a strategy meeting. As alone as we could leave him on the inside of a boat, we all watched him boot up Top's small laptop, popped in one of the CDs, and watched his eyes as he typed in a search option. We knew exactly what he had done as he searched his own name and whispered, "Oh shit, you've got to be kidding me," after seeing how many entries there were.

Sorensen stuck his head down the hatch and said, "A speedboat just went by the mouth of the inlet and I am sure they saw our boat. They did not slow down but there were two, white, military types that looked hard and long as they passed by." He said he did not believe they had seen him, as he was sitting on the gunwales on the other side of the salon roof.

I told everyone, "We have used up our welcome here, folks. It's time to move."

We all climbed into the two rubber boats except Top. He stayed aboard the *Semper Fi*. I took the Major, his suitcases, and two of the disc copies from the computer. Sorensen took the bigger Zodiac and loaded Calvin and Wilson in with him for safekeeping, Top hid his laptop computer in the secret compartment where he kept his guns. He hid the remaining copies of the discs in the CD music and DVD stand in the salon. It would take hours for any searcher to go through the hundreds of discs Top had stored there!

Top said he would stand fast, wait a couple of hours, and then set sail for Nassau harbor and wait for us to catch up.

Sorensen left first and turned to the north. As he turned, he waved me on my way, telling us he didn't see any threatening boats north or south as he got into the open water. I took off and followed the bigger Zodiac about a mile behind. When Sorensen was almost out of sight, I turned west into a small harbor where there was a large condo complex with a number of docks and a small cleared beach for the condo owners. I drove our rubber boat up into the brush on the south side of the beach and, from the brushy area, we could see the road and the vehicles going to and from Nassau.

We just sat there for a while, watching the road and the condo area next to us. We didn't see anything that seemed out of the ordinary. Sometimes, you have to look for what looks ordinary but is out of character for the surroundings.

There was a small passenger bus parked next to the condo office and a few people with their luggage milling around in the guest parking lot. I told the Major we had a good chance to get to the airport by appearing as guests from the condos. We each grabbed one of his bags, walked across the corner of the beach, and joined the folks near the bus loading area. We were greeted with big island smiles and a couple of cheerful hellos, but no sign of any suspicion. A few minutes later, a young Bahamian man came out of the office, greeted us all, and proceeded to open the door to the bus. We all boarded, took our seats, and the driver drove off down the road toward Nassau and the airport. So far, so good.

Well, things can change in a New York minute, because about a half-mile down the road, we came to a police roadblock. They were searching a couple of cars that they had pulled off to the side of the road. The drivers appeared to be Americans. As we approached, I saw one of the American military types with the Bahamas police asking questions of the drivers of the cars. I looked at the Major and he immediately moved from where he was sitting to beside a woman who was traveling alone. I then moved my position to the opposite side of the bus, away from the view of the police and the Americans doing the questioning. I had two S&W M&P 9mm compact pistols in my waistband under my shirt, but I could not picture myself shooting any of these Bahamas police. Well, not unless I absolutely had to!

There was a small VW car stopped in front of us with a policeman leaning over and talking to the driver. The driver appeared to be a Bahamian. The cop let him pass. The cop then walked over to our small bus and motioned for the driver to open the door so he could speak with him. I could not hear what they were saying but they both broke out in laughter at some remark as the cop pointed to the VW driving away. It appeared the police officer and our bus driver knew each other—or they were otherwise related.

Our driver looked back into the bus and said something to the cop. He then turned again and looked directly at me. He turned back around to the cop and said something that caused more laughter and the cop shook the driver's hand, stepped off the bus, and waved us through. As the driver passed the checkpoint, I saw him look up at me through his large rearview mirror and give me a wink!

We rode the bus to the small shops near the airport and, when the driver stopped for a stop sign, I signaled him that we wanted to get off. He said, "You'd be better to wait a few minutes cuz I got better shops for you and your friend to see just down the road a bit."

Moves like this normally make me very nervous, but after getting us through the checkpoint earlier, I decided to trust him a bit longer. The driver picked up his CB radio mike again as he had when we were leaving the condo area. I tried to hear what he was saying but the road noise was too great.

After about a half-mile, he turned down a short road and stopped next to an old warehouse. He pointed to a door at the side of the building and asked us to give his love to his cousin Calvin. These really were small islands!

I led the way through the door into the large building. The Major was carrying his two suitcases. To be safe, I told the Major we had to wait just a minute for our eyes to adjust. I already had my semi-automatic hanging from my right hand and pointing at the floor as my eyes adjusted to the low light. In front of us was a long hallway that seemed to stretch about a hundred yards. I tried each door along the way only to find them all locked tight. There was a faint light at the end of the hall, and we could hear music playing off in the distance.

As we approached the door, I moved my position to an angle where I could see through the crack of the door. With my 9mm leading the way, I pushed the door open until I could clearly see the room's interior.

The source of the music was a small MP3 player hooked up to two small speakers sitting on top of a file cabinet next to a window. The window was grimy yellow but clear enough to see through. As I looked out, I found it hard to believe that I was looking at the tarmac of the airport. The building we were in stretched across the airport perimeter with no gate or guards to stop anyone from breaching the security of the airfield. Such a breach of security was shocking based on the extreme measures our law enforcement took back in the states.

The Major moved into a position to look into the room and, after a moment or two, realized the enormity of what we were looking at. We literally could walk right out the side door of this building and into the International Airport! Now, all we needed was an airplane!

First things first, though. Who used this office? And, where were they right now?

I looked around and found some files and receipts lying on the desk. They looked like maintenance records and purchase orders for typical aircraft parts. I pushed the door open to look outside and saw a man working on a Cessna 182T with a brand-new shiny paint job.

There was no one else around, so I walked over to him and asked if he had any small aircraft for lease.

He looked at me with little to no surprise and asked, "Did you close and lock the door leading from the hallway?"

His question surprised me, but I turned and asked the Major to go back and make sure to close and lock the door. The Major looked as confused as I felt. I asked him how he knew we were here and he said he knew we were coming as soon as we jumped on his cousin's bus at the condo complex earlier. He introduced himself as Ronald Waters, employed by the Bahamas government and working for his cousin, Calvin Green. I was wondering if there was anyone on these islands not related to Calvin. Believe me, though, I wasn't complaining!

Mr. Waters replied, "I have access to a number of planes for lease."

He asked me specifically what I was rated for, and I told him that the 182T was right up my alley. He bowed and swept his hand toward the pretty little single-engine plane like a gentleman might motion to a lady to cross in front of him. He told me it was quite fast, had a pressurized cabin and a good oxygen system. He then added that it flew great at low altitude just over the top of the waves into the States.

I tried to pay him for the rental with the remaining cash I had and some the Major had produced from his pocket, but he refused my money.

He said, "She is topped off with fuel and ready to go, so you can be on your way whenever you are ready". As we walked up, he said he had just done a complete maintenance check and that she was as fit as a fiddle. He advised me to file a visual flight plan with the airport authority and to tell them that we were going sightseeing around the islands. This way, I could fly wherever I wanted without arousing any suspicion.

The evening was still young and there was still too much light to take off back toward the mainland and Miami. Someone in the control tower with a good pair of field glasses would be able to see the Major and me clearly sitting in the windscreen of the plane, so I did a pre-flight on the plane and reviewed its handbook on takeoff and landing speeds. I recalled that this craft's capabilities and flight factors meant that this plane was referred to as a "complex" because it had a constant pitch propeller and retractable landing gear. Everything else about her was pretty standard.

I told Mr. Waters that he had a fine craft and asked if I could use his cell phone to call a friend of mine in Miami. I asked the friend to meet me at Miami-Opa Locka Executive Airport north of Miami at about ten o'clock that night. I figured that I could fly low to the ground clutter to avoid detection by the Coast Guard and defense folks in south Florida since I had done it many times before. I'd chosen Miami-Opa Locka because it was the Coast Guard's base of flight operations in the Miami area.

Mr. Waters left for a few minutes, then returned with sandwiches and bottled water for our flight. I could not remember when we'd eaten last and the Major is always hungry. The food was met with great enthusiasm by both of us.

The sun was just about on the western horizon as it approached six-thirty. I did another quick preflight check and radioed my intentions to the ground controller in the tower. The plane was in near-perfect condition and, as I started her rolling, she handled great on the ground. I had the Major sit in the co-pilot's seat and we both wore ball caps to hide our features from anyone watching the aircraft with binoculars.

I saluted Mr. Waters, gave him a big smile of appreciation, and then taxied as instructed to the end of the runway. There were no spotters visible on the taxiways and the tower was too dark to see if anyone was tracking us. I did my warm-up and switched frequencies, telling the tower that I was going to get in some night flying on my log, would be heading west, and would be back in a while to do some touch-and-go landings.

When I was told to take-off, I lined the plane up on the centerline of the runway. As I looked down the runway for take-off, the Major tapped my arm, pointed his first two fingers at his eyes, and then pointed toward a dark green truck parked on the side of the swale to our right. There were two Caucasian men sitting in it and watching our plane through field glasses. I thought the structural post on the side of the windshield blocked any direct view of our profiles and our hats hid our faces well.

148

We were both wearing large communication headphones over the hats and we kept our heads turned slightly to our left as I pulled back on the throttle. We ran down the runway with ease and lifted off nicely into the early evening sky just as it was turning orange from the setting of the sun.

I climbed out a few hundred feet and turned west as I had advised the tower. As I turned right and climbed through a thousand feet, I looked over my right shoulder at the airport and saw a number of vehicles racing down the taxiway with flashing red lights as if they were preparing for an emergency landing.

The air controller in the tower called out my tail number and asked me to change radio frequencies to a restricted number I was not familiar with.

I looked at the Major, said, "No way," and reached over and switched off my beacon signal and turned off my running lights. I immediately turned south and, with a special stall tactic, dropped out of the sky until my altimeter read three hundred feet. That still gave me a safety margin of about one hundred feet above the ocean.

I told the Major, "Well, it seems we must have been identified by the watchers when we took off, but our Aloha party was too late to wish us farewell."

I took a bearing on the compass, steered a course due south, and watched for any aircraft lights on the planes landing and taking off from the airport. I asked the Major to use my sat phone to call Top and advise him to stand by for our rescue if we needed one. I turned to the east around the south end of New Providence Island. If they had an aircraft searching for us, they would be looking to the west, not east.

The Major picked up my cell, dialed a number, and said, "Hello, Top." He then passed it to me.

The cockpit was fairly quiet compared to a non-pressurized cockpit, but I still had to listen carefully to tell if it was Top on the other end.

Top said he was anchored just off Cable Beach west of Nassau harbor. I gave him a basic debriefing on what had happened after we left the boat and about the van driver bringing us to the airport. I then told him that we were about fifty miles south of his location and heading east. I explained that I was going to double back to try a run at Miami to drop off the Major.

He said Sorensen and Calvin had just come back aboard the *Semper Fi* a few minutes ago and they'd had no problems after they had left the boat earlier. They had decided that coming aboard was safe because other boats were anchored nearby. Top said several aircraft circled him a couple of times during the day as he cruised away from the cove but seemed more interested in searching the inlets and coves than hassling a big sailing rig flying the U.S. Marine Corps flag off its mast. Many of the security working the San Andros matter were probably former Marines; they would not even think about bothering a fellow Marine. I asked him to standby in case we had to ditch the aircraft and needed to be rescued.

While I was talking to Top, I turned south and reversed my course to head west toward Andros Island. We were still flying at three hundred feet and I could see the phosphorus in the water as the waves broke up below. I had the radio turned down low but every few minutes I could hear a call for us requesting that we change frequencies and return to the airport.

I looked at the Major and said, "Fat chance of that!"

I tuned into the Miami information channel and received a weak signal at this low altitude, but it was enough to use as a beacon to home in on the Radio Directional Finder the plane was equipped with. As I saw the lights on the horizon at Nicholls Town, I turned northwest to stay out of earshot of the folks at San Andros.

I flew just fast enough to keep aloft with minimum noise. The Major took advantage of the close proximity to the cell tower on San Andros to call a lawyer friend of his in Miami to meet him at the airport—when and if we made it to Miami. The "if" part was what I was most concerned about.

I could see two sets of lights south over the San Andros airport. One of them had the light pattern of a helicopter and the other was more than likely a KC 130. I dropped the plane down another hundred feet and watched out of the port side of the plane. I was flying due west now and held that course for about thirty minutes, then turned north and flew about fifty miles off Florida's east coast.

I could finally see the glow of the lights of Miami on the distant horizon. I kept the plane low and steady at about 130 knots until I thought we were about even with West Palm Beach. I increased my altitude and popped up just behind an airliner. It was rough trying to stay out of the jet wash, but with my lights off and my transponder on standby, I was just where I wanted to be—invisible!

The larger aircraft descended into Palm Beach but I kept going west, dropped from eight thousand feet to about three thousand, and turned south. At the same time, I turned on my transponder and called Miami Center announcing that I was thirty miles north heading for a landing at Opa Locka Field for a refuel and then heading back to Orlando

International Airport after a short break. I knew we had slipped through the cracks again, and I gave the Major a hearty thumbs up as I turned toward my approach heading.

We landed and turned onto the first taxiway. The first Fixed Base Operation (FBO) was right in front of us and I announced to the ground controller that we were stopping there.

The ground controller gave me the A-OK, and I signed off. From where we were situated, the tower would have a hard time reading or even seeing our tail numbers.

After I shut down the engine and turned off all of the electronics, we climbed out onto the tarmac and I told the Major not to go inside but to walk out through the side gate and hail his friend from in front of the small terminal down the way. I advised him to stay in the shadows and not let anyone get a good look at him. I told him I would catch up with him later. He took his two suitcases and left the plane.

I finished tying down the aircraft and looked around the FBO. Looking through the window, I could see a clerk at the desk looking down at some papers. He never paid me or the plane any attention, so I placed the keys to the aircraft under the wiper on the pilot's side of the windscreen and followed the Major out of the side gate.

I told the Major, "I will call Mr. Waters in the morning and tell him where his plane is and have Gage call my accountant to send him a check for the fee of getting the plane shuttled back to Grand Bahamas Island."

The Major looked at me, "You always remember to take care of those who take care of us."

Before the Major left, I asked him something that had been bothering me during the entire trip. Why did he think the Middle Easterners stayed in the Bahamas after they had left the states following 9/11?

He said, "Simple! Their business interests in the States were as close to San Andros as they were to Miami or Orlando. They could fly from San Andros to Miami or Nassau and go anywhere they needed and not be bothered!"

called Top as soon as I was clear of the airport to tell him that we'd made it safe and sound. He told me he was still in the same spot and that nothing had changed since we last communicated. A few speedboats had cruised by with a couple of nosy people on board, but they paid no attention to his boat. I told him I expected to be back within a few hours and asked him to set sail for Andros Island. I needed to get to the *Big Mamoo* and all my gear from the boat.

He said he was hauling up anchor as we spoke. I could hear Sorensen saying something to Top in the background and then he came on the line. He told me that he had spoken to one of his associates earlier who told him that there was an "Intelligence Alert" issued by Homeland Security a couple of days ago that described some terrorist activity in the Bahamas. It requested air and surface surveillance from the Coast Guard and other military forces in the immediate area. Sorensen told his guy a bit about what we had observed and then explained the sighting of the undersecretary in Nassau. Sorensen asked his friend for some unofficial "heads up" on anything else he could find out.

After signing off with Sorensen, I called Dave up on Merritt Island and had him call me back on a safe phone. I gave him the short version of our adventures. He said that he would keep staying at my place at night to be sure all was secure. I told him I needed my camera equipment from my safe room in Isla Del Sol and asked him to fly it down to me right away.

Dave was an even better pilot then I was but had lost his pilot license some years ago in a child custody dispute with the courts. My Cessna 182 was tied down at the little Merritt Island Airport, and no one there would ask Dave for his license before he took off. My Cessna was not a Turbo, nor did it have a pressurized cabin, but it was quick and reliable. I asked Dave to fly visual to the Fort Lauderdale Executive Airport. He would call me just before takeoff and would land about an hour and forty-five minutes later.

I then called my nephew JR and asked him to pick me up outside a Starbucks near the Opa Locka Airport as soon as he could. He was visiting with my brother, his Dad, and said he would be there in thirty minutes. I made a quick call to Gage to have him call my accountant regarding payment to Mr. Waters for the Cessna. Gage said that when I had more time, he needed to update me on a few matters, but they could wait for now.

I went into a 7-Eleven and bought three more burners and four disposable digital cameras. I grabbed a couple of snacks and energy bars and waited for JR on the corner of the building across the street from the Starbucks. From this vantage point, I could see if he was being followed and if anyone was snooping around and looking for me. I saw no one when he pulled up in his souped-up pick-up truck.

JR was looking for me when I jogged across the street, came up along the side of his truck, and climbed in the passenger side. The look he gave me was one of *Okay, Uncle Jake, what did you step in now?*

I looked at him and said, "What?"

He just shook his head and gave me a big hug across the center console.

About the time we rounded the first corner, Dave called me and said, "I am lined up for take-off now and estimate my arrival will be in less than two hours, Chief."

He had the equipment I'd asked for and had packed a bag of clean clothes for me. I thanked Dave and asked him to call me as soon as he was at the Executive FBO on the south side of the field. I could hear the familiar winding up of the engine of my plane over the phone and, as we signed off, I wished him a safe trip.

I had JR bring me out to west Broward County to see Ralph, a friend of mine for many years. Ralph was an old spook from the Cold War days when our CIA made regular sorties in and out of Cuba. Ralph would meet their boats and ferry them through the swamps to dry land and safety. Ralph was known to have a great armory at his disposal at all times. I needed a special article for Sorensen and figured Ralph would love to get back into the game.

Ralph greeted us in his driveway with a big bear hug for each of us and asked, "So, Jake, are you the one causing so much trouble in the Bahamas?"

I've learned long ago not to even ask Ralph how he knows things. He had an endless source of information that amazed even me. It stood to reason that he was another one of my information sources in South Florida and all-around America—besides Gage, of course!

JR and I followed Ralph into the house. I gave him some of the basics and let him go on about what a bad idea it was to mess with these particular guys. I asked him about the goings-on in San Andros and he said he knew a lot about it that and it was very complicated!

Ralph had been collaborating with Gage and comparing notes. (That's how he knew about my involvement.) They found out that in the early 1950s, a group of former German citizens and military officers were moved from various locations where they were being hidden to San Andros. These Germans were part of a secret program called Operation Paperclip and Operation Overcast by the U.S. Government. They were former military and German government officials who helped the Allies after the Second World War. Even though many of them were hardened war criminals, they became extremely valuable to our military efforts against the problematic Russians threatening the U.S. and the entire free world.

They were hidden on San Andros to protect them from not only their enemies from the war but also their own countrymen who thought they were traitors to the Third Reich!

They were all provided with pensions and new identities that included American and Canadian passports. They were fairly well hidden there and supplied with ample security of their own choosing. Most of them lived a quiet, peaceful life and very seldom left the small community, though some of them traveled a bit to meet family members at various locations around the world. When England granted the Bahamas their independence in 1973, they stayed closer to home. They did not trust the Bahamians as much as they had trusted their former British landlords.

Ralph went on to say that Gage did some in-depth research and found a few more interesting stories about the small community and how they became a political liability as time went on.

A group of former government and intelligence folks were put in charge of "caretaking" the community. These aging senior citizens would soon die off and the liability would fix itself—or so they thought. The group charged with running this program was coasting along with few or no problems. They held annual meetings in Washington D.C. every year that were more of a formality than anything else. They went over the budget for the coming year and voted healthy pay raises for themselves. Many of them owned condos in the Bahamas, paid for by funds out of the annual Overcast Fund!

I said, "Go figure. Do taxpayers pay for everything in this world?"

Ralph detailed more about the secret operation and then revealed that he had taken part in escorting some of the Germans to San Andros over the years. He said it was a quick and easy buck and that they were mostly elderly men and women who said little and just got on and off his boat at Nicholls Town.

Ralph went on to say that it all came alive again after 9/11, when he and a group of friends in the business were contacted and asked to carry supplies and building materials to San Andros. He said that judging from the cargo and food items, some Arab-type folks were being moved there. Many of these folks came from the Orlando area. They were flown by helicopter to San Andros. He supervised about four loads of goods to Andros for these Arabs but never actually went to San Andros.

I told him about seeing a few of them firsthand and that one or two of them looked like Osama Bin Laden himself! Ralph said that a number of them were thought to be relatives of his.

I asked Ralph if I could borrow or buy a good long-range 30-06 rifle with a decent scope for a couple of long shots I might have to make.

He said, "I have just the thing, pal, but I will not accept any money from you. Use it wisely."

We walked around the inside of the house and into Ralph's office in the back where he opened a wide closet door. Behind the door was another door made of reinforced steel. The door had a digital keypad where he punched in six numbers and the bolt clanked like an old dungeon cell door.

He laughed and said, "That's just a prank sound effect that the safe manufacture added for effect, but I like it."

Beyond the steel door was a room completely filled with professionally made gun racks. Each rack was loaded with rifles and pistols. There were three M-60 machine guns on the floor on their tripods. There was even a fifty-caliber machine gun on its stand against the opposite wall. I had been in this room a few times before, but it never ceased to amaze me what an amazing arsenal Ralph had. It was rumored that Ralph kept all of these weapons as a supply point for soldiers and federal agents in case of an invasion from Cuba or a civil war. I believe he is a consummate collector of guns and keeps every firearm he comes in contact with instead of disposing of them after an operation.

I once stayed in Ralph's home with a group of civil rights lawyers and caseworkers during a big anti-government court case. Ralph was just as protective of and friendly with those folks as he was to militants and spooks. Ralph seems to have no political center. He is like a good soldier. "Mine is not to wonder why. Mine is just to do or die!"

He went to the back of the room and picked up a black matte aluminum case about four feet long with nylon straps neatly riveted to its center. There was a small tag hanging from one of the handles that said "CheyTac!" When Ralph opened the case, I thought I was seeing a ray gun used in science fiction movies!

It was a rifle like no other I had ever seen. It was dark grey and appeared to be completely made of metal. No wooden stock or grips. Ralph lifted it from its case and cleared the chamber. He passed it to me gently and I was surprised it didn't weigh as much as I thought it would. It had a strange-looking sight mounted on its top bracket and more little nooks and crannies than I had ever seen on any weapon. Ralph explained that it was a .408 caliber Intervention sniper rifle built by Cheyenne Tactical in the good ole' U.S.A. He said it was the best sniper rifle ever made.

I asked him how he had this little beauty in his gun locker. He just smiled and told me it was a gift from some nice folks from Israel. I didn't question him any further. I thanked him but said I wanted a good sniper rifle, nothing this complex. I didn't want to have to go back to school and learn "Sniping 101" all over again!

He smiled and put the Cheyenne Tactical weapon aside, lifted another case from a shelf, and passed it to me.

I flipped the hinged locks, opened the case, and found what looked like a modified Remington 700 rifle that I was very familiar with.

Ralph told me it was an M24 sniper rifle made by Remington. I took the rifle from the case and held it up to the light. It felt familiar, like an old friend. I had used a 700 in Vietnam many times. I still preferred the M14, but this rifle was lighter and used the same 7.62 NATO round that the M14 used. It was a bolt action, which gave the shot more power and range. It had a Léopold fixed-powered scope mounted on its top. Just perfect for my purpose, which even I had not figured out quite yet! But, having what you need when you need it is paramount when in survival mode.

I took out my cell, called Sorensen's seaplane friend, and requested another ride to San Andros.

He said, "Not a problem," and then added that he would be ready in about three hours and that I should meet him at the Old Chalk Seaplane Ramp near Miami Beach.

I told him I knew exactly what he was talking about, thanked him, and then called to check on Joel.

I told Joel that he should be hearing from attorney Doug Parton shortly. He told me his family had collected a large sum of money for his defense and it would be available when we needed it. I told him not to worry about it right now, as we would add it all up when we had the time to breathe. He laughed and it was a good laugh. Something I had not heard from Joel since I had met him, and I was glad he was acting somewhat normal now.

I called Top and asked him to sail over to Nicholls Town and meet me at my boat. He told me he was already underway.

Ralph said he was going to call Gage to let him know that he had conveyed the most recent information to me. He then asked me if I would rather he boat me over to San Andros in his Sea Ray Boat. I thanked him for the generous offer but said that I needed to get there even faster. I told him about Top and the help he had been so far. He said that Sorensen was being missed and that a few of the area spooks suspected his involvement in the Bahamas excitement.

Ralph then asked me about Jason Patrick and his mysterious disappearance. I just gave him my most innocent look.

He smiled and said, "Good job, Jake. No one liked that guy anyway—not even those who worked for him!"

I told Ralph, "Thanks for everything," and then had JR drive me to the Fort Lauderdale Executive Airport so I could meet Dave when he landed.

As we drove up I-95, I saw my Cessna approach the runway at FLEA. As old as she is, she's still pretty to me. One of these days, I was going to buy a larger, faster plane. But, right now, she suits my needs just fine.

JR dropped me off at Sentry Air with a hug and a wish of, "Good luck. Don't get dead, Uncle Jake!"

I asked him to tell the rest of the family that I loved them and then climbed out with my new rifle in its case and numerous boxes of ammo. I was ready for just about anything.

The problem with carrying a rifle case is that it draws attention right off. I walked into the FBO and all the folks in there turned in unison to look at me and my case. See, I said it draws attention.

I walked to the counter and told the clerk I was meeting the Cessna that just landed and showed her my pilot's license. I asked her if I could leave my case with her while I walked out to the flight line.

She said, "Certainly."

I lifted it around the desk and placed it on the floor behind her.

I walked over to the security door leading out to the flight line and she buzzed me through.

Dave was tying the plane down, but he looked up with a smile. We greeted and I told him I needed to get going within the hour to meet a friend in Miami. He opened the passenger door, lifted out a case, and passed it to me. He also passed me a stack of hundred dollar bills I desperately needed. I briefed him on the past few days and bid him a safe trip back to Brevard County.

I went through the FBO, picked up my rifle case, thanked the young lady, and out the door I went. No eyes flashed at me as I left. I hailed a cab from the parking lot and asked the driver to take me to South Beach. When working an operation like this, I seldom tell a stranger my final destination until we get close. Again, I use one of Gage's mottos: "Be extremely cautious in everything you do!"

I called the Major and briefed him on what I was up to in code so the driver could not accurately repeat what I'd said, should anyone ask. The Major told me he was meeting with Joel in an hour and was trying to get a Bahamian prosecutor to agree to his conditions prior to presenting Joel at trial.

I told him that I was going to document as much of San Andros as I could so he could use it as leverage before the trial.

He said he believed that only a few in the Bahamas government knew the extent of the goings-on at San Andros. He would return to Nassau as soon as he was guaranteed that he would not be roughed up again, and, even then, he was filing a complaint with the State Department over the incident in Nassau. He had figured out that one of the assistants to the prime minister had set him up that day and sicced those thugs on him.

I told him that, according to Ralph, we had stirred up a hornets' nest!

When the driver arrived on the islands near Miami Beach, I asked him to bring me close to the seaplane ramp on the bayside. When he got to within a hundred yards of the ramp, I asked him to pull over in front of a wide driveway to one of the many Miami Beach mansions. As far as he knew, the mansion was my final destination. I paid him his fee and gave him a fifty-dollar tip.

He smiled at me and said, "Happy hunting, pal!"

I smiled back and gave him a thumbs up.

Instead of walking right to the ramp area, I strolled across the street and lingered in front of another mansion. The large old house was familiar, as it had been used as a movie prop many times over for TV shows and movies.

As I stood looking at the house, I saw in the reflection of a brass plate a rather large man watching me from the shadows of a tree inside the short fence surrounding the mansion.

I continued to walk toward the seaplane ramp. The man walked out of the shadows and toward me. I stopped and faced him with my hand on a knife in my pocket. As he approached, I recognized my friend Ralph. He smiled and passed a small package over the fence. He told me to open it when I got on board the plane.

He said he would watch my back until we took off "for old time's sake!"

I asked him what he was doing in front of this mansion and he said he owned it and the other four houses on the street. I should not have been surprised!

I thanked Ralph again for everything as he stepped over the fence and walked me over to the ramp at about the same time the plane landed out in the river. I still had no idea who this pilot was, but he sure was handy, and he hadn't complained about my spur of the moment requests.

As the plane powered toward the ramp, I noticed someone sitting in the right-side passenger seat. When the plane spun around back toward the water, I saw that it was Senator Jackie Lyons. Lyons was the Democratic senator from Florida who chaired the Senate Panel on Intelligence. She was also known to be "more than a good friend" to Doug Parton!

When the single, running engine of the plane wound down and the pilot reached over and pushed the door open for the senator to deplane, Ralph walked over and helped her to the ground. He hugged her and kissed her cheek warmly as they passed pleasantries with one another.

She turned to me, smiling, and said, "Long time no see, Jake!"

I smiled back and kissed her cheek.

She told me she had heard that there was trouble going on in the Bahamas and she'd had a strange feeling that Doug and I were involved somehow.

I told her that the Major was in Miami now and that I was sure he would love to see her and tell her everything.

She said, "Jake, I am way ahead of you."

She had just left him and already knew most of the story. "The reason I came to see you, Jake, is to warn you that the people you are up against are not some low echelon peons but some of the top career intelligence folks in Washington."

She told me she would do all she could to get the media to start exposing the San Andros matter, but that it would be difficult because these high-profile thugs had a lock on most TV, cable, and newspapers around the country. As usual, the politicians would not even address an issue unless it is staring at them from a TV or newspaper headline.

Senator Lyons promised to make an issue of the San Andros matter as soon as she arrived back in Washington.

We hugged again, said "Good luck," and I climbed into the cockpit of the seaplane.

I made a quick call to Mr. Waters at the airport on Grand Bahamas and told him his plane was parked at the Opa Locka Airport. He told me he had already arranged to bring it back. He said one of his best friends ran the FBO where the plane was parked. I thanked him and told him I would reimburse his expenses soon. He said he knew I was good for it—as long as I stayed alive.

I noticed that while I was talking to the Senator, Ralph was speaking to the pilot. I also noticed that Ralph had passed the pilot an envelope that the pilot accepted and held in his left hand until he boarded the aircraft. It seemed to be a banking envelope holding a great deal of paper currency. The pilot slipped the envelope into a slot on the dash of the plane and started his take-off procedures.

I didn't bother making small talk with him, as I already knew he wasn't interested. I asked him to fly toward the Island of New Providence so we could see if we could find the *Semper Fi* along the way to San Andros. He just nodded and pulled the throttles to their limits as we skimmed over the water and took off.

We'd flown for about an hour and forty minutes when he tapped me on the leg and pointed to the horizon. The unmistakable sail of the *Semper Fi* was full out and the boat was leaving a one-mile wake behind it as it cut through the emerald water. We circled the boat, and once Top recognized us, we landed into the wind and taxied as close as we could to the boat.

Top reefed his sails some and Wilson hauled the big inflatable over the side, jumped in, and sped over to the plane to pick me up. Wilson was all smiles as he pulled the Zodiac up to the plane's pontoon and held it steady while I climbed aboard.

As I stepped onto the wood deck of the Zodiac, I noticed Wilson's smile fading as he looked beyond me at the pilot. I made note of it as I piled my cases into the boat. I waved thanks to the pilot as he powered up to take off. We pushed off and Wilson turned the Zodiac toward the boat and hit the throttle.

As we cruised toward the *Semper Fi*, I asked Wilson about that look on his face when he saw the pilot. He looked at me and said he had seen that pilot and his plane the day he arrived at San Andros. He said that he and another sentry were sent to Nicholls Town to pick up two civilians from the docks and that they flew in on that same seaplane—and it was that same pilot.

I told him that I had no idea who or what he was, but I was sure he was a government spook who flew many folks many places. I told him I wasn't concerned, as a very dear and trusted friend of mine knew him. I didn't tell Wilson, but I planned to call Ralph as soon as we boarded to get more info on our mutual pilot friend. Wilson and I boarded the *Semper Fi*, we hugged all around, and I went below to call Ralph.

I stuck my sat phone out of the front hatch to get a signal because the cell service was weak to nothing out here between the islands. Ralph answered on the first ring and asked if everything was all right.

I told him about the pilot and he said, "Not to worry. He told me his name was Frank Tobin." Frank was a former Air America pilot from back in the Sixties and Seventies. Many agencies used his services for the same purpose as we had used him.

Despite working for the bad guys, he was one of Ralph's best sources of information and one of his best allies, thus making him my friend, too. I signed off from Ralph and joined everyone in the cockpit where Top was running the boat engine flat out. There was little breeze on the boat as we were running before the wind and, thus, our speed and the wind were nearly equal. I briefed Sorensen on the pilot and then told him what Ralph had said. Sorensen said I should have asked him, as he had known Tobin for thirty years!

I filled everyone in on the past few hours and told them about my meeting with Senator Lyons. Top told us he was a personal friend of the senator and said she was a fine, upstanding lady. I told them she was going to start passing the word around D.C. about what was going on in the San Andros matter and was going to try to get the news media fired up enough to ignore the influence of the powerbrokers in Washington.

After about an hour, we could see some of the fishing boats off of San Andros, which told us we were within an hour of seeing land near Morgan Bluff and Nicholls Town. Except for Top, all of us went below where no one on the other boats could spot us. But we were not below more than ten seconds when Top stomped his foot on the deck three times. I went to the hatch and he called down that there was a helicopter heading our way from the west.

I told Top to keep his heading and to wave to them if they did a flyover. As the bird got closer, Top said it was a military-looking helicopter painted black or a very dark gray. We all could hear it thumping as it cut through the air as it traveled east.

I went over to my belongings, took the new sniper rifle out of its case, and loaded it. I had not practiced with it yet, but I was a fair shot with any weapon at any range. Everyone eyed me with much curiosity. I guess they were a bit surprised that I had such a rifle on this mission and were wondering exactly what I planned to do with it. I also knew that Sorensen would find a good use for this weapon when the time came.

As the helicopter came closer and closer, Top gave us a blow-by-blow narrative of its actions. It kept its course from the west and its elevation and speed. About two minutes later, it passed by about a mile to the north and then kept going. I warned everyone to stay calm and remain below until it was over the horizon. About ten minutes later, we could no longer see it and relaxed a bit.

I nonchalantly wiped the rifle down and unloaded it. Sorensen gave me a raised eyebrow and that look of *What exactly were you going to do with that thing anyway, Jake?*

I just smiled and put the rifle neatly back in its case, telling him that the weapon was intended for his use.

Within the hour, we were in sight of the island and I could just make out the mast and hull of the *Slim Molly* (aka, the *Big Mamoo*). We found a mooring toward the center of the other boats and dropped the anchor. I surveyed the other boats around us for any unusual activity and saw nothing suspicious. I could clearly see the public dock and boat ramp on the shore, and there was no sentry or any vehicles parked near the dock in the adjacent parking lot. I asked Sorensen to come with me to check out my boat and so he and I could get some time away from the others.

We took the Zodiac and cruised in the opposite direction of the *Slim Molly*. I looked into all the boats we passed to make sure there wasn't anyone on board watching my boat. I didn't see anything out of place and none of the boats were running generators for their air conditioners—which they would have to be doing or have all their hatches open because of the heat. So, we tied up to the east side of the boat where shore eyes wouldn't notice us. I found all my markers still in place, so no one had come aboard in my absence.

I cranked up the motor after checking the fluid levels and, after another ten minutes, cranked up the Onan generator to charge the auxiliary batteries. I have a built-in solar charger that keeps my engine batteries up and ready at all times. I have been meaning to install the same system for the auxiliary battery system. I left the air conditioners off for the time being.

The one drawback of being under power on a boat is that you can't hear anything outside the cabin if you're down below and you can't hear another boat approaching when you're on the deck.

However, I did hear three warning blasts from Top's boat's air horn. I also felt the boat shift as someone climbed aboard. Seconds later, I saw a long black barrel, topped by a silencer, emerge from the hatchway and point toward the salon. What was most interesting about the entire fifteen- to twenty-second ordeal was the sound of the man's head hitting the hatchway frame a millisecond after Top's 7.62 round hit him in the back of his head!

The second round struck the head of the second attacker, who'd been standing out in the cockpit next to my helm stand. As I rushed the hatch to the aft section of my boat, I could see Top standing in his cockpit, still sighting down the barrel of his old M14 rifle. I saluted him, grabbed the two men lying in my cockpit, and threw them into their rubber inflatable. I looked around the bay area and saw no one looking at us or at any of the boats moored there. The breeze was coming from the west and it would have dampened the sounds of the rifle, but for no one to be interested at all was very unusual.

Sorensen unhooked Top's Zodiac from the cleat of my boat, grabbed the bowline of the dead attacker's rubber boat, and headed east out of the harbor. As he was winding between boats, I saw him cover the bodies up with a green tarp. They must have been waiting for us by hiding behind one of the bigger boats at anchor as we cruised over to my boat.

I grabbed the hose out of the side locker in the cockpit and washed the blood, skin, and brain fragments from the deck. I wiped down the bulkheads and teak with a wet rag, and then I took a bottle of white vinegar from the galley and sprayed all the surfaces of the boat. This would help eliminate any "material" left on the boat from what had occurred.

I now had two more pistols and a handheld radio that one of the intruders had dropped. I turned the volume knob and found it had been turned down low. I then discovered that its battery was dead. That may have explained why we were not being overrun with troops right now!

I decided to haul anchor and motor out of the harbor. I came up alongside the *Semper Fi* and told Top we should head down the coast a bit. Top agreed. I told him that he did some fine shooting. He grimaced and told me that he was sure they were going to fire on us as soon as they cleared the hatch on my boat.

I told him Sorensen and I had been taken completely off guard, and then I thanked him profusely. I knew then that I was far too tired at this point and needed some sleep before we went any further.

A moment later, Sorensen appeared alongside my boat. He said a small fishing boat had flagged him down. When he stopped to speak with the Bahamian, the fisherman pointed at the towed, rubber inflatable and said, "I just received a call from my wife that there may be some fishing chum that needs to be disposed of on its way east."

Sorensen understood and unhooked the inflatable, passing the line to the fisherman. Sorensen said there was not another word spoken. He didn't look back as he powered away. He was just happy that matters had been taken care of.

I told Sorensen we needed to go down the coast, secure anchor, and get some much-needed rest before we made any more mistakes. He agreed and tied the inflatable to the stern of the boat. I saluted Top, powered around the outermost boats at anchor, and turned to the southeast.

As we distanced ourselves from the island, I watched the harbor and air for any signs of pursuit. I saw none, but I did discover that the attackers' handheld radio had the same charging plug as one of my radios, so I plugged it in to charge it up so I could hear who was transmitting.

Both of us traveled about ten miles down the coast and dropped anchors about a mile from the beach. We then tethered the two boats together and drew up a watch list to take shifts so we could all get some sleep. Top and his crew took the first watch. Sorensen and I took the dawn watch.

When I lay down, resting my head on my soft goose down pillow and looked around, it seemed like I hadn't seen my rack in weeks. There were once again all the familiar sounds and smells I loved and recognized from the years I had spent on this wonderful boat.

Because of my love of the sea and the *Slim Molly*, I had always dreamed of sailing her around the world, a voyage I had planned that would take about four years of leisure time during which I could write all my stories for publication. I had always felt that many of the things I had seen and personally taken part in would be interesting and educational for future generations to come. That hasn't happened yet, and I'm sure not getting any younger. I thought maybe if I survived this matter, it would be a good time to cut my losses and sail east to the Mediterranean and points south. It would be nice to visit Africa and not have anyone shoot at me!

The sound of the waves lapping against the hull put me right out and, soon, I was dreaming my normal nonsense and at total peace. The world was a different place when I was in a deep sleep.

It seemed like only ten minutes had gone by when Wilson called to me from the hatch of my cabin. It was my watch already, and all was well, according to Wilson. He told me they had heard and seen a helicopter far off on the horizon. It patrolled back and forth most of the night around the northeast sector of the island. They also saw searchlights up the coast from the boats. They were obviously searching for their missing would-be assassins, but they would never find them unless they did a DNA analysis on a few sharks' stomachs!

Dawn was breaking and it was now light enough to see the coast to the west. I could see some of the small fishing boats on the northern horizon, which meant any patrol boat up the coast that was looking south could see us.

I checked one of my cell phones and, to my surprise, found I had a signal. I called the Major in the States and he answered on the second ring. I told him in code about the day before and he whistled in response. He said that this would prove to be the costliest matter we had ever had to deal with in our forty-some-odd years working together.

I responded, "We have only just begun, Major. I am sure these folks won't give up until we all are silenced for good!"

I went on to tell him that I had some plans of my own. The Major advised me to gather as much evidence as I could about what was going on at San Andros. He would use it to set Joel free from the charges and expose the goings-on in the Bahamas. I told him he had to make his deals from the States and to stay in hiding until we were able to clean up some of the mess here. A mess it already was, but a bigger mess it was about to become.

There was too much corruption surrounding this matter to expect a fair trial, or even a fair hearing for Joel. I told him about Senator Lyons and her commitment to spreading the word in Washington. He said he was already aware of it and that it was part of his overall strategy. Of course, he knew about her involvement, as she was most likely laying there beside him as we spoke!

I signed off with the Major and saw that Top was just climbing out into the *Semper Fi's* cockpit. He had a mug of coffee in his right hand and saluted me good morning with it. I greeted him back and asked if he had heard from his daughter lately. He said she was doing fine and was studying for the LSAT exam. She had decided she wanted a career in law. I told him that she now had a whole new group of uncles who would coach her every step of the way!

I suggested that he might want to head back home now as things were going to heat up very soon. I reminded him that if he was caught and convicted of a felony, he would lose his retirement and possibly even his liberty.

He grinned and said, "I wouldn't miss this for the world, Jake. The four million-dollar boat that I am standing on was not paid for by Marine Corps retirement funds, so don't worry about me!"

I said, "All right then, Top. Let's form a plan."

After the others had had some strong coffee and cold cereal, and I had, as always, tea, we went below into the salon of the *Semper Fi* to discuss the next step in our minor war in the Bahamas. We needed to come to a consensus on a plan.

Sorensen stayed sitting in the hatchway so he could watch the horizon for any unexpected company. I looked around at our small army and wondered how much I could trust these guys when the going got tough. I mean really tough! I am used to depending on myself and no one else, but I knew I could always count on Sorensen, no matter what. The others were about to be tested!

The first concrete decision we made was that right after dark, Sorensen and I would do a night recon of the perimeter of the entire San Andros community. We would move the boats back up the coast and anchor near the shallow reefs on the northern shore. I needed to recover my scooter from the bushes on the old logging road so we could use it for supply runs into Nicholls Town.

We hauled in the anchor on the *Semper Fi* and untied my boat from its side cleat. I motored up the coast. Top let out a little sail as he cruised up the coast and close to Nicholls Town before turning northwest to hug the coastline. I continued to stay out on the horizon and watched Top with my field glasses. If he saw anything threatening, he would signal me by taking his ball cap off and dropping his sail.

We cruised around Morgan's Bluff. I could now see the house where we had spent some time last week. There was still no sign that the folks who owned it were there. I decided to keep it in mind in case we needed to use it again.

We cruised due west and passed the approximate area where the road went into San Andros. When we were about a mile west, I came about, turned south toward Top, and signaled him to drop anchor when he found a suitable spot. The *Semper Fi* turned south and then slowly drifted north. Top had dropped his anchor and I knew he was secure where he was for now.

I headed a little farther west of his moored position and dropped anchor using my electric Windless. When the anchor bit into the sandy bottom, my boat, like his, spun around and pointed north. I thought it best not to tie our boats together as that would present a larger target for any would-be attackers. Sorensen pulled the Zodiac up snug to the port side of the boat and we both climbed in, bringing with us some special equipment that we may need if things heated up sooner than we anticipated.

I was watching the shoreline with my Bushnell high-powered binoculars, looking for any sign of sentries, when I noticed what appeared to be a line of footprints beyond the high tide mark. I didn't know how old they were and I was not sure when it last rained, but I figured they were recent. We had to be cautious during daylight hours.

Sorensen and I motored over to Top's boat and passed our gear up to Wilson. I could hear Top in the salon speaking on his ship-to-shore radio. He was talking about how great it was here in the Bahamas this time of year. It sounded like he was giving someone an invitation to come down and join him on his boat on vacation.

I stepped down into his salon and he put his finger to his mouth, then winked at me as he spoke. After a little more conversation, he told whoever was on the radiophone that he would watch his email for the flight times and see him then. He signed off and looked at me with a big smile on his face.

Top explained that he just got off the radio with his former commanding officer, who was also retired and a good friend. He wanted someone a little more specially trained to support our efforts and could get about five more former Marines from his old outfit.

Wilson chimed in and said he thought he could contact a few of the guys he met at San Andros for some more up to date intelligence. He knew many of them were very turned off by the assignment, and he was sure they would defect in an instant.

I wasn't so confident. I also was not sure that I wanted outside help in the form of former Marine Recon troops. I certainly didn't want the responsibility. I don't have enough eyes to watch out for that many guys, and when guys are under my watch, they are my responsibility!

I asked Top to hold off inviting any of his friends to our operation until

Sorensen and I had a chance to survey the setup over at the village.

Dusk turned to dark, and so Sorensen and I put our gear into the small Zodiac and cast off. We slowly drifted away from the *Semper Fi* until we could clearly see the shore about a half-mile in every direction. Sorensen took a night vision monocular out of our gear bag and scanned farther in both directions.

There was no sign of sentries or movement on the beach or in the bushes. I motored west about two hundred yards and then eased through the coral reef to the edge of the beach. We dragged the boat up into the bushes, covered it with brush, and then used some brush to obscure our footprints and the boat's drag marks through the sand. We then checked our gear and set out on foot back toward San Andros.

The first thing we did was locate my moped. It was exactly where I had hidden it, and it started the second time I kicked the starter lever. We knew no one had found it or messed with it as it still had a full tank of gas and was ready to go. We decided to leave it right there until we needed it later. I turned the fuel flow valve back off and covered it back up with loose brush.

We were about a half-mile from the road that led to the Village of San Andros, and we walked on the edge of the road in the light brush and trees. There was a strong breeze coming from the east and I could clearly smell food cooking and smoke. The breeze was also good for covering up our footfalls as we stepped on the occasional twig and dead leaves.

When we were about fifty yards from the road into San Andros, I could hear voices and smell cigarette smoke, so I hand-signaled to Sorensen to squat down and stand fast as I assessed the situation. We sat quietly and the voices sounded as if it was a new checkpoint at or near the entrance to San Andros. We had to determine if there were outposts along the road on the way in or on the main highway where we were now hiding. We heard a truck coming from the west and dropped down onto our stomachs. It was a Hummer with a large antenna sticking up at its right rear quarter. I was beginning to believe that these folks had just as much military surplus as a third-world nation. There were two men in the front seats and at least one in the rear. I could see a large rifle sticking up in front of the front seat passenger.

As we were better informed now, we decided to head south through the wooded area parallel to the road into the village. We stayed low and made as little noise as possible. Sorensen used the night scope to diligently scan the woods ahead and look for the heat signatures of hidden sentries.

We were about a hundred yards in when he grabbed and squeezed my arm. With his right-hand index finger, he pointed ahead and to the left. I took the scope and focused in on two men in a small clearing. From what I could tell, they appeared to be digging in the ground with military-type shovels. They were making a lot of noise as they jammed the shovels into the ground and threw the dirt aside. We crept up as close as we could and then had quite a shock! Two bodies were hanging out of a wheelbarrow next to them. The bodies appeared to be Bahamians.

Two diggers were wearing head wraps and were speaking Arabic with a mixture of broken English. What they were saying made no sense to me, but I did understand when one of them spit in the wheelbarrow onto the two dead bodies.

At that point, one of the seemingly lifeless bodies began to groan and then lifted an arm. The two diggers looked mad, lifted their shovels, and beat the person in the wheelbarrow. As I saw blood and flesh flying up from the wheelbarrow, something snapped in my mind and, in a moment of rage, I stood up and walked slowly over to the two. I stood there for a moment as they looked back at me as if I was part of the landscape. I looked at the two bodies and saw they had been mutilated severely prior to their deaths. The scene was horrific as I realized that they had suffered gravely for some unknown reason.

Sorensen walked to my left and, without any signal at all, pulled out his Combat Marine knife. With one long slash, he cut both of their throats, nearly severing their heads off. As they fell silently to the ground, which felt like slow motion, we commenced beating the two diggers into two piles of bloody pulp with our rifle stocks. I guess I had really underestimated just how emotional I was feeling about this case. I was now ready for anything!

We pushed the mush of the two Arabs into the hole they had dug. I took a few photos of the scene with the camera on my phone and texted them to the Major and to Gage as evidence for the trial. I then noticed a small bracelet on the arm of one of the dead Bahamians, so I slipped it off and placed it in my cargo pocket. We pushed some dirt over the remains and placed the two Bahamians on top before pushing the dirt into the hole. We would inform any family the two Bahamians had of where they could find them once this mess was over.

We were far from finished with these San Andros folks. I believe that the entire village, both German and Arab, must have felt my negative energy, because the moment I had that thought, everything went completely quiet. Even the birds and insects were eerily silent. I had not experienced that kind of inner darkness since I was crawling around the corpses in Africa some years before! We humans have far more energy and influence over the environment and our surroundings than we could ever imagine.

Sorensen hand-motioned for me to follow him and we made our way farther south and then closer to the village to the east. We went beyond the German part of the village, skirted the Arab section to the west, and settled in for a surveillance of the area. There was quite a bit of activity around the houses and around what appeared to be their Mosque. There were a few Americans speaking with the men of the village, but neither Sorensen nor I recognized any of them. Sorensen pointed at one of the men and said he thought that one was a "whacker" from Miami—"whacker" meaning a hitman! Hell, they all looked like hitmen to me.

We stayed there in place for a few minutes and then moved farther south through the heavily wooded area where we were told earlier that there was a training compound of some kind.

We came to the edge of a clearing where there were some small, hut-like structures. It reminded me of the John Wayne Training Facility at Quantico, Virginia. We sat silently for a few minutes at the compound's perimeter and, when we could see that there wasn't anyone around, we carefully kneeled up and surveyed the area.

There were about ten small buildings surrounding a central pavilion. Next to the pavilion was a large cage that looked like it would hold four lions or maybe six, full-sized men. The floor of the pavilion was wet and sticky, so I turned on my small Maglite and found it was blood. At this point, with no circus in town, I was guessing it was not lion's blood!

I found a few human teeth and some chunks of flesh that looked fresh by just a few hours. It didn't take much to guess who had been the entertainment here. With disgust, I looked at Sorensen and told him this entire area needed to be shut down as soon as possible and forever.

Sorensen just stood with his rifle over his shoulder and his hand on his hip, looking at the blood and carnage, and said, "Jake, when you're right, you're right, pal!"

It was now quite evident that there was a great deal more going on here than we had previously thought, or even imagined. We had former Nazi war criminals, Arab types carrying sophisticated weapons, and now we'd found they were committing torture and murder. On top of it all, we had

U.S. government officials, U.S. government military-type sub-contractors with U.S. military equipment, and Bahamian officials all directly involved. Among other hideous things, there was a conspiracy by these officials to prevent one old Jewish man from getting a fair trial for a crime that was both trumped-up and defendable.

We made our way back through the woods to the village area and Sorensen and I took note of the security positions on the west side of the village. There were only two checkpoints on that side. One at the main entrance and one at the entrance to the Arab section on the south end of the German village. From what we could tell, it did not appear that there was any mixing of the two groups. The gate near the Arab section was manned by several white, American, military-looking men and two Arab-garbed men. All the sentries were holding assault rifles, and the Americans had pistols on their belts.

From years of experience, I noted that these men and the main entrance guards were very lax in their duties. They were milling around and acting as if there was no threat at all. That also answered my earlier question as to why there were no patrols on the north side where our boats were anchored.

I thought to myself, *It will only be a short while before they feel our sting!* Very soon, the Arab community would be missing their gravediggers. Someone would certainly sound the alarm once they realized their security had been breached.

Sorensen and I made our way back to my moped and rode it west to the shoreline where we'd hidden our Zodiac under some brush. We uncovered the Zodiac, hid the scooter in the same brush, and walked the Zodiac to the beach.

We could see the two boats out on the reef by their navigation anchor lights bobbing up and down on the swells. As we hit the waves leaving the beach, I asked Sorensen if he thought we should involve Top and Wilson in our next step.

Sorensen replied, "Jake, we have little to no choice, pal, just because of the numbers."

I knew we would need a major diversion once we hit the camp. We both knew that the element of surprise was the only hope we had. It was paramount to finding where they had their prisoners housed so we could get them out. I also needed a couple of eyewitnesses to the murder charges against Joel. That was going to be the hard part, as any witnesses had to be bad guys who had nothing to gain by helping us.

We quietly motored our way out through the reef and to the *Semper Fi*. Top was sitting in the cockpit. He greeted us with a smile and a salute as we came alongside.

Top had his long gun leaning on the gunwales beside him. He said he had seen a small boat to the east near Morgan's Bluff about an hour ago, but it turned back east and disappeared around the point shortly thereafter. "It was too far away to see if it was a patrol boat."

We had not seen any Bahamas Naval vessels for quite some time—and that was very unusual in these waters. The only thing we could figure was that they had been advised to avoid the area until this mess was wrapped up.

Sorensen said he would make a few calls to gather more intel on the San Andros front. I told him that I would confer with Gage to see if he had any new intel so we could compare notes. I also needed to call the Major and find out what his agenda was and what the time frame was to deliver any info we could gather for Joel's defense.

As we sat in the cockpit of Top's boat, I saw a flicker of light on the beach to our south. I immediately warned everyone to get down and grabbed the Yukon night vision monocular from my gear bag. I got down on my belly on the edge of the gunnels and looked through the Yukon toward the beach. I could make out the heat signatures of two people standing near the brush just off the beach. One of them flashed a small flashlight toward our boats in what must have been some kind of Morse code. I'd never learned anything except SOS so it was totally lost on me.

Top popped his head up when I described what I was seeing and, as he turned toward the flickering light, he read the message just like he was reading a book.

The men on shore were messaging that they wanted to meet with us to join up with us. I could think of no reason anyone would know who we were or what we were up to in these waters. I asked Top to signal back for them to identify themselves and explain what they were talking about.

Top did as I requested with his Maglite. They immediately replied that they were senior security for Mentor Corporation and a mutual friend in Washington, D.C. had contacted them. They were former Marine Military Police and had no idea what they were getting into when they joined Mentor Corporation. I was surprised by the amount of information transmitted in such a short period of time between Top and the folks on shore. Then again, Court Stenographers blew me away at how quickly they could read back my statements upon request. Not to mention shorthand!

Top signaled them to standby. We all sat together on the deck below the gunwales and tried to figure out our next move. We were concerned that if we granted them an audience, it would confirm who we were. We were also concerned that it would open us up to a barrage of automatic gunfire that would shred the *Semper Fi* and us along with it. After a short, but very serious, discussion, we all agreed that we had no choice but to continue communicating with them.

Top signaled them and asked who the mutual friend from D.C. was. We had a fifty percent chance that we would be chewed up by hot copper and lead. Instead, we received a signal back that said a certain lady politician was a family friend of one of the men on shore. They further signaled that they had been watching for us all day from the marina at the eastern end of town.

I told Top to signal them to lay their weapons on the ground, move away from them, and then I would bring the small Zodiac to the beach to speak with them.

Top and Sorensen would be watching through the scopes and would have the soldiers in the crosshairs of their long guns if they made any move to assault me. Top did not beat around the bush and signaled them that they would be the first to go down if anyone assaulted me in any way. I put my Smith and Wesson Air Weight pistol in my side pocket and climbed into the small Zodiac for the trip ashore. I asked Wilson to watch with the Yukon night scope to see if he recognized either of the two men on the beach.

At first glance, he said, "I do not, Jake."

I had one of Top's small walkie-talkies on my belt and locked the talk button to "on" so they could hear what we were saying at all times from the boat. As I slowly crossed the shallow water over the reefs, I could see the two men now more clearly. One of them was of medium-height and wore a baseball cap with the New York Yankees logo on the front. The other was a bit shorter and bald or had shaved his head.

The closer I got, the more confident I was that they were legitimate. The shorter of the two guys kept his hands up and the other held his out in front of his body as if he was going to do deep knee bends.

I beached the boat and pulled it up out of the small waves lapping on the shore. They both stood off to my right and didn't move a muscle. I let my eyes adjust, then looked around the bushes but saw no sign that there was anyone else hiding nearby. The shorter of the two men requested permission to speak. I put my hand up with my palm out and my right index finger to my lips, telling him to be quiet for a moment as I continued to listen for any sounds that might give away an ambush. After two or three minutes, I walked over to them. Top and Sorensen had a clear shot if they became stupid or cute. They wouldn't be cute for long, and it would be the last stupid thing they ever did, that was for certain!

In a stern voice, I asked them both to take off the light coats they were wearing and turn around with no fast moves. I shook each one of them down and found nothing but a clip knife in the pocket of the taller man. They seemed to be relaxed and positive in their movements and demeanor—enough for me to start asking questions.

The shorter one identified himself as John Martin from Tampa, Florida. He said he had spent eight years in the Marine Corps and Mentor had employed him for about a year. He had just arrived back from Afghanistan two weeks ago. He was immediately sent here to the Bahamas.

The taller man introduced himself as Jim Vann from Oceanside, California. He was originally from Salt Lake City, Utah. Vann said his wife and two kids lived in a house they bought in Oceanside while he was in the Marine Corps. He spent ten years in the Corps and got out after his fifth tour of duty in Afghanistan. His family was sick and tired of his being in the crap of war ever since they had been married. His wife gave him an ultimatum—get out of the Corps or she was leaving him, and she meant it. He got out of the Corps and had worked for Mentor as a Security Trainer for about a year. About a week ago, he was sent down to the Bahamas from his training base in San Diego. Vann's father-in-law was a friend of Senator Lyons, and the man contacted her with the information about the goings-on here in San Andros that Vann had given him. Vann stated that he did not like what he was seeing and feeling about the place and had decided to be a whistleblower if he could get away with it.

After some further questioning, I stepped away and released the send button on my walkie-talkie, then pressed it again and asked Sorensen and Top what they thought. Wilson did not recognize either of them and mentioned that he had been gone from the village before they arrived. Sorensen advised that we bring them over to the *Big Mamoo* and let them chill there while we came up with a game plan.

I asked both men to place their guns, clips, and backpacks on the deck of the Zodiac and we pushed off into the surf. I radioed Sorensen and asked them to watch the brush on the shore for any sign of movement as we motored to my boat.

After I pulled alongside the boat, I tied the aft line to the transom, climbed aboard, and told them to pass their weapons to me and then climb into the cockpit.

Before I left the two on my boat and motored over to the *Semper Fi*, I asked Vann what his relationship was with Senator Lyons. He said his father-in-law and his wife's uncle had been friends with her for many years, and that his father-in-law worked on her campaign during the last two elections. Vann had called his father-in-law the day before yesterday to tell him what he had seen at San Andros and to tell him that he was afraid for his safety if he tried to leave. It might even cost him his life.

His father told him to call him back in two hours and, when he did, he said to watch for my boat. His father-in-law told him that Aunt Jackie wanted him to find me and ask for my help, and that my boat would be a thirty-eight-foot Morgan sloop with a wide spreader on the mast.

Vann had confided in Martin as he knew he felt the same way, and they both decided to try to leave together to find us.

They both stated that they had been AWOL since yesterday morning and had a Hummer hidden in the woods not far from where I picked them up. I told them to stay on the boat, stay down below, and I would consult with the others and be back shortly.

I left the two men and motored over to meet with Sorensen, Top, and Wilson. After telling them the rest of the Mentor men's story, Wilson confirmed most of what they said. I needed to call the Major to confirm Senator Lyons' roll in this and get his guidance. Meanwhile, we had to do a bit more surveillance on the island. The uniforms our new guests were wearing gave me a good idea of how that would come about.

I called the Major and he answered on the second ring. "You're getting slow these days, Major. Letting the phone ring more than once."

He chuckled, then confirmed what Vann and Martin had said. I told the Major that I was doing some recon the next morning and would brief him as soon as I could. The Major said that a number of folks in Washington were putting pressure on the White House to intervene in Joel's case, but so far had met with denials about the safe haven for the Germans and Arabs on San Andros.

He said that the Bahamian prosecutor, the man who set the Major up last week at the Government Building and could not be trusted, was demanding Joel's return to Nassau for trial. I told him I was going after some info in the morning and that I had a number of folks prepared to give testimony regarding the goings-on on San Andros Island.

We signed off, and, after telling everyone what he said, I told them to hit the sack and rest up for a very long day tomorrow. I scanned the beach one more time with the night scope and then went below to get some rest myself. Sorensen took the first watch. I would take the last two hours before dawn.

As I started to slide off into REM sleep on the couch of the *Semper Fi's* salon, I was jolted awake by a quick stomp of Top's foot on the deck directly above me. I turned, grabbed my rifle and sidearm, and slid up the ladderway to the cockpit.

Top was hunched down on the deck, aiming his rifle toward the shore. I picked up the Yukon scope and focused on the beach. There were four people who appeared to be civilians walking east on the shore. One had a walking stick and the other three were waving at our boats. There was just enough light from the stars and clear sky to see them walking on the white beach.

Sorensen came up on deck, took the glasses from me, and said he was sure they were trying to get our attention. I took out my small flashlight, flashed it three times in their direction, and all of them waved frantically. I looked at Sorensen and he nodded as we got ready to go ashore to see what this latest surprise was all about. We sure were gathering a lot of attention while we were trying to hide.

Sorensen, helming the Zodiac, turned toward the beach and powered over the reef heads. As we got closer, I saw that at least one of the people on the shore was a woman. They all appeared to be unarmed. As we slid up onto the beach, they grabbed the bow and pulled us out of the waves. I recognized a woman from Nicholls Town whom we had met last week—or was it the week before? Time was running together now.

Sorensen climbed out of the boat like a Viking ready for battle, looking large and mean as usual with his rifle, and stepped toward them.

They backed up a few steps and the woman said, "Whoa, big guy, we're here to help!"

I asked her how she knew we were here and she replied without hesitation that everyone on the island knew about us. She then quickly added that everyone except the folks at San Andros knew where we were, but not to worry. Our location was safe with the locals.

She introduced herself as Nancy White and said she was a Nicholls Town Deputy Police Commissioner. The three men with her were her cousins, Moe, Paul, and David, and that all of them were from Nicholls Town. Nancy and Moe were going to stay here with us and the brothers, Paul and David, would go back to Nicholls Town to gather additional information for us.

She added, "Calvin is my cousin and he sent us to help you, Jake."

Again! "These islands sure are small."

Nancy had received a call from Calvin about two hours ago asking her to contact us and aid us in lining up some witnesses for the American who had been charged with murder. Calvin was still hiding in Nassau with some relatives, but he promised that he would be over here to help as soon as he had enough support from some government people that he knew he wouldn't be arrested on sight.

The brothers left and we took Nancy and Moe aboard the Zodiac and headed back to the *Semper Fi*.

As we cruised over the reef, Nancy said she was in constant contact with Calvin and added that, because of him, she'd learned a number of foreigners who worked at San Andros were reported missing by their families.

I asked her if she managed to save any of the names of those missing and she handed me a red USB jump drive. She said that all the names and contact people were on the drive, including the Bahamians who turned up missing or whose bodies were found around the island under strange circumstances. Her boss, the local Head Commissioner of Police, was reluctant to pursue the investigations into these deaths, and she believed he was involved—and coincidently very wealthy man as a result! Those incidents were on the USB drive, as well.

After we boarded the *Semper Fi*, I asked Sorensen to make copies of the jump drive onto four or five CDs in case we ran into foul play before getting them to the Major. I knew from experience that CDs can survive water damage, but I was not sure about the jump drive.

I introduced Nancy and Moe to Top and Wilson. She said she had heard that many soldiers had deserted and/or asked for help from the local residents.

We still had a few hours before daybreak so I suggested that we post a watch and get some much-needed sleep. We showed Nancy and Moe to the Salon where they could get a couple of hours of sleep before sunrise and Sorensen and I took the bow V-berths up forward. I fell asleep as soon as I put my head down on the pillow.

I was startled awake at 0630 by the bright sky shining through the glass hatch over my rack. I took a moment to allow my memory to catch up with last night's discoveries. I could also smell the aroma of strong coffee and good old fatty bacon coming down from the galley.

Top and Nancy were busy fixing a great smelling breakfast while Sorensen was already up and cleaning his rifle and two pistols. I've never known Sorensen to have a dirty weapon for more than a few hours. I could see Wilson was standing in the cockpit, though I could only see his legs as I looked through the hatchway above.

I didn't see Moe yet so I figured he was in the forward head. I looked through one of the portlights and saw my boat at anchor. I saw no sign of our newest mercenary teammates, but that was a good thing since, if I could see them, then folks on shore could see then, too.

I picked the walkie-talkie up from the com-table and hailed them. I wasn't sure if it was Vann or Martin, but one of them answered right away and told me all was well and they had plenty of food and water. I told them we were working on a plan and would come over and brief them shortly. I asked them to maintain their positions below deck until after our meeting. They said they would remain below deck and wait for further orders. I was beginning to like these two guys.

I could see that our immediate job was going to be to try to find some of these witnesses and get their official statements to the Major as soon as we could. We also needed to get into and search the so-called training facility.

I asked Nancy if she knew if there was any way to sneak into the south of the village without being detected. She said there was an old dirt trail that used to be the main road before the logging industry shut it down. Her younger brother still used it to gather land crabs to sell.

Moe spoke up and said, "I know the old road well. Years ago, my father told me it was used by the Americans during the Second World War to bring supplies to the airport from the eastern shore."

I asked if either of them knew if the security forces were using it as a supply route. Moe and Nancy didn't know. We definitely needed to check it out. The only problem was the visible exposure across the runway at the airport.

Sorensen and I crossed to my boat using the small inflatable and briefed Martin and Vann on our meeting. There was no practical way I could think of to get them back to the States right now, so I told them they were welcome to stay aboard my boat until there was some form of transport. They said in unison that they wanted to stay, become part of our team, and help us clear up this mess. I asked Martin if I could trade clothes with him so I would fit in over at San Andros. He eagerly consented and I put his military garb on. He took a set of my clothes for a replacement.

I thanked them both and said, "Sorensen and I are going to do a recon this morning and come up with a plan to expose what is going on here at Andros Island."

Martin replied, "We're ready when you need us, right, Vann?"

Vann said, "Ready as anything, sir."

I switched on the generator so they would have air-conditioning to offset the hot sun on the rise. I also showed them the satellite system that they could use to watch TV. They thanked me and said they would monitor the news coming out of Miami that might be of interest to us.

We went back to the *Semper Fi* and sat down with Top, Nancy, and the others to plan our recon mission.

We finally decided that Sorensen, Nancy, and I would go ashore and walk to the airport. We could stay in the tree line along the runway until we reached the old road. From there, we could reach the south side of the village. Most importantly, we needed to stay alive!

We used the small inflatable to go ashore. This time, Sorensen and I carried our M14 assault rifles with the short barrels and breakdown stocks. These were easy to carry and easier to conceal than a conventional weapon.

We also carried our semi-automatic pistols, and both had a small, digital movie camera clipped to the front of our shirts to video as much as possible.

We concealed the inflatable in the brush and crossed over the old logging road. The woods here were easy to move through and the underlying brush scarce but still good concealment if we hunkered down and stayed still. Getting across the main road to the airport was relatively easy, but the woods along the runway were thinner and showed a lot of recent activity with both tire tracks and military boot prints

We cut further east and stayed low as we moved south, stopping every five yards or so to listen for any sound or movement that might give us advance notice of a patrol or sentry post. We saw a civilian pickup going north alongside the runway with one man driving and one man riding on the tailgate. Nancy said she knew them and that they worked at the airport doing general maintenance.

When we got to the clearing that was, according to Nancy, once the main road to the east coast of Andros, we found it was no longer a road but just a dirt path used by trucks with military-type tires, by the look of the tracks. We decided to continue walking south out of the view of the airport workers in the truck.

Nancy told me that a newspaper reporter came to Nicholls Town from Miami a few years ago. Three men claiming to be customs officers picked him up. She only heard about the incident from a former police officer she worked with. He told her that he had never seen these three men before and that he believed them to be Americans, not Bahamians. Soon after, she heard that this police officer was transferred to some faraway island, and she never saw or heard from him or the reporter ever again.

Nancy's story seemed unrealistic in these days of mass communication and organized news reporting. How could human rights violations go on in the Western Hemisphere without the entire world knowing about them overnight? Then I thought about Haiti, Mexico, Venezuela, and some of the other countries that had many of the same problems that the alleged free world ignored.

We moved slowly through the brush until we smelled food cooking and some distant murmurs from the residents of the village. There was still no sign of any guards or early warning systems as we crept closer to the village. Based on the lack of security, I wondered if hidden cameras or some kind of ground movement sensors were observing us. I signaled Sorensen and Nancy to stop and gather around me.

I told them that we were going to separate, one across the road in the bushes and the other on the north side from our current position. I was going to walk right down the middle of the trail as if I belonged there and see what I could see. If there was a confrontation, Sorensen should cause a distraction enough for me to scramble back into the cover of the woods.

I hung my rifle over my shoulder and walked east down the trail. I was wearing dark green cargo trousers and a lighter green, multi-pocketed shirt. I had a black UCF ball cap on pulled down to just above my eyes. So, other than my remarkable white hair sticking out around my ball cap, I looked like all of the other security men in the area.

I walked into a clearing that had the village road running north and south through it. There were a few people standing near some small buildings to my right and a larger building on the east side of the clearing. It had a garage door in the front that made it easy for me to see inside and spot a small sound stage or a movie set. The light wasn't good enough for me to see it clearly, but it appeared to be set up to look like rock formations in a desert—and, it looked vaguely familiar.

As I walked south toward the training area, an armed, Arab-looking man walked out of the building, pushed the door up, and held the door as four other men walked out. One of them was extremely tall—well over six feet tall—and very thin. He was wearing headgear that nearly covered his face and hair. The other men with him were similarly dressed in robes and headcovers. The armed man looked over at me, nodded in greeting, and then looked to the four men. He then closed the large door, locked it with a heavy-duty padlock, and they all walked north toward the village.

I watched as they strolled away from me and thought that I recognized, but couldn't quite place, the tall man as he disappeared around the corner. I turned to the south and walked through a wide path and into a cleared area. I was surprised to find an obstacle course similar to the one I'd run at Parris Island years before. A few small buildings were part of a mock-up of a "John Wayne" close-combat training area. Further south was a wooden mockup of an airplane frame, complete with doors and rows of seats as in an actual airliner. There was no doubt in my mind that this was not only a combat training area but also a terrorist training facility. We had bumped into something down here that no one wanted the world to know about. We needed to get this information out to the Major and the rest of the world as soon as possible!

I turned back toward the trail and saw three Arab men walking toward me. They carried assault rifles and looked unhappy! I kept walking toward them and, as I approached them, I snapped them a proper salute and held it until one of them returned it, slow and proper.

I stopped in front of them and asked how they were doing. The man who saluted me answered with a very proper British accent, "We are fine, thank you. But what are you doing in a restricted area, sir?"

I said, "I am Colonel Jackson Brown and have been charged with the southern camp security."

He said no one had informed him of any such arrangement, as it was his responsibility to secure the Muslim area. I told him to check with the folks at headquarters. Because of the recent problems, things were changing and they were beefing the security up.

I told him a few outsiders were causing problems near the northern village where the Germans were living. We wanted to secure the southern area so it wouldn't spill over and cause them similar problems. I added, "I am looking around to see where I can place sentry positions until the matters get resolved and things get back to normal around here."

I could feel Sorensen's energy focused down through the sights of his rifle the whole time I was talking with these men. I knew if one of them was to make the slightest move to touch me or draw down on me, Sorensen would put all three of them down in two seconds or less. I didn't want to be the recipient of their body waste as Sorensen's large-rounds pulped them.

I took a step backward and told the three men I was going west a few paces and then I was going to report back to my boss about what I thought was needed to secure the southern perimeter. As I moved away, I saw the man in the middle who had been talking to me slip something shiny out from under his shawl. I knew instinctively that it was a knife without clearly seeing it.

I casually put my hand in my pocket and said, "Oh, let me show you something I found on the ground over there." I closed my hand around my ever-present .22 derringer that I always carried in my pocket and shot the Arab two times in the crotch and abdomen just as he lunged toward me with the knife. He continued forward and bent over as if someone had hit him with an ax.

Before I could readjust my aim for the other two, both of their heads exploded from the two quick shots from Sorensen's rifle. The shots were so fast that it almost sounded like one shot. One of the men dropped a wallet-type folder from his shawl as his body collapsed in front of me and I grabbed it up. I quickly turned west and dove through the brush, did a roll, and when I hit my feet, I kept running. Adrenaline is a wonderful thing when you need it.

I ran about twenty-five yards and Sorensen popped out of the brush. He put his hand up and signaled for me to follow him. I saw Nancy to my right holding Sorensen's pistol and facing backward toward the village. We crossed to her side of the path and headed north through the woods toward the main road. With any luck, we would make it to the Zodiac and be onboard the boat before the security folks at the village got their act together to track us. Nothing they had done had impressed us so far. Hopefully, the trend would continue.

As we approached the main road to the airport, we heard three distinct shots coming from the south. They were far off, but no doubt aimed at flushing us out. We crossed the main road and hunkered down in the brush to see if anything was moving to our north before we reached the old logging road near our hidden Zodiac. A dark green Hummer with two men in it raced toward the airport. The Hummer didn't hesitate near our position so we knew we were safe for now. We moved farther north through the brush.

I radioed Top with my walkie-talkie when we got close enough for a signal. I gave him a quick brief that we had stepped into some pretty deep crap and were hightailing it back to the boats to regroup. I asked him to prepare both boats for a quick departure.

We made our way over to the beach and quickly cleared the brush from the Zodiac. Top was just turning north towing the *Big Mamoo* and I could see that Martin and Vann were up in the cockpit wearing body shirts and ball caps. The shirts and caps looked strangely familiar.

We had just cleared the reef when Sorensen bumped my leg and aggressively pointed toward the east. There was a fast-moving boat coming our way and it looked like trouble. Quickly, I radioed Top to stand by with his big rifle—the one that could literally stop a boat dead in the water.

I decided to do what they would least expect of us and turned toward them to take them head on. Sorensen lay down on the deck of the Zodiac and Nancy sat on the deck just forward of me. I told her to reach up and hold the handle to the outboard steady while I prepared my rifle for battle.

The patrol boat was dead ahead and coming at us at high speed. I could see the *Semper Fi* turning east towing my boat. I could also see Top holding his rifle case, which I knew meant *Those guys in the patrol boat are in for a big surprise.* I radioed Top not to let Wilson or the guys on my boat take part in the shooting, as I was worried about any conflict of interest when it came to testifying about their former employer.

As the patrol boat approached, it turned slightly northwest and I could now see the passenger aim his rifle directly at our Zodiac. I looked at Sorensen and nodded. He winked back at me just as the guy on the patrol boat fired.

Sorensen never flinched. He fired and I could see his round striking the shooter right smack-dab in the middle of his forehead. I could actually see the man's head contents spray out the back of his head and fly through the air behind the boat in a red mist.

The only other person on board, the boat driver at the helm, must have panicked because the boat swerved to the right, flipped up into the air, and rolled over into the water. The boat stayed upside down and the huge outboard motor roared and then shut down as it sucked water into its air intake. Everything was completely quiet.

All I could hear was our small outboard idling as we drifted toward the upside-down patrol boat. I goosed the throttle as we looked for the boat driver to pop out from under the boat. There was no sign of him. I pulled our boat closer but still could not see him in the water. Sorensen hung over the side of our boat and, with some effort, pulled one man up that he saw floating just under the surface. It was the man he had shot. He tied the man's body off to the side of our boat with the bowline.

Nancy jumped into the water, went under, and moments later came up with the other man in tow. He was clearly dead. It appeared he had broken his neck when the boat flipped and, as this looked like an accidental death, I told her to leave him floating and pulled her up into our boat. I once again turned north and passed behind the two sailboats floating about fifty yards away. I radioed Top and told him I was going to drag the other guy north and release him where no one would find him. Hopefully, when the capsized boat was found, they would think it was merely an accident and believe that the sharks got the other body.

We towed the body out about five miles, dug the guy's wallet out of his pocket, and removed a ring and his watch. It was an expensive Rolex, probably worth ten thousand dollars. We untied the body and watched it float off and start to sink as we headed back to meet up with Top, who was a couple of miles south and headed in our direction.

When we turned to the *Semper Fi*, I pulled Top aside and asked if our new guests said anything at all regarding the two dead boatmen. Top said Vann knew the two men and that both of them were bad guys

From my boat, being towed by the *Semper Fi*, Vann hooted, "That was an amazing shot Sorensen made."

I nodded in agreement. They both smiled back like they were proud to be part of our group. I asked Top to haul them alongside so they could come aboard and join us.

We continued northwest toward the Gulf Stream. It wasn't as crowded as I thought it would be on Top's boat. In fact, he had berths for everyone should we decide to drop my boat at one of the numerous islands in the area. I placed a call to the Major and told him what we had seen at San Andros.

I had not found any witnesses to the actual killing of the commandant. This troubled the Major. I told him we would circle back to the island and continue our investigation. I didn't mention the latest deaths, as I felt even the Major had his limits on bad news. I told him we were moving the boats and would call him soon with the next update. He said he was getting a lot of pressure from the U.S. State Department to turn Joel over to the Bahamian authorities. I told him to tell them to go pound dirt!

I requested input about our next move from my fellow boat mates. Nancy said she knew a number of Bahamian workers at San Andros and added that the father of one of her friends had worked there for many years. He was retired now and living near Nicholls Town. She said the workers there were a closed-mouthed bunch who were afraid of losing their jobs if they discussed anything about the village.

I asked her to start thinking about who would be the most likely to give us information so we could address the question of who would testify later. I could tell that her wheels were turning regarding my request.

I decided to sail my own boat back into Nicholls Town harbor with Sorensen on board with me. Top took the rest of the crew in the *Semper Fi* about a mile south and dropped anchor. At that distance, our walkie-talkies would still work and we could cover each other's backs without looking as if we were together. As I sailed by the north coast of San Andros, I could see through my binoculars that two boats were near where the patrol boat had flipped over. Our new course back to Andros made us look as if we were just sailing into the area.

I let out the sails as Sorensen manned the helm. Top was now about a mile east of us and making for Morgan's Bluff. I had Sorensen turn south so we could get closer and have a better look at the salvage operation of the overturned patrol boat. We turned east again about a half-mile north of the wreck and saw two other patrol boats near the crash site. Both Sorensen and I stayed low in the cockpit just in case, but the searchers never glanced in our direction.

We dropped anchor as close to the center of the other moored boats as we could. We did not seem to attract any attention. I could see the *Semper Fi* about three-quarters of a mile off our starboard side. He had dropped anchor and was standing in the rear of his cockpit, looking back at us. I radioed Top and told him that Sorensen and I were heading ashore. I asked him to bring Nancy to the beach. We would walk down and meet her after we checked that all was in order.

We took the small Zodiac to the beach. I ran a zigzag route through the other moored boats to see if any of them were occupied. There must have been fifty good-sized sailing yachts and cruisers anchored in the harbor, along with a few really nice catamarans. Most with U.S. homeports or U.S. State boat registrations on their hulls. There did not seem to be any people on the boats. I figured they must have left their boats there to have them available for cruising around the islands and just flew back and forth.

Since there was no sign of anyone, we went ashore at the public landing. I could see the customs agent sitting under an awning and talking with a local. I made sure he saw us. I waved at him and he waved back. He recognized me from my numerous stops here over the past few weeks.

We walked south toward an area where we could see Moe Taylor bringing Nancy ashore near a couple of old buildings on the beach. She looked up at us and shook her head as if to say "Back off!" I nudged Sorensen and we turned to cross over to a small food store. We went in and I looked out the window but pretended to look at the goods on the shelves in the front. I saw Nancy come from the south and stand there for a few seconds. She must have seen them before I did, but I could now see two men—white guys—walking from the back of the buildings and down the way.

Both were carrying sidearms and looked like military types. Nancy, seemingly very confident, greeted them and showed them her credentials in her waist pack. They seemed satisfied and, after a few minutes of speaking to her, turned around and walked back the way they had come.

Nancy walked into the store and nodded as she entered the door. She looked to the rear of the store and asked whoever was back there for three cups of tea. I hadn't seen anyone tending the store, but I now saw that Sorensen was engaged in a conversation with a very large Bahamian lady who stood nearly as tall as he did.

Nancy introduced her as "Momma" to us.

Momma shook our hands like a man and winked at Sorensen with a coy smile. She held his hand a little longer than she did mine. She said to Sorensen, "You are one tall drink of water, now, aren't ya, boy?"

Sorensen didn't say a word, just politely smiled and took a step backward.

Nancy asked Momma how long the two men she had encountered outside had been hanging around the area.

Momma said they, and others like them, had been around for about two days now. They came around asking if anyone had seen two men and their boat, as they were missing. She told them that some guys fishing had mentioned seeing a boat with two men meeting the description heading west toward Miami. They seemed satisfied with that and left, but there had been a sentry presence ever since that day.

She said she had been watching from her side window and saw two different patrol boats cruise around the harbor for a couple of days as they checked each moored boat in the harbor. She thought it was weird, but she hadn't seen the patrol boats in a few hours and had heard that one of the boats capsized earlier today off the north shore.

When she said that, she looked directly at me with that all-knowing look that I was beginning to recognize from these Andros Islanders. They were definitely a special lot with extra-sensory perception!

I took my walkie-talkie out of my trouser pocket and radioed Top, telling him to have his passengers stay low until we dealt with these guys. It dawned on me that they never approached us as we came off the water, and that worried me now. I motioned to Sorensen and Nancy that we should go out the back way and right now!

When we got outside, I scanned the buildings to the left and right and, as I didn't see anything unusual, we ran to the brush line about twenty-five yards to the west. When we were in far enough for cover, I radioed Top and explained that we may be in some trouble.

He said, "I am pulling up anchor as we speak and am moving north toward your position right now, Jake."

We waited a few seconds and started back toward the public landing. All we had for weapons were one sidearm each. I only had two clips for my

9mm, and I was sure Sorensen was just as short on ammo. Nancy didn't carry a firearm, as was the custom of most of the Bahamas Police. Just as we arrived in our Zodiac, I heard the roar of vehicles at high speed coming from the west but heading in our direction. This was not a good sign.

Sorensen looked at me, then at Nancy, and nodded to the west. I knew exactly what he was thinking.

I told Nancy, "We know where there are guns and plenty of ammunition, and that's where we need to be."

I radioed Top and told him there was company coming—and not the kind you invite for tea. I told him to sail back west to where we had been moored earlier. He asked if we needed some cover fire from the waterside, and I told him no, as we were headed for the village through the woods.

We had traveled another hundred feet when we saw the two huge Hummers drive by, headed into Nicholls Town. There were four men in each vehicle and they were all heavily armed. Not what I was hoping for today!

Top radioed that he had the vehicles in his sights and would cruise along the north shore while we cut through the woods about a mile inland. He said Wilson had the helm and he would cruise behind his boat in his Zodiac.

Top added, "If you guys need assistance or a quick ride, I will be ready to go. Just let me know."

As we walked through the woods, Nancy directed us to a small path that led us away from the main road. After about a hundred yards, she put her index finger to her lips and, with the palm of her right hand, motioned for us to stay where we were.

I could smell food cooking and the smell of wood burning. Sorensen and I hunkered down in the brush and waited for Nancy to return.

Sorensen signaled for me to listen and I heard Nancy laugh two or three times. Shortly afterward, we heard someone walking through the woods toward us. Because I could not see them, I pulled out my pistol and stayed low. Nancy walked right up to us, shook her head, and motioned for us to follow her.

As we followed her, I noticed that the narrow path we were on was once a fairly wide dirt road. I looked directly behind us and could see that it ran back to the main road. We turned southeast and I saw a clearing, but no sign of any buildings. I could smell the smoke and food much stronger now.

I asked Nancy, "Where are we going and what are we doing?"

She smiled and said, "I want you guys to meet someone. I think he could be a huge benefit to us."

We walked around the clearing and into the shade of some large trees. I now realized that the smell was corn or some other grain cooking and, I knew before we arrived, that it was an old-fashioned alcohol still. One of my first assignments in the Marine Corps was to seek out these illegal stills and destroy them before they killed or sickened the many civilians—as well as military men—in the coastal South Carolina area. I don't recall those stills ever smelling as good as this one!

As our eyes adjusted to the low light from the umbrella effect of the trees, I saw the stills. There were two of them and they were working hard. Steam was rising from the valves and the collecting bottles, which were old, three-gallon water bottles, each about half full. A small man was kneeling down next to the farthest still and stoking the wood fire below it.

He stood up, brushed off his hands as we approached, and shook our hands when Nancy introduced us. I was shocked to see it was Moe, who was supposed to be on Top's boat! Nancy saw my surprised look and laughed at the confusion on my face. It then registered that she had called him "Larry" Taylor.

Sorensen apparently was not suffering the same confusion as I was. "So, when do we meet 'Curly?'"

Nancy didn't hesitate for a second and told us that there was indeed a third brother and his name was Curly. He lived in Miami, Florida. Mr. and Mrs. Taylor were obviously big fans of *The Three Stooges*. I just chuckled.

Nancy explained that she and the Taylors had been friends since they were small children. Larry had been running this illegal still for many years, making high-quality liquor for the local community. She said that some of his biggest clients were the Germans at San Andros.

He said he wasn't even born when the Germans arrived in the early-to mid-Fifties, but he learned soon enough after being around them that they liked their booze, and they liked it strong. He had been supplying them for over thirty years now. He tried to sell to the Arabs when they arrived both before and after 9/11, but they were teetotalers. He had a brisk business going with the Americans since their arrival after the old German fellow was killed.

I asked him if he knew anything about the killing of the German and he said, "Yep, I saw the whole thing."

I was shocked!

Larry offered us each a drink from his still, but, as we like our eyesight and life, we nicely declined.

I asked him to describe what he saw and he told me.

"I saw the old German leader skulking between two buildings. The old man was carrying what looked to be a large sword in his hand and it looked menacing." Larry's voice went up a notch. "I then saw another, smaller, old man come from behind an old Volkswagen. He was definitely trying to get away. The big German ran up to him and swung the long sword at the smaller man, striking him on the top of his arm. The small man fell, got up, and tried to get away again, but was struck a second time with the sword as the big German rushed him in a rage. The smaller man fell on the ground again, and then the big German tripped and fell onto the smaller man.

"There was a piece of pipe stuck in the big German's face. Then about ten more Germans grabbed the smaller old man and held him down on the ground. These people were kicking and stomping on the man as he lay there, screaming for mercy! They were all shouting that the commandant was dead."

Larry said he waited quietly for a few minutes, then decided to run back through the woods to his home and only told his wife what he saw. They both talked about it for hours but decided to keep quiet for fear of being arrested for his alcohol dealings.

I knew that Joel had acted in self-defense, but was flat out amazed to hear that the commandant had attacked him with such rage as if he knew who Joel was. I wondered how the German recognized Joel after so many years.

I asked, "Who else may have seen this, Larry?"

He said there were at least ten people standing near the attack who saw the German attack the smaller man.

My next problem was standing right in front of me. I badly needed Larry to write and sign a sworn statement and agree to testify at trial. The problem was his illegal occupation—which was his livelihood. Somehow, we would have to try to protect him from prosecution.

I pulled Nancy aside and asked what the laws were in the Bahamas pertaining to illegal alcohol. She said they were more or less the same as they were in the U. S. I explained my dilemma to her and she said that everyone on the north island bought from him and, in fact, the prime minister favored Larry's brew above all others on the islands. This still didn't help. Perhaps the Major could work out a deal with the politicians. It was at least worth a try. I was thinking that maybe now I needed that drink from Larry's still!

I used Sorensen's cell phone to record Larry Taylor's statement. I told Larry to leave out the part as to why he was there in the first place, as well as his current occupation. Afterward, I sent a text of the entire statement and comments to the Major's cell phone. In a separate text, I sent our current dilemma status. I figured that he would find a way to get Larry's info into court without endangering the man's liberty and further pursuit of happiness.

he next order of business was our present problem of staying alive while being hunted by numerous para-militants searching for us on the main road. Larry volunteered to take us through his special path, which took us to within a hundred yards of the German village. He said he would be available to speak with the Major when it was time.

I thanked him and asked him to make a list of all of the people he could think of who may have witnessed the attack on Joel by the German fellow. I asked Nancy to get this list to me as soon as possible.

I also told Nancy it was probably best for her to head back to Nicholls Town while Sorensen and I made our way back to Top's boat. She agreed and headed east with Larry. Sorensen and I decided to walk right through the village and see if we could bluff our way through to the beach.

As we entered the village, we could see a few militants milling around the road back to the Arab sector. We could not see the front gate area from where we were but we could hear a number of trucks or Hummers running on the road. We walked casually west and talked about some made-up nothings so we looked relaxed and normal.

As we neared the woods on the west side of the village, a man with a strong German accent asked us to help him with something. Sorensen looked at him and said, "Sure" right away.

We walked with the older man to a small, ranch-style house. He introduced himself as Von Viegle. He was pleasant and thanked us twice for our time before we went into his house.

Inside was like going back in time. The furniture had wooden arms that you would see in most American homes going back a few decades, with heavy upholstery on the larger pieces. The walls were covered with large black and white still photos from the 1930s and 40s. They were mostly pictures of cities from a bird's eye view. Most of them were framed and crossed with target lines as if they'd been taken through a rifle sight. In fact, I quickly realized that that was exactly what they were; they were bomb sightings taken through a bombardier's site!

There were also photos of German officers in group poses, and many photos of German aircraft. It looked like a war memorial. Every wall was covered with photos or memorabilia from the German Army. I noticed one picture that nearly froze me in my tracks. It was a photo with a title below in German. I quickly recognized one guy as Von Viegle and the other as a very young Col. Stefan Braun, the dead commandant Joel was accused of murdering. His sleeves were rolled up and he was clearly showing off the tattoo on his right arm. He was standing with a group of other German officers. They were at the forefront of a group of half-starved POWs. It was a black and white photo framed in black wood.

I glanced over at Sorensen and nodded toward the framed photo. He winked and as the old German and I walked into the next room, Sorensen stayed behind. I knew that when we came out, there would be a missing photo or two on the wall.

Von Viegle took me into his kitchen, showed me a large wooden box, and asked me to carry it back to the checkpoint. I said sure and lifted the box slowly. The articles inside rattled some and I could smell oil. I asked him what was in the box and he said it was his guns and that the security men had asked for them. I did not know what he was talking about but I carried them anyway.

I could see that Sorensen was standing in the doorway, waiting for me to come out, so I got out of the way and let the old man pass into the living room. Von Viegle went out of the front door and we followed. I told Sorensen that the box held the guns they asked for and Sorensen nodded in acknowledgment.

I told the man that we would bring the box to the checkpoint and that he could stay here at home. He looked at me and said he would go with us to check them in because he wanted to get them back after the crisis had passed. I looked at Sorensen and raised my eyebrows to signal him that I knew we were in deep crap unless we did something quickly. I looked around and could only see two other people some distance away from us.

I considered decking the old man but thought better of it when I realized a blow to the face or head would probably kill him at his age. I sat the box down on a lawn chair in front of his house and pretended to answer my cell phone. I mimicked a conversation and signed off. I told Von Viegle we had to handle a matter right away and would come back for the box in a few minutes. He said he would wait and Sorensen and I walked farther into the village and away from the old man.

Sorensen complimented me for the quick thinking and mentioned that Von Viegle would have believed a monkey at his age. Sorensen said he had the photo and a couple of others showing Von Viegle much younger and in uniform with the commandant at a POW camp. He said he had also taken a couple of other random photos that could be used to prove what was going on here at San Andros.

We walked toward the Arab area and, as I looked for a path that would lead us to the airport, a couple of security men walked toward us. Sorensen moved about two feet away from me to give us both room to maneuver, as it appeared, we were going to need it. One of the militants started to pull his sidearm out of its holster when they were within ten feet of us.

I greeted them with a hearty nod and asked, "Is it always this hot and humid here, guys?"

The man with his hand on his gun hesitated just a moment when I said that, and it was enough time for me to sucker punch him to the ground. He slammed down and didn't move a muscle. I didn't have time to look over at Sorensen, but I knew his guy was out cold, too. I grabbed the fallen man's pistol and Sorensen took the rifle the other man was carrying.

I quickly looked around and saw only civilians watching us. I grabbed Sorensen's arm and we walked double-time toward the Arab area. As soon as we cleared the first corner, we headed west through the woods toward the airport. We were looking for the path we had taken earlier with Nancy.

Suddenly, I heard some shouts behind us and the sound of a vehicle coming from the front of the village. I stopped and said to Sorensen, "Like it or not, we need to change our direction and head back toward them, buddy."

If we could join them during their confusion and pursuit, we might have a chance of surviving this ordeal and escaping to live another day.

We came out of the brush about fifty yards north of where the two militants had confronted us. There were half a dozen militants running toward the fallen men and perhaps another ten already at the scene. I could see that one of the men on the ground was shaking his head as he was talking to the group and pointing south away from us.

We were back in front of the Von Viegle house, so Sorensen picked up the box from the table where I had left it. We continued walking toward the front gate and the area I thought might be the headquarters building. Sorensen had the militant's rifle hanging over his shoulder as he carried the box out in front of him. I noticed that he had his pistol in his hand underneath the box. I had my pistol and the other fallen militant's pistol stuck in my belt under my loose shirt.

As we approached the main gate, we noticed that there were only two guards posted outside and no movement in the gatehouse.

Sorensen looked directly at one of the sentries and asked, "Where do you want the German's weapons to be placed? He said they were supposed to be brought over to the security office in the Community Center."

Sorensen set the box down on a small table next to the guard building and, out of curiosity, I opened the top and looked inside. I was shocked to see two Ingram Mac-10 machine guns and an old German Luger pistol in perfect condition. There was no ammunition in the box, but about two dozen clips for the automatics and pistol. What in the heck was Von Viegle doing with this much firepower, especially in a country that did not allow firearms at all—at least as far as I had been led to believe?

I asked the two guards if we could leave the box there for a while as we patrolled the main road. I told them we needed to secure the perimeter. Both guards treated us as if we belonged there and had rank and said, "Yes, sir," every time we spoke.

One said, "That will be fine, sir. We'll look after the box until you come back for it."

Sorensen and I stepped away from the guardhouse and only got a few feet when we heard a vehicle coming up the road behind us from the village. We continued to walk, paying no attention to it.

We heard it stop at the gate. I signaled Sorensen to turn left into the woods off the road and we continued a few feet into the brush until we were out of sight from the gate. I then tapped Sorensen's arm, double finger-pointed to the woods, and we took off running through the trees.

As we were running, I heard a man shout, *"Halt!"*

I glanced over my shoulder and could not see anyone, so we continued on our course. Just then, a shot rang out from the road. We turned slightly south and then ran due west until we came to a path that went north and south from the main road.

I could hear limbs snapping, some muffled shouts, and some heavy running in the brush. We figured the chase was on!

There were a couple of more shots fired from the pursuers, but they had no idea yet where we were. As far as they knew, they could have been shooting at their own men.

Luckily, the ground under our feet was covered in pine needles, so we didn't leave any footprints. We were in good shape unless they brought out the tracking dogs. But, we still hadn't seen any sign that they had any dogs, so we figured we were safe.

We followed the path until we got to the airport road. We half-walked and half-trotted through the woods next to the road. I stopped every few minutes and tried to get a radio call to Top on his boat. I figured he was too far away and the trees were blocking the signal. We headed for the old logging road. I tried to contact Top again and still had no response. We were now close enough that I should have had a good signal, so I started to worry that all was not well with Top and the boys.

We picked up our pace, made it to the beach in record time, and lay down on the sand where it met the brush. From our current position, we could see the *Semper Fi* had a small patrol boat tied to its port side and two other boats slowly circling around it. There were two men in each of the circling boats, one man in the boat alongside Top's, and one standing in the cockpit of the *Semper Fi.*

The men were definitely militants and holding combat rifles. The man standing in the cockpit was aiming down toward the deck—and that was where I thought Top and the others must be kneeling or lying down. At a closer look, I could see that the man in the cockpit was shouting at whoever was down on the deck.

We needed a plan and we needed it quickly or the militants were going to bring Top and the others ashore. And, I was sure that the American militants rather than the local authorities would hold them. That thought gave me an idea.

I pulled out one of my cell phones (I was now carrying three) and called Nancy White. She answered almost before the first ring. I told her what was going on aboard the *Semper Fi* and asked if she could do anything to override the Americans. She said she was at Nicholls Town and would call me back in a few minutes.

Sorensen and I stayed low in the brush and watched the boats, feeling helpless. About ten minutes later, Nancy called back and said she was on the police commissioner's boat heading for the *Semper Fi.*

I asked Sorensen what he thought the range was with the strange-looking assault rifle he had taken earlier from the militant.

He said, "I can probably get some rounds to hit the water around the boats if I aim high enough, but that's about it, buddy."

I told him that we might have to cause a little diversion when Nancy arrived.

As we watched the ocean, we heard a boat coming from the east—a large cabin cruiser with a stripe on the side. As it approached Top's boat, it lit up its blue light bar attached to a stainless-steel tubular frame on the roof. It was Nancy and two uniformed Bahamian policemen. They circled the three boats and Nancy spoke through a loudspeaker and told the militants to lay down their weapons.

The two uniformed policemen did not appear to be armed. One of the militants raised his rifle and aimed it at Nancy.

I told Sorensen to see how close he could place a round next to the boats. Sorensen took a few moments to look down the barrel of the rifle and then fired three rounds that struck the water just short of the boat carrying the militant pointing the rifle at Nancy.

The man swung around and randomly fired a volley of rounds toward the shore, but none struck even close to where we were. He then turned back and again pointed his weapon at Nancy and her policemen. I looked at Sorensen and nodded.

Sorensen took only a fraction of a second to fire two rounds. I couldn't believe my eyes—especially as far away as we were—as the blast blew the militant off the boat. The air on the other side of him turned crimson with blood as he flew through the air and fell into the blue waters below. I was amazed at the shot—as was Sorensen.

He looked at me and said, "What the hell, Jake?"

And, we both looked down at the rifle.

It was a strange-looking black composite stock with a large magazine. I picked up one of the spent shells and saw that it was a standard 30-30 cartridge. I then noticed that the primer and shell were wax coated the way some self-loaders were. This round was definitely special loaded for sure and probably held far more grains of powder than a normal round.

While we were still looking down at the rifle, we heard the roar of outboard motors and saw that the three militants' boats were roaring off toward Morgan's Bluff. Top was now standing up in the cockpit as Nancy's helmsman pulled the patrol boat alongside the *Semper Fi*.

I called Top on the walkie-talkie.

His first comment was, "Holy shit, Jake! Who fired those rounds?"

"I have no idea what you're talking about, Top." I winked at Sorensen.

I told Top to stand fast and we would talk about it later. For now, I advised him to get under sail and motor as fast as he could north. I told him to stay in international waters until I contacted him in the next couple of days. I was very specific that he should not go to any port in the States until we discovered what the militants knew, as we did not know what they might report to the authorities.

I asked if he had enough food and water for five days. He said he did. He also reminded me that he had an onboard desalinizing filter system for converting seawater to fresh drinking water. I told him either I or the Major would be in touch with him soon. Even as we spoke, I could see his sails running up on their electric winches. Top was on his way.

I then called Nancy with a little bit of an attitude. I told her she needed to go back to Nicholls Town and file a formal complaint against Mentor Corporation for as many charges as she could nail them with, including threatening to shoot a Bahamian police officer.

I said, "I don't know who in the hell they think they are, but it's time to take some action against these assholes!" I asked if she could have one of her friends with a boat pick us up from the beach west of where she was and take us out to my boat. She said she would call her cousin to see if he was heading back in from fishing and could give us a ride.

She said, "Jake, there is a reef about a quarter-mile west that extends out into the water. It would be a good pickup location.

"Great, and thanks for being there when we really needed you, Nancy."

She smiled a smile I could see a half-mile away and waved goodbye.

Sorensen and I looked at one another, shrugged, and walked into the brush just off the hot, sandy beach. We could hear no other boats in the area, nor could we hear any vehicles on the old logging road. We eventually came to the reef elevated from the surf, just as Nancy had described and waited for any sign of Nancy's cousin.

Neither Sorensen nor I had eaten anything since yesterday and it was catching up with me. With Sorensen's muscle mass and size, I don't know how he endures long, extended periods of time without eating.

We stayed down low in the brush until we saw a small fishing boat slowing and turning into the beach. We could see an older Bahamian man at the wheel. We left the brush and ran straight to the boat. The water was shallow next to the reef, but the boat had a wide bottom so he could fish the shallows.

His name was Patrick White and he looked to be about fifty years old. I figured he looked older than he probably was because of the many years in the harsh, burning Bahamian sun.

I politely said, "May we come aboard, Captain?"

He nodded, shook both our hands, and showed us the cleared area under the bow cover of his boat. We climbed in out of sight and, as we settled in, he backed the boat with its small, diesel engine into the deeper water.

Patrick turned the boat to the east and, over the sound of the diesel engine chugging, I asked him if he could drop us off south of Nicholls Town so we could meet up with Nancy. He said his own dock was about half a mile south of the town and was secluded from the other houses. I told him that would be a better choice. I thought it best not to tell a local something he knew more about than I would ever know.

When Patrick pulled up to his dock, Sorensen and I stayed put until Patrick walked out to his house and scanned the road for any dangers. A few minutes later, I heard Nancy call to us that all was safe and that we could come out.

Nancy and Patrick were standing on the shore as we climbed out of the boat. They walked down the dock. Nancy had a bag with some nice-looking sandwiches and bottles of water for us. Patrick was already eating his.

Sorensen and I ate with relish and my stomach thanked me with every swallow! I wasn't even sure what I was putting in my mouth.

I again called the Major in Miami and advised him of the day's events. I left out the part about the amazing long shots by Sorensen. The Major said he had been meeting with Joel and that he was holding up well for a man nearing ninety years old or older

Joel was a pretty tough guy. I told the Major that I would do what I could to keep Larry Taylor safe, as he was our only eyewitness at this time.

The Major said he was meeting with some Bahamian officials and would decide if he should reveal what we knew about the assault on Braun. I asked him to be cautious with the information as I thought these folks would do anything to continue to cover up what had been going on here.

I know the Major well enough to know a smiling face and a happy handshake can influence him! It worried me that he would give up our information source too early in this fight.

When I got off the phone, I took Nancy aside and asked her about getting Larry to hide out for a while until we could get his testimony. She knew it was a good idea but said Larry would never go for it. His business was too competitive and he would lose his income, and maybe even some of his customers.

With this problem in mind, I now needed to get Larry some personal security that could overlook his illegal activities and protect him. I contacted Calvin for some help.

Nancy led us to a small, beautifully painted house on a back road near the center of Nicholls Town. When we walked inside, I saw that it was quite modern, with a large-screen television and comfortable furniture around the small living room. The dining area of the kitchen had two laptop computers and two multi-function printer-fax machines. She explained to us that this was the North Andros Island Office of Intelligence. Primitive compared to U.S. standards, but quite sufficient for Bahamian needs.

I noted that the doors were not locked and the windows had no locks or alarms on them.

She said, "It isn't necessary as no one would bother us here without being observed immediately. Not to worry, Jake." She added that there was little to no significant information on the old computers.

I asked her how far back the historic information went. She said it had some facts and stats that predated the Bahamas' independence from Great Britain. I thought for a second, then asked her to please look up the arrival of the Germans at San Andros. She said she would, but added that there were many folks still around who lived here during and after World War II. She remembered her mother telling her, when she was very young, that there were very bad people living there and never to go there with her friends.

I was still finding it hard to believe that an entire town of former Nazi senior officers had lived this long right under the public's nose—and no one had ever discovered them other than Joel and his friend. I knew there were Nazi hunters all over the world and even knew the headquarters for these groups was in the Miami area.

It goes to show that governments can wield a great deal of power and cover up anything they want—anywhere!

Our present problem was getting around the manhunt for us without losing any ground. I was not sure where we needed to be, but I knew we needed more witness information for Joel's defense. Having just one witness was dangerous for both the witness and for Joel. The Major said that Joel was doing well, but a man that age was surely feeling the pressure.

Sorensen and I needed to clean up and change our clothes. We were ripe by now and our enemies, if professionals at all, would be able to track us by smell alone. I asked Nancy if someone could tow my boat a little farther south so we could board without drawing too much attention, freshen up, and regroup. She consulted with Patrick and said it would be handled in short order.

We finished our food—though I still wondered what it was—and drank some more water before walking out of the back door. I got my sense of direction and we turned north to move closer to the port where Patrick was towing our boat.

Nancy said that Patrick was pulling the *Big Mamoo* into a small boat repair area where he would hide it from the waterside or anyone driving or walking down the road. We patiently stood in the bushes by the road, waiting. A number of Bahamians walked by and could clearly see us but no one so much as glanced our way. It was amazing how united these folks were. I am not sure I will ever understand their ability to communicate with each other so swiftly and quietly—a trait the U.S. could learn from.

About thirty minutes later, I saw the mast first, and then Patrick's boat towing my sloop around the point and into the inlet. The old boat looked pretty damn good as I studied its sleek hull and massive custom mast. It seemed like I hadn't slept in my rack in weeks, and there was no sleep like the sleep on that boat as it bobbed at anchor in a safe harbor with the waves lapping at her sides.

Patrick pulled the boat in and then swung it around so it was facing east. He backed up and released the anchor, then hauled the aft mooring line to the dock where we were standing and passed me the line. Sorensen stepped aboard and opened the cabin hatch using the combination on the lock. If someone had tampered with the lock, it would have failed to open on the first attempt. Sorensen carried his pack and weapons down into the cabin salon.

I stayed on the upper deck for a while and talked with Nancy about lining up a couple of more witnesses regarding the death of the German, Commandant Braun. She said she would get the constable who was on duty that night to meet with me, as he had expressed doubt over the story concocted by the Germans the day after Joel was taken into custody. I told her I would meet with him at her little intelligence office in a couple of hours. Nancy was a godsend and was making our lives much easier than she would ever realize.

I looked down into the cabin and saw that Sorensen was already in a sound sleep on the side seat next to the galley. Sleep sounded good to me, too, but I needed to shower and change my clothes before I was expelled from the Bahamas for smell pollution! Nancy told me there was a shower facility in the building next to the dock area. I grabbed some clean clothes and made my way to the building. As I approached it, I heard a sound, looked down the road toward town, and saw a Hummer driving slowly toward the center of the small town.

Nancy walked by me and said, "Not to worry, Jake. They won't get any information from the villagers."

Although I was leery, I went into the small building and turned on the much-needed shower. As I let the warm water flow over my sweaty body, I heard the Hummer pull up outside by the small marina. I stood on tiptoes and saw Nancy speaking with the two occupants of the vehicle. The driver smiled, laughed at something Nancy said, and then drove off.

It dawned on me that I hadn't told Sorensen that a vehicle was coming after seeing it down the road, and knew immediately that I could have made a fatal mistake.

Just then, I saw movement out of the corner of my eye. I saw Sorensen slip out of a brushy area next to the marina carrying his newly claimed rifle. He was bent low to the ground as if he was stalking, and he looked pretty menacing. I knew him well enough to know exactly what he was doing.

I tried to signal him from the window but he was too low to see me in his peripheral vision. I quickly wrapped a towel around my midsection and rushed out the door. I spoke his name as he came even with the building. He looked over at me and started to tell me that we had company just as I told him that Nancy had defused it already. Sorensen took a deep breath and calmed down.

When I finished showering, Sorensen did the same. Afterward, we met with Nancy at a picnic table in the marina courtyard. I made a satellite call to Top and he reported he was about five miles off Miami. He was going to dock and drop off one or two of his passengers and collect some provisions before heading back to San Andros in case he was needed here.

Nancy said she was going to set up a meeting with some of the townspeople to see who had any knowledge of the German's death that night and who would be willing to speak to me. She said there were people who had lived their entire lives on the north side of the island and had never seen even one of the Germans.

Sorensen and I went back to my boat and cleaned our weapons— something we hadn't done for days. I believed this was the longest period of time that Sorensen had ever gone without cleaning his weapons. It was a wonder that they still functioned with all the sand and saltwater they had been exposed to. Afterward, we chose the weapons we were going to carry next and placed the rest in their proper hiding places. I put enough ammunition in my backpack to sink a small ship and gave Sorensen about twenty clips for his two pistols and the special AR he was now carrying. That rifle was amazing as it folded out to about eighteen inches and, without a clip jammed into the bottom, was only about six inches wide. It fit nicely under his jungle jacket and hardly produced a bulge. I carried two 9mm semi-autos that I stuck in my belt. I also carried the rifle I had secured in Miami. Fortunately, the case looked more like a small briefcase instead of a rifle case. It had one quick-release flap that was easy to open if an emergency presented itself.

Patrick had generously put a case of spring water on the back of my boat and Sorensen and I put two bottles each into our pockets. I saw Nancy standing near the road so I waved at her to join us.

When she arrived, I told her we needed to check on Larry Taylor to make sure he didn't disappear if or when the Major released his statement to the other side. The only way to preserve his safety and keep him alive was to get him on Top's boat and out of harm's way. Nancy thought this option didn't have a snowball's chance in hell but was willing to give it a shot. She said we could look him up after she finished with her meetings with the townsfolk in just a little while.

Sorensen wandered into town to make sure there was no ambush waiting for us. The Hummer that had passed us earlier returned, and it headed toward San Andros. I called Top again and he said he was docked at Fort Lauderdale. He would be setting sail in less than an hour. He said he tried to get rid of a few of his passengers, but with no luck as no one wanted to abandon the cause yet.

I signed off and called the Major. I got his voicemail and left him a message. To round off the calls, I contacted Dave and gave him an abbreviated version of what was going on and asked him to keep the plane fueled and ready for action.

He said, "I have been staying on the island to watch it more closely during the night and there have been very few flyovers."

Flyovers were normal as my island was just west of Patrick Air Force Base near the shore of south Merritt Island.

He said, "The plane is already fueled and ready to fly, boss."

The nice thing about where I keep my plane is I could get to it by water in less than fifteen minutes from the island. I signed off from Dave and tried the Major again. This time, he answered on the first ring.

The Major said that he let his friend Senator Lyons listen to the interview of Larry Taylor. She was going to start spreading the word around Washington regarding the village on Andros Island. She had heard there were many very important people involved in the operation for years.

The Major said there were many prominent politicians and corporate CEOs sweating that their names would be associated with this exposure. This, he said, was our most dangerous front. If there was government involvement surrounding this then we could expect an army of resistance before it was properly exposed. He said that he had already tried to get the media involved but the stories were being immediately squelched.

I told him I would continue to build our case by gathering witnesses and that he should keep me informed of his moves. He agreed and signed off.

As Sorensen and I waited for Nancy to get back from her meeting, I noticed the sky to the west was starting to darken. When the sun sets in the islands, you either get multi-colored skies or it turns a deep blue just before the dark of night settles in.

I asked Sorensen to suit back up so we could leave our little hideout under the cover of the rain. We found Nancy speaking with a few people across from the marina. As we approached, I looked at Nancy and pointed to the sky. She nodded.

It wasn't long before it started to pour. The storm built to near hurricane winds and included pounding rain and raindrops the size of quarters. The three of us jogged down the muddy road, staying close to the brush, and as the ground was soaked, it became a quagmire. We had to keep to the grassy areas or we would get bogged down.

We saw no patrols or Hummers along the way so we figured staying on the road a bit longer was our best option. About a half-mile out of town, Nancy took a left and went down a narrow path to the southwest. I recognized the path and knew that it would lead us to Larry Taylor's stills. The rain was still coming down hard and furious and the path was starting to flood and flow back toward the road. I wiped the rain from my eyes and noticed that there were a lot of deep boot prints that were filling with water.

This wasn't a good sign as far as Larry was concerned. I tapped Sorensen on the shoulder, pointed to the boot prints, and Sorensen nodded. I quick-stepped up to Nancy and touched her arm. She stopped and I pointed out the quickly fading boot prints.

She looked at them, then back at me, and said, "Larry has early warning systems in place. It won't be easy to catch him off guard, Jake. He is a real professional at this game."

I suggested that we get off the trail and cut through the woods in case there was a reception party waiting for us. We all agreed and moved toward the south.

Sorensen took point with Nancy between us. I was focused on our rear flank in case we had missed anything along the way. The rain was still coming down steady and that was good for us. However, it could also be good for an ambush party up ahead.

As we moved slowly along, I saw Sorensen tense up and stop. He raised his arm with his fist clenched. We all stopped and kneeled down so the brush concealed us. He pointed up ahead and, as I moved the brush aside, I saw what I believed to be two Americans standing in a clearing not fifty feet in front of us. They were wearing camouflaged jungle utilities. Both had rifles and sidearms. When I looked closer through the rain, I saw Larry sitting next to a tree with his hands tied behind his back. I could see a mixture of rain and blood running down his face. He looked as if he had been beaten badly about the face and neck.

We looked around to see if there were any other militants in the surrounding area. Sorensen signaled me with two fingers that he could only see two men. I pointed to the man on the left and nodded at him. He nodded in return.

I placed my hand on Nancy's shoulder and pressed her lower to the ground. I took out my small Beretta 9mm and placed it firmly in her hand. I whispered that the safety was on and a round chambered. She nodded. I looked at Sorensen and we both moved at the same time.

There was a loud crack of thunder. We took three steps each and were on the two men before the flash of lightning had time to dissipate. I slammed my right fist directly into the right side of my guy's head as he was facing away from us and, as he went down, I saw Sorensen's guy already on the ground, out cold and in the mud. From where I was standing, both guys looked like pigs in slop.

Nancy jumped out of the brush and was at Larry's side in a flash. Sorensen and I were still making sure there were no other hidden militants in the area. We didn't see any but, at that moment, one of the two downed guys' radios chirped and a voice came on asking for an update. No other voice responded so I knew they were trying to reach these two.

I grabbed the radio out of its holder on his ammo belt and then Sorensen and I picked Larry up while Nancy untied his hands. He was still conscious and able to stand on his own. After a second, he shook himself loose from us, stepped over to one of the guys on the ground, and delivered one hell of a kick to the side of the guy's face.

I said," I bet that is going to hurt in the morning!"

I then told everyone that we needed to get lost, as I believed the area would be swarming with bad company soon. The man on the radio was getting more and more insistent and asking for an update.

Larry was very weak from his beating, so we helped him back along the trail toward the road. It was still raining quite hard and the wind was picking up and making so much noise that we were unable to hear anything ahead of us. Nancy pointed to the woods to the east and we turned and started walking quickly back toward the village.

Larry started telling Nancy how when he arrived at his still this morning he noticed the footprints on the path. He turned to leave, but four white militants who had been hiding in an ambush near his still equipment apprehended him. He said they questioned him about anyone coming through his area in the past few days. He told them he had seen no one and that his area was well hidden from the general view. They questioned him thoroughly for a couple of hours but he told them nothing. Two of the militants left and the other two stayed and continued to interrogate him.

Larry said there was nothing nice about their interrogation tactics. One of them, the one he kicked before leaving, started looking around his stills and found the note from me with my cell numbers on it. That was when the guy came over, called him a liar, and started to punch him in the face and kick him all over.

He kept telling the militant that the numbers belonged to a couple who wanted to buy more of his shine for delivery to Nassau, but the militant kept beating on him until the other militant stopped him.

They were waiting for a vehicle to take Larry to San Andros for more questioning. Larry added that when he made a delivery yesterday, there was a lot of activity at the Village. It looked like some of the Arabs were packing and getting ready to leave.

This presented an entirely new problem. We needed photographs to prove what we had seen here and we needed them right away. The videos we took with our mini-cams did not show enough of the village to prove how large an operation San Andros was. I asked Nancy if she and Larry could get back to Nicholls Town without me and Sorensen. She said she could.

I told Sorensen that we needed to do a photo survey on the village right now. He agreed.

As we headed west toward San Andros, I saw Nancy and Larry continuing east. I had two small HD digital cameras in my backpack. I gave one to Sorensen and kept the other.

We stayed in the brush for about a mile and then turned south. It was still raining very hard. It was a good cover for any noise we might be making. We watched for any outpost guards who may have been placed around the village but saw none.

We could hear voices coming from the village just west of us. I really needed photos of the Arabs to bring back to the Major. We lay down in the brush about twenty-five feet from the back of the houses in the Arab compound. It was still raining like hell and I didn't want to get the cameras wet, but I knew the photos would be blurry anyway.

There was some activity going on in and around the houses. It appeared that they were packing up boxes and bringing them to the front doors of each house. There were a few militant-looking men carrying suitcases and boxes in front of the houses. They were trying to stay out of the rain, but they were not having much luck. There were two Hummers parked in the clearing at the center of the common area. I didn't see how all the boxes and cases were going to fit into just those two Hummers.

The rain began to slow so I told Sorensen that I was going to go to the other side of the village to photograph as many of the Arabs as I could. I told him to stay put and take pictures from that side so we had them from different angles. I reached over, turned my tiny flash off, and reminded him to do the same on the camera I'd given him. We didn't want to light up the whole forest when we started clicking off pictures!

He smiled at me. I wasn't sure if it was a smile of thanks for the reminder or a smile of, "Do I look that stupid?"

I walked some then crawled until I was beyond the houses. I then made my way to the other side of the compound. The rain was much lighter now and I could see farther into the compound. There were boxes and suitcases stacked up on the front porches at every house. For the first time since we had arrived, many of the Arabs were wearing western clothing--shirts and slacks. The women were wearing dresses and slacks, something very taboo in their culture. And, for the first time, none of them were wearing head coverings. This told me they were leaving and covering up their ethnicity! After all these years here, they were ready to vacate the islands.

The rain had turned into a drizzle, so I took a few photos of the men and women on the porches. I also took a few shots of the militants assisting them with their belongings. The small cameras didn't have a sophisticated zoom feature so I zoomed about halfway to their limit so the pictures wouldn't lose too much resolution.

I took about a dozen photos with my camera phone and, as I lay there, I sent them to the Major and to Gage across the Gulf Stream. At about that time, I saw four militants come out of the largest of the buildings with the tall Arab who resembled Bin Laden. I took a few pictures of him and the people he was with. He looked just like Bin Laden, but shorter at about six feet tall. I shot about ten good photos of him and his entourage.

Two of his fellow Arabs were carrying AK rifles with folding stocks so they could conceal them. They were also carrying extra magazines on shoulder harnesses. They were definitely security and looked highly professional.

I tried to find Sorensen's position across the clearing to be sure he was completely hidden, but I could see no sign of him or his camera. These bodyguards looked as if they would shoot first and ask questions later. I, in turn, would retaliate in kind. A lot of folks would die before the dust settled!

The rain had stopped for a while but the sky was looking like it had more in store for us soon. The wind was blowing quite hard and making enough noise that I could have banged my rifle against a tree and no one would have heard me.

I clicked my walkie-talkie twice to Sorensen and he immediately clicked me back twice, signaling he was okay.

I moved south, cut across the clearing, and made my way back to Sorensen's position. As I looked back at the training area, I saw the mockup buildings that looked like a John Wayne shooting range for military training. The thing that really caught my eye this time was a section that looked like a section of a mountain or stone cliff just like an area of Afghanistan, including old, dried plants and rocks. It resembled the background of at least one of Osama Bin Laden's videotaped messages seen on U.S. national news reports! I moved closer to that area and took a number of pictures of the stone looking stage with my smartphone and sent them directly to the Major and Gage.

I shifted back to Sorensen's last position and we both went a few yards north to the older section of San Andros. We again took pictures of the buildings and the older German folks wandering around. After sending the photos to the Major and Gage, we moved back south, skirted the training area, and cut west toward the airport.

When we were a safe distance from the village, I decided to check-in with Top and give him an update on our progress. I called him with one of the burners I still had.

He said that he was about halfway back to San Andros aboard the *Semper Fi* and making good time with the wind and his engine. He would be close by mid-morning tomorrow, about fifteen hours from now. He would anchor off the north shore again and stand by to move briskly if we needed him. I was amazed at the speed the *Semper Fi* could achieve under sail and power.

As we made our way toward the airport, we heard some noises about twenty-five yards away. We knelt down and remained still. The sounds turned into low voices and the sound of feet on the path coming from the airport. Sorensen and I quietly moved south a few yards and patiently waited.

A few moments later, about ten militants walked east toward the village, all heavily armed and wearing backpacks that appeared very heavy. They all seemed fairly seasoned. A couple of them were mature-looking enough to be retired military. This was a sign that either the people running this show were getting tougher or this was an exit escort for the people leaving the village. For me, it meant that I was about to lose any potential witnesses for Joel's case.

Over the years, the Major has told me time and again about the importance of letting the public know about political crimes and misconduct, and that the best chance for justice is exposure. If politicians cover up an event, then it never happened. But, to do that, they needed the help of the news media. To get the news media to help in a cover-up or a successful spin, the politicians make promises and offers rewards for a publisher's cooperation! "Quid pro quo."

When the rain stopped completely, we heard the sound of a large plane behind us at the airport. This was more than likely the means of transport for all these folks who were going to disappear from this island.

I called the Major and told him that he needed to call a quick press conference to expose what has been going on here at San Andros. He agreed. If the village was found deserted, it would be washed over and Joel would never get a fair trial or be able to expose the decades-old crime of harboring these war criminals. The Major said that there were already rumors spreading that the village was a secret military training facility used to train troops for special missions on foreign soil! He requested that we do all we could to slow down the evacuation until he could interest the media in flying to San Andros and witnessing for themselves what has been going on here!

I got off the phone and looked at Sorensen.

He smiled at me and said, "Let's go shut down an airport!"

214

We reversed our direction and headed west toward the runway. We could still hear at least one large airplane rumbling in the distance. It sounded like a KC-130, a large transport plane widely used by the military around the world. Each one could hold about a hundred people for short distances and fifty or sixty with cargo for long distances.

As we cleared the woods on the east side of the runway, we didn't see one but two KC-130s near the terminal building. A number of crewmen were moving around the aircraft parked off to one side. The other aircraft was running and appeared to be doubling as a meeting place. The top part of the rear ramp door was partially open and I could see a few men inside. They were both military- and civilian-clothed and facing the interior of the plane. The plane was making a great deal of noise as one of its four engines revved up.

Sorensen and I made our way to the spot closest to the aircraft still running. I asked Sorensen how well he thought he could place a couple of damaging rounds into two or three engines on both planes. He said he would do his best. The KC-130 can take off and fly with two engines so we had to disable at least three engines on each plane.

Sorensen laid down at the edge of the woods, took careful aim with his newly secured tactical rifle, and fired one round into the outside starboard engine on the plane that was sitting quietly on the apron. The sound of the other aircraft's engine drowned out the sound of the rifle firing.

The men standing behind that aircraft never even looked up. Sorensen continued to shoot carefully placed rounds until three of the engines were visibly dripping oil. He then shifted his position and fired on the other aircraft. He avoided shooting the engine that was running as that would have shut it down and alarmed everyone that something was amiss. We slowly moved back to the tree line and Sorensen slipped a fresh clip into the rifle. Once we were clear and saw no activities out of the ordinary, he took aim and flattened the front tires on both aircraft.

The shifting of the front of each plane to a lower position drew the attention of the men on the ground. They ran to the front of the planes, looked at the tires, and all hell broke loose.

Two or three of the men started firing their pistols in all different directions. We weren't sure exactly what they thought they were shooting at, but, fortunately, it wasn't at us!

Another one picked up a rifle from somewhere, fired in our general direction, and then shifted his fire to a point farther north than where we were. Sorensen lifted his rifle and started aiming it at the guy with the rifle, but I pushed the barrel down and told him that they had no clue as to where we were, so giving up our position was not a good idea.

He nodded. We knew they were confused and disoriented, so we crept backward, as we watched the airport area for any patrols coming our way. When we were totally concealed in the woods and sure that they weren't pursuing us, we got up and ran to toward the main airport road.

When we reached the main road, we heard a couple of vehicles traveling at high speed from the direction of the village. The sound was distant enough that we knew we still had time, so we crossed the road and hid in the brush just as two Hummers raced by.

They were moving so fast that we could not be sure, but there appeared to be two or three men in each vehicle. At least one of them had a rifle leaning out of the window. They were frantically looking left and right, obviously looking for the "terrorists" who shot up the planes at the airport.

None of these men appeared to be seasoned soldiers. After so many years, you can tell the seasoned guys from the noobs.

After they passed, Sorensen and I continued north until we got to the old logging road. We found a small clearing and took a short break. I called Top and gave him a coded breakdown of the last couple of hours. He said he was still a few hours away but could arrange a seaplane if we needed to evacuate right away. I thanked him but said no. We still needed more witnesses for Joel.

While we were resting in the brush, we heard a large helicopter fly in from the west. As it neared, we could see it was a large military copter with no markings on its fuselage. It appeared to be well armored and even had rockets mounted on its sides. I couldn't imagine that a private militant group like the one here on San Andros could afford such an expensive multi-million-dollar aircraft!

It was becoming more obvious that this was a government-funded operation. Now that I thought about it, neither of the KC-130s at the airport had any markings on them, either—not even November numbers.

More than likely, the copter had seats for a few of the more important members of the community so that they could leave immediately! Unfortunately, we couldn't go back to the airport and disable the copter. We got a little crazy at times but never stupid. But, as I thought about it, I came up with an idea that could slow them down a bit.

Sorensen and I started moving toward the entrance to the village. There were four guards standing outside the gatehouse. We could see some movement a short distance down the road in the larger building used as the headquarters for the militants. As usual, I didn't have to discuss my thoughts with Sorensen. He instinctively knew what I was thinking.

I called Nancy and asked her to pick us up near Morgan's Bluff in about thirty minutes. We were going to attempt to stop the folks trying to flee by holding up in their compound until members of the press and some cameras arrived from Miami.

We moved back toward the road, then moved about fifty feet from one another and laid down on the ground.

Sorensen looked at me and gave me his *I am ready* nod.

I gave him a small salute and he fired his first round.

It struck the small air conditioner on the wall of the guard shack and caused it to spark, roar, and spew a white powdery smoke inside and out of the shack. I took aim. My first round struck the radiator of the Hummer parked next to the headquarters building. As the engine was still hot, it started to steam and bellow out smoke. The guards were slow to react to the first two shots so we took advantage of the confusion to start pouring rounds into everything we could.

We avoided the humans but left little else untouched. A couple of the guards haphazardly fired back. Soon, all of the guards, including the men in the office building, ran back toward the village area to the south. What made no sense at all was that most of them left their weapons on the ground by the guardhouse. Sorensen and I looked at each other and just smiled.

We picked ourselves up, ran deeper into the woods south of the road and, as we ran, we fired about ten more rounds at each of the houses through the trees. We fired in short flurries so it would appear that there were more than just two people attacking them. We took out the electric transformers on the telephone poles to knock out the power, and we fired on the water tower to cause further confusion to an already panicked crowd.

There were people running and limping all over the common areas. The militants were nowhere to be seen. They were either hiding or defending a couple of disabled aircraft at the airport. Whatever the case, we needed to become scarce!

I signaled Sorensen to head back to the beach. I took off after him, but a little to his left so we didn't create too big of a target. When we reached the road, we looked in both directions and ran along the edge of the brush. After about a hundred yards, we crossed the road and made like greyhounds chasing a rabbit for the beach.

When we got to the edge of the beach, we started to hear gunfire from the direction of the village. It was erratic and sounded like they were shooting everywhere—exactly the result we were looking for. Confusion creates further confusion when no results come from your efforts. And, they were getting no results. Perfect!

We again heard the big helicopter lifting off at the airport and watched it climb high into the sky as if it were under fire. Once at a safe altitude, it turned west and raced over the horizon toward Miami.

I called Nancy. She told me that she was just down the road, not far from our current position. She said all was clear. We ran back out to the edge of the road where I'd seen her little car about fifty yards away. We dropped back into the brush and carefully made our way to her.

We jumped into the rear seat of Nancy's car and she sped off east toward Nicholls Town. With the size of the two of us, Sorensen and I filled the rear area of the car. We were hardly able to move. Our rifles were tucked under us in such a way that it would take a crowbar to move them. It was far from comfortable as the rifles jabbed into our bodies.

Nancy, with a chuckle, said, "Welcome aboard boys. Having fun yet?"

She told us that the entire north end of the island was in turmoil since someone had shot up the airport and disabled two expensive airplanes. She glanced over her shoulder and smiled a bit as we looked innocently back at her.

I started to say, "Don't look at us!" but thought she knew better than that, so I just kept my mouth shut.

Nancy also told us that she had set up a few interviews for us with people who knew about the death of the old German.

We arrived back in Nicholls Town without incident. I asked Nancy to drop us at the Marina so I could get some much-needed supplies from my boat. Sorensen sat down in the bushes to watch for trouble while I pulled the boat close enough to get aboard. What I needed most was my small video camera and some tapes for my tape recorder.

I inspected the boat and checked my fuel and battery power. Everything was up to snuff and ready to sail as soon as we needed the boat. Sorensen boarded the boat and went below.

I called the Major and he informed me that a number of reporters and cameramen were flying to San Andros from Miami and that a number of the reporters had leased a large helicopter. I told him that they might have to land on a shortened runway! He said that it was all over the news that a group of terrorists had shot up the airport at San Andros,

I suggested that he pass the word to the news media higher-ups that there were militant Arabs living on the island and to warn them by radio that if they flew over the village, they could be fired on because the militants were a bit agitated at the moment. I could tell by his demeanor that the Major wanted to ask, "What did you do now?"

I told him that once the media were there, Sorensen and I would try to get back over to the village.

We hung up and I went back down into the cabin to change my clothes. I chose a light khaki jungle shirt with extra pockets and a small pocket on the inside to carry my small .22 magnum derringer. I noticed that Sorensen was sound asleep on the divan. That guy could sleep through a hurricane—or a terrorist attack, even if he was one of the terrorists!

After I woke Sorensen, we made our way down the road to the south where Nancy said she would meet up with us. There still wasn't any sign of the militants in town so we were able to stay on the road. Both of us were carrying our rifles and sidearms now, and we both had numerous clips of ammunition for both types of weapons. Not to be too obvious about it, but we were both carrying our rifles low beside our legs.

As usual, we saw very little movement around the small homes the locals lived in, but I always felt as though we were being watched. All your senses go into overdrive when you need them to.

We came around a sharp turn in the road and noticed Nancy speaking to a few folks near a small building. She caught us out of the corner of her eye and waved us over. She introduced us to ten people that she said had pertinent information about the killing of the old German and the horrible treatment of Joel after his capture. She said that all of the statements were positive for Joel, and all contradicted the Bahamian prosecutor's case.

Nancy led the group behind the small house where she had a few lawn chairs arranged for their comfort. Sorensen and I wrote out their statements for their signatures. Nancy signed all statements as a witness and took them to her office to make numerous copies. She wasn't gone but a few minutes and then returned with the copies and large waterproof sandwich bags to store them in.

Understanding the inner workings of legal proceedings, I had the witnesses sign each of the copies again to attest to their authenticity. I asked Nancy to take the originals to her office and immediately fax them to a number the Major had given to me in Miami. She thanked all the witnesses, then left right away to return to her office to take care of business. Nancy was so pumped that she didn't even turn to wave goodbye! She was on a mission—a mission that had severe consequences!

Sorensen and I left the area with caution and made our way back to my boat. I called the Major and advised him to look for the fax coming through from Nancy. I told him the originals and some signed copies were at Nancy's office in Nicholls Town. He said he would review the documents then get the copies to the news media.

He told me he had retained a Bahamian lawyer to present the defense case at the Nassau court. He also said that the judge had demanded that Joel be brought back to the Bahamas before any court hearing could be conducted.

I told the Major that it was my opinion that the judge was not on our side and told him not to give in. The Major stated that when the news media finished with their stories about San Andros, the Bahamas government would be hard-pressed to demand anything except forgiveness!

I replied, "Major, I think the finger-pointing is going to be rampant."

It would have been so good to be aboard the *Big Mamoo/Slim Molly* again, but we needed to get back to the north side of the island and wait for Top to arrive. From there, we could also watch for the arrival of the news media as they descended on the island. I would have enjoyed watching from my boat as they approached the village, but that would only put us in a position to be apprehended by one of the patrol boats in the area. We decided to take my small inflatable to the north shore. We loaded our equipment into the boat and took off north toward Morgan's Bluff and then west to the beach area where Top would be in a few hours.

As we made our way around the north side of the island, I spotted a larger than usual speedboat coming in at high speed from the northwest. It was about fifty feet long and rode low on the water. It looked like the kind of boat the drug runners use to run up the coast when they are trying to avoid the Coast Guard and DEA.

As we got closer to the north shore, I saw a group of people standing on the beach. Sorensen took out the binoculars and held them as steady as he could. He sighed and said, "Well, Jake, it seems that the Arabs decided to leave before their TV and news debut today, buddy."

I didn't want to hear that at all. Sorensen looked at me and I said, "For the full effect, Joel is going to need to expose all that has been going on here for the past fifty or so years, pal."

I asked Sorensen how he felt about disabling the four large outboard motors on the back of the boat with his new toy. He said he would give it a shot—or two! That new toy was more like an elephant gun than anything else I could compare it to.

I continued west across the top of the island and then drove ashore about a half-mile west of the folks on the beach. Sorensen got a few extra rounds, grabbed his rifle, and ran into the brush to the south. I never had to wonder if Sorensen was going to be successful. He was the ultimate professional and Success was his surname.

I waited for a few minutes, pushed the inflatable back out into the surf, and then continued west. The speedboat was so large that it was turning back and forth along the beach, looking for a passage through the reef. Knowing this area and the reef system like I do, there was no way those big outboards were going to clear the reef anywhere on this north shore. The only way those people on shore could board that boat would be by rubber inflatable or swim like hell over jagged reef heads.

The speedboat went farther west as its captain looked for a place to run the bow up onto the sand. He passed where I thought Sorensen should be in the brush lining up his shots. As the boat passed to the west, I saw a bit of smoke, a slight flash, and then three more flashes. The engines were so loud in order to push a boat that size, I couldn't hear the shots coming from Sorensen's rifle.

I could tell that the captain and his one-man crew were unable to hear the shots either as they continued to look forward as, one by one, the engines stopped running.

A moment later, one of the engines caught fire. I could see the fuel pouring out of the side of it like wine streaming from a wine barrel with the flow constant.

The captain took out a fire extinguisher and attempted to put the fire out but soon gave up as the entire rear of the boat was ablaze!

I was about a hundred yards away as the crew dove into the water. The smoke was now thick and black, and it bellowed from the entire back deck and all four engines. With a surprised look on my face, I pulled up next to them and threw them floating seat cushions and a rope, which they both grabbed and used to pull themselves to the deck of the boat. They looked like waterlogged rats as they plopped down into the bottom of my boat. They thanked me for picking them up.

Their boat was now totally engulfed in flames. I asked what happened and they said the engines had been running hot ever since they slowed down after crossing the Gulf Stream coming in from Miami. Neither man had a clue that they had been fired upon, so I called Sorensen on his cell and told him we had a couple of guests that needed transportation to the beach.

He said, "Don't ever ask me to give up this weapon, Jake, as it now has the name 'Sorensen's Eliminator.'"

I laughed, hung up, and told my guests that my friend was tending to some business and I would take them to shore.

I asked them what they were doing on the reef when their boat caught fire and they told me they were trying to get close enough to the shore to take on some passengers who needed transport to Miami.

I asked, "So why aren't the passengers flying out on the island hopper airlines that fly in and out of San Andros about every two to three hours?"

They said that they didn't know. A guy from Washington, D.C. contracted them that morning and had offered them a huge payment to get here right away. They agreed to the deal and were on their way.

I told them I had a cell phone in case they wanted to make a call to their family or employers. They took my phone and, without even thinking, placed the call. I could only hear one side of the conversion and it was not pleasant. I guessed they called the guy in Washington and he was extremely upset. Their twenty-five "Yes, sirs!" were a pretty good indication of the guy's mood on the other end. My new guests were getting chewed out damn good!

I motored toward the beach and told them I had to drop them a little west of where we were because of the reef. Our guests seemed satisfied that I was a Good Samaritan and thanked me again. I quickly asked them for their full names and addresses for my captain's logbook. They complied with no hesitation.

I quickly called the Major, gave him an update on the latest events, and passed on the men's names and information. He said he would pass that along to the press. I gave him the Washington, D.C. phone number that the speedboat's captain had called from my cell phone.

He said he would have it checked out and asked if any of the press had arrived yet. I told him we had not seen any aircraft arrive yet. I signed off from the Major and called Dave to update him on the past few hours. He said all was well on the island and that he was standing by to fly down when we needed him. I explained that the runway was a bit cluttered at the moment due to some trouble earlier in the day. He said he could rent a seaplane and be here in about three hours, if need be. I asked him to stay by his cell phone for my call. I called Gage and left a brief message to keep him in the loop.

Sorensen returned from up the beach. He told me that he put two rounds each into the outboards of the big speedboat. He said he placed them low on the covers so they did the most damage and the men on board wouldn't notice. How he got eight shots off that fast and that accurately is beyond me, but accuracy is the name of the game with Ron. He informed me that a number of Arab types were down the beach and that they may be waiting for a boat ride.

We pushed the inflatable back out through the surf and headed back east. The two men from the burning boat made it back to the group of Arabs and their keepers that they were supposed to have picked up. Judging by their body language, there were many upset folks standing there, waving their arms around like they were swatting flies.

I looked at Sorensen, threw my arms around for a few seconds, and said with a bit of an accent, "Is that burning boat how I am to get off of this island?"

He laughed and pointed to the sky.

It was about that time that the first of the media helicopters from Miami appeared over the island. As the big bird flew over the people on the beach, I could see cameras pointing down from the open doors on both sides of the copter. The Arabs scattered like cockroaches when the lights came on, running back toward the brush as they covered their faces from the cameras.

The big helicopter settled down on the beach and, before the blades even slowed, about ten reporters and cameramen leaped out onto the beach. In a matter of seconds, they overtook the Arabs and were shouting questions to them so loudly that even we could hear from a hundred yards out on the water.

"Why are you hiding on the island?"

"Who facilitated your hiding here?"

At the same time, four militants holding rifles stepped in between the reporters and the Arabs and started pushing the reporters back. One of the militants pushed a cameraman back so hard that he slipped and fell to the sand. The other cameramen filmed this event and shouted at the militants to leave them alone. It was a newsperson's dream. American military types were attacking Americans on behalf of a group of Arabs, and it was all being filmed for the world to see. This was news worth watching!

I called the Major to inform him about the beach incident and so he could send an alert to news reporters and stations about what was currently happening on the island. I feared that the militants would confiscate the news films and detain the reporters until the San Andros Germans and Arabs could be taken away and hidden.

As I was speaking to the Major, a second helicopter flew over and began filming the incident on the beach. The Major gave me two cell phone numbers of two reporters who were on or near the island. He told me to call them and direct them to where these incidents were taking place. I hung up and called one of the reporter's numbers. He answered on the second ring. I told him about the beach incident and that we were on the inflatable boat just off the beach. He said he was in the helicopter circling overhead now.

While we talked, I saw a man hanging out of the open side door of helicopter number two and waving at us. When he was back inside the copter where he could hear me better, I told him there was a man who may be one of Bin Laden's brothers among the Arabs. As they made another pass over the beach, the militants pointed their rifles away from the reporters. I couldn't see if the Bin Laden look-alike was among the people on the beach, but the reporters were photographing and interrogating them all.

So as not to look too suspicious, we cruised around the point to

Nicholls Town, climbed into the Big Mamoo, and cruised back to the beach area. We figured that the two stranded boaters had told their stories and everyone believed that the motors had caused the fire. At least there were no patrol boats out looking for anyone.

We passed the area where the Arabs and the reporters had been. The beach was now clear. The big helicopter that had landed on the beach was gone. The wreckage of the speedboat was also gone, but we could still smell the smoke from the burning fiberglass.

I called my voicemail and had a few routine messages. One was from Joel's son saying he was in Miami and was meeting with the Major that afternoon. He asked if I was going to be at the meeting. It was good to know that what Sorensen and I were up to here in the islands was not common knowledge. I knew it had been too long since I had made contact with Gage, but with all that was going on, the Major had probably touched base with Gage to clue him in.

We dropped anchor, climbed back into the inflatable, headed inland to beach the boat, and then pulled it into the brush. I pulled out the rubber satchel containing our weapons and supplies. We both checked and loaded our rifles and handguns. With everything going on, we needed to be prepared for anything. And, the most important "thing" for us was to stay alive!

All was clear, so we grabbed our rifles and gear packs and made our way to the old logging road.

As we moved closer to the village, we could hear some shouts and an occasional scream that sounded Arabic. We decided to stay in the brush for our own good as we approached the outskirts of the village. We could see a number of journalists attempting to interview the residents and photographers taking random pictures of people and structures. We moved north toward the German village and, to our surprise, there were no journalists there. This greatly concerned me!

We could see the Germans looking out of their windows but no reporters were attempting to interview them or take any pictures of them. Uncovering the fact that some governments were hiding Arabs and supporting them here on San Andros was important, but that wouldn't help Joel in his defense. We had to interest the reporters in the old German residents before the news was sent to the States for the 6:00 and 6:30 news reports. This was so much bigger than just Arabs being hidden and protected!

225

Sorensen and I stashed our rifles, ammo, and gear packs in the brush, broke out of the woods near the border of the Arab village, and walked calmly up to a group of reporters. I introduced myself to them and told them about the Germans. We noticed that there were no longer any militants in sight. I told them to look in the Community Center and the vacant houses for them. I explained that there were numerous U.S. citizens guarding these two groups of people and that they were seriously armed like an army. One of the reporters told us they had seen a few armed men a couple of hours ago when they first arrived but hadn't seen one since. Sorensen and I pointed to the Community Center and told them to be careful but to go through the back door with their cameras running!

We moved back toward our stash of guns and gear in the brush in case the reporters were threatened and just waited and watched.

The first thing to happen was that the door of the Community Center was pushed closed when the reporters pushed it open. Then, a second later, the front door flew open and ten militants with towels or magazines over their faces came running out of the front door and toward the path to the airport. There were four or five photographers on the road in front of the militants, and they turned their cameras toward them as they rushed forward.

Sorensen winked at me, picked up his pistol, and fired five rapid rounds into the ground in the brush, which made the militants drop their facial covers and aim their rifles in every direction. This gave the cameramen a clear shot of their faces, their outfits, and their weapons. To make matters worse, four of the old Germans came hobbling out of the Community Center with old German Luger pistols and started aiming them at the cameramen. I doubted those old pistols still would fire and, if they did, the old men aiming them would be lucky if they hit the sky.

Nonetheless, Sorensen and I stood by with our pistols at the ready in case we needed to stop a major incident from occurring.

The old men dropped their pistols to their sides, calmed down, and started answering the reporters' questions. They told the reporters about the U.S. and Canadian governments bringing them here to retire. One man claimed that he received his monthly retirement income from a Canadian Bank.

We would have enjoyed listening to all of their statements, but we had to put together a few more witnesses for Joel's defense and we needed to get back to Nicholls Town to do it. As we walked back toward the main road, still in the brush because of our rifles, we saw two Hummers parked partially in the brush near the front guard gate. There was no one watching them, so we opened the driver's doors and found they both had the keys in the ignitions.

Sorensen gave me a thumbs up, took the keys to the Hummer he was closest to, and threw them far out into the brush. I climbed into the other Hummer and started it up. It was quite the vehicle, with oversized seats, lots of interior space, and gadgets all over the place.

Sorensen climbed into the passenger seat and said, "Now, this is my kind of ride."

And, off to Nicholls Town, we went. In military-style—first class, I might add!

As we approached the outskirts of town, we saw Nancy driving toward us in her small car. I blinked the lights a few times, stopped, and stuck my head out of the side window so she could see us.

She stopped alongside us and said, "A new ride, Jake? You never cease to amaze me." She went on to say she was driving out to the airport to meet some Bahamian officials who were arriving soon in a small plane. They were officially on a fact-finding mission for the prime minister.

I told her that we would follow her to the airport and stand by as backup as she answered any questions about the goings-on here on San Andros.

We followed her little car to the airport. As we passed the entrance to the San Andros road, three militants jumped out of the brush and tried to wave us down. None of them had any firearms visible, so I looked at Sorensen and he nodded to stop.

They asked for a ride to the airport so they could get out of the area. I looked at Sorensen and he shrugged, so I had Sorensen climb in the rear seat to keep an eye on the one that I was putting in the front seat next to me and the other I put in the rear stowage area where he could do us no harm.

I asked them where their weapons were and they said their supervisors advised them to ditch them and not to acknowledge that they had ever had them. They were told not to talk to the reporters or they may be arrested. They'd been told it was a government-sanctioned operation and didn't know it was an illegal gig! One of the militants said the supervisors had all moved over to a house on the beach at Morgan's Bluff. They described the house as the one we'd borrowed a few days ago. Well, the owners may never use it, but it seemed everyone else was enjoying their beachfront view.

We dropped them off at the terminal, they both said, "Thanks a lot," and we parked next to Nancy's car in the visitors' parking lot. I didn't have the heart to tell those boys that they would fly farther if they flapped their arms. No way was any fixed-wing aircraft going to land at or take off from this airport anytime soon.

We caught up with Nancy on the tarmac near the disabled KC-130s. She shook her head and asked us how they were ever going to get a vehicle big enough to drag these huge aircraft off the runway.

I told her, "They can always blow them up and move the smaller pieces!"

She didn't laugh or even smile. In fact, she gave me a deadly stare.

I looked at her and asked, "What?"

She just looked away.

Shortly thereafter, she told us that she was beginning to feel we were more trouble than she needed for her small island. Even though she spoke sternly, I could see the sparkle of admiration in her eyes as she reflected on what we had accomplished here in such a short period of time.

We told her the leaders of the militants were hiding in a house over on Morgan's Bluff. She called someone and told them about the hiding place. When she got off the phone, she told us that the reporters would be advised where they could find the leaders for an interview. Now, she was smiling again.

A few moments later a twin-engine, high-wing STOL (short take-off and landing plane) passed overhead, turned, and landed with many feet left to spare on what was left of the blocked runway. The STOL taxied around the two KC-130s and stopped right next to the small terminal building. The door opened and four Bahamian men climbed out and walked toward us. Nancy stood at attention and respectfully greeted the four men. I noticed two reporters and a cameraman walking out of the small FOB office. They saw the STOL and continued toward the men who had just deplaned.

Sorensen and I stood off to the side and watched the four men and Nancy as they spoke. As I studied the men, I realized that one of them was the same Bahamian I had seen in the room where the Major had been held and manhandled a week ago in Nassau. He was giving Nancy a hard time. I decided to walk over and confront him with my knowledge of his involvement with the militants and the U.S. spooks that day in Nassau.

It is always good to have *size* on your side. I walked up to the man, Sorensen at my side, and asked him if he remembered me. The man looked at me for a moment and put out his hand as if I was someone, he should remember but didn't. I passed on his offered hand and told him and everyone else within earshot that I was present in the Government Building when he took part in the kidnapping and false imprisonment of lawyer Doug Parton while he was attempting to meet with Bahamian legal officials.

The man immediately withdrew his hand and said he had no idea what I was talking about. I told him not only did he know, but he was also about to be served with a civil lawsuit naming him as a major defendant in a civil-rights complaint. I made that last part up, but it was enough to get him shouting and blaming some other people and saying they misled him in the facts.

Sometimes, you have to pull one out of your hat to get the right reaction, and I did! A wise man once said, "A good time to keep your mouth shut is when you're in deep water." With the camera running and pointed at his face, this guy was going to drown!

I pulled Nancy aside and asked her who this guy was. She said he was the Bahamian ambassador to the U.S. for the past thirty years. His name was Phillip White, related to her and Calvin many times removed. I had never heard of him. Or, if I had, I had forgotten.

He was raging about his integrity to his three plane mates and did not appear to be making any progress with any of them. Nancy smiled at me behind their backs. She reminded him that he had been to the island twice in the past two weeks to meet with the Americans at the San Andros Airport.

The ambassador turned his attention to the young female constable and gave her a look that made me step in front of him and glare back. We stared each other down a moment, and then I told him he had a great deal to explain and now was a good time to start.

Mr. White looked at me and said he didn't need to explain anything to me and then, after a second take, asked, "Who in the hell are you and why are you here, anyway?"

I told him I was not the one who needed to explain anything. However, if he wanted to question me, we could do it before even more reporters arrived by helicopter and by boat.

Mr. White walked away from us and said something to the pilot who flew them into San Andros. The pilot looked at the other three gentlemen standing with us, and all of them shook their heads!

After the three men walked a short distance away to speak quietly among themselves, Nancy smiled at me and said, "Jake, you have a fine way of making new friends, now don't you?"

I told her I had a feeling that Mr. White was a big part of the problem and we hadn't heard the last from him. Nancy agreed.

I walked to the airport building to be alone and called the Major. I told him about the ambassador being here on San Andros and explained to him that he was one of the men in the room where the Major had been taken after he was abducted.

He asked me to photograph the guy with my phone and text it to him.

While I was talking to the Major, I walked over to Mr. White and said, "Mr. Ambassador?"

When he turned to look at me, I took his picture.

He screamed at me to *"Stop!"* and then he made the mistake of lunging for my phone.

I stepped aside and he fell right down on his face there on the tarmac. Of course, I was glad to see that the nearby cameraman who had come with the reporters was filming the whole thing. I immediately sent the photo to the Major's cell in Miami.

I told Nancy that Sorensen and I were going to make our way back over to the village while the reporters here were grilling these guys and that I would call her later. I told her we still needed a few more witnesses for Joel. She told us she would keep working on it.

We jumped back into the Hummer, which we were now treating as our own, and drove directly across the runway to the small road we used to get to the Village. It sure was nice having wheels instead of having to walk through the woods everywhere. I parked the vehicle in the bushes a few yards from the edge of the village. We locked our rifles in the rear compartment, checked our sidearms, and then took off on foot to see what had transpired in the two hours since we were gone.

There were now about twenty-five cameramen and reporters wandering around the two villages. This was exactly what we wanted to see happening all over this mysterious place. When they saw us, they charged over to film us, thinking we were more of the U.S. militants.

I held up my hand, stopped them, introduced myself, and then told them I could not answer their questions because of attorney-client privilege. They asked me who the attorney was and I told them Doug Parton of the United States. They all immediately recognized the name and then retreated from us as if they were afraid, they would interfere with our operation.

Sorensen said, "Man, I am impressed. I haven't seen a crowd disperse like that since I farted in a full elevator at CIA headquarters last year!"

I told him that the Major must be working the media overtime in Miami on this issue.

Everything was now fairly peaceful at the village. There were still some of the old Germans barricaded in their homes, but there were no militants about to cause any problems—at least as far as we could tell.

We walked to the Arab compound and saw about the same thing going on there with reporters giving the residents the third degree. What I didn't see was the Bin Laden look-alike. I asked Sorensen to go to the south end of the houses and work back toward me as he searched for the rest of the Arab residents. I began at the north end and worked my way south. There were a few boxes and suitcases on the floors but no signs of anyone hiding. Where in the hell did they all go?

A few minutes later, Sorensen caught up to me and shrugged in puzzlement. I told him that I was fairly sure that they had not left the island yet. There were no boats or helicopters near the village large enough to evacuate people that we had not already disabled. I looked at Sorensen and both of us realized at the same time that there was more to this area then what we'd seen. It seemed the mysteries of this place just kept coming at us!

I pointed at the training field to the south of the Arab village. Sorensen walked over and spoke to a couple of cameramen. They loaded up with extra equipment and followed us as we walked through the field of makeshift buildings, combat training obstacles, and staged scenes. They filmed us as we moved along.

A small opening in the bushes at the edge of the field looked as if someone had recently trodden on it. I took point and Sorensen followed with the cameramen in tow. I cautioned the cameramen to stay back and to stay low.

As I turned the corner on the path—*bang!*—a shot rang out and, at the same time, I felt a sting on my left side. I hit the dirt and felt my side with my right hand. I had a small crease in my flesh and a lot of blood staining my shirt. I bleed profusely when first cut or injured, so I wasn't that concerned—at least for now.

Sorensen crawled up to me and lifted my shirt to check out the wound. He said, "It will play well to the cameras, but I have done more damage shaving with a dull razor, Jake."

I pushed his hand off my shirt and said, "You are such the comic, aren't you?"

At that moment—*bang!* Another shot rang out and the bushes shed a few leaves over our heads. All Sorensen and I had were our handguns, so we stayed low and kept the cameramen down to try to keep them out of harm's way.

One of the cameramen held his camera up high and turned the viewfinder down so I could see in it. He said I might be able to see something if I looked into the little screen hanging from the bottom.

I could see a large mosque-like building that we had never seen before set in a group of oversized pine trees. There were three or more Arab gunmen in the front windows with AK-47 rifles pointed in our direction. I heard some noise behind us and saw a number of reporters and cameramen crawling toward us, trying to see and film where the gunfire was coming from.

I waved for them to stay down as another three shots rang out and leaves and pine needles fell to the ground. I continued to watch the gunmen through the camera view lens.

Sorensen sided up to me and asked if I thought he should run back to get our rifles. I said no as I felt the more these Arabs stayed holed-up in their mosque, the more newsworthy this story would be and the more it would lend credibility and attention to Joel's story. Eventually, these Arabs would have to be neutralized, but for the time being, it was great news. The cameras were running and filming the shooters, and they were clearly Arab militants. As long as the reporters stayed low, they were not in much danger of being hit. Meanwhile, the film footage was being beamed back to the States via satellite for the entire world to see.

I told the reporters and cameramen to stay put and signaled for Sorensen to follow me. We left the reporters behind and crawled to the training field area. I told Sorensen we needed to search the German compound for some evidence that would aid Joel's case. I never stopped collecting evidence until I felt I had more than enough to make the case a slam-dunk win!

We started with the small office next to the Community Center. The

Germans had clearly ransacked it as they were preparing to leave the island, but there were still thousands of papers all over the floor and in drawers. We started to read some of the papers but there were far too many for us to sort through. I found a number of large black trash bags and we began to throw papers and binders into the bags. We then ran out of the building and threw the bags into the brush in case any of the many government authorities that were bound to be here before long intercepted us.

I told Sorensen, "We know they are coming. We just don't know when, pal, so let's get as much as we can."

We went back into the office and continued to sling papers into the trash bags. Sorensen stopped me and said, "Jake, look at this!"

I walked over and saw he was holding a large scrapbook. It was old and worn and contained hundreds of photos taken in what appeared to be a German concentration camp. The old German that Joel had killed was featured in almost every photo as a very young officer. This had to be one of the most significant discoveries we had found in this case so far!

Sorensen and I took some of the photos, gathered together five of the news photographers, and laid the photos out for them to see and photograph. Many of the photos clearly showed the commandant in various acts of violence against the prisoners of a concentration camp. I explained to the reporters that the large German officer in the old photos was the man Joel was accused of murdering. I also asked them to contact Doug Parton in Miami to get the details of the charges against Joel if they were not familiar with them. This was exactly the type of breakthrough that makes the difference.

While we were speaking to the group of reporters, we heard more gunshots from the area where the Arabs were still holding their position. I told the reporters that there was a man among them that looked very much like a member of the Bin Laden family, that they were hiding in a building to the south, and had a number of their fellow reporters and cameramen pinned down on the path leading there. They said they would take it from here and left us to join their comrades.

I told Sorensen that we should take a run down to Morgan's Bluff to see what was going on with the militants and the news media there. Sorensen ran down to get our Hummer as I gathered the trash bags full of documents out of the bushes. When he arrived, I threw the bags in the back and we took off like a bat out of hell for the beach.

I called Top to see how far out he was from the island and what he thought his ETA was. He said he was within three hours of dropping anchor off San Andros. I briefed him on what we had found and told him we would be leaving the bags in the brush next to the beach where we had been picked up before. I also asked him if he would grab the bags and my little moped that was still stashed near the old logging road.

He said, "No problem, Jake. I got it handled."

When we were a couple of hundred feet away from the house on Morgan's Bluff, we saw numerous reporters and cameramen. I pulled the Hummer off the road and we jumped out to continue on foot.

There were two police cars parked across the road, blocking access directly to the house. As we approached the crowd, Sorensen pointed to a half-hidden path to his right through the brush. Following the path, we cut through the brush and found it came out onto the beach two houses to the west of the house the militants were holed up in. We also noticed a large yacht closing in on the beach from the east. It was towing a very large rubber boat with two outboards fitted to its rear section. There was no doubt in my mind that it was the militants' escape route from here, the reporters, and the past.

I double-timed it back to the road and informed the closest reporters that there was a way around the private road that went to the house and that the militants were about to make a run for it on a large boat just off the shore. The beaches, as far as I knew, were public property and they could gather right behind the house and film the men as they ran for the raft.

They collected their equipment and raced down the path to the beach. As Sorensen and I watched, the reporters crowded around the rear of the house, set up their cameras, and shouted questions to the militants gathered on the rear patio of the house. Many of them were attempting to hide their faces from the cameras.

While some of the cameramen filmed the back of the house, others turned their attention to the large boat off the beach. The boat had turned to the northwest a bit and I could see two men with binoculars looking at the reporters and camera crews. Shortly afterward, the boat turned north and then back to the west. The militants had just lost their ride.

Just then, I received a call from Top that he was dropping anchor west of us. I told him we would meet him on the beach when he came ashore to pick up the documents. Sorensen and I ran back to our Hummer and headed west to meet up with Top.

As we passed the road leading into San Andros, we saw some of the reporters filming for the nightly news. I recognized one of the reporters as a famous face from the Iraq and Afghanistan war front. I figured that this would generate a great deal of information regarding Joel. The more information the public had regarding Joel and his plight, the safer he would be when his case went to trial. If it went to trial at all!

I pulled the Hummer over to the side of the road where I had hidden my moped. It was still there and looked to be in fair shape. I was tempted to lift it into the back of the SUV but decided it would be better off going aboard Top's boat. We walked to the beach and saw Top motoring back out to his boat. I could see the tops of the black trash bags showing above the sides of his Zodiac. There were four more black trash bags hidden in the brush and waiting for Top's next trip. Sorensen rolled the moped to the trash bags and laid it on top of them.

We saw there were no other boats visible in the area. We recognized an all too familiar sound, turned, and saw two more helicopters coming in from the west. They were large Chinook transports typically used by the military. As they flew closer, I saw that there were no markings on them. This reminded me of the planes that Air America used in Southeast Asia during my years in Vietnam. I knew why they were there right away!

Sorensen and I ran back to the Hummer and I turned it back toward San Andros. I drove as fast as I could, and when we arrived at the entrance, I shouted to the reporters that the two big helicopters now circling overhead were going to airlift the Arabs out. We then raced to the south end of the compound where the Arabs had gathered in the mosque. Camera crews and reporters swarmed the clearing at the training field, waiting for the Arabs to come out. They were all looking up at the helicopters and some were filming as best they could with the wind from the blades churning up dirt as they landed.

I knew their plan was to blow all the reporters out of the way with wind and debris from the blades so they could evacuate the Arabs. I turned to signal Sorensen, but he had already grabbed his rifle from behind the seat and was running off into the brush to the south. I knew what he was up to. He was going to put the "Sorensen Eliminator" into action one more time!

Less than ten seconds later, I heard his rifle report and saw the lead helicopter veer off to the south like it was under attack. The next helicopter must have received a radio call from the lead bird as it too maneuvered away from the area.

Sorensen stepped out of the brush and quickly stored his rifle back in the Hummer. I asked him where he had aimed and he said that he put four rounds behind in the fuselage of the craft. There was nothing of vital importance to the copter's controls there and the rounds could make a great deal of noise in the steel cabin.

I was worried that the birds would come back and start shooting, but, instead, they turned and headed back to the west. They disappeared over the horizon and soon we could no longer hear them.

I called the Major and briefed him of the events over the last couple of hours. He said that all hell was breaking loose on national and international TV stations. He was getting phone messages and photos from Top of the documents and pictures we had confiscated. He was having these documents downloaded and printed and later would visit with Joel to see if he could identify any of the folks depicted in them. He would also have him read the documents to see if the information would be helpful to his case. Most of the documents were in German, but some were in English and already they were showing some knowledge of the U.S. and its allies regarding the atrocities at the prison camps.

The Major said he had received a call from a high official in Washington requesting a private meeting! I warned him not to wind up alone with any of these dealmakers, and he said he was going to ignore the request for now. He added that he was getting serious pressure from Washington to return Joel for trial soon or they would be forced to extradite him.

I told him I did not want to bring this fight to Miami, but I would if that was what it took to win.

After I signed off, Sorensen and I walked back to the Arab stronghold and spoke with the reporters still staged there. They said that some of the Arabs came to the front of the building when the helicopters appeared and then fled back inside when they heard shots and the helicopters retreated. One of the reporters stated that he saw one of the armed Arabs talking on a small handheld radio and that it appeared that they were in communication with the birds. One of the photographers said he got a couple of close-ups of the pilots and that they were white men for sure—probably Americans.

I asked everyone to be quiet for a moment so we could hear the big choppers to the west. It sounded as if they were landing at the airport. I suggested to Sorensen that we skip over there to see what they were up to. To know your enemy is the first line of defense in beating them.

We ran to the Hummer, jumped in, and headed to the north side of the airport where the two large helicopters were on the ground. A black Hummer was making its way from the main road to the two birds. A number of heavily armed men were sitting in its cargo space. I sure didn't like the looks of that.

I turned the Hummer around and headed back to the village. I warned the reporters that the helicopters may be heading back to pick up the Arabs and that any chance of filming the Arabs when they boarded would be lost if they were not in position when they arrived. I warned them that the copters would be heavily armed this time. This time, they meant business!

I had to think fast. I had an idea that I passed by Sorensen and he agreed that anything was better than doing nothing at this point. There were four abandoned Hummers in the German compound. I got two volunteers to go with us so we could drive the Hummers back to the field just north of the building that the Arabs were using as a stronghold. We lined up, spaced the vehicles about three feet apart, and then pointed the Hummers at the building across the field.

While we waited for the copters to make another run for the Arabs, we poured about ten gallons of diesel fuel from the spare fuel cans over the vehicles. Just as we finished, we heard the copters winding up for their take-off and evacuation run.

We waited until the copters were in the air and well on their way and then we lit the backs of the Hummers on fire and placed them in low gear. The Hummers started crawling across the field at a slow pace with smoke billowing out of their rear quarters. We jumped from the cabs and watched as the field, the only landing zone they could use to evacuate the Arabs, became a smoke-filled arena with no visibility. The helicopters circled four times and then flew back toward the west. The sky was black with smoke from the burning SUV's!

As we watched the burning Hummers closing in on the mosque, the Arabs looked out of the door and the windows in sheer panic. All of a sudden, the door opened and the Arabs started running to the left and right of the burning vehicles. I still didn't see the Bin Laden-looking fellow or any of the armed Arabs that had been shooting at us earlier from the windows.

One of the reporters shouted to us that there were some men escaping out of the back of the building. As the reporters hauled their crews and camera equipment to the rear of the building, we heard a burst of machine gun fire and the two lead reporters went down, bleeding badly from their wounds. The rest of the reporters dove to the ground with equipment flying everywhere as another burst blew by from the rear of the building.

Sorensen looked at me, and I nodded a "you betcha." We ran to our Hummer and retrieved our rifles and spare clips.

We ran as fast as we could around the side of the building, staying low. After only fifty yards, I saw an Arab aiming a sniper rifle at the reporters. I pointed him out to Sorensen and he nodded. To make sure we appeared to be playing fair, I stood up briefly after Sorensen lined up his shot and whistled at the shooter. He quickly fired a round at me and Sorensen took the entire top half of his head off with one nicely placed shot. As soon as the guy went down, another very large Arab popped up of the tall grass and blasted automatic rifle fire in our direction. I took him out with a three-round burst to the chest and midsection.

We were in an area that was denser with brush than where the Arabs were so they had no idea of our exact location. And, I was glad that we were hidden from camera view on the north side of the building.

I signaled for Sorensen to move to the south and I moved to the east another ten yards. We had no real protection in the brush. All the Arab shooters had to do was spray some automatic fire into the brush and they would have chewed us up! Fortunately for us, they didn't think of it or just weren't that smart.

We could still hear the big choppers to the west, and we knew it was only a matter of time before they returned to attempt hauling the Arabs out. This wasn't over yet!

One of the crawling Hummers must have struck the building, as we heard the crunching of wood breaking and the engine making noises as it labored to a stop. It was only a matter of time before the building caught fire, forcing the rest of the Arabs out.

Sorensen had moved farther south and I could barely see him in the brush. He waved his hand above his head and pointed in the direction of the Arabs in the woods. I understood that he was going to make a move on them and I was to divert their attention while he got in position.

I quickly found a group of bushes and lay as flat as I could on the ground. I could just see some blurs where the Arabs were grouped together. I took careful aim and started firing just above their heads so the branches and leaves were falling on them.

They all dove for cover and scattered left and right. Within seconds of firing my gun, I heard the distinct sound of Sorensen's rifle blasting away to the south of my position. He must have been right next to them as they all started running toward me—and the burning building! I watched for anyone with a rifle or handgun but saw none. It was hard to distinguish men from women as the panicked Arabs ran directly at me. I heard two more shots from Sorensen's rifle and more came running out.

Just as the lead Arabs cleared the brush into the field surrounding the building, the back door of the building flew open and five large Arabs burst out, firing their rifles at their own people. They didn't care what they were shooting at, just that they were firing at something. Behind them, three Arabs stooped down as they came down the stairs. I recognized the Bin Laden-looking guy in the middle being protected by the large Arab shooters.

Sorensen made three quick shots and before I could count them, he sent the Arabs to Allah. One more ran out of the door and I took out both his legs with one clean shot. The Bin Laden-looking man ran around the building and right into the clutches of the cameramen and reporters. He stopped short, tried to cover his face, but it was no good. A couple of reporters shouted questions, calling him "Mr. Bin Laden" as they fired questions at him like a machine gun. He turned and looked back at the burning building behind him and then went to his knees like he was praying for some unseen guardian to lift him up and away from this mess he was in. I didn't think his prayers were going to be answered.

I saw three or four reporters lying on the ground. They had been badly shot by this guy's thugs. The other reporters were treating them—and now it was time for the helicopters to land. Not to evacuate the Arabs, but to bring the wounded to Miami for medical attention.

As I was looking for one of the radios the Arabs were using to speak with the helicopters, I saw Nancy and two other constables pull up in her small car. The two guys were so big that they hardly fit in that little thing of hers. She ran over to me and said that the Bahamas army was arriving by helicopter in the next few minutes. The U.S. government informed them that a "terrorist group" was attacking American journalists on San Andros.

I had to laugh because the Arab guards were shooting at the reporters, and there was no doubt that these same government sources and officials were supporting them. If the army was on its way, then there was no need to call the helicopters to aid the reporters. I threw the radio down that I had picked up when Nancy arrived, looked at Sorensen, threw my thumb over my shoulder, and told him we needed to make ourselves scarce.

He looked at me and said, "This has been the most fun I have had in days, boss." And he smiled as he walked away.

I gave Nancy a big hug and we made our way back up the trail to the west. When we arrived at the airstrip, we saw the mess everything was in. Two KC 130s and two very large helicopters were grounded with one copter looking very broken. The Lord only knows how many souls we provided Him in the past few days.

We walked north until we reached the edge of the beach. We put an ear to the air and heard the army's helicopters landing at San Andros. I slipped out of the brush enough to see Top's boat anchored about five hundred yards from the shore and called him on one of the burners I was still carrying. The batteries were about dead but it rang and he answered on the first ring.

Top told me the Bahamas Navy patrol boat had been cruising back and forth for some time now. He suspected there was a highflying plane also doing recon in the area. He had retrieved the rest of the black bags with the documents, but he was unable to float my moped out yet. He had left it hidden in the brush as a result. He was concerned that if he made another run ashore to pick us and the moped up, it would draw attention to us.

I agreed and told Sorensen we were going on another wonderful moped ride into Nicholls Town.

We walked to the moped in the bushes. It cranked on the first kick and ran smoothly even with all the dirt and mud on it. Sorensen and I put our caps on backward and took off down the road into San Andros. I thought of that scene in *Dumb and Dumber* where the two fools rode that little scooter to Colorado and laughed to myself. I really hoped we didn't look that dumb. We had left our rifles hidden in the brush and the spare ammo a few feet away so they would not pose a danger to anyone discovering either of them.

As we approached the entrance to San Andros, we saw two Bahamian soldiers standing on the side of the road. I waved at them and they waved back. We drove on by and continued to Nicholls Town with little fanfare.

As we approached Morgan's Bluff, we saw a few newsmen walking up the road toward San Andros. I stopped and told them that the other reporters had found some Arabs and a Bin Laden relative hiding in the village. They all started running to the west with big smiles on their faces. I guess something I said really made their day!

Sorensen gave me a strange look and said, "I hope you are right regarding the Bin Laden guy, Jake."

I told him it would keep the powers that be busy trying to combat all the negative info—at least for a while.

As we pulled up to the little marina where the *Big Mamoo* was moored, we saw the Bahamas Naval patrol boat cruising north not far off the coast. I wasn't sure how much they knew about me or my past few days of action in their beautiful country. It was a little less beautiful because of Sorensen and me. If they had a clue, they would be looking for me and my boat for sure.

Sorensen and I stood in the shadows until the cruiser had passed us and sailed far to the north. I then untied the line from the piling and pulled the stern of my boat over until we could climb into the pulpit. Everything on the boat seemed secure and showed no signs of having being searched. The leaf I had jammed into the handle of the deck hatch was still there--except that it was waterlogged from the rain. I signaled to Sorensen that everything was okay.

I settled in, cranked the engine, started the generator up, and let them run for a while. I then hauled the anchor in. We decided to cruise south for a while to make sure no one was following us. I then brought the boat about and headed north-by-northeast. I figured I would sail over the horizon and then meet up with Top on the *Semper Fi.*

We sailed back to the north shore where we had left my moped and took the inflatable to the beach. I retrieved the little bike and we headed back out to the *Big Mamoo.*

While Sorensen was securing it, he stopped short and spoke loudly enough to be heard over the sound of the diesel engine. "Jake, we have a big problem!"

I set the autopilot and jumped down into the hold. I didn't like what I saw, but I saw it right away. There was a small bomb fastened under the deck with enough C4 plastic explosives to send us and the boat to Davy Jones's Locker for good.

quickly examined it and saw it was attached to a basic cell phone, which was itself attached to a homemade detonator. It wasn't sophisticated looking, but it was done well enough to work. Examining it further and with extreme care, I detached the phone and then the detonator. Sorensen released the zip-ties that held it in place and brought it above deck for us to examine. As he looked it over in more detail, I went about checking the rest of the holds for any other surprises that might ruin our day. I found nothing of interest and went back to where he was still checking out the bomb's system.

A simple bomb made up of the military type C4 that we typically used in Vietnam. The blasting cap igniter was of the same vintage. There were two AA batteries made by Eveready and they were candle wax coated to keep them from corroding. It looked much like an IED, but Sorensen knew better. He said it was the work of a U.S.-trained widow-maker and had the earmarks of the folks he worked with at Langley. He said he was very surprised that there was only one, as that was not typical of the way they worked. He explained that more often than not, two devices were planted for good measure. One main one and one acting as a backup.

We searched everywhere but still found no signs of another device. I found three damp plastic trash bags stuffed in a storage slot under the port gunnels that were not there prior to our leaving the boat. That told us that a swimmer or SCUBA diver most likely floated the device in. The bag was still wet, which told us it had come in today after the rain. No one but the villagers knew the boat was connected to us, so a call to Nancy was in order.

Nancy was still at the village when I raised her on her cell phone. She said she would call a couple of her sources in town to see if anyone saw or knew anything. She said that the Bahamas Naval cruiser had been patrolling back and forth for a few hours off Nicholls Town. She would call back as soon as she had anything significant to report.

I reflected on our earlier confrontation with the Bahamian ambassador at the airport. I was discounting the militants from the village as they had their hands full—what we refer to in our business as "golden handcuffs"—with the problems we had recently created with the world press.

We could see the naval cruiser turning west near Morgan's Bluff about a mile from shore. Sorensen took the binoculars and said it was the same boat that we had been on some days ago. There were two U.S. spooks on board when he joined them. He said they were communications and surveillance specialists. He didn't think they were the bombers, but they would definitely know who was.

I would have loved to see the communications log for the past couple of days, as I am sure it would have shown a bit of interest in our presence in the Bahamas. Being popular isn't always a good thing, especially in our business.

About ten minutes later, I received a call back from Nancy. She said that a launch had come ashore from the naval patrol boat this morning to pick up some supplies. Her friend who lives across from the marina saw a SCUBA diver roll off the back of the launch near my boat and then saw my boat rock a bit shortly thereafter. She thought that was a little strange and said the diver was definitely a white man. She also told us that the Bahamas army had taken control of San Andros and that she and her department had arrested a number of the U.S. militant leaders for not having official permits to work in the Bahamas. It wasn't much but it was all she had to hold them for a while. She had five prisoners that she was transporting to Nassau by slow boat in order to hold them longer.

I asked her to get me their names, social security numbers (if possible), and the names of their employers so I could pass it along to the Major as soon as possible.

Sorensen took the cell phone formerly attached to the bomb and checked its memory for any recent call activity. There were four separate numbers in its memory and they had been recorded in the past twenty-four hours. Only one of the numbers called the phone. Three of the numbers were in the 202-area code—Washington, D.C.—and the other number was from area code 305—Miami! It was the Miami number that had called the phone. We were fairly sure the Miami number was the bomb trigger operator.

One thing I have learned over the years is that when one of these spooks makes an attempt on your life and fails, he or she is very likely to try and try again until they are successful. I was pretty sure there were two or more men on that cruiser tasked with getting rid of Sorensen and me.

I called Top and asked him if he could see where the naval cruiser was from his current position. He said it was off Morgan's Bluff and appeared to be dropping its anchor two miles from his boat. He said it had been cruising back and forth since he arrived a few hours earlier.

While we were talking, he said, "Wait a minute, Jake. I just saw them put a launch over the side and two white men got in the boat and it is heading back to the east."

I said, "Thanks Top," and came about in the *Big Mamoo* as Sorensen came up from below. I asked Top to stand by for my call to haul anchor and broke the connection.

I told Sorensen, "Our spooks from the Bahamian cruiser are on the water in a small boat about ten miles east of us and I believe they want to get closer to our boat so they can watch as we're blown to hell."

Sorensen looked at me and said, "We are both going to die, but today is not the day, Jake."

I set my Decca 101 on its eighteen-mile range and could see the shore and the blip of the cruiser on the screen. The smaller boat the two men were on would not show up on my old unit, but it would tell me if the cruiser moved from its mooring position. I had my mainsail and jib fully forward and catching the wind perfectly from the west. I also had my little diesel engine at its full throttle position. We were making about ten knots or better, which was slow in comparison to the launch the two men were in. They would be turning south in a few minutes to cruise down off the beach of Nicholls Town, if I didn't miss my guess.

"Prepare the Sorensen Eliminator for a couple of long shots, buddy," I told Sorenson, then added that I would do the honors.

He said, "Not on your life, pal!" He was supposed to be one of the charred remains floating around the clear blue waters of Andros. I couldn't disagree, so I asked him to prep my rifle, as well.

As we continued to race back to Nicholls Town, I saw a small boat turn south about two miles off our bow. I grabbed my binoculars and focused on the boat, then gave them to Sorensen. He confirmed that they were the two spooks from the cruiser. I altered my heading a bit to intersect their wake.

As we continued, I saw the man on the passenger side of the boat look at us with a small pair of binoculars. He then pointed to us and the boat turned in our direction. I could tell they had sped up by the size of their wake.

I told Sorensen to stand by for some action.

He looked up, gave me a thumbs up, and prepared his rifle for the first shot.

As they approached us, the passenger started frantically waving his arms in the air as if asking us to stop.

I looked over at Sorensen as he was lining up his shot and told him to stand down for a moment.

He looked up and said he had a clean shot if they made any move to arm up, but I had a strange feeling that these guys were on the level.

We held our guns on them as they slowed down and approached us. They started screaming that we needed to get off the boat right away and that a bomb had been planted on it.

I ordered them to stand down, to keep their arms in the air, and asked them to explain themselves. They began to shout at the same time that there was no time.

In my best drill sergeant's voice, I yelled at them that we had found and disabled the device. They looked bewildered but calmed down. I ordered them to pull to our port side away from the view of the cruiser that was now about five miles away but within binocular range and could identify us.

The men identified themselves as Tom Walden and Pete Mont. They openly admitted they were CIA communications specialists and told us that a man from Miami boarded the Bahamian cruiser that they were on last evening. The guy was carrying a small, unassuming briefcase. He spoke with the captain and, as a result, the boat cruised about ten miles off the east coast of Andros.

They said that early this morning, they cruised south of Nicholls Town, where the man got into a launch boat with two Bahamian sailors. They watched from their sidelight on the ship as the man took off his shirt, placed a dive mask on his face, took a plastic trash bag from the bottom of the boat, and went over the side. The launch continued on to Nicholls Town, where it generally picked up supplies and mail. They saw my sailboat rock a bit shortly after that and only then put two and two together.

They said they knew from reliable sources that Sorensen was on a small sailing vessel and were convinced that he was part and parcel to the shenanigans going on over in San Andros. They demanded to be let off the boat and were granted their demand when the cruiser anchored off Morgan's Bluff. They did not see us until they had started turning south around the point but recognized our boat.

Sorensen asked Walden and Mont to describe this diver as best they could. Mont said he had strikingly blue eyes and dark brown hair but noticed a small white streak of hair coming from a scar on his left temple.

Sorensen turned to me and said, "Jonathan Landis. I know that asshole all too well!" Sorensen said Landis was a washed-out field agent who'd been caught taking cash from the payouts to the Iraqis back in the early days of the war. He was thrown out of Iraq and fired by the CIA. Sorensen had heard that he was contracting himself out for wet work to some of the smaller security companies in Afghanistan. He said he confronted Landis in Miami when he learned he was seen meeting with some young Cubans in Little Havana. He never discovered the true reason for the meetings but was sure it was to assassinate someone! Sorensen said he bruised Landis up a bit and escorted him to the Florida Turnpike on his way back to Baltimore, where Landis currently lists his residence.

Sorensen made a tight fist and said, "Landis is a very bad man and I should have removed him from society long ago!"

We thanked the two men and sent them on their way back to the Bahamian cruiser.

Sorensen turned to me with a strange look on his face and said, "Jake, we need to find Landis and put him down for good!" He said Landis was not the type to give up and would be doubly motivated now that we had foiled his first attempt.

Just as Sorensen said that, we heard a phone ringing from down in the cabin. Sorensen swung down and returned with the phone that had been attached to the bomb. I looked at my watch and saw it was straight-up noon. So, Landis had wanted to take us out at high noon so he could always remember the specific time. Well, noon came and went, and we were as alive and whole as ever.

I looked at Sorensen and said, "Yep, time to take Landis out, bud." I hauled in the jib and turned north, away from the island. We were about three miles from the beach at Morgan's Bluff and about five miles from

Top's *Semper Fi*. We were on our way.

I called Top and briefed him on what was going on. I told him we were going to go over the horizon to the north and come back to his location from the northeast so as not to be detected. I asked him to prep the Zodiac so we could use it when we reached his position. I figured that Landis was on the shore somewhere and had expected us to explode when he signaled the cell phone trigger.

The phone rang twice more while we were sailing to the north. My guess was that Landis thought the phone wasn't getting the signal from the cell tower while it was down in the hold of my boat.

It took us about four hours before I started our compass heading back toward Andros. Meanwhile, I called the Major on the sat phone and briefed him on the last few hours of our continuing adventure. He said that the news media's official line was that the problems in San Andros were terrorist-related. Most of the government-leaked information tried to make it look like known terrorists had committed all of these heinous acts. Now, many of the reporters were starting to acknowledge that there appeared to be a mass cover-up of a secret government safe haven for Nazis and Arabs fully supported by America and other unknown countries. He said he was still holding off on bringing Joel back to the Bahamas for a hearing until the situation cooled down more.

As I was signing off from the Major, one of my cell phones gave a couple of chirps and then went quiet. Sorensen picked it up and said it didn't reflect any number on its screen and was out of range of the cell towers on San Andros.

I looked at the phone, one of the burners I had picked up along the way, and realized it was the phone Top often called me on. I turned the sat phone back on and called Top. He said he tried to call me a number of times. There was a fast-moving boat headed in our direction from the Bluffs area with three white males on board wearing camo clothes and, he thought, touting long-range rifles. It looked suspicious to him and he thought he would give us the heads up.

I told Sorensen and he said he could see a boat on the horizon heading straight in our direction. I thanked Top and asked him to haul anchor and head north in case we came in second in a skirmish and needed to be picked up from the warm Gulf Stream.

He said, "I am already underway and I'll be there as fast as I can!"

I put the phone away in the dry storage bin and asked Sorensen to pass my long gun up to me. He was busy checking his new best friend, the "Sorensen Eliminator," and passed me my weapon. I checked the chamber and the action on mine. It was ready.

As the boat rapidly approached, I dropped the sails and kept the engine running at full throttle. When they were just within range, I turned hard at them and Sorensen, not waiting for an invitation, fired two well-placed rounds into their windscreen.

Bang-bang!

All three of the heads disappeared below the bow at the same time. They steered to their right and presented us with their port side. Two of them popped up and shot a couple of bursts in our direction that missed completely.

I fired my .50 caliber and peppered the side of their boat. It looked like top-grade Swiss cheese as my rounds tore huge holes through their hull.

Sorensen started shooting well-placed rounds at the waterline and at where the deck met the gunnels. He shot about twenty rounds into the hull and the boat seemed to slow down and turn away from us.

I turned my autopilot off and steered aft of the speedboat. It was taking on more water than its bilge pumps could pump out and starting to list to port. Sorensen stood up on the roof of the cabin of the *Big Mamoo* and said there were three bodies in the prone position on the deck of the boat and a lot of blood! There was no movement whatsoever. I turned again.

As we approached the boat's stern, we could see that all three men were pretty chewed up by our rifle shots. They were all facing the gunnels of the boat as they lay there on the blood-soaked deck. As I maneuvered in close, Sorensen jumped onto the swim deck of the boat. He jumped into the cockpit and looked at the three dead men. He grabbed the hair of the middle man, pulled his head up off the deck, and turned so I could see him.

He shouted, "Meet the former Mr. Landis!"

Sorensen opened the hatch to the small cabin on the boat, unceremoniously shoved the three bodies inside and shut the hatch. He turned off the idling motors, threw a couple of switches on the console, and jumped back on board my boat. As we watched, water quickly filled the cockpit, as Sorensen had turned off the power to the bilge pumps.

I looked at the horizon all around us and saw nothing but blue-green ocean and white, puffy clouds. I knew Top would be sailing into view very soon and did not want him involved in this latest matter. Sorensen took my .50 caliber and shot a dozen larger holes through the deck and hull of the speedboat. Water gushed up into the cockpit and the transom went below the waves very quickly. We waited and watched and, five minutes later, the boat was completely under. I could still see some of the smaller debris floating on the water, but very little, and most of it was floating away with the current.

I hauled up my sails and zigzagged a course to the south until we saw Top's boat coming at us over the horizon. Sorensen had already cleaned up all the loose brass from the deck and put the rifles away. Top asked on his radio if the speedboat that he thought was heading in our direction had confronted us, and I said no, we hadn't seen it. Top said it must have headed back to Miami.

As he said that, a shiny object caught our eye as it rolled across the deck of my cockpit— a .50 caliber shell casing that we had missed earlier during our clean up. Top didn't see it as he was looking in the other direction. He said he thought he saw that boat go over the horizon on its way to Miami. I shrugged and threw the casing over the side. Wilson, who had been riding with Top, was looking in my direction but never let on that he'd seen the shell!

Sorensen, Top, and I discussed the fact that my boat had been identified as belonging to me. We decided that we could no longer use it as a refuge. Upon realizing this was a fact of life now, I asked Wilson if he thought he could pilot the *Big Mamoo* to Miami or Ft Lauderdale under engine power. He said that not only could he navigate it under power, but he could also sail it as he had a little experience from sailing as a young man. I asked him to sail to any of the harbors from Miami north and I would have my friend Dave meet him once he docked.

Sorensen and I unloaded our weapons, ammo, and other devices from my boat and transferred them to Top's boat. I gave Wilson some cash so he could buy a plane ticket back to his home and thanked him profusely for his help and loyalty during the past few days.

Wilson said, "It has been my pleasure, and if you guys ever need another helping hand, don't hesitate to contact me…really, I mean it."

Top had built-in hiding compartments on his boat similar to mine, so we used these to secret away our tools of war.

As I watched my boat sail off to the west, I was impressed with Wilson's ability to properly set the sails and run off the wind as well as I could. She sure looked pretty as she moved away from us. With one last look at the *Slim Molly/Big Mamoo,* we turned our attention back to San Andros and our next move. What our next move was going to be was still under serious discussion.

A fter setting the *Semper Fi's sails* up with different colors and numbers so we were less obvious, we sailed farther north and then east before turning back to the southwest to make it appear that we were sailing in from the island of New Providence or from some eastern port of call.

As we approached Nicholls Town, we could see the Bahamas Naval cruiser still anchored off the Morgan's Bluff area. The small launch was back, tied up alongside the cruiser. Sorensen said he was going to call Tom Walden and ask him who Landis was supposed to meet at Morgan's Bluff. We knew one thing for sure—Landis wouldn't be making that meeting.

Sorensen came back a while later and said that there were two Mentor Corporation Officials there at the house on the Bluff that seemed to be running the show and that they were on the phone continually with some higher-ups. Walden told Sorensen that he was trying to get the numbers off the air that these men were calling and would get back to him.

Top asked how in the world he could get the numbers and Sorensen told him that the two CIA men were communications specialists and had intercept equipment on the cruiser. He said Landis had met with these two men and made about ten calls before he jumped into the boat with two guys that sped in from the east earlier in the day. Walden told Sorensen that these two big shots had been trying to reach Landis ever since they left earlier in the day. He thought Landis was coming after us as he had seen them load some high-power explosives on board the bigger launch before they left.

Sorensen said, "Well, we never saw them, but we will sure keep an eye out for him." And, he said it with a straight face!

Top anchored the *Semper Fi* about three miles south of the harbor. I called Nancy and asked for an update. She told me that the central government in Nassau was going absolutely bonkers and had ordered her boss, the head constable, to stand clear of the American militants. Her boss, stationed down south, had decided to take a vacation and disappear for a few days until this whole affair blew over.

I was about to say, "What a frickin' chicken!" but held my tongue. I briefed her on our general location and told her we were going to need to gather the witnesses together and get the original written statements from her regarding the village and Joel's matter. She said she had already put together most of the additional statements and she was going to produce multiple copies just to be safe. She was on her way back to her office from the airport.

As we continued to talk and started to make plans to meet, her phone went dead. I called her back a couple of times and then waited for her to call me back. After about thirty minutes, plenty of time to have driven into Nicholls Town, we saw no sign of her whatsoever. Sorensen and I climbed into Top's Zodiac and double-timed it to shore!

We docked the inflatable on the beach next to the town pier. We each had our sidearms, plus two rifles and some extra ammo in a gunny sack, which Sorensen carried. We both were carrying our sidearms concealed under our shirts. I saw one of Nancy's cousins across the street and waved him over. I asked him if he could get us a car and that we would gladly pay for it.

He said that the only cars for rent came from the old Germans at San Andros. Well, we knew that was a wash, but he said he had a friend that had an old Toyota pickup truck that he knew he could borrow.

I told him we would pay handsomely for it, and we would even fill the fuel tank when we were finished. He took off down the road like a chicken with its head cut off and in less than ten minutes he was back driving an old sun-bleached and rusted-out red Toyota pickup. I gave him a couple of one-hundred-dollar bills and said that there would be more when we gave him the truck back later.

I got behind the steering wheel, looked at all the broken gauges, shook my head, and drove the truck while Sorensen continued trying to reach Nancy on her cell phone. It kept ringing and then went directly to voicemail. We stopped a couple of times to ask some locals along the way if they had seen Nancy pass by. No one had seen her in the last few hours.

As we sped along the main road—if you could call it speeding at thirty-five MPH because of a wobbling front wheel— a small car appeared. It was coming the other way but flagged us down. The man driving the car told us there was a roadblock up ahead and that some American soldier types were searching all the cars near Morgan's Bluff. He said that Constable Nancy White's car was smashed into the brush right next to the roadblock. He said he didn't see her at the roadblock. We thanked him and drove west a bit slower now.

When we were about a half-mile from where we thought the roadblock was, we parked the truck in a little turn off and gathered our weapons and backpacks. It was starting to turn dark now so we had the cover of darkness to perform our next move. Darkness was definitely our friend tonight.

We stuck to the brush about ten feet off the paved road as we approached the makeshift roadblock. Four men were securing and manning the blockade, and they were using two Hummers as rolling gates. We couldn't see if there were any more troops off the road in the brush, but there didn't appear to be. Two of the militants were carrying rifles and the other two were wearing sidearms and had extra clips on their ammo belt. I was sure their rifles were close by. We could also see Nancy's little car stuck in the brush as the man had said. She must have run off the road as she came around the corner from the airport.

Sorensen and I were on the north side of the road, and we could see the house that the militants were using to our north next to the beach. We waited a while and listened to the conversations of the sentries. Not once since we'd arrived, some fifteen minutes earlier, had any of the sentries been in radio communication with the house. We could easily have shot all four men in less than two seconds with our silenced pistols but decided we had done enough killing for one day. I told Sorensen that we should walk north a few feet and then walk down the small road from the beach as if we were coming from the house. That would catch them completely off guard and we could take them down quickly with a couple of butt strokes from our rifles. Sorensen agreed.

We walked up to them, holding our rifles as naturally as we could by our sides, and, as we walked, we laughed a couple of times as if we were telling jokes. The four sentries stood there looking at us with smiles on their faces. One of them looked at his watch and said that there was supposed to be four replacements for them in about an hour. I told them that they decided that only two were needed and that they were relieved of duty. They all said that was great and started to walk up the road toward the beach.

I cracked the second man in line on the back of his head with my rifle and followed up with a horizontal butt stroke to the first guy. Their knees buckled and both went down hard. At the same time, I spun to cover Sorensen and found his two guys already lying on the ground.

Sorensen looked at me and said, "That was too damn easy."

I checked each man to make sure everyone was still breathing and then Sorensen and I tied them hand to foot with some thin nylon rope I had brought from the boat. We relieved two of them of their jungle jackets and transferred our ammo clips and cell phones to the multiple pockets of the new jackets. We dragged them into the bushes and then moved the Hummers to the side road leading to the shore where the militants were holding out.

We walked up the road and saw that the militants had taken over the house we had used. We counted about fifteen in the area—well-armed with either rifles or sidearms.

No one seemed to pay us any attention. There were no reporters left in the area, which told us that they had been forcibly removed. It would take a great deal to convince a reporter or news photographer to willingly leave a once-in-a-lifetime news source.

We stayed in the shadows away from the lights and waning sun. We needed to find Nancy quickly before the real relief guards discovered that we had moved the Hummers and there were bound guards in the bushes down the road. I walked around the back of the house toward the beach and Sorensen walked to the front door. I caught up to him at the front door as he was peering in the front window next to the three-step porch.

He pointed to the window and, when I looked inside, I saw Nancy was handcuffed and her mouth duct-taped. Sitting across from her was none other than the Bahamian ambassador himself. This asshole was really starting to get on my nerves! Nancy had some fresh blood on her shirt and her hair appeared to have been pulled back as if she had been held by it. My blood was starting to boil and that was never a good sign for the next person dumb enough to get in my path.

There were ten men in the room—most of them older executive types or possibly politicians. If Nancy wasn't in there, I would have been more than happy to throw a grenade or two in the middle of them. Then again, if Nancy weren't in there, I wouldn't be as pissed off as I was.

I tapped Sorensen on the arm and we slipped behind the house to the patio area where the barbeque grill was set up. We both had the same idea at the same time as we moved in unison to the propane tanks. One was hooked up to the grill and the other was sitting to the rear as a spare. When we checked, we found that both were full.

I disconnected the one tank and we carried it to the side of the house. I went back to the grill, grabbed the long-necked firelighter, and walked back to Sorensen, who was jamming a piece of driftwood into the nozzle opening of one of the tanks. He then opened the valve and gas began to hiss out. He did the same thing to the second tank. Now, the propane gas smell was starting to become pungent.

We carried them under the rear porch near a sliding door leading into the cellar area. There was no one inside the lower level of the house so we walked in and set the tanks down. I flicked the lighter and it flamed up. I held it to the valve and, after a couple of tries, a long blue flame shot out about two feet. I let it burn a few moments and moved it to the wood-paneled wall. The wall began to smoke almost immediately. We lit the second tank the same way and placed it facing some cardboard boxes in the front of the cellar.

Smoke and some low flames began to rise up to the first floor of the house. Sorensen and I ran up the stairs and began shouting, *"Fire! Fire!"*

I ran around the front as Sorensen ran through the rear sliding glass doors into the house. As I rounded the corner to the front, I saw men running out onto the front lawn and into the bushes. I cut between them and pushed my way into the front door. Sorensen was already beside Nancy, telling a militant he would take her out. The militant was reluctant to be relieved of his duties, so I walked up behind him and smashed him in the head with the stock of my rifle. He went down like a rock! It wasn't a great move because now I had to carry him out of the burning house, too!

Sorensen lifted Nancy up with little effort and carried her out the front. I picked up Tweedledee, carried him out, and dropped him down on the front lawn. I told one of the many militants he fell down the stairs inside and hit his head. Two men began examining him as I walked over to where Sorensen was holding Nancy. I cut her plastic cuffs off and helped her stand. I told them both to walk with me as I acted as if I was in complete charge of all things great.

With the fire and chaos all around us, no one challenged us as we walked back toward the main road. We did not look back and everything was going smoothly until someone shouted from the end of the road that someone had attacked the guards.

We were about halfway there when a group of militants started running down the road toward the roadblock. I steered Nancy, who was still in a daze, into the brush away from the long driveway. Sorensen lingered behind us on purpose to block anyone from challenging us. We thought we were in the clear as there was a great deal of confusion at the house and there was no leadership giving any direction.

As the four or five militants came abreast of Sorensen, he pointed toward the main road and they ran on by.

I asked Nancy if she could make it another hundred yards or so and she said, "Yes, I can, Jake, lead the way."

We continued through the brush until we were about ten yards from the road. We then turned east until we came to the pickup truck where we had pulled it into the brush at the side of the road. I told Sorensen to take Nancy back to Nicholls Town so she could be treated.

She said she was so pissed that the Bahamian ambassador caused this and that he was planning to fly into Miami. A helicopter was scheduled to arrive in a few hours to take the Mentor executives back to the States.

I sent them off in the old truck and turned back toward the burning house.

As I returned to the scene, I saw total chaos surrounding the grounds. Many of the militants were pointing their pistols and rifles at each other, thinking they were confronting me. They were acting like a gang of clowns with weapons. Even the Keystone Cops looked like seasoned professionals compared to these guys.

I scouted around the outside of the yard near the house and saw that the Bahamian ambassador and Mentor Corporation executives were standing near the brush to the east of the house. There were no armed militants near them while they were talking quietly among themselves. The ambassador was visibly upset over something and the other two men were trying to calm him down. I waited behind them for a while until one of the executives moved away to talk with a group of men near the back of the house.

I casually walked up behind the Mentor guy with the ambassador and butt-stroked the American in the back of the head. In that same movement, I grabbed the ambassador around the neck and dragged him into the woods.

I didn't make a sound and the ambassador stumbled backward out of pure terror. I think he was probably thinking he was about to meet his Maker!

I dragged him as far back as I could to get out of the light from the flames of the fire and then ordered him to face forward and walk ahead of me. He continued to beg for his life with every step. He even offered me a great deal of cash that he had tucked away in a Miami bank. I kept quiet and shoved him in the middle of his back every four or five steps. When we got to a clearing and the sounds from the house were far behind us, I stopped him and ordered him to sit down on the ground Indian style. By making him cross his legs in this manner, he could not stand up without a great deal of effort. I took out my cell phone, set it on video, and told him I wanted a complete and detailed narration of what had been going on here at Andros Island as far back as he could remember.

Ambassador White asked in a panicked and shaky voice if I would let him go if he did what I requested. I told him I would first consider the validity of his information before making any decision. I made him sit up straight and face me as he began to unveil a story even I had problems believing.

He had been a clerk in the prosecutor's office at the Nassau Court House and saw some complaints filed in the mid-1950s by longtime residents of Nicholls Town. They complained about foreign workers building homes off the road to the old airport who were not using local labor. Much of the good land around the islands was being bought up cheaply by people from all over the world—and much of the good fishing grounds were becoming "off-limits" to native Bahamians.

Americans had taken over the entire area and restricted Bahamians from any access to their own properties. This had forced the ambassador's entire family to move to New Providence Island almost overnight.

White said that he learned at an early age that there were some former German citizens living on San Andros Island and he eventually learned that a delegation of Canadian officials was cutting a deal with the British government to place even more of them there. For a while, there were even armed soldiers stationed at the village to protect the Germans, and he said he was pretty sure that the soldiers were U.S. or Canadian.

He gathered all the information he could about what was going on there on San Andros and then brought it to the attention of one of his uncles who worked for the Bahamas government after they gained their independence from Great Britain. About a week later, his uncle called him to a meeting at a hotel near Cable Beach. When he got to the meeting, he found his uncle and three men, all Americans, in a small conference room. None of the men introduced themselves but got right down to business, telling him how important it was for him to stay silent about what he knew was going on at San Andros. They promised him that he would be rewarded for his loyalty to what they called "world peace."

He soon learned about Operation Paperclip and Operation Overcast, American policies that allowed Nazi leaders and scientists to live in the U.S. and other places without being prosecuted for war crimes. He described how governments relocated the Nazis to the Bahamas and hid them away from the rest of the world—and especially from the Jewish Nazi Hunters who sought to bring them to justice.

White was given a good job at the American Consulate Office in Nassau and, after working with the Americans as a lobbyist to the Bahamas government, he was appointed Ambassador to the United States. He had been the Ambassador for over thirty years. He said he never wanted to be a part of anything so wrong, but political position and very good compensation were too hard to pass up.

The Germans had been here since the early 1950s, and they were allowed to come and go as they pleased with no scrutiny or challenge to their passport. Many Bahamians and American government officials looked the other way while war criminals were being hunted all over the world.

After 9/11, when the world was looking for Osama Bin Laden and his family members, White said that many of his family members and associates came to the Bahamas and stayed in secret at the nicest hotels and resorts on New Providence and other islands until their new homes and mosque were finished at San Andros. Like the Germans, many of the Arabs and Middle Easterners came and went from San Andros without any scrutiny at all. A deal between the U.S. and the Bahamas prevented the Bahamas Customs and Immigration Authorities from stopping or questioning these people at any time or for any reason during their stay in the Bahamas.

Year after year, White was given large sums of U.S. currency to distribute to his government officials. The funds never seemed to slow down, and when he asked for more, it was always there without question. He had a complete record of all the funds on his private computer at his home on New Providence, and he promised he would provide this list if I needed it.

I asked him to empty his pockets slowly and, as he did so, he took out a computer flash drive attached to some keys. I asked what I would find on the USB drive and he reluctantly admitted it had a lot of information relating to what he had already told me. He said it was part of his insurance protection, as he knew this day would eventually come. I took his keys with the flash drive attached and put them in my pocket.

He told me he had also been getting huge payoffs from Mentor Corporation for about five years and had accepted money from other U.S. firms in the past. He said he'd shared the funds with other Bahamian politicians over the years and acted as the middleman for gifts, vacations, and money to others in the Bahamas and the UN.

I asked White if that was all true to the best of his recollection while the video was still running. He answered, "Yes," so I turned the video off and sent it to the Major's phone and email address. I also sent a copy of the video to Gage up at Patrick Air Force Base and to my own email address for safekeeping!

I forced White to his feet. His legs were almost asleep from the position I'd had him in so I gave him a second to regain his composure, then pushed him through the brush toward Nicholls Town. He asked me to let him go so he could get back home to his family before the news of San Andros Island reached Nassau. I told him that that would be up to Constable Nancy White, who I believed was a distant cousin of his. He said he had nothing to do with the way she was treated at the house, and I told him he had everything to do with the way she was treated because he did nothing to try to stop it. He hung his head and began to cry.

As soon as we were clear of the beach house, we crossed the main road and stopped at a clearing about a mile from town. I called Sorensen and told him where we were. He said that a number of folks had been asking for the ambassador and that he had heard that a contingent of Bahamas' military were on their way to San Andros. I asked how Nancy was doing and he said she was on her feet and doing far better. I suggested that she come by and place White under arrest herself before the military arrived so at least that legal process could start before the cover-up began. He asked me to hold for a moment and then put Nancy on the phone who said she would be right over as soon as she found a driver. I hung up and called the Major back.

I asked him if he had seen the video, I sent to him earlier. He said he had quickly scanned it and had assigned one of his legal assistants to transcribe it so he could get it to the national press. I asked him if perhaps it should be sent to the masses right away before anyone screamed, "National security!"

He reflected on it a moment, then said he felt I may be right. I suggested he send it to his private or office computer so he could distribute it quickly. He agreed! He said he would configure it and send it to everyone in his media group. I told him that I was turning Ambassador White over to Nancy and was waiting for her now. He told me to be cautious, as things were heating up quickly! He said he was meeting with some Bahamian prosecutors in Miami later that afternoon.

A few moments later, Nancy called me and said she was west of town. She told me there would be two cars coming.

She said, "I am not taking any chances until this is all over, Jake, so I have two other constables with me as backup."

We waited next to the road until we heard them coming. I sent the video to Nancy's phone so she had his statement for grounds to hold him on.

I told White I would testify on his behalf that he was cooperative if he continued to be so. He said he was afraid they would kill him if they had him in custody. I told him I would kill him if he tried to recant his confession. I told him to think about the last few days and all the disasters that had come about and then asked him to think about me verse them! He looked at me for a moment with a blank stare and then, as if it was all dawning on him for the first time—who we were and what we were capable of—he said in a low voice, "I'll take my chances with them."

Nancy, Sorensen, and two constables got out of their cars and she cuffed White, called him cuz, and the other two police authorities placed him in the backseat of the small car they drove up in.

I asked her if there was anyone on these islands she wasn't related to. Nancy said, "For me to know and for you to always wonder, I guess?"

Nancy pulled me aside and asked if I would mind cruising on a small boat that belonged to a former friend of hers to Miami. I did not question her use of the word "former," and as she described the boat to me, a thirty-eight-foot Sea Ray fast-mover, I eagerly agreed with no questions asked. This boat would be nearly as fast as a plane ride back to the States.

Sorensen and I cut through the brush back toward town. We still had our weapons and sidearms, but I figured folks by now were getting used to seeing white guys carrying guns. I called Top and told him we were heading over to the speedboat and would catch up with him in a couple of hours or less. I briefed him on Ambassador White's info and his arrest. Top said he would sail over to cover our flank as we left the north side of the island.

As we located and boarded the boat, I received a call from the Major saying he was about to go on the air at a news conference in Miami. He had just sent out a mass emailing of White's videos and had already seen news bulletins on the tube.

We searched Nancy's boat as best we could for any surprises and checked all seacocks to make sure there were none damaged or tampered with. I cranked the engines after checking all the cooling levels, including the generator.

Top called me on his Marine Band radio and told me to tune into any Miami radio or TV station and to listen. I did so and heard the familiar voice of Doug Parton gracing the airways with his deep mellow voice. He was informing the world that numerous governments, including the United States, had been harboring war criminals and possibly 9/11 collaborators! He went on to describe the Bahamas Ambassador to the U.S. and the UN as a co-conspirator and offered verbal proof in his own words of what has been going on since World War II.

Top said, "Jake, this is on right now on every radio and TV station that I turn to."

I could just imagine the heads that would be rolling around Washington D.C. over this news!

Top went on to tell us there was a news bulletin on CNN showing a group of well-known senior government officials and White House and congressional advisors gathered in an alley next to a Washington, D.C. building. They were all carrying large boxes and attempting to load them into two long, unmarked panel trucks. He explained that some of the reporters had been poking the boxes while they questioned the men. Some of the boxes had fallen to the ground, and the cameras started filming official letterhead documents and what appeared to be ledgers scattered all over the place. Some of the men were pulling their jackets up in an attempt to hide their faces from the cameras, but everyone could clearly see who they were.

As we were preparing to leave, Nancy came over to the boat to see us off and tell us where she wanted the boat moored in Florida. She described a mooring that sounded a lot like my island in the Banana River. After her request, she kissed me on the lips in a way that was far more than a friendly comrade smooch. That answered my question on the mooring. At that

262

point, I saw Sorenson's attention focus on me.

I looked over at Sorensen, he stuck out his fist, and we struck knuckles!

Jake Storm Will Return

ABOUT THE AUTHOR

William Johnstone Taylor has been an active investigator for more than forty years and is the Director of the William J. Taylor Agency. He was Chief Investigator and a consultant on a number of high-publicity cases, including The Karen Silkwood case, featured in the movie *Silkwood*, the kidnapping and murder of Charles Harmon in Santiago, Chile, depicted in the movie *Missing*, and many other nationally and internationally renowned investigations.

Mr. Taylor is a former Marine Corps Criminal Investigator and Intelligence Officer. He served three tours of duty in the Republic of South Vietnam. He has been a featured speaker for The Association of American Trail Lawyers, Florida Bar Association, Pace University School of Law, Connecticut Bar Association, and many other organizations throughout the years.

Mr. Taylor is a Lifetime Member of The Federal Criminal Investigators Association, a past member of the International Police Congress, a former member of the Florida Secretary of State Private Security Council, Florida Association of Licensed Investigators, Central Florida Criminal Justice Council, Private Investigators Association of Florida, and Past President of the Florida Association of Private Investigators.

Stolen Angels was his first Jake Storm novel. *San Andros Fault* is his second.

He lives in Pickens County, Georgia, with his wife, dog, and two cats.